W9-DEL-960

TWISTED
WEBS

Also by Darlene Quinn

Webs of Power

Sizzling Cold Case

TWISTED
WEBS

A NOVEL

Darlene Quinn

EMERALD
BOOK CO.

Published by Emerald Book Company
Austin, TX
www.emeraldbookcompany.com

Distributed by Emerald Book Company

For ordering information or special discounts for bulk purchases, please contact Emerald Book Company at PO Box 91869, Austin, TX 78709, 512.891.6100.

Design and composition by Greenleaf Book Group LLC and Publications Development Company
Cover design by Greenleaf Book Group LLC

Publisher's Cataloging-In-Publication Data
(Prepared by The Donohue Group, Inc.)

Quinn, Darlene.
　　Twisted webs : a novel / Darlene Quinn. -- 1st ed.

　　p. ; cm.
　　Sequel to: Webs of power.
　　ISBN: 978-1-934572-71-9

　　1. Twins--Fiction. 2. Kidnapping--United States--Fiction. 3. Rich people--United States--Fiction. I. Title.

PS3617.U562 T9 2010
813/.6   2010929170

Part of the Tree Neutral™ program, which offsets the number of trees consumed in the production and printing of this book by taking proactive steps, such as planting trees in direct proportion to the number of trees used: www.treeneutral.com

Printed in the United States of America on acid-free paper

10 11 12 13 14 15 10 9 8 7 6 5 4 3 2 1

First Edition

DEDICATION

With love to my fantastically supportive husband, Jack Quinn, who is always there for me, keeps me going, and makes it all possible.

Acknowledgments

I am grateful to many fine people who have made their beloved department stores a magical, successful place, including Allen Questrom, master of merchandising, retail, and company turnarounds, who led Federated Department Stores out of bankruptcy and onto the acquisition of R. H. Macy & Company, Inc., and the Broadway/Emporium Stores; Terry Lundgren, currently chairman, president, and CEO of Macy's, Inc. (formerly known as Federated Department Stores, Inc.)—a true believer in "a balanced life"; Jack Chestnut, executive vice president, regional director of stores/Macy's West; and Anders Ekman, general manager of Nordstrom Cerritos.

Others to whom I owe my firsthand retail education and authenticity throughout this work of fiction are the former executives and the sales and sales-support associates of Bullock's and Bullocks Wilshire.

In matters outside the world of retail, I would like to thank Gainer Pillsbury, MD/hospital administrator; Stuart Anderson, MD; Kim Anderson; Nikii Benson, Lieutenant Raymond P. Lombardo (officer in charge, West Los Angeles Police Department, detective section); and Brennan Harvey, who does his level best to keep my website updated.

I couldn't do without the folks at EMSI: Marsha Friedman, Steve Friedman, Tony Panaccio, Rachel Friedman, Rich Ghazarian, Lisa Hess, Damon Friedman, and Ginny Grimsley (who keeps us all sane and on the same page). It's a joy to work with this savvy group of publicists, all of whom are dedicated professionals with great senses of humor.

I must also thank Greenleaf Book Group, and in particular Justin Branch, senior consultant; Bryan Carroll, production manager; Lisa Woods, book trailer designer; Neil Gonzalez, cover designer; Caryn Lusinchi, marketing manager; Carrie Winsett, marketing associate; Kristen Sears, distribution manager; Linda O'Doughda, editor, who is detail oriented and in tune with my characters, and who has an excellent eye for story; and freelance copy editor Amy D. McIlwaine, for assuring accuracy and order with her fabulous sense of time and place. Your collective enthusiasm and dedication have not only enhanced this work of fiction but also made the journey to publication an exciting and enjoyable adventure.

And finally, a special thanks to Kathy Porter, my administrative assistant and author of *Earth's Ultimate Conflict* (A Gray Guardian Series), who is an invaluable part of my team.

PART ONE: 1990

PROLOGUE

Mario Christonelli pulled his silver Taurus into the only remaining parking spot behind St. Joseph's Church, his trembling hands damp and cold. Between jagged breaths he wiped his palms on his trousers, then leaned over to check the large canvas bag on the passenger seat beside him. Inside, the tiny baby still slept soundly in the soft cradle he'd crafted for her. Suddenly he crushed both hands to his chest, as if to slow the thundering beat of his heart. *What have I done? What in hell have I done? God forgive me.*

Mario's eye shifted to the digital clock on the dashboard. It read 6:55. In the glow of the illuminated church, he sat stiffly. Time stood still.

His thoughts shot back to Erica, and his guilt shifted to unspeakable regret over what he'd done. Regret over what had driven him to commit this sin against God. Regret that his actions would bring so much pain to innocent people. But what choice did he have? Deep in his heart, Mario knew that if it were possible to turn back the clock, he still would not alter the course he had taken.

Moments later, parishioners began to pour out of the church's open doors. Mario watched Father O'Reilly bid his final farewells in the vestibule and then turn toward the corridor leading to his small office. Mario gently scooped up the baby, snugly wrapped in a pink receiving blanket. *No, not "the baby,"* he corrected himself. *Our daughter.* He flung open the car door and headed toward the church steps, calling out, "Father? I need a few minutes of your time."

Father O'Reilly smiled in recognition. "Mario. Of course." He paused, his empathy transparent. "How is Erica?"

The priest had been privy to Mario and Erica's despair. Well into her ninth month, Erica's appendix had burst, infection dashing their hopes of ever having a child of their own.

"No better, I'm afraid." Mario saw the questioning look in Father O'Reilly's eyes as the priest's gaze drifted down to the small bundle held awkwardly in his arms. Not caring to elaborate, Mario plunged on. "I've something . . . something I must confess."

Father O'Reilly nodded and said, "Well, my son, then you must come to confession tomorrow morning, before our next mass."

"But . . . I . . ." Mario paused, groping for the right words. They didn't come. A moment passed, and then he blurted, "Forgive me, Father. What I have to tell you cannot wait. You must hear my confession now."

Ashleigh Taylor stared straight ahead, oblivious to the silver-haired nurse behind her wheelchair, oblivious to the hum of voices that echoed off the walls of Long Beach Memorial Hospital's enormous lobby. Oblivious to anything but her tiny daughter.

From the moment this nightmare began, her room on the maternity floor had been flooded with people—hospital staff, members of the hospital administration, police, plainclothes detectives. She'd talked to scores of individuals, so many that their faces and words were no more than an unfocused kaleidoscope.

As Ashleigh gazed down at her baby, her vision blurred. She blinked back tears. *Who did this? Who could have taken her twin? And . . . why? Oh my God, why did this happen?* She prayed once more for strength.

Ashleigh's only relief was that she would finally be leaving the upheaval on the maternity floor and the endless litany of questions she could not begin to answer. Neither the nurse who pushed the wheelchair nor the two uniformed officers accompanying them had spoken directly to her since leaving the fourth floor. What was there to say?

The instant the automatic doors hissed open, Conrad rushed to her side, his dark hair slightly disheveled, a light stubble shadowing his jaw. He took her hand in his, then tenderly ran his index finger along their daughter's soft cheek.

Ashleigh sat up as straight as she could, trying to show her husband that she could be—she *would* be—strong. Her gaze drifted from Conrad to the black-and-white police cars, one directly in front of their rented Lincoln Continental, the other nearly touching the back bumper. Behind the rear police car was a black sedan. The driver's door swung open, and a tall man in a dark suit headed in their direction—perhaps one of the plainclothes detectives? Ashleigh felt her resolve begin to waver.

Conrad followed her eyes toward the tall man beside the black Crown Victoria. The man was well over six feet, with thick salt-and-pepper hair and a serious expression on his thin face. "Be right with you," Conrad called out. Turning back to her, he said tenderly, "We're going to get through this."

"I know." Ashleigh squeezed Callie lightly and then raised her to meet her father's outstretched arms. Before either he or the nurse could utter a single word in protest, she rose from her wheelchair. "I rode in this thing only because I was given no choice," she said in a strained voice. "I don't need to be pampered. I need to be strong."

"Ashleigh!"

"I'm sorry, love. I know I must sound like a petulant child. But I can't allow myself to be weak or fall into any kind of self-pity. We both have to be strong. Callie needs us, and I pray that whoever has taken Cassie will . . ." Tears filled her eyes again, this time spilling down her cheeks before she could stop them.

Conrad pulled her close with his free arm.

"I'd like to sit in the backseat, beside Callie," she said, knowing her husband would understand.

"Of course," he said, pulling open the rear car door.

Ashleigh slid into the backseat, then froze. A single infant car seat had been secured to the beige leather seat. Conrad must have dashed out to purchase it that morning. There was no sign of the one they had bought in anticipation of the twins—the double one that had been strapped to the seat the day before. The day their life had been torn apart. The day Ashleigh had reached into Cassie's bassinet beside her own bed and scooped up a rubber baby doll, swaddled in a pink hospital receiving blanket and staring up at her with bright blue, plastic eyes. The day her heart had come to a full stop.

Taking a steadying breath, Ashleigh looked up at Conrad and word-lessly held out her arms for Callie. He held her gaze silently. There was no need for words. He gently placed their daughter in her arms and then strode toward the detective.

Callie whimpered, and Ashleigh's thoughts temporarily shifted from her own loss. She held her infant daughter for a moment or so, rocking her back and forth until she quieted, then carefully maneuvered her into the car seat. Fumbling with the unfamiliar latches, Ashleigh had to smile at her own awkwardness. But Callie immediately settled down and appeared to be taking in her surroundings.

Ashleigh thought of the mysterious bond between identical twins—she'd read that it could be powerful. From the moment she'd learned that she was carrying twins, she had devoured every relevant book and article she could get her hands on. Did that bond develop in the womb? Could Callie, even now, sense the loss of her sister? *Oh, let it be temporary!* Callie would not be missing her twin for long. Whoever had taken Cassie would be found, and she would be returned to them. Their family would be whole again soon.

Ashleigh willed herself to believe it.

"The detective said everything is in order." Conrad sighed and slipped behind the wheel of the Continental, then turned the key.

"Meaning what?" Ashleigh responded.

"Long Beach PD has set up their equipment in Charles's home. They'll be monitoring all the incoming calls." His voice was less than reassuring as he told her all that he'd learned from the lanky detective.

After a short exchange about what the day might bring, Ashleigh soon became lost in her own thoughts.

She would not dwell on the twins' delivery away from their new home in Dallas, three weeks early. Instead, she willed her thoughts to Charles Stuart and the effect this catastrophe might have on him. Charles had always been there for Ashleigh—his wisdom, his strength, and his values had been a part of her life for as long as she could remember. Her parents had been killed in a plane accident when she was barely two years old; Charles and her grandmother were the only "parents" she'd known. Since Gran's death, there had been only Charles.

Ashleigh had arrived in California a few days ahead of her husband, to take care of the last-minute details for the spectacular birthday celebration she'd been planning for Charles. Having recently been appointed CEO of the prestigious Michael Nason Specialty Stores, headquartered in Dallas, Conrad had been unable get away earlier.

Charles Stuart's birthday celebration had attracted widespread media coverage. The distinguished list of those who had come to honor the razor-sharp ninety-year-old could fill several pages of the Who's Who directory. His white hair thick and his posture erect, Charles looked decades younger than his age and was still an impressive figure in the world of retail. He had remained a valued member of the Consolidated Department Stores board of directors, up until the hostile takeover by the nefarious corporate raider, Philip Sloane—a shrewd Australian real estate tycoon who knew nothing about department store management or how to manage a leveraged business.

Conrad pulled into the driveway in front of Charles's four-car garage and put the car in park, snapping Ashleigh back to the present. She shuddered at the vision of this beautiful home being transformed into a surveillance headquarters for a possible ransom attempt. And yet she prayed that whoever had taken their daughter would call. And that the call would come soon. She refused to consider the alternative.

Charles stood for a moment or so beside the open gate of his two-story home in the quiet Long Beach community of Naples, then approached the car. He pulled open the back door, a tentative smile playing across his aristocratic face. As Ashleigh searched for words, her composure slipped another notch, and tears flowed down her cheeks unchecked.

Conrad leapt from his seat and dashed around to the rear passenger side of the car, extending his hand to greet Charles while keeping an eye on Ashleigh and their baby.

Ashleigh swiftly pulled herself together and forced a warm smile, though it failed to reflect in her tearful eyes. "Would one of you like to hold Callie?" she offered, unhooking the buckles on the car seat and lifting the baby into her arms. Charles smiled and reached for the small bundle. Ashleigh gently placed Callie in his outstretched hands.

Once Conrad had assured himself that Charles had a firm grasp on his daughter, he said, "I hope the police haven't turned your home upside down . . ."

"Just relieved they were able to set up so quickly." Charles hesitated for a second. "So far, there have been no incoming calls of any significance." Together, they walked toward the front door.

When Ashleigh stepped into the large kitchen of her childhood home, her tenuous hold on her emotions nearly gave way. More than half a dozen police officers milled about. Two folding tables had been installed in the middle of the room. The tabletops were covered with recording machines, telephones, open notebooks, and notepads. Phone lines were strung across the room, held down by duct tape. The odor of strong coffee and an unnerving hum permeated the air.

She gave Charles a warm hug before transferring the sleeping child from his arms to her own. She spotted a small cradle by the familiar kitchen table, but rejected the idea of placing Callie in the midst of all the activity. Yet Ashleigh wanted her daughter near. She did not want her to wake up all alone. Peering into the dining room, she saw men sitting around the oblong table and turned back to Charles. "Is there anyone in the library?"

He shook his head. "No. Only in the dining room and here in the kitchen."

A woman strode into the kitchen carrying several plastic bags. "Ashleigh!" It was Elizabeth, a registered nurse who was Charles's personal assistant. She seemed surprised to see Ashleigh, and instantly dumped the bags on the sink and made a beeline across the room. "When I called the hospital, they said you wouldn't be released until afternoon," she said. "I'd planned to get you set up in the library." Elizabeth's eyes pooled with tears, but her voice did not waver as she greeted Conrad, then pulled Ashleigh and the baby into a motherly hug.

Before Ashleigh had a chance to respond, she noticed that Elizabeth's gaze had drifted down to Callie. She slowly pulled the blanket away from her daughter's face so the warm-hearted woman could take a peek.

Conrad pointed toward the cradle and said, "I'll move this into the library," pausing to make sure that Ashleigh approved. She nodded, then noticed a tall, lanky man step into the room. It was the detective whom Conrad had spoken with outside Memorial Hospital.

"Mrs. Taylor, I'm Detective George Davis, LBPD. We spoke briefly in the hospital yesterday evening. When you get the baby settled, I'd like to go over the details of the disappearance of your . . . other daughter."

Ashleigh stared at the detective. She didn't remember him. Steadying herself against the doorjamb that led into the dining room, she attempted to stay focused. And yet she couldn't dispel the recurring vision of the rubber-faced baby doll, its plastic eyes staring up at her from the pink blanket. Again and again, as if on a continuous loop in her mind, she felt herself reaching into Cassie's bassinet and finding only those lifeless eyes staring back at her. The floor seemed to shift beneath her feet. Ashleigh couldn't push a single word past her constricted throat.

Conrad put his arm around her and glared at the detective. "Detective Davis, we have cooperated fully with law enforcement. My wife has gone over every detail of what she knows about our daughter's disappearance. She has spoken to untold numbers of detectives, police officers, hospital staff . . . The police have the doll that was left in Cassie's bassinet." He took a heavy breath. "She's told you everything she knows—"

Ashleigh held up her hand. "It's alright, love." Her eyes stung with unshed tears. With an effort, she fixed her eyes on the detective again. "I don't know what I can tell you that you don't already know, but as soon as I get Callie settled, I'll join you in the living room."

There was nothing else for her to do.

Ross Pocino found a parking spot opposite the entry to Long Beach Memorial Hospital. He noted the abundance of black-and-whites parked at the top of the winding driveway beside the hospital. *Surprise, surprise.*

Heaving his ample girth from beneath the steering wheel of his red Mustang, he wasted no time mounting the broad staircase toward the hospital entry. Next to the sliding doors, he recognized one of the police officers posted at the hospital because of the kidnapping.

"Hey, Joe. Is Lieutenant Flynn around?" Pocino asked.

"Didn't see him leave. Was headed back up to Maternity last time I saw him." He paused, checking out Pocino's rumpled sports jacket. "Sort of thought you might show up."

It wasn't much of a stretch.

After Pocino had left the force and served a short stint as head of security for Bentley's Department Stores, he'd signed on as an investigator with the Landes Agency. So when Consolidated had fallen victim to Philip Sloane's hostile takeover bid—and Conrad Taylor and Mark Toddman had found their every move being shadowed—the investigations firm was hired and placed on retainer. Pocino had served the personal as well as the business needs of the former principals of Bentley's and Bentleys Royale, part of the retail giant's West Coast divisions. Taylor and Toddman had refused to work with Sloane; they had moved on to the prestigious Michael Nason's in Dallas, while Sloane had sold the West Coast divisions of Consolidated to Jordon's and then run the remainder of the retail empire into bankruptcy.

But despite all these changes, Pocino's loyalty to the Taylor and Toddman families had remained constant. When Conrad had called him early that morning, he had jumped at the opportunity to help them out.

"Conrad Taylor and his wife are more than clients," Pocino acknowledged. "We've covered a lot of ground since I worked security for Bentley's." Without further elaboration, he pulled out a small spiral notebook and asked, "Has a kid ever been snatched from this hospital before?"

"Never. Memorial Hospital has an impeccable reputation and, the security staff is excellent. Unfortunately, there are so many goddamn exits . . ."

Anxious to get to the lieutenant, Pocino said, "Thanks, Joe. Need to see Flynn ASAP. Catch you later."

Pocino strode to the elevator bank and pushed the UP button. The doors to the first elevator hissed open, and he stepped back to allow its occupants to pass by: a young woman in a wheelchair, holding an infant wrapped in a fuzzy blue blanket, and the heavyset nurse who was pushing them. The nurse gave him an apprehensive glance, then proceeded to the lobby. A police officer was just a few steps behind.

Before he had a chance to step into the elevator, the door to the middle elevator slid open and Lieutenant Gary Flynn strode out.

"Figured I'd be running into you." Flynn gave a knowing smile and a firm handshake. "Come on back and I'll fill you in."

Heading toward the administration offices, Pocino said, "All I know is that someone took one of the Taylors' twins. That's it."

"Can't tell you much more. We've posted officers at all exits and swept every inch of the maternity ward. The other floors are being covered as we speak."

"How in the hell can someone just waltz out of the hospital with someone else's baby?" Before giving Flynn time to respond, Pocino added, "Got to be an inside job."

"That's the line we're taking." As they entered the administration complex, Flynn lowered his voice and gestured toward the first conference room to their left. Inside, Pocino got a whiff of strong coffee and noted half a dozen abandoned Styrofoam cups and wads of crumpled paper strewn across the long oak table. Chairs had been left askew, but the room did not reek of the usual stale smoke—surely the hospital had prohibited smoking. Still, it was obviously the meeting place of the investigating officers. Flynn pulled out a chair and gestured toward the far wall, where a coffeepot sat on the counter above some cupboards.

Pocino pulled a Styrofoam cup from the holder and poured some of the inky black liquid into it. "How about you?"

"Been here since around seven last night," the lieutenant informed him. "I've had enough coffee to keep me jumping all month."

Pocino took his coffee to the table and plunked himself down in the chair beside Flynn. "So fill me in."

"The case was immediately kicked up from missing persons when . . ." He inhaled slowly. Then, meeting Pocino's stare with piercing eye contact, he continued, "Got to keep this under wraps as long as possible." Again he paused, a frown furrowing his brow. "Considering the victims, it's not likely to be too long. Anyway, as I was saying, we kicked the case up to kidnapping as soon as we found the doll."

"A doll?"

"Yeah, a doll wrapped in hospital blankets. It was left in the missing baby's bassinet."

Barely listening now, Pocino jumped to a rapid conclusion. "Got to be more than one person involved. This place is huge and there's a lot of exits, but there's also a helluva lot of people milling about. Not easy to walk out with a baby." He paused. "Aren't all the new moms taken out in a wheelchair?"

"Standard procedure. The hospital administrator and the entire staff are up in arms. Everyone's baffled. Nothing like this ever happened before. No one can fathom how a baby could be carried out undetected."

"Are you thinking about bringing in the FBI?"

"Not at this point. They're typically involved only in cases when a kid is taken across state lines, and we have no evidence of that. In fact, we have zilch in the way of evidence. Anyway, with all the domestic shenanigans these days, the FBI stopped investigating even those types of kidnappings a few years back." After a slight hesitation, Flynn added, "But hell, you know all that. You know it all too well."

Pocino didn't respond. He gulped down the remainder of his coffee and refocused. "With these high-profile victims, there's a damn good chance this case'll involve ransom."

"Right."

"And they don't come a lot higher-profile than Taylor and Stuart. Wonder if Stuart's big birthday bash was what triggered some low-life's plan."

Flynn shrugged. "It's a possibility. We've set up surveillance at the Stuart home."

"What are the odds on a ransom call?"

"Because the delivery of the Taylors' twins was three weeks early and away from their own home—"

"Not much time for planning," Pocino cut in. He turned over the possibilities in his head. "In the kidnapping of an infant, the motive generally boils down to one of three scenarios." Holding up an index finger, he said, "Number one, someone can't have a kid of their own and wants one." Raising a second finger, he continued, "Two, someone is selling babies to couples unable to have their own. And third," he said, lifting his ring finger, "is for ransom—when the victims are affluent, like the Taylors and Stuart."

Before Flynn had a chance to interject, Pocino concluded, "Seldom are infants harmed by a kidnapper." Looking straight into Flynn's eyes, he sought confirmation. "Right?"

Flynn nodded. "You're on target."

"All the hospital personnel been interviewed?"

Flynn nodded again. "Everyone on the maternity floor, the entire hospital staff, visitors, even the other patients. You know the drill." He leaned back in his chair before continuing. "The instant the baby was found missing, the hospital was locked down. No one's been allowed to leave the building before being interviewed. Major problem is, we aren't sure how wide the window was between the time the baby was taken and when the mother discovered her missing." Lieutenant Flynn leaned forward again.

"So, what's your take on the whole affair?"

In the subdued elegance of the living room, Ashleigh dropped down beside Conrad and sank back against the plump sofa pillows. She tried to focus her attention on Detective Davis, attempting a smile. Every few seconds, she forgot to breathe.

Davis broke the tense silence. "Mrs. Taylor, we'll make this interview as brief as possible. Let's begin with your last recollection of either seeing or holding your infant . . ." He glanced down at his notes. "Cassie."

For a moment, Ashleigh did not look directly at the detective.

Cassie . . . The image of her tiny daughter came clearly to her mind. "Cassie is the more active of the twins. She awoke about three o'clock in the afternoon. After nursing her, I held her for a while, and then Callie let me know that it was her turn, so I put Cassie back in her bassinet. She was sound asleep."

"And that's the last time you saw her?"

His words pierced her like an icy needle. "I . . . I'm not sure. I . . ." She took a breath to steady herself, her throat too dry to push out a single word. She dropped her head and gestured that she needed a moment.

Conrad put an arm around her shoulder, his concern palpable. Silence permeated the room as the detective waited for Ashleigh to continue.

"Both bassinets were beside my bed. I checked on the babies constantly. How could I stop looking at them? They were both so . . . so beautiful. When I saw that they were both asleep—I don't know when . . ." She couldn't go on.

"So someone must have taken Cassie and put the doll in her bassinet while you were asleep," Davis filled in.

Ashleigh squeezed Conrad's cool, dry hand and nodded.

"And you found the doll in the bassinet"—Davis paused again to check his notes—"at around five thirty-five."

Ashleigh nodded again, not trusting her voice. She heard the constant tick of the grandfather clock and the ragged sound of her own breathing. Finally, she spoke the thought that kept echoing in her head. "I don't understand how someone could have come into my room without my hearing them. Since the moment the twins were born, I've been super-sensitive to even the quietest of sounds." She was sure she had dozed only moments at a time since she'd delivered the twins. So how could she have slept through someone walking into the room and taking her baby away?

"Well, Mrs. Taylor, after giving birth to twins, it's not surprising that you'd need your sleep," Davis said. "The hospital is a busy place filled with all sorts of noises."

You just don't understand! Ashleigh wanted to scream, but his next question sent her in another direction.

"Do you recall any of the hospital staff coming into your room after you put the babies back to bed?"

"Sure," she said, although her attention had not been on the hospital staff. "Nurses and nurse's aides were coming in and out of our room constantly. Some to see if I needed anything and others to just take a peek at . . ." Once again, she tried to visualize the features of each person who had come into the hospital room. But it was no use; it was all a blur. The only thing that was crystal clear in her mind's eye was her daughters—healthy and whole. She'd checked each one's ten fingers and ten toes, over and over, in awe. So tiny and so perfect. The look of adoration on Conrad's handsome face when he'd first laid eyes on Ashleigh and their tiny daughters would be etched in her memory forever. Conrad had flown back to Dallas after Charles's party for an important management meeting at Michael Nason's. But when she'd rung two nights ago to say she was going to the hospital, he'd raced to catch the next plane to Long Beach, practically out the door before she'd finished telling him that her water had broken. He'd arrived just after the delivery, while she was still in recovery. It seemed like a hundred years ago.

The phone shrilled, bringing the interview to a halt.

Conrad sprang from the couch. He stood, unmoving, beside the phone, until the officer in charge of phone surveillance signaled that his team was ready.

"Hello." Conrad's baritone voice filled the room. Ashleigh leaned forward on the sofa, her gaze unwavering. His eyes met hers, but he shook his head. "I'll have to get back to you," he said, and ended the call.

Throughout the day there was the steady hum of detectives and police officers discussing what was or was not happening. Each time the phone rang, Conrad's wild eyes shot to the surveillance officer. He waited for the signal, then snapped up the phone, praying to hear the kidnapper's voice with news of his infant daughter. Although he'd never imagined himself actually hoping for a ransom demand, now it was his vehement desire. He wanted it more than anything. He wanted it *now*.

After several false alarms, Ashleigh had agreed to take Callie upstairs and try to get some rest. All the hustle and bustle was surely taking its toll, especially the press conference they'd thrown together on Charles's front lawn. Ashleigh's on-camera plea for her baby's safe return had been shown by all the local TV networks. Conrad marveled at the way she appeared to be taking things in stride, revealing few signs of weakness. But he knew her too well to be taken in; she must be near the breaking point. His wife was the most compassionate person he'd ever known, but somehow she could never allow herself to be on the receiving end of compassion. If only she'd let down her guard. *But how can I ask her to do that? It might be all that's keeping her sane.*

The events she'd been through in the previous forty-eight hours were enough to send anyone over the edge. Even he was totally undone—he had to force himself to remain focused. The words Ashleigh had spoken moments before she'd taken Callie upstairs kept replaying in his head. "There's not going to be anyone calling for ransom," she had said, her voice barely above a whisper, her liquid brown eyes full of sadness. He wished it were possible to block out those words. Conrad didn't want to think about that. Raking his hands though his hair, he rose and headed back into the kitchen for another cup of strong, bitter coffee.

He, too, feared that whoever had taken Cassie intended to keep her.

CHAPTER

5

Paige Toddman padded into the kitchen of her Greenwich home and drifted toward the aroma of freshly brewed coffee. As she filled her cup, she noticed Mark's empty mug on the countertop and remembered his early morning meeting with Cyril Stein, the CEO of Jordon's. She hoped it was going well, though she had no doubt that her husband's vision would soon become a reality. Against all odds, Mark had wooed Consolidated's creditors and persuaded the majority of them to become investors instead. The bankruptcy would soon be lifted; the end was now in sight. As far as Paige was concerned, her husband could do anything.

Climbing up on one of the bar stools to enjoy a few moments to herself, Paige sipped her coffee and let her mind drift. She recalled the night of the extravaganza at Carlingdon's in Manhattan, when Mark's role in the Consolidated rescue plan was first unveiled. No one would have believed then that the troubled retail empire would be turned around in just a few months. Through Mark's leadership, disaster had been diverted. Not only that, but Mark and his management team were now setting the wheels in motion to acquire Jordon's—the very department store conglomerate that had taken over Consolidated's West Coast divisions.

We've come so far, thought Paige. Just a few years back, there had been that brief misunderstanding between the two of them, coinciding with the hostile bid for Consolidated. But aside from that, she and Mark had always been an invincible team. While he made the ultimate decisions for whatever venture he was involved in, she was never kept on the outside. Paige was an active participant in various charities and in the arts, in a big way. And she, as well as Mark, held the position of director on several boards. They shared freely in each other's successes. And that night at Carlingdon's had been one of the shining moments of his career.

She'd been a little nervous as their limousine had passed the blinding klieg lights outside the Carlingdon's Lexington Avenue entrance and pulled up to the curb. But when a uniformed doorman had pulled open the door and she and Mark had emerged from the limo into the warm spring evening, those jitters had disappeared.

They'd been greeted by scores of blinding flashbulbs and hordes of partygoers eagerly awaiting their arrival. Buyers, vendors, and manufacturers alike had been invited to "Broadway 90" to preview the fall fashions while enjoying a five-star meal. But the number-one reason they had come was to meet and appraise the merchant prince of retail—the man whom the board of directors had somehow convinced to break his contract and leave his prestigious position as CEO of Michael Nason's. The man who had come to lead Carlingdon's and its bankrupt parent company, Consolidated Department Stores, through their greatest challenge. Mark Toddman had been touted as Consolidated's only hope for rescue from bankruptcy and rebuilding. Everybody had wondered: Could he really pull it off? Could he restore the nation's greatest group of department stores to their former grandeur?

Inside, men in square-shouldered suits and women in short black dresses were served champagne and hors d'oeuvres by tuxedoed waiters. Show tunes had rippled in the background, drowned out by the buzz of voices and bursts of laughter. That night, the theater of retailing had been at its grandest, enveloping both the optimistic and the pessimistic members of the throng.

Mark and Paige had smiled broadly as they made their way across the foyer, stopping to talk with friends and colleagues who had come from Fifth Avenue and beyond. The Toddmans had planned to enjoy every moment of the evening, despite the unavoidable hushed tones that reached their ears. Between sips of Perrier-Jouët, there had been murmurs of Carlingdon's former ambience and the humiliation of Chapter 11, from which no major retailer to date had ever survived. But Paige had held her head high, thinking, *Mark will show these doubters.* She knew her husband, and she'd had the utmost confidence that he would prove to be the exception to the rule, with his simple mantra *Carlingdon's will survive . . . Consolidated will survive . . . Department stores will survive.*

To her, his words had held more than the ring of hope. She'd known Mark would make them ring true.

As Carlingdon's CEO Duncan Bradley, dressed in a beautifully tailored dark blue suit, had walked to the microphone and given a weary smile to the crowd milling around the escalators, Mark—standing beside him, a full head taller—had continued laughing and joking with the press. In a white double-breasted blazer and gray slacks, he'd looked relaxed. Since entering the store, he'd been shaking hands and slapping backs.

Duncan had cleared his throat and, with a dazed expression, introduced his new boss—and the new CEO of Consolidated Department Stores.

Paige had watched her husband grin as he looked out over the crowd. His curtain was rising, and he'd known it. It had been a long wait, but Mark was back where he belonged, and he would make a difference.

"Tonight is a night for celebration, so I'll keep my comments to a minimum," he'd begun, his Boston accent still as thick as a Kennedy's. Throughout his address to the audience, he had made no reference to the company's many creditors—neither those who were behind him one hundred percent nor those who remained skeptical. "Please enjoy the fashions as they are informally modeled throughout the evening. Let these fabulous creations remind you of the reasons our customers love to shop with us. Clearly, a department store is the most exciting place to shop. And with the lightning-pace of our world today, consumers desire our convenience along with our quality and selection. Yet throughout my twenty-five years at Consolidated, people have talked about department stores being an anachronism. It just isn't so. The department store is no dinosaur. Just walk through Carlingdon's. Feel the energy within these walls."

Paige had caught the sparkle in Mark's eyes and felt his excitement. It was contagious. She felt a tingle even now, sitting there in her bathrobe at the kitchen counter, as she thought back to the vitality and conviction his words had conveyed.

"Since most of the things we sell are not necessities," he'd continued, "it's up to us to create the excitement and the demand. Unfortunately, we've gotten away from that in the past few years—particularly after financial people were brought in to lead the department store business. But while we must keep our eye on the bottom line, we can't afford to miss the big picture. We owe our stockholders a substantial profit; however, we must not fail to provide the type of service and ambiance that our patrons expect and deserve from us. Merchandising is an art. It doesn't always 'add up.' It's the unknown. It's the romance. It's the sizzle that makes life interesting."

As promised, he had brought his talk to a speedy close. "I don't gamble. When we emerge from Chapter 11, it will be with the same principles we've always had. Those principles are our strength. In this business, size means nothing. We make our money by being creative and by being unique." With a broad grin, he'd concluded, "Now, please follow Paige and me onto the dance floor. Let the party begin!" Then Mark had pulled her close, given her a kiss on the cheek, and guided her across the floor to the escalators that would take them to the top floor.

Taking hold of her husband's hand, Paige had hardly been able to wait for his arms to wrap around her. After twenty-two years of marriage, her heart still beat a little faster when Mark was beside her and they could close out the rest of the world. No matter that they were sharing the evening with five hundred business associates. On the dance floor, he was all hers.

Sipping her coffee again, Paige thought now about how Mark had approached the dance floor that night as he approached most areas of his life: with confidence and enthusiasm. How they'd glided across it that evening to the mellow strains of the thirty-seven-piece orchestra. How, in the essence of his brief statements, he'd sounded confident—and he was. But of course he'd been candid with her.

He'd confessed that it was the biggest risk of his entire career.

6

Mario checked his rearview mirror and backed out of the driveway of his sister's Westminster home. When he'd strapped his newborn daughter into the infant carrier in the backseat, her cry had pierced his heart. *If only I could keep her here in the front seat beside me, like Mom did Jean when she was a baby.* But those days were long gone. Mercifully, the baby drifted off to sleep only seconds after Mario rolled out of the driveway. All was silent save the hum of the motor.

His mind raced back to the previous night, when he'd taken his infant daughter into his sister's home and lowered her into the dainty, pink-and-white bassinet Jean had lovingly refurbished for his and Erica's baby. The baby had awoken and begun to cry, and she did so throughout the night, settling down only when he held her. He could still feel her soft finger wrap around his own, changing his world forever. "I will do everything in my power to give you a beautiful life, to protect you and never let anyone take you from us," he had murmured into her ear.

She'd rejected the bottle of formula Mario had prepared for her, and she cried whenever he tried to return her to the bassinet. As long as he rocked her or walked with her, she appeared content. He felt an irrefutable bond between them, and so he tried to ignore the throbbing in his gritty eyes. He hadn't had a moment's sleep—not that he could have slept last night under any circumstances.

Jean was out of town on a buying trip for her antiques boutique, but she'd left the key under the doormat and a note on the kitchen table, reminding her brother not to forget the bassinet or the other gifts she'd left for Erica and the baby. She didn't know that Erica had lost their baby. Mario hadn't told her. He hadn't told anyone. And he didn't intend to.

No one must know that this baby wasn't the one Erica had carried nearly to term. Now that they were moving to New York, where he would begin his career as a fully credentialed nurse practitioner at St. Vincent's Catholic Medical Center, there would be new friends and associates. Erica would find new colleagues, too, as a sales associate and fashion designer at De Mornay's, a fancy Fifth Avenue boutique. No one need know—ever. He might live an eternity in hell for taking this child, but there had been no other way to save his wife. He couldn't allow her to sink further into depression.

He'd told no one of their loss. Instead, he'd told his former peers—the staff members at Long Beach Memorial Hospital—that although Erica's delivery had been a couple of weeks early, while she was at her brother's home in Laguna Niguel, she had given birth to a healthy baby girl.

Now he had a trunk full of gifts the staff had given him the night before, at his going-away party. Gifts that one of the security guards had helped him carry to his car, never suspecting that a missing baby was tucked inside the canvas shoulder bag he'd carried.

Mario's scalp tingled, and he broke out in a sweat along his hairline as he thought back to how long the security guard had stood alongside his car, as if he had all the time in the world. Thank God, the baby had not awakened.

Leaving Westminster now, Mario drove right past the on-ramp for the 405 Freeway and headed toward Pacific Coast Highway instead. Soon he was traveling south in his silver Taurus. He flicked on the radio and turned the dial to 640 AM, wondering if there was any news yet of the missing child—and praying there wasn't. Tuning in at the end of the hour, he caught only a small portion of the news. What he heard made his blood turn cold. It was worse than he'd feared. Far worse.

. . . known about what's happened to the missing twin. However, we have been informed that the infant taken from Long Beach Memorial Hospital was the child of Conrad Taylor, CEO of the renowned Michael Nason Specialty Stores, headquartered in Dallas, and the great-granddaughter of Charles Stuart, builder, original owner, and inspiration behind the Bentley's

and Bentleys Royale department store empire. Stuart's vision of building a unique, upscale specialty department store in the suburbs, rather than in the downtown sector, was known as "Stuart's folly" before the Depression, when construction began. It was only later that Stuart's forward thinking was heralded as pure genius and his cathedral of merchandising became a protected California monument in . . .

Gripping the steering wheel so tight that his knuckles turned white and his fingers grew numb, Mario panicked, his thoughts going into overdrive. *Oh my God. Holy mother of Jesus. Not only have I committed the most unforgivable of sins and devastated a young mother, I've also taken a baby who's bound to attract widespread media coverage.* His heart gave a dull kick before settling into rapid rhythm. It was too late to turn back. He desperately needed to talk to Ian—alone. If his brother-in-law wouldn't help him, his life might as well be over. The sound of pounding surf roared in Mario's head, but as he gazed out over the Pacific Ocean, it appeared tranquil.

I've got to get a grip, he told himself.

Nearing Crown Valley Parkway in Laguna Niguel, Mario glanced at the clock. It was nearly a quarter to one. He wanted to avoid his sister-in-law. Ian had said that Leslie was going to some sort of charity meeting at one o'clock. She'd most likely left already, but Mario dropped his speed just in case she'd had a late start.

On Camino Del Avion, he turned right into the gated community and stopped in front of the guard's kiosk. "Mario Christonelli," he called out.

"Yes, Mr. Christonelli. Dr. McDonald is expecting you. Said you would be staying at their home for a while, so you'll need one of these." He handed Mario a plastic card and gestured to the residents' entrance.

After thanking the guard, Mario slowly wound his way up to Windham Lane. Rounding the cul-de-sac, he pulled into the driveway, thankful that Leslie's Lexus was not parked in the open garage.

Mario scooped up the sleeping baby and cautiously mounted the front stairs. The door stood ajar. Peering through the glass of a side panel, he let out a breath and slowly pushed open the door. Cautiously taking in the room, he tiptoed across the tiled entry to the living room couch, lay the baby against one of the cushions, and needlessly placed a couple of flat pillows beside his daughter. *Best not to greet Ian with a baby in my arms.* Having made sure his baby was safe, Mario called out, "Ian?"

"Back here in the study."

Mario jogged across to the hallway, stopping in front of the door to Ian's study. "Are you taking care of the death certificate?" Ian looked up from his paperwork, his expression puzzled. "Yes. But you'd better tell me what this is all about."

"You didn't say anything to Erica, did you?" Mario asked, his anxiety echoing in the rise of his voice.

Ian swiveled his chair so he could face Mario, a worried expression on his angular face. "No, I didn't. She's in the guest room. Hasn't stepped foot outside that room since you left. Leslie and I are worried as hell. Leslie takes meals to her, but as far as she knows, Erica seldom ventures out of bed. She hasn't eaten more than a few bites."

Even though it came as no real surprise, Ian's words cut through Mario like a sharp blade. *My wife is dying a slow death, if not in body, then in mind and spirit.* If it hadn't been for Erica's inconsolable state of mind, he never would have considered the irreversible act he'd committed the night before.

He had to make Ian understand. He'd done the only thing he could conceive of that might possibly return Erica to the vivacious young woman he'd married. In his heart, he knew that this was the key. Now he must convince Ian that his support was critical to Erica's recovery. He had nowhere else to turn. Ian was her brother, and he knew her—and loved her—better than almost anyone.

The family history that Ian had shared with Mario so many years ago, before he and Erica were married, dominated Mario's thoughts.

Erica's birth had been an accident in the midst of a troubled marriage, when her parents were in their mid-forties. Their father suffered an early death by stroke at age forty-nine. Much later, a month before Ian was to enter medical school at University of California, Irvine, their mother had been institutionalized. She'd fallen into a deep depression following the death of her eldest son, and the full responsibility for her teenage daughter had fallen to Ian. With the support of a healthy trust fund—passed down from his paternal grandfather and made available to his mother (and in turn, to him)—Ian was able to remain in school and go on to earn his medical degree in obstetrics and gynecology. Ian had confessed to Mario that getting through med school while being responsible for his teenage sister had been a formidable task. Although Erica was bright and, most of the time, good-natured, she'd also been strong-willed and, like their mother, prone to bouts of depression.

"Ian, what I have to share with you—it will shock you to the core, but I need you to hear me out."

"That sounds pretty damn ominous. You've got my ear, but let's move to the kitchen so we can grab some coffee. I have a feeling we're going to need it."

Mario followed his tall, lean brother-in-law into the room and then waited as Ian poured steaming coffee into two oversize mugs. When Ian gestured toward the kitchen table, Mario yanked out a chair and prayed the baby did not awaken before he was able to get Ian's full support. God knew how much he needed it. Without Ian's help, he'd be left without a hope.

Like an automaton, Paige set the phone back in the cradle, her eyes brimming with tears. She glanced over at her seven-year-old daughter, who sat cross-legged on the living room floor, surrounded by pink tissue paper.

April appeared deep in thought, a baby's rattle in each hand. Then, nodding her head as if she'd made an important decision, she held up the rattle with the soft pink bear and said, "I think this one should be for Callie because she is the oldest, and this one will be for Cassie." With her other hand, she shook a nearly identical rattle in the shape of a bunny.

Her legs suddenly rubbery, Paige sank down to the couch. The echo of Conrad's words pounded in her head: *One of our twins has been kidnapped.* He hadn't told her much more, but the image of a baby, of any child, being kidnapped rendered Paige weak and shaking with fear.

The roar of the air-conditioning kicked in, muffling April's next words. The sight of the packed suitcases by the door chilled Paige to the bone. Uncharacteristically, she was at a loss for words.

Paige and Ashleigh had formed a strong bond during the past two years of living in Dallas. While their husbands were immersed in enhancing both the ambiance and the bottom line of Michael Nason's, the women threw much of their time and energy into the community, as ambassadors for the upscale department stores. Although Paige had been thrilled to return to Manhattan and the Toddmans' new home in Greenwich, she missed Ashleigh's intelligence, missed her optimistic outlook, and missed the younger woman's companionship most of all. So when Ashleigh had invited Paige to stay with her after the birth of her twins, she'd accepted without hesitation, and April had been counting the days until their expected delivery. The day before—the instant they'd received news of the early arrival of two perfect daughters—Paige had escalated their plans.

"Now we don't have to wait anymore, Mommy!" April had squealed in glee as she danced about the room. Paige had been equally excited, though a bit more practical. She'd outlined all the things they must take care of before their departure, even as she assured her daughter that they would leave the very next afternoon. She'd been confident that Mark, who was working night and day to restructure and take Consolidated out of bankruptcy, would not mind their brief absence. Her only concern had been taking April out of school, but the early delivery had meant that was no longer an issue. The school year did not begin for another three weeks.

Paige thought about how different their own lives would have been without April, their beautiful, doe-eyed daughter. It seemed a lifetime ago, but in fact it was just a little more than two years since the adoption had been finalized. As the result of a series of miscommunications, Paige and Mark had separated, and she had pursued her early dreams of counseling the underprivileged. It was during this period that April and her young mother had entered Paige's life. April, only four when her mother had been murdered, had forever changed the course of the Toddmans' lives.

The thought of April being taken from them turned her blood to ice. What kind of a monster could take a child from her family? *Family, family . . .* The thought echoed in her head. *What about our family?* Now that Mark's mother and Martha Winslow, April's surrogate grandmother, were gone, the need to find her own mother hit Paige squarely. Ever since adopting April, Paige had promised herself that when they returned to New York, she would begin to search for her. There were so many unanswered questions. What kind of person was the woman who had abandoned Paige as a toddler? Had Paige been a horrible, unlovable child? Was the woman who had given birth to her a drug-addicted lowlife? Or had her mother simply been too young, a victim of circumstances, as April's biological mother had been?

April clambered up on the couch beside Paige, bringing her back to the here and now. "What's wrong, Mommy?" Her voice was soft, and she sounded worried.

Pulling her close, Paige said, "I'm sorry, my love. I . . ."

She knew she must tell April that one of Ashleigh's twins had been kidnapped, but how could she explain? As both of the babies' names echoed in her head, Paige realized that she didn't even know which one was the missing twin, and she didn't know what to tell April. As she searched for words, she felt April lift a small hand to her face and wipe away the tears. Paige hadn't even realized they had spilled down her cheeks.

Ian set his mug on the table and fixed Mario with an appraising look. His brother-in-law looked as though he'd slept in his blue Izod shirt and chinos. But judging from Mario's unshaven face, his hollow, bloodshot eyes, and the puffy, dark circles beneath them, he'd obviously had little, if any, actual sleep.

Already puzzling over Mario's request to change the names on the death certificate of their stillborn, Ian knew, before his brother-in-law uttered his first word, that something was wrong. Terribly wrong.

"No one must suspect that Erica did not give birth to a healthy baby girl."

Ian froze. "What in the—"

"Please," Mario broke in. "Let me tell you the whole story. After I get it all out, you can ask all the questions you want. And I pray to God I'll have some answers."

Ian slumped back in his chair. "Go ahead."

"Our friends, family, and work associates knew that Erica and I were expecting our first child. Only you know the truth about what happened . . ."

Ian knew only too well. After two miscarriages, Erica had been unable to conceive another child. Before turning to in vitro fertilization, his sister and Mario had tried to adopt. Having bought a crib and created a nursery in their small apartment not once, but twice, the couple had learned that the mother of each baby they were waiting to adopt changed her mind at the last moment. The heartache of losing a second baby they'd already felt was theirs had sent Erica into her first full-blown bouts of depression.

But Mario had not stopped talking.

". . . never saw any signs of manic depression before Erica's first mis-carriage. We've been so happy together. I don't have to tell you how sweet and funny your sister can be. She has a heart of gold." He paused, then shook his head as if to dispel something unpleasant. "Oh, hell. I'm not telling you anything you don't already know."

After taking a small sip of his coffee, Mario continued, "I won't deny that Erica could get down in the dumps at times. But who wouldn't? The string of disappointments she's endured would get anyone down. One goddamn disappointment heaped on another. We knew the odds were against us with the in vitro. Only thirty percent, right?"

Ian nodded. He knew exactly what Mario was about to say, but let him continue anyway.

"After eight months, we were sure we were out of the woods," Mario said, almost to himself.

Ian broke in. "No one could have predicted that twist of fate."

Mario's head dropped down. Pressing his temples with both hands, he took a moment before blurting out, "This last loss has thrown her over the edge. Nothing will bring her back, other than having a baby of her own. You know—"

"Stop," Ian commanded. *Has he completely lost his mind?* When Erica's appendix had burst, and she was rushed into surgery at South Coast Medical Center, Ian had scrubbed in. It was he who'd had to tell Erica that the infection from her ruptured appendix had taken the life of their unborn child—and eliminated any chance of her ever conceiving another child. Ian was still reeling from the pain of being the messenger of such devastating news. The hollow stare he'd seen in the eyes of his fragile younger sister was emblazed upon his soul. His voice was harsher than he'd intended when he said, "You know full well that adoption is your only option."

Mario ran his stubby fingers through his dark hair and stared directly into Ian's eyes. "I understand, only too well, that Erica cannot carry another child. So I've done the only thing that will bring her back to all of us who love her. Attempting another legal adoption is not an option. Even if she was up to it, I couldn't put my wife through that again. And you of all people know that she's not up to it." Mario's voice did not waver. "You also know that adopting a baby is not nearly as easy as most people think, and now that Erica is thirty-six and I'm almost forty, the deck is definitely stacked against us. So let's not consider traveling down that road."

Mario took another sip of the still-steaming coffee and winced. "Let me start from the beginning. When you gave us the news that we could never hope to have another baby, I was totally unstrung. Not for me as much as for Erica. Sure, I'd like to have a kid, but it goes a lot deeper with her. This loss has thrown her over the edge, I tell you. And it's up to us to get her back." He paused.

Ian stared at Mario. Things were starting to fall into place, and somehow he knew he was about to be told something he didn't want to hear.

"Everyone at Memorial believes we had a baby girl. Last night they threw me a big going-away party. Most of the gifts were for the baby."

Ian frowned, concerned that his sister might not be the only one who'd gone over the edge.

"Please. Let me get this all out," Mario demanded. "Try not to judge. Just think about Erica. Last night I . . . I took a baby that was not mine."

Ian's mouth dropped open. "You . . . you kidnapped an infant?"

"I did," Mario said. "But please, Ian—please hold your judgment. I know it's a sin against God, and I'm willing to take any kind of retribution. But this baby is our only hope of bringing Erica back to us."

Ian shot up, knocking the kitchen chair to the floor. Unable to contain himself, he shouted, "Have you lost your bloody mind?" A chill spiraled up his spine, his horror mixing with a fair amount of incredulity. "You kidnapped a baby?" he repeated. Then, before Mario could respond, he asked, "How?"

"Please, hear me out. I'll tell you whatever you want to know. I know it sounds crazy, but I did it—I took a baby. And I did get away with it. God help me! I didn't have a choice."

Ian picked up the chair and sank back down, pressing his spine against the hard, straight back, trying to take it all in. "Hold it," he demanded. "Say that again."

"I didn't have a choice. I knew about Rose, about the possibility . . . I think it was late June when I first met her," Mario began. "I was returning from my lunch break when I saw this young girl in front of the hospital, her face streaming with tears. No one else was around, so I stopped to see if there was anything I could do. She shook her head, and I was about to walk away when her knees buckled. I caught her just as she began to topple down the stairs. I helped her over to that bench beside the coffee kiosk. Once she settled down, we talked for a while. She told me that she was only sixteen. Her parents refused to allow her to have an abortion, yet they wouldn't let her give the baby up for adoption either . . ."

Ian was having trouble concentrating. Nothing could possibly justify what his brother-in-law had done. As Mario droned on, Ian tried to curb his racing mind and tune in to what he was saying.

". . . and she knew she wasn't ready to take on the responsibility of raising a child. When I asked her if she'd like me to talk with her parents, she said no. She told me that her doctor had talked to both of her parents about putting her baby up for adoption, but they wouldn't hear of it."

"Mario," Ian interrupted.

"Please, hear me out. I saw Rose now and again at the hospital. She never changed her mind, all throughout her pregnancy—she knew she wasn't ready for that baby. At that time, all I could offer was a noncritical ear. But when Erica lost the baby, I thought of Rose. Of her unwanted child. I realized that her needs and desires meshed with ours. She was due to deliver, and we cooked up a plan for me to take the baby before Rose's parents could inflict their agenda on her."

Ian had heard enough. But before he could interject, Mario held up his hand and continued at a very rapid pace. "The timing was perfect. Rose was overdue, you see, and her doctor had scheduled to induce labor on my last day at Memorial."

"Mario," Ian said, his voice harsh.

"One more minute." Mario's voice was unsteady, but he plunged ahead. "Rose felt that a baby would destroy her future, and she trusted me to give the child a good home, so it would have been a win-win situation. She delivered early yesterday morning. My friends and associates had planned a going-away party for yesterday afternoon. The timing was perfect. I planned to keep my uniform on and go to the maternity ward after the party. I prepared a soft cradle inside a canvas shoulder bag, and I bought a baby doll and wrapped it in a hospital blanket. I planned to leave the doll in the bassinet and put Rose's baby in the cradle bag."

Ian stared at his brother-in-law. How on earth had levelheaded, intelligent Mario devised such a mad plan?

"But after the party," Mario continued, "when I arrived on the maternity floor, I found that the poor teenager's parents had whisked her and the baby away. In less than twenty-four hours! My gut was doing cartwheels. I'd already promised Erica that we would have our baby daughter when I returned, and that there would be no complications. Nothing to fear." Mario stared at Ian with hollow eyes. "But Erica didn't believe me. She'd given up hope. The last time I talked with my wife, she told me she was nothing but a useless vessel. She said she wished she could die! She recited a litany of reasons why she thought she was turning into her mother and would end up just like her, in a loony bin. God, Ian, I knew right then and there that there was no way I could return without a baby girl."

Ian stared back at his stocky brother-in-law, whose face was twisted in agony, but couldn't push a single word through his constricted throat.

"I was desperate. Had no idea what to do. Then I saw that a woman had delivered twins the same day as Rose. Two baby girls. She was young and could have more babies." Mario held up his palm. "I know . . . I know, I'm rationalizing, and it's still a sin against God, but so help me,

I couldn't turn back. I quickly checked the room number and took off toward it. When I passed by the room, I saw that the mother had dozed off. Two bassinets were beside her bed. No one was in the corridor, so I slipped inside the room and . . . and scooped up the baby nearest the door. I put the doll in the empty bassinet and the baby in the cradle inside my shoulder bag. It was a perfect fit. But when I walked out the door, I broke out in a cold sweat. I prayed that the mother wouldn't wake up. That the baby wouldn't cry. And that I would make it back to my wife, with this beautiful baby girl, safe and sound."

Incredulous, Ian felt unable to breathe. *This can't be happening.* But he quickly gulped in some air and pulled himself together. "Weren't you seen by the hospital staff?"

"Sure, I was. Knew I would be, so I made a point of saying good-bye to all those who couldn't come to my party. As well as the shoulder bag, I was carrying two sacks full of gifts. I'm sure no one suspected. Strange thing is, when I came out of the hospital, one of the security guards saw that my hands were pretty full and helped me take the gifts to the car. When he kept talking, with no signs of being in a hurry, my heart beat so loud, I was afraid he might hear it. So, after what seemed an eternity, I told the guard that I needed to get home to my wife and our new baby pronto."

Ian was baffled, and disoriented. "So . . . you stayed in Long Beach last night?"

"No. Figured it would be safer to stay at my sister's in Westminster. She's out of town." Mario seemed to be looking for a sign of understanding, but Ian had none to give. He remained silent and stoic.

Finally, Ian spoke. "My God, Mario, you've taken *someone else's child.* Are you aware of the consequences?"

"Of course I am! I've also thought about losing Erica forever. My warm, loving wife. Goddamn it! I know what I did was wrong! It's eating me up inside! I even stopped at St. Joseph's to confess my sin to Father O'Reilly."

"And he forgave you?"

"No. He told me I must take the baby back to her mother." He met Ian's eyes. "Don't you understand? Unless Erica has this chance to realize her dream of motherhood, she'll continue to feel worthless. Her depression will never go away. Worrying about turning into her mother—it'll become a self-fulfilling prophecy."

Ian was still aghast at Mario's confession—to him and to the priest. "I really don't understand your religion. How can a priest hear a confession like yours and remain silent? How can he keep that sort of information to himself?"

Mario just stared at his brother-in-law. Heaving a sigh, he explained, "What is said in confession is between the person and God, not the person and the priest. The priest is only a messenger. It's a holy covenant, one that provides great relief. But I'm not one to preach, especially not now." He paused and then said, "You're the only one who can help us."

"What do you expect me to do?" Ian felt the color drain from his face.

They were interrupted by a soft cry from the living room.

Ashleigh trudged up the carpeted staircase toward the guest room, and away from the area where the detective and a score of other policemen were still milling about. Rhythmically patting the fretful Callie on the back, she began to relax. She had managed to keep Callie away from the TV cameras but was relieved that newscasters and cameramen were no longer on the premises. A cradle, identical to the one downstairs, sat just inside the bedroom door. Ashleigh stopped midstride and stared at the empty cradle, which had been meant for Cassie and now seemed to fill the room.

Where is she? My baby girl? Will she ever be returned to me? Who has her? Is someone feeding her, taking care of her? Ashleigh shuddered. Her thoughts, as well as her gaze, turned to Callie, whose cries had risen to an alarming pitch. Gently stroking her daughter, Ashleigh pushed all thoughts of her missing baby from her mind, shifting her full attention to the precious gift she now rocked in her arms. An old, familiar lullaby played in her head—the one that Gran had sung to her. Softly, Ashleigh began to sing, "Lullaby and goodnight . . ."

Held tight against her mother's chest, Callie grew still, seeming to look straight into Ashleigh's eyes. Then, reaching out her doll-size hand, she caught a loose stand of Ashleigh's hair.

With tears welling in her eyes, Ashleigh brushed her fingertips over the light silky hair on her daughter's head. It was impossible to predict whether it would be blond like her own or dark like Conrad's. What was far more important to both her and her husband was that their daughters be healthy. Neither cared about the color of their hair or eyes. What did it matter?

Ashleigh lowered Callie onto the king-size bed, changed her diaper, and wrapped the blanket snugly around her, just as the nurse had shown her. Reluctantly, she lifted the heated bottle of formula and wiggled the nipple between Callie's rosebud lips. The baby wrinkled her nose but soon caught on and began sucking in the warm liquid. *Only temporary,* Ashleigh thought. And she prayed it would be. She had been intent on nursing, and was devastated when she was told that she wasn't producing enough milk for her tiny daughter. *When Cassie is once again in my arms, everything will be as it was meant to be.*

When the bottle was nearly empty, Ashleigh patted her gently on the back, then leaned down and placed her sleeping daughter in the cradle. Callie whimpered only once, then drifted back to sleep the instant the cradle began to sway.

Charles Stuart stood in the doorway of Ashleigh's old bedroom. His heart fell as he saw the young woman rocking the cradle. As if it were only yesterday, the vision came to him of Louise, the love of his life, kneeling beside the toddler's bed in which Ashleigh had slept. That vision from the day Ashleigh's parents had died was etched in his mind and locked in his heart. It would live with him until the day he died.

"Charles." Ashleigh's voice jolted him from his memories. She not only looked like her grandmother, he realized, but also was like her in other ways: strong but at the same time soft, so warm and loving. Under these heartrending circumstances, a less disciplined young woman would have a breakdown, and yet Ashleigh showed little sign of the strain she was under. *But at what cost?*

Rising from her spot at the side of the cradle, Ashleigh looked up and smiled. The sparkle was absent from her soft, brown eyes.

Stepping into the room, he said, "Can we talk?"

"Of course. I'm so sorry—"

"Don't apologize." Charles's voice was sharper than he intended.

Ashleigh blinked.

"Forgive me for being so blunt, but darling girl, you have nothing to be sorry for. You're certainly not responsible for any of this."

"But—"

"But nothing, Ashleigh," he said, his words overlapping hers. "You are not responsible for someone taking your baby. You did nothing to deserve this." He hesitated, but not long enough for her to respond. "What concerns me most is the fact that you're holding it all in."

Ashleigh's eyes met his, a stubborn expression written across her face. "You didn't raise me to wallow in self-pity."

"Darling girl. I'm afraid your grandmother and I may have done you a great disservice. If we, in any way, implied that you should remain stoic when faced with a tragedy of this magnitude, we were wrong."

Her eyes glistening with tears, Ashleigh said in a voice just above a whisper, "I was a very lucky little girl to have grown up with such loving parents as you and Gran. No one could have had better role models. I am very thankful for my early training."

Looking away briefly, she wiped her eyes before returning them to his. "Yesterday, when I picked up that doll, I felt as if I'd been ripped in half, and I did totally fall apart. It took a long time for me to pull myself together. It wasn't until Conrad walked in, until he took me in his arms, that I was able to think about all that I have—to think about Callie and what a blessing she is. About how important it is that she not feel as if . . . as if she isn't enough. The fact that I can keep my most powerful feelings under wraps is a blessing. It's a talent that's as automatic as breathing, and it has served me well."

"But this is hardly—"

"Please don't worry about me, Charles. I did all my real crying yesterday. Losing Cassie is by far the most devastating loss of my entire life, and I want her back. More than anything in the whole world." She spoke rapidly, leaving no room for Charles to comment. "Since our prayers have not yet been answered, and we have not received a single ransom call, I have to face the fact that whoever kidnapped Cassie intends to keep her."

"Surely you're not resigned to that?"

"Of course not!" Ashleigh replied vehemently. "Part of me has to believe the police will find her. We will do everything in our power to get her back—every last thing. But I can't hold out hope forever for what seems unlikely to happen. I can't neglect Callie in the meantime. I must go on as if Cassie . . . my baby girl . . . is beyond our reach. I can only pray that whoever has her will be good to her." She held out a palm, again preventing Charles from interjecting his thoughts. "I've done a lot of thinking since yesterday; in fact, I've been thinking nonstop."

She walked over and sat down on the bedroom sofa and gestured for Charles to come sit beside her. "Do you remember my college project in psychology? The one where I attended a meeting of Parents of Murdered Children?"

Charles nodded. He remembered it well. It was the first time he'd seen Ashleigh totally at a loss.

"I couldn't believe how each of those parents would walk around wearing a button displaying the face of their murdered child. How they could devote all their time and energy to bringing the murderer of that child to justice. It just seemed like their other children, their *living* children, became victims of neglect. I won't do that to Callie."

Charles was speechless. It was true that as a college student, Ashleigh's views on this had been strong. So strong, in fact, that her community service project had ended up with a focus on siblings of murdered children. But at that time, of course, she had not been the victim of such a catastrophic loss.

Ashleigh went on. "I anguish over Cassie—whether she's being well taken care of." She stopped and took a breather. "And I pray that she will be returned to us unharmed. But we can't allow ourselves to get so absorbed in finding Cassie that Callie—the daughter we *do* have—is given less than she deserves. She needs our love and our full attention now."

Ian froze. The cry in the next room had jarred him. *The kidnapped infant is in my home?*

Mario shot to his feet; his fleeting eye contact begged for understanding and support. Ian did understand. His sister was very sick. The man was desperate, and desperate people often take desperate measures. But how could he possibly support such a heinous act?

Ian rose and silently followed Mario into the living room. He watched his brother-in-law—saw the love and tenderness in Mario's eyes as he gently picked up the infant and swayed to and fro, cradling the bundle in his muscular arms. He thought of his sister, who had eaten nothing, and spoken to no one for days. *But this is wrong, so very, very wrong. This baby must be returned to her mother. Erica must never see her. That would surely be a point of no return. I can't let that happen.*

Ian searched for the words that might bring Mario to his senses. At the same time, he tried to formulate a plan—how could he discreetly get this child back to her mother without destroying Mario and Erica's future? But before he had a chance to utter a single syllable, the bang of the garage door, followed by the familiar roar of Leslie's Lexus, turned him in another direction. His heart skipped a full beat. His eyes froze on Mario, who was standing stock-still now. "Wait here," he said, and with no time to think things through, he raced toward the kitchen and the door leading to the garage.

Sensing trouble, Mario quickly withdrew a bottle from the thermal bottle warmer, then did the only thing that was sure to tip the scales in his favor. Taking long, even strides, so as not to disturb his tiny daughter, he headed straight to the back bedroom—the guest room in the McDonalds' spacious home.

He paused in front of the closed door, then slowly turned the knob and stepped inside.

Erica appeared to be dozing, her tangle of curly blond hair spread across the pillow. She looked so very young. He wanted only to protect her—to make her whole again.

She didn't stir when he straightened the bedclothes; nor did she move when he carefully lay the baby in her arms. For a few breathless moments, Mario stood staring down at the tranquil picture of mother and child. He prayed his wife would smile once again when she awakened with their daughter in her arms. At the same time, he feared the questions she might ask. She must never know that this baby was not the one he'd told her about—the infant of the young girl named Rose, who hadn't been ready for a baby, who had wanted a better life for her child than the one she could give her.

That was a wonderful fairy tale, but it had turned out to be a lie. Surely it was not the first lie between them, and it wouldn't be the last. But those had been white lies—could this unending string of fiction he was about to weave be considered the same? Lying to Erica, even for her own good, felt like a razor blade twisting in his gut. And yet there was no alternative. She must never know what he had done. She must be protected from the mountain of guilt he would be saddled with for the rest of his life. He could rationalize till eternity, but he knew the truth. He had committed an unforgivable sin, one for which he would pay dearly.

The baby whimpered, distracting him from his thoughts. Erica's eyes shot open, and she murmured something—words he could not hear. He leaned closer and saw her eyes fill with tears. She stared down at the infant, pulled her close, and began patting her on the back. The baby quieted, and although she was only two days old, she appeared to look up at Erica. While Erica struggled to a sitting position, Mario arranged the pillows behind her, unconsciously holding his breath. Neither spoke a single word.

Finally, Erica spoke. "Is she really ours?" Her voice was soft and unsteady as she asked the only question he felt capable of answering.

Mario inhaled deeply now and nodded. "She's really ours. No one will ever take our baby from us. Never again." He spoke the words with conviction and prayed they would remain true.

Leslie, her fiery red hair neatly arranged in a French twist, reached down to pull the lever that popped open the trunk before she climbed out of the Lexus.

The kitchen door flew open. Ian's frame, backlit from the kitchen, filled the doorway.

"Just in time," Leslie said. "Everything is in place for next week's charity auction, so the meeting was actually pretty brief, and I had time to stop by Staples and pick up most of the school supplies for the kids. Could you—"

Ian, now beside the car, slammed down the trunk. "I'll take care of that later. Right now we need to talk."

"What's wrong?" Her mind went immediately to the kids. The girls were expected home from camp that evening.

"Kids are fine. Should be home within the next couple of hours," Ian assured her, knowing that her first thought would be for their safety.

He knew her so well. It made her smile. Glancing back down at the closed trunk, she asked, "Is it Erica?" She'd seen Mario's car in the driveway.

"Leave the things in the trunk. I'll take care of them later," Ian repeated. And without another word, he took hold of her elbow and guided her through the garage door and onto the patio.

Ian pulled out a couple of chairs from the patio table and gestured for Leslie to be seated. She did not immediately move forward. *Why the mystery? What's going on? This is not at all like Ian.* Wary of what he might say, Leslie fixed her eyes on her husband and reluctantly sank into the chair.

"What is this all about?" she asked, her eyes shifting toward the house. "Is it Erica?" she asked again, panic starting to set in. Ian took the chair beside her. And then he told her everything.

Almost everything.

Registering the same shock and disbelief that Ian had felt earlier, Leslie shot to her feet. "That baby must be returned to her mother immediately."

Ian sprang to his feet too. "Wait, Leslie. There's no question about that," he said, standing between his wife and the house. "But we must think this through."

"Think this through? Have you lost your mind? The sooner we get the baby back to her mother, the better it will be for everyone. I know how concerned you are over Erica, but she won't gain any peace by stealing another woman's baby."

Ian could find no fault in that. Leslie was absolutely right. The child must be returned to her family as soon as possible. He nodded quickly. "I agree. But this is a delicate situation. Mario could lose everything he's worked for. Unless this is handled discreetly, he could be prevented from ever walking the halls of any hospital. He could be in terrible trouble. We can't allow that to happen. We—"

Leslie attempted to step around her husband, but he shifted squarely in front of her and put his hands on her shoulders. Her Irish blue eyes glinted. "It's clear that Mario has gone 'round the bend," she said. "I just pray to God that he hasn't taken you along with him!" Taking an uneven breath, she continued, "Aside from the moral issues involved, Ian, there is no way—*no way*—you can afford to be a part of this. Just think about your own career! Are you willing to place it in jeopardy? Are you willing to play Russian roulette with all of our lives?"

It hit Ian then that his wife didn't even know how right she could be about this gamble. Because for some reason, he hadn't told her that the baby was a twin—from a high-profile family. He wasn't quite sure why he'd left that part out. Well, maybe he was.

The thought filled him with icy dread.

14

Ian slipped his arm around his wife's shoulders. He knew he had to calm her down. And he knew Erica must never see or hear about this kidnapped baby.

"Come with me while I speak to Mario," he said. "He's in the living room with the baby." Noting the hard-set determination in Leslie's eyes, he added, "After I've said my piece, you can tell Mario anything you feel you must, but we've got to keep our voices low. Erica must not know the baby is here."

Leslie nodded her understanding, if not her approval, and they headed to the living room.

Still engrossed in formulating his plan, Ian was alarmed when he found the living room vacant. The only sign that his brother-in-law had been there was the shoulder bag that lay on the sofa. "Oh my God," he whispered as panic crept up his spine.

He stood frozen next to his wife at the far end of the living room. The disaster they had discussed moments before had escalated to a full-blown crisis.

Without another word, Ian bolted toward the back bedroom. Leslie did not follow. Instead, wordlessly, she sank down onto the sofa.

Outside the bedroom door, Ian came to an abrupt stop. *What am I going to say? What in the hell am I going to do?* He contemplated several different scenarios but instantly rejected each one. What Mario had done was monstrous. Despite whatever good intentions he'd had, what he'd done was utterly wrong. And now he had taken this stolen baby to Erica. Ian braced himself, then pushed the door open.

Stepping inside, he felt as if the wind had been knocked out of him. Erica literally glowed as she smiled up at him.

"Ian! Isn't this the most wonderful miracle imaginable?"

She was so childlike and alive. As if the nightmares of the past week had evaporated, his sister appeared whole once again. How was he going to tell her this baby was not hers?

Mario stood protectively beside Erica and the infant, his eyes challenging Ian.

Ian could not formulate a single phrase, and to his utter horror he felt a lump grow in his throat. He had felt his sister's desperation, her heartbreak, and now her relief. She seemed to be at peace, as if there had been a rebirth within. *How am I going to tell her?* The situation could not possibly get worse.

Then Ilise, his six-year-old daughter, charged into the room.

"I'm home, Daddy, and look what . . ." But the instant she laid eyes on the baby nestled in Erica's arm, Ilise seemed to forget all about what she was going to share with her father. She sprang up onto the bed beside Erica and reached out for the baby's tiny hand. Her eyes wide, she asked, "Is she real?"

Erica, her eyes brimming with tears, said, "Very real." She scrunched over a bit to make room for her niece.

"So, what are you going to call her? I like the name Taylor!" Ilise said excitedly.

Mario squeezed Erica's hand. Just back from camp, Ilise and ten-year-old Laura did not know that Erica had lost her baby. No one had told them. "We were just talking about that when your dad came in. Mario and we have decided on a name we like even better for our daughter. Your new cousin's name is Marnie."

Ian's heart sank to new depths, and his mind came to a full stop. Things had gone too far. Erica had given this baby a name, and she believed the infant was truly hers. They were all stuck in this nightmare story, this runaway automobile careening down a steep mountain road with a severed brakes line. There was no stopping it now.

CHAPTER

15

Sun streamed through the bay windows of Ashleigh's bedroom in the Stuart residence. She awoke with a start and bolted upright. A quick glance at the bedside clock alarmed her; it was already after ten. The cradle beside her bed was empty. Trying to curb her rising panic, she grabbed her robe from the foot of the bed. Calling out to Elizabeth, she flew down the stairs and rounded the corner to the kitchen.

The downstairs cradle was empty too. The kitchen, now free of police surveillance, was deserted. Frantically, Ashleigh spun around and cried out, "Elizabeth! Where are you?"

"In here," Paige called from the living room as she strode toward Ashleigh. "Elizabeth and Charles have taken Callie and April out for a walk."

The tension eased from Ashleigh's body as she shrugged into her robe. "How could I have slept this late?" She hadn't had a full night's sleep since the birth of the twins, more than two weeks before. Then, with sudden clarity, she eyed Paige with suspicion. "You didn't bring Callie back to my room last night, did you?"

Paige grinned. "Guilty as charged." Before Ashleigh could say another word, she explained, "You were exhausted, and we all felt a full night's rest was in order." Then she admitted, "Besides, it was a special treat for April and me to have Callie in our room." Taking hold of Ashleigh's hand, Paige began tugging her toward the living room. "It's about time we had some time to ourselves."

Astonished, Ashleigh followed Paige's lead. "But how could I have slept so long and not known Callie was missing?"

Paige's voice rose as if she were offended. "Callie was not *missing*." Then her voice softened. "She was with us. Besides, with Elizabeth hovering, it would be impossible for any harm to come to Callie."

"Oh, Paige, I didn't mean to imply—"

"Of course you didn't," Paige said, waving off Ashleigh's concern. "Callie was an angel. She didn't awaken until nearly seven. I picked her up at the first whimper. Her tiny cry was so soft, it didn't wake April up, but somehow Elizabeth appeared instantly beside me with a clean diaper and a heated bottle." She hesitated for an instant. "What a godsend Elizabeth has been. Not only does she take care of Charles, but she also seems to take everyone else under her wing."

Ashleigh nodded. "She has a wonderful way of always being there without intruding," she said absently.

"Right," Paige agreed. "After she changed Callie's diaper, she handed her back to me and gave me the heated bottle. I knew she herself was dying to feed her, and I might have let her, but by then April was up and she asked if she could hold Callie."

Ashleigh gave a slight raise of her brow.

With a twinkle in her eyes, Paige continued, "Don't worry, I didn't hand your precious bundle to a seven-year-old. We came out here to the sofa, and I cradled Callie while April held the bottle. We made quite a good team. I think you would have approved."

Ashleigh nodded again, still appalled that she could have slept all night and all morning without even realizing that Callie was not beside her.

Misreading Ashleigh's lack of response, Paige continued, "Well, I know I don't have experience with the dirty-diapers-and-baby-bottle routine, but—"

"Hush. I'm sure you and April were superb and Callie was well taken care of. What concerns me is the fact that I could have been so unaware that—"

"Whoa," Paige interrupted. "Give yourself a break. We led you on a merry chase yesterday . . ."

That's certainly true, Ashleigh recalled, as visions of their long trek the previous day played in her head. Wanting to introduce Paige and April to the Long Beach area and show them as many local highlights as possible before their return to New York, she'd initiated a rather ambitions walking tour the previous morning. Even with the baby, temperatures in the high eighties had not deterred them, though they had all welcomed a stop at the air-conditioned Teacher Supplies store, where Ashleigh had purchased for April a copy of *Heidi,* one of her own girlhood favorites. After lunch at Hamburger Henry's, at the far end of Belmont Shore, they'd taken April to Mother's Beach that afternoon.

Last night, after she'd changed Callie into her fuzzy pink nightie, fed her, and placed her in the cradle they kept downstairs, they had all enjoyed an early dinner and talked about the day's activities. Ages seven to ninety, they had no trouble diving into the lively conversation, though Ashleigh remembered now the difficulty of keeping her eyes open. As was the case so often lately, she'd been just too distracted to stay tuned in. She thought about Cassie, and prayed she was being fed and well cared for. She'd drifted in and out of sleep as she sat on the sofa, all the thoughts and emotions that she could share with no one passing through her mind. She remembered Paige tapping her on the shoulder and offering to feed Callie her next bottle, then bring her upstairs to her cradle beside Ashleigh. Though she didn't remember going upstairs, apparently she'd taken Paige up on her offer—and had been dead to the world for more than twelve hours.

Paige was still talking. ". . . keeps asking about a sister!"

Pulling herself back to the present, Ashleigh realized that she had not been listening. "Sorry," she confessed, "I'm afraid my mind wandered off."

"Not important. I just said that April now wants a little sister."

"Well?" Ashleigh teased her friend.

Paige shook her head, then instantly changed the subject. "I can't believe April and I have been here nearly a week, and this is actually the first bit of time you and I have had totally to ourselves."

"I know." Ashleigh wished Paige and April did not have to leave the next morning, but April was beginning a new school in Greenwich next week, and Paige was very much involved in planned events with Mark. Besides, yesterday Paige had admitted that she missed her husband and all the excitement involved in the negotiations for taking Consolidated out of bankruptcy. "When did Elizabeth and Charles leave with the girls? How long did they think they'd be gone?" Ashleigh asked, hoping for some time. She desperately needed to talk to someone. No, not just *someone*. If she couldn't talk with *Paige* about all the things relentlessly drumming around in her head, she might explode.

"No more than ten or fifteen minutes ago." Paige hesitated. Sensing the reason for Ashleigh's question, she said, "It's about time we had a good talk." At the shrill of the teakettle drifting in from the kitchen, she went on, "Let me make a pot of tea. We'll have a good hour or so to ourselves."

"Thanks," Ashleigh sighed, relieved to have her friend by her side. "I could use a good chat."

God knows, I need it.

CHAPTER

16

At the squeak of crepe-soled shoes across the linoleum floor just outside his office, Ian's head jerked up from the thick stack of medical files.

There stood his brother-in-law, still as a statue, his thick-bodied physique filling the doorway. Neither man spoke.

Ian motioned him in. With his heart slamming against his rib cage, Ian flung open his desk drawer, withdrew the parchment paper, and shoved it past the stack of files toward Mario.

Over the past two weeks, he'd had no chance to talk alone with Mario about the dreadful crime he'd committed. His brother-in-law had been back and forth, to and from Long Beach and the apartment they would be leaving behind. Although the packing and preparing for the move to New York had begun months earlier, the treks back and forth from Laguna Niguel had not been part of that plan. But soon they would be gone, on the other side of the country. Ian's kids would be sad to see them go—they'd already accepted the baby as their new cousin. It was simply too late to alter the course, but the urgency to talk with his brother-in-law had never been more real.

Now, without a second's hesitation, Ian stammered, "Have . . . have you totally taken leave of your senses? Did you actually think you could get away with this?"

Mario stepped forward and snatched the birth certificate from the desk. "I did what I had to do. Our daughter needs a birth certificate, so when I saw the door to Records unlocked and the area vacated for some sort of staff meeting, I took care of it." He cleared his throat. "Unless you report this document as fraudulent, there is no reason—"

Ian was on his feet in a flash, for once not giving a damn about remaining calm or controlled. "That fraudulent document is the least of our problems. The damage you've done is irreversible. You can't possibly get away with this." Pointing at the document in Mario's hand, he went on. "This trumped-up birth certificate for a Marnie Christonelli doesn't make that baby yours. You know good and well that kidnapping any child, of any age, for any real or perceived reason, is wrong."

"Calm down, and let me—"

"No! No more of your goddamned rationalizations. No matter how you choose to justify your actions, at the end of the day you can come to only one conclusion. What you've done is . . . *monstrous.*" Swallowing the knot in his throat, Ian took a couple of short breaths before he continued. "Do you have any idea of how many lives you've thrown off course? And presenting that infant to Erica as her own . . . Losing another baby could easily land her in a mental hospital."

"That's not going to happen. Erica will not lose this baby."

"Damn it, Mario. Kidnapping is a heinous crime in and of itself—but the baby you've kidnapped isn't just any child. This child is an identical twin from a prominent family. They will leave no stone unturned until that baby is returned to her mother. And where will that leave Erica?"

"We went over all this already, Ian, and—"

Ian slammed his fist on the desktop, and his voice rose an octave. "Have you turned on the TV?" Without waiting for Mario's response, he went on, "That mother's plea for the return of her baby was heart-wrenching." He leaned up against the desk for support. "Thank God, I didn't tell Leslie that the baby you kidnapped was the twin."

"What *did* you tell her?" Mario's voice shook.

Ian remained silent for a few heartbeats. Leslie's reaction to the news that Mario had taken a baby was bad enough. If she found out that it was the baby of the mother she'd seen on TV, he didn't know what she might do. But he knew her too well to count on her silence. "I didn't tell her much at first, but when I had to tell her something, I could only explain your original plan about the young girl . . . about Rose."

Mario nodded, a series of thin lines creasing his forehead.

"I told her a goddamned lie. I told my wife that fictional, win-win situation you drummed up. That Rose would be able to go back to school, and you and Erica would have the daughter you longed for."

"And?"

"She didn't buy it. She was incensed. Asked how I'd feel if it was Laura or Ilise who had that baby."

"What did you tell her?"

"If one of our daughters were in trouble, I'd never . . ." Ian stopped suddenly. Running a hand through his thinning hair, he glared into Mario's troubled eyes. "Damn it, what I told Leslie is beside the point. A kidnapping for any reason, with or without the mother's permission, is abhorrent to Leslie and to me as well."

"What are you saying? Are you telling me that she's going to—"

"What I'm telling you, Mario, is that it's a good thing you and Erica are moving to New York. The sooner, the better. It's too much of a strain on Leslie to remain silent about a stolen baby in our home." Walking back around to the other side of his desk, Ian sank down into the desk chair. "Sit down," he said.

Mario remained standing.

"There's no point in running this into the ground. You've got me up on a mountaintop, between a blazing inferno and a leap to sudden death. On one hand, I can't be an accomplice to a kidnapping. On the other, I can't be responsible for sending my sister into a depression from which she may never recover." Shaking his head, Ian asked, "What have you told Erica?"

"The same thing you told Leslie. I told her Rose had given birth to our child."

"And if she finds out that you lied?"

"She won't."

"How in the hell do you intend to get away with keeping the baby?"

Mario sank down into the chair opposite Ian. His face was sallow and strained, as if he held the weight of the universe upon his shoulders. "Let's not rehash good and evil—what's right, what's wrong—or even whether I'm being rational. The fact is, everyone knew Erica and I were expecting our first child. No one knows that our child was stillborn—other than you, Leslie, and a handful of strangers at South Coast Medical Center. No one here or at Memorial Hospital knows . . . not even my sister knows. They all believe that Erica delivered a healthy girl."

"When the detective from the LBPD called, his questions were about what I might've seen the night the baby disappeared. I told him about my going-away party. Even told him I stopped by the maternity ward to say my good-byes to everyone else, in case anyone reported seeing me there. I told him that the security guard helped me load the baby gifts I'd received into the car. The detective made no future plans to interview me or come down here."

Ian could only hope those plans would never be made.

Mario heaved an exhausted sigh and glanced down at his watch. Now that everything was coming together, and Erica was once again the happy, optimistic girl he'd married, he would not allow his brother-in-law to rattle him. Still, he wasn't quite sure how much his wife had shared with Ian about their upcoming plans before they'd lost their own baby. "Let me make this short and to the point," he said. "For Erica, this opportunity in New York is her dream come true. Remember when she called you a few months ago to tell you about her interview at that fancy Fifth Avenue boutique? She wanted you to know that her education at the L.A. Fashion Institute was finally paying off. Her new boss is somewhat intimidating, and she'll have to start out in sales, but she's enthusiastic about being surrounded by all those top designers and their creations. And she told me that once she's conquered her fear, it'll be an inspiration to work with a designer the likes of Viviana De Mornay. A dream come true," he repeated.

Rapid-fire, Mario concluded, "I've rented an apartment with an extra bedroom so that my brother can stay with us. He was recently laid off and has split up with his partner, Jeff, so he no longer has any ties to the West Coast. He's decided to pick up stakes and head east with us. He's setting up his own business, designing company websites. He'll work from our apartment while looking after Marnie when Erica and I are at our jobs. It's a perfect situation for now, and when Mike moves on, we'll have a separate bedroom for Marnie."

In fact, his brother would be at Ian's house any minute now, and Mario needed to help him load the car. "We'll all be out of your hair within the next hour. I need to be in New York tomorrow, so Mike is taking me to the airport, then he'll be driving Erica and Marnie cross-country in our car."

It seemed that Ian was only half listening. "Say you get away with this for a few years," he said finally. Then he leaned forward, resting his elbows on the table and his chin on his folded hands. "How long do you think you can conceal an identical twin?"

Ashleigh adjusted the umbrella over the round patio table while Paige set down the sterling silver tray. It was a beautiful morning, cool and sunny, with the sun glinting off the bay about twenty yards from the patio. A perfect day—and Paige was the perfect friend with whom she could share her troubled thoughts and fears.

"Finally we have some time to ourselves."

"About time," Paige said, wearing a mock expression of irritation. Then she smiled and transferred the teapot and all the paraphernalia for their morning tea from the tray to the table.

As Paige set their table, Ashleigh took a long breath, then plunged in. "These past couple of weeks have been . . . have been . . ."

Nodding her head as she poured the tea, Paige said, "I wish there were something I could say or do—"

"For now, please, just be my sounding board. I have so many conflicting thoughts that I may very well come across as someone ready for the loony bin. Try to be patient with me."

"Milk?" Paige asked.

"You know I do."

Then, as if they hadn't been interrupted by the tea ceremony, Paige said, "You are the least likely person I know to be a candidate for the loony bin. With what you've been through and how—"

Ashleigh raised the palm of her hand. "Please, no sympathy. You know I absolutely can't handle sympathy directed at me." She looked intently at her friend, pleading with her eyes. *I might break down, and that is unacceptable. Even with Paige.* She stirred her tea, her mind working out just where to begin.

Paige began for her. "Conrad returning to Dallas right now for business—it must be totally devastating."

Ashleigh shrugged. "He stayed here as long as he could. Besides, he'll be back on Sunday." And yet it *was* devastating; she needed her husband now more than ever. Although she knew all the rational reasons for his return to Dallas, she couldn't help but feel that he should have made Cassie's kidnapping a higher priority. There were other department heads who could fill in. Who could possibly fault him for taking some time? And yet she knew the demands of the retail business, particularly for someone in Conrad's position. She also knew, only too well, what it was like to be torn between actual needs and emotional needs. This was new to neither of them.

"This Sunday?" Paige asked.

Ashleigh nodded. "It's too soon to take Callie on an airplane, so Conrad is taking the train back to Dallas with us. Really, I'm alright. Anyway, you know the demands of the retail industry as well as anyone."

"Of course I do. But I've never had to experience"—she hesitated—"the loss of a child. I don't think I could handle it if anything were to happen to April."

"None of us really knows what we can handle until we come face-to-face with it and have no alternative. My grandmother used to tell me that God will never give us more than we can handle. But there are times when I wish that God didn't believe I was so darn capable."

Paige laughed empathetically. "Do I ever understand what you mean!" She paused and met Ashleigh's eyes. "I don't know how you've managed to stay so upbeat."

Ashleigh sat quietly for a moment. "My grandmother's words keep echoing in my head. Her philosophy was 'Count your blessings. And always focus on the portion of the goblet that is full.'" She paused again, an image of her loving role model crystallizing in her mind. "That was Gran's version of the old cliché about looking at a glass as either half full or half empty." And for the most part, that was the way of life that Ashleigh had adopted. She'd often been accused of being a Pollyanna, which was alright with her. She would much rather be overly optimistic and occasionally disappointed than worry about what might go wrong but usually didn't.

She continued, "When I was very young, Gran played the Glad Game—you know, from *Pollyanna*—with Charles and me every night before bed. I had to find something to be glad about every day. And when I couldn't find anything, Gran would help me. God knows, it's been hard since Cassie was taken. But I do my best to focus on Callie and how blessed I am to have such a happy, healthy baby. I've started playing the Glad Game with her, to let her know that she means the world to her mommy and daddy." She smiled wanly. "Of course, at this point it's a monologue."

Paige gave Ashleigh a broad grin. "I like that. I really like that—a lot. I think tonight April and I will play the Glad Game." She leaned in a little closer to her friend. "Ashleigh, I think it's important that you talk to me about what's troubling you. You can't keep this all bottled up inside."

Ashleigh sighed, looking tired. "Okay. I'll try to make this as coherent as possible. My thoughts—they're terribly conflicted."

"It's a wonder you can string together a single coherent sentence, Ashleigh. Don't be so hard on yourself."

Ashleigh closed her eyes and shook her head. "Paige, I have to confess: I don't think my baby . . . I don't think Cassie will be found. That TV plea was a waste of time. I just sounded pathetic and—"

"Hold on. You handled the interview fantastically. And it may still bring the results we all pray for. You were anything but pathetic. You came across as a strong woman and a caring mother."

"It was something we had to do. Otherwise, we'd never know what might have happened. If the person who took Cassie was listening . . ." Pausing, she took a sip of tea and then said, almost to herself, "I know Cassie is alive, and I believe that whoever took her will take care of her. But damn it, Paige, Cassie is mine! I carried her for nearly nine months. And Callie needs her twin."

Paige moved her chair closer to Ashleigh's and draped her arm around her shoulders. "I know. I know how you must be struggling. I know you dug into every aspect of bringing twins into the world, of their personalities. It's not fair that . . ."

Ashleigh felt a lump rising in her throat, and the tears she'd been trying to keep inside for so long began to slide down her cheeks. Picking up a napkin to dab her eyes, she gently pulled away from her friend. In seconds, she managed to regain control. "I'm sorry. I didn't mean to come across with the 'poor me's. I didn't mean to. I learned a long time ago that real life is never one hundred percent fair. On the one hand, I would do anything in my power to get my baby back. On the other, I don't ever want to do anything that might make Callie feel that she's only half of a whole—that she's not enough."

Ashleigh took several quick breaths. Then she told Paige about the meeting she'd gone to in college, the Parents of Murdered Children support group. "The murdered child caused a ripple effect throughout the entire family. The murderer took not only the life of one child, but in a way caused the death of the entire family—the only real difference was that the hearts of those left behind continued to beat."

"You said you know Cassie is still alive. How do you know?"

Ashleigh nodded. "Sounds crazy, I know. I can't explain it, but I think I'd know if . . . if something really bad had happened." She shook her head before continuing, "Maybe I've read too many novels or seen too many movies. Anyway, I try to tell myself that I have a wonderful baby girl and that I should be thankful. The person who took Cassie might not have been able to have a child—so that person is taking really good care of mine. But damn it, Paige, that doesn't really help. Worst of all, these . . . these conflicting thoughts are not something I can share with Conrad."

This revelation appeared to startle Paige. "Why on earth not?"

Ashleigh took another sip of tea, searching for the right words. How could she tell her friend why she feared telling the love of her life exactly how she felt? Conrad was her soul mate—and yet she felt a wall beginning to grow between them. "Since Cassie was taken from us, Conrad has become a very angry man."

"You've been through so much, Ashleigh—it's only natural that there is some tension." Paige hesitated. The worried expression on her face made Ashleigh cringe. "Your marriage isn't in trouble, is it?"

"No," Ashleigh quickly responded. "At least, I don't think so," she added, not daring to think differently. "Conrad couldn't be more loving to me or to Callie. But whenever we talk about the kidnapping, he becomes so angry and vengeful . . . It scares me. He's hired Landes. He says we'll keep them on retainer, no matter how long it takes."

"Well, that's a good thing, isn't it?"

Ashleigh looked out toward the bay, as if the words she was searching for were written somewhere out there. *How can I express just how this feels?* "It is," she said hesitantly. "Right now it's the only sensible thing to do. But . . ." Paige remained silent while Ashleigh refilled her cup, took a sip of her tea, then set the cup on the table. "I simply have no faith that Cassie will be found. She was taken two and a half weeks ago. The police have run into nothing but dead ends, and so far Ross has no good leads."

"You've hired Ross Pocino?" Paige asked.

"Yes. Despite his lack of delicacy, there isn't anyone better equipped to work on Cassie's abduction. He's finally found his niche with the Landes Agency."

They both knew Pocino well. Ashleigh had first encountered him during his stint as director of security for Bentley's, which had been a colossal mismatch. He'd been like a salmon trying to run downstream. While he lacked nothing in the way of brains or savvy, he'd displayed the diplomacy of a toddler when it came to dealing with the department store's upscale customers. However, Dick Landes, who was also a former police officer, had recognized Pocino's potential, and now Pocino was a valued investigator in his agency. Landes was a suburb diplomat who could easily adapt to any social class or situation. The two polar opposites made a great team.

Paige knew all this as well as Ashleigh did, of course. But with Ashleigh's next words, a look of incredulity spread across her friend's suntanned face.

"Did you know that Ross's four-year-old son was kidnapped at the Thousand Oaks Mall?"

Paige set down her teacup, her eyes filled with alarm. "When?"

"A long time ago. Before Ross came to Bentley's. He was a police officer at the time, or maybe a detective. With the Hollywood division of LAPD, I believe." She took a sip of tea, then went on. "His wife . . . his ex-wife, was having some sort of makeup demonstration at Robinson's. Apparently, she took her eye off their toddler—their only child—and he disappeared." Ashleigh glanced toward the bay. Recalling what she'd heard, her eyes pooled with tears, and she cleared her throat. "The little boy's body was found three days later. The case is still unsolved."

"Oh my God."

"Obviously, it's not something Ross is comfortable talking about. I found out about it during the investigation of the fraud at Bentleys Royale and the disappearance of Danielle McIntire." She was sure Paige would recall the disappearance of the young buyer some years ago, if not the elaborate scam at Bentleys Royale.

Paige nodded. "Of course. That was headline news."

Ashleigh tried to push the murder of Ross's son out of her mind. "Anyway, I thought Ross was a real jerk when he first showed up at Bentleys Royale. His endless clichés and less-than-immaculate grooming threw me. But it didn't take long to discover that he's lacking neither intelligence nor loyalty. He's a gruff old teddy bear, but one I've learned to rely on."

Paige grinned. "I know what you mean. I remember my first encounter with him only too well. When he was assigned to Mark as a bodyguard during the takeover. I wandered into the kitchen for my first cup of morning coffee—my hair uncombed, wearing only my bathrobe—and found Ross seated at my kitchen counter, just as rumpled-looking as I was." She shook her head as if to clear her mind. "That was the roughest period in our entire lives, and it wasn't just the takeover." She paused, her eyes meeting Ashleigh's. "But I'll share all the personal drama later. Right now there are more important things to talk about."

Ashleigh realized something had happened between Paige and Mark during the takeover three years before, but at the time the two women had been only acquaintances. All Ashleigh knew was what Conrad had been able to tell her, which wasn't much. She did know that the Toddmans had been separated for a short time, but she figured it couldn't have been too serious or lasted very long. Otherwise, she would have heard more, considering how close the two women had become. But surprisingly they'd never gotten around to talking much about the past, only the future.

"Ashleigh," Paige said, snapping her fingers.

"Sorry, my mind was wandering." Ever since Cassie's disappearance, Ashleigh had been so distracted, unable to keep her mind on anything for long, preoccupied with her missing child but also fighting to keep the unknown at bay, with thoughts of other events and other times. But now her mind returned to the tragedy enveloping her life. She sighed. "You know, I trust Ross to do everything possible for Cassie. And those statistics I told you about earlier, about the recovery rate for infants—they're pretty positive."

Ross had given Ashleigh a rundown the previous day. In the past eight years, he had told her, out of 119 infants that had been kidnapped in the United States, 110 were recovered and returned to their parents. "But it still doesn't help a whole lot," she said sadly. "Those who were recovered were found in the first few days; the other nine were never found. What is it they say about kidnapping in general?" She hesitated, trying to pull some other statistics from her head. "I can't remember the breakdown, but for every hour the child is missing, the chances of her being found go down. It's already been nineteen days, and we are no closer to finding Cassie than on the day she was taken."

Suddenly realizing how far their conversation had gone off course, Ashleigh pushed back her chair and rose. "Let's move inside and get out of this sun." With so little time left before the others returned from their walk, and only one day before Paige boarded the plane for Manhattan, Ashleigh couldn't afford to squander any more of their time together. She must get to the strictly personal things—the things she could share only with her closest friend and confidante.

Unable to reach Paige at the Taylors', Mark stared at the phone. Checking the clock at the far side of his executive desk, he saw that he had another forty minutes before his next meeting. Enough time to give his friend and former partner a call. Conrad must be going through hell. Not bothering to have his secretary place the call, Mark picked up the receiver and dialed.

He quickly got through to his former secretary, who had stayed on at Michael Nason's after he left and who now seemed as dedicated to Conrad as she had been to Mark when he was at the helm of the prestigious store. Leaning back in his desk chair, uncharacteristically ill at ease, he propped his feet on the cherrywood trash can and impatiently waited for his friend to come on the line.

Mark had little time to contemplate how he would broach the subject of the search for the missing infant. After the obligatory greetings, he plunged straight ahead. "I understand you have Landes on retainer?" Without waiting for a response, he added, "Does that mean the police department still hasn't developed any substantial leads?"

"Just a lot of dead ends so far," Conrad answered in a heavy tone. "But I'll do whatever it takes to get Cassie back. She's our daughter, and she belongs with us and with her twin." After a brief pause, he went on. "It's an open case on the LBPD books, but I'm afraid it's slipped to a low priority. Good thing I brought Landes in from the beginning. He and his agents . . ." The line went silent for a heartbeat, then Conrad said, "Sorry. That's like the choir preaching to the preacher."

Mark chuckled. Both men had worked with Dick Landes and knew that his agents were the best. "How's Ashleigh holding up?"

There was a prolonged silence before Conrad said, "She's doing amazingly well under the circumstances."

"But . . . ?" Mark said, knowing there must be more to it than that.

"She's coping. But I'm afraid she's holding a lot inside." Then, abruptly switching gears, Conrad asked, "What's new on the restructuring front?"

A bit stunned at the sudden change of topic, Mark decided just to follow his friend's lead and plunged ahead with the more comfortable topic of business. "New playing field. Not at all like the LBOs we were dealing with a few years ago." He and Conrad had gained a firsthand education in leveraged buyouts after Philip Sloane had launched his hostile bid for Consolidated. "We've got a great team of attorneys working round the clock with our creditors. Leaving that largely in their hands. My job is clear-cut at this point. Like in the past, my goal is to make this company mean and lean." Again he let out a chuckle. "I'd better watch the clichés. I'm beginning to sound like our pal Pocino." He paused. "But seriously, we are working on downsizing in a big way, while being very careful about what gets downsized."

"Ashleigh's definition of downsizing is simply fewer people to do the same amount of work. But I assume you are focused more on downsizing the head office and middle management rather than sales associates."

"That's the model. Customer service must remain one of our highest priorities." Feeling his eyelid begin to twitch, Mark continued, "I wish I could say we were accomplishing superior customer service across the board. But at this point, we aren't. It drives me insane. But we're making inroads, cleaning up the mess we inherited from Sloane, and most of our creditors have agreed to share the risk in lifting this bankruptcy."

While it wasn't fair to blame the entire collapse of two of the nation's largest retailer empires on the feisty Australian alone, he'd been a major player. The bankruptcy courts were now clogged in the aftermath of the leveraged buyout frenzy of the '80s. "Fortunately, our attorneys have convinced a large number of creditors that they have more to gain by betting on us than by collecting pennies on the dollar through the bankruptcy courts. Already many of our creditors have become investors. We're leaving those negotiations in the hands of the attorneys, so our management group can concentrate on the actual restructuring." Mark dropped his legs from his desk and leaned forward. "I don't need to ask how things are going at Nason's. I just got a glimpse of your third-quarter sales report. Congratulations! I knew you wouldn't miss a beat."

A few moments more of shop talk was followed by the standard good-byes. Returning the receiver to the cradle, Mark frowned. There was something that Conrad was not telling him. He could feel it hanging over them throughout the whole conversation. In the business arena, Conrad could be counted on to be candid—but like Mark himself, he tended to keep personal matters close to the chest.

Paige held the door as Ashleigh glided across the threshold, gingerly balancing the tea tray. After a quick trip to the kitchen, they settled in the formal living room of the Stuart home. Paige dropped down on the plump sofa, which, according to Elizabeth, had been recently recovered in a delicate, floral chintz fabric. As she struggled to get into a comfortable position, she smiled. Although she and April had been there with Ashleigh for the past week, they had seldom been in this room, and when they were, she'd always been seated in one of the overstuffed armchairs. "I'm afraid I need to grow another few inches for this sofa," She teased. Her legs dangled about an inch above the floor.

With a smile, Ashleigh said, "I never noticed how wide those cushions were before."

"Well, with your long legs, it wouldn't be a problem." She went on to the real topic of conversation, with hardly a breath in between. "But you have more important things on your mind, so let's take advantage of our time together before we're invaded."

Ashleigh bit down on her lip, searching for the words or a place to begin.

"Before we were sidetracked, you were telling me how difficult it was to deal with Conrad's anger."

Ashleigh nodded. "That, and the constant rehashing of events. I keep thinking of Gran. She had to deal with the loss of her only child, and yet she was always so positive and a pleasure to be around." With a faraway look in her eyes, she murmured, "Right to the end she was a strong, positive woman—never a hint of the 'poor me' syndrome."

Over the past few years Ashleigh had shared with Paige many wonderful memories of her grandmother and Charles Stuart. Paige had great admiration for Charles and was sure she would have felt the same for Ashleigh's Gran. "From all you've told me, I know she was a strong woman, but I'm sure she must have gone though her own period of grieving. After all, you were only two years old when you lost your parents, so—"

"Of course she must have," Ashleigh broke in. "But I can't picture her moping around."

"Nor have you." Paige leaned forward. "But I've been worried about you keeping everything inside. It isn't healthy."

The new mother nodded, and silence filled the room. Paige waited for her to go on. After a long, awkward lull, Ashleigh said, "As I told you, I'd do anything to get Cassie back. But there is literally nothing I can do. Nothing! So I want to concentrate on my blessings."

Paige nodded. She was beginning to understand what her friend was attempting to put into words.

"I have a beautiful, healthy baby girl. A gorgeous, loving, and successful husband. Charles is doing well—incredibly well." Her mouth turned up in a smile, which was reflected in the brief sparkle of her luminous eyes. "And we have wonderful, supportive friends." She held out her hand, and Paige squeezed it.

"It is fantastic that you can be so positive after . . . ," Paige began, but she trailed off as Ashleigh pulled her hand away and rose to her feet, then crossed to the bay windows and gazed out, a look of anguish on her lovely face.

"Paige . . . does that make me sound as if I don't care about Cassie?"

Ian slammed the microwave door and punched in one minute on the timer when he heard the peel of Leslie's tires and felt the vibrations of the motor reverberating in his aching head. He rushed to the front door, threw it open, and dashed out onto the porch just in time to see the back of the Lexus rounding the corner. *Has the bloody woman lost her mind?* Thank God, most of the neighborhood kids and their parents had probably departed an hour or so earlier for school or work.

Kneading the muscles in the back of his neck, Ian slowly returned to the kitchen and pulled his steaming coffee mug from the microwave. In the twenty years since he'd first laid eyes on Leslie, Ian had never seen this side of her. No matter what was going on around her, Leslie never got rattled. She'd been the picture of calm and reason, even in the midst of chaos. But these past two and a half weeks felt as if he'd taken a trip to Purgatory. Whatever he said, or didn't say, would set Leslie off. He found himself continually defending his brother-in-law, against his better judgment, and he was sick of it.

He no longer regretted not telling Leslie the entire truth about the baby who had been in their home. Even the version he'd told her—the false tale about Mario's original plan—was to Leslie nothing less than an immoral and reprehensible act, one that was absolutely wrong as well as totally illegal. Her holier-than-thou attitude grated on him and made him defensive. The truth was catastrophic, he had to admit, but the damage had been done. There was nothing they could do about it now. Ian took a sip of the strong Columbian coffee. Thank God, Leslie did not know the real story.

The phone, blaring from the wall above the kitchen counter, interrupted his thoughts. He was on call, and he hoped to hell it wasn't the hospital. He needed to be here when Leslie returned, to try to clear the air and put the past few weeks behind them.

"Hello?"

Without returning his greeting, a cold, businesslike voice asked, "May I please speak to Mrs. Christonelli, please?"

"Erica is on her way to New York."

There was a moment of silence. "Do you have a number where she can be reached?"

"I'm afraid not. But I have a number where her husband can be reached." Ian stretched across to the Rolodex and began fingering his way through the Cs.

The voice on the other end of the phone quickly said, "It's *Mrs.* Christonelli we need to speak with. Do you have a number for her?"

We? The word echoed in Ian's head. *Who in the hell does that refer to?* "I told you, she's en route to New York," he said with as much patience as he could muster. "She's driving across the country with her brother-in-law. Could I help you?"

"Do you have the number of the hotel where she'll be staying tonight?"

"Who *is* this?" He knew something must be wrong. He had to get through the staccato questions and get some answers.

"Dr. Danica Wygod, calling from St. Luke's–Roosevelt Hospital."

"St. Luke's?" Ian repeated. Then it wasn't the LBPD inquiring about an abducted infant. Had the call come from anywhere other than a hospital, Ian would have felt a sense of relief. But he wasn't relieved, and he had no information to offer. Not knowing where they might end up each night after a day's driving with a newborn, Erica and Mike had not made reservations. Ian had no idea where they might be—and no way to get in touch with Erica unless she called.

"This is Dr. Ian McDonald." Though he seldom used his title like this, he knew it was the only way to end this question-and-answer routine and get to the reason for the call. "Erica is my sister. Has something happened to her husband?"

"I'm afraid so, Dr. McDonald."

CHAPTER

22

The past few days had flown by. The party Paige and Mark had hosted Sunday evening at their French manor house in Greenwich had been instrumental in bringing another investor on board for Consolidated. Monday had brought exciting news: April loved her new school. Not even the anticipated hiccup of being the new kid at a new school had surfaced. April had become fast friends with Madison, a girl in her class. This had been a big plus, Paige realized, and had smoothed the transition for her precocious young daughter. Getting her up and about this morning had been a piece of cake, and now Paige wouldn't be worrying about how the seven-year-old was faring in school all day.

The squeal of tires and brakes sent Paige to the door. Flinging it open, she dashed to the veranda and immediately saw a crop of unruly red hair. The convertible top of her former trainer's red MG was down, leaving him windblown and rosy-cheeked.

"Sonny!" she whooped, and flew down the steps.

Climbing out of the sports car, Sonny eyed Paige from head to toe, then smiled. "Top of the morning," he sang out. He threw his arms around her, lifting her off her feet.

Regaining her balance, Paige asked, "Is it really true? You're moving to New York?"

"Aye, colleen. Sonny's been a-missin' you and a-wantin' to get to know the wee one. So when my friend Brad mentioned he had an opportunity with Morgan Stanley, my only question was, how soon could we book a flight?"

Paige laughed. "I've so missed that lyrical tone of yours."

Sonny cocked his head, his cheeks dimpling in a wry smile. "And . . ."

"The gym's all set, so all I need to know—"

Sonny shook his head, spilling stray hairs across his forehead. "You're a-skirtin' the issue. Not sure what the issue is, but Sonny knows his little colleen is a-skirtin' it."

How does he always seem to know when I have something I need to air? "Busted," she said, and laughed. Taking Sonny's hand, she led him into the house.

"Passing through another wee storm in a teacup, are we?"

Paige nodded as they entered the library. "And speakin' of tea, I'll be askin' Wilma to get us some tea, then we'll have a wee natter," she said in her best imitation of Sonny's in-and-out Irish brogue.

With Ashleigh on the opposite coast facing problems of her own, Paige was especially grateful to be with her old confidant once again. Sonny knew more about her history than anyone. He'd been there with her in her darkest days, long before she'd known Ashleigh. She wanted to discuss something with him that she couldn't share with Mark, who was supportive but disapproved of digging up the past. "It's about my mother."

Wilma appeared with a large silver tray holding their tea. As she set the cups and saucers on the coffee table, Paige introduced Sonny as someone who was like a member of the family. Wilma welcomed Sonny, poured the tea, and silently disappeared.

With a curious tilt to his head, as if there had been no break in their conversation, Sonny repeated, "It's about your mother, you say?" Not waiting for a response, he continued, "Aye, colleen. Once you've decided to open up, you've never been one to beat around the bush, but I'm afraid you better bring me up to speed. Last I knew, you had no idea who your mother was and had no desire to find her."

Paige nodded. "That's before I *was* a mother. With the passing of Martha Winslow over a year ago—"

"I was sorry to hear about her passing. She was a great lady, and you told me how close she and April were."

Paige again nodded, not trusting herself to speak. Martha was the widow of Mark's mentor and the one who, representing the Consolidated board, had asked Mark to come back to Consolidated and rescue her late husband's former legacy from bankruptcy. She had been the closest thing to a mother Paige had ever had, and she loved her, as did April, who called her Grandma. Clearing her throat, she said, "And Mark's mother also passed away last year."

"So you're looking for a granny for the wee one?" A deep frown furrowed his brow. "If the woman abandoned you—"

"I'm not sure what I'm looking for, and I have no idea what I might find. I just know I must find my mother. I need to know if she's still alive. I need to know what kind of a person she was when she left me in foster care. What kind of person she is now . . . and why she abandoned me."

CHAPTER
23

Ian swallowed thickly, a kaleidoscope of images shooting through his mind. He attempted to concentrate on the doctor's words, which she delivered in a detached monotone.

"Mr. Christonelli was in a very serious car accident on the Brooklyn Bridge. He was hit head-on. It seems the driver of the minivan—"

"Dr. Wygod," Ian cut in. He didn't give a damn about the details of the accident. Not now. "What is my brother-in-law's condition?"

"He is still in Emergency, but his condition is critical."

Ian wanted to strangle the officious doctor. They should be talking doctor to doctor. "Critical" didn't tell him a damn thing—it was a bullshit generalization. *How* critical? That was what he was desperate to know. "What's . . . the . . . prognosis?" he punched out though dry lips, keeping as much of the irritation out of his voice as possible.

"He has a broken collarbone and two broken ribs. No other fractures."

Ian felt some of the tension drain from his body. Mario was alive.

"But he has not yet regained consciousness." That was no cause for great alarm. He was alive. "As you know, Dr. McDonald, it's too soon . . ." The doctor continued in her condescending tone, but Ian's mind was focused now on Erica. Clenching his fists tight enough to turn his knuckles white, his mind raced. *How in the world am I going to reach her?*

Hours later, Ian still had gotten no opportunity to talk privately with his wife. From the moment she returned from picking up the girls from school, they had gone nonstop from homework to dinner and then back to the nightly barrage of homework.

Finally, after tucking the girls into bed, Ian said, "It's such a lovely night. Let's go out on the patio. I have something important to talk over with you." He reached out and took Leslie's hand as they descended the stairs. She did not resist. "I want you to know that I realize how horrific these last few weeks have been for you, and I regret having placed you in such a compromised position."

Leslie's blue eyes glistened in the light of the overhead chandelier. "You are not to blame. And I'm truly sorry for being such a bitch these last few weeks."

Squeezing her hand, he grinned. "Not exactly a bitch." He understood her moral outrage. Knowing the whole truth about the infant that his brother-in-law had kidnapped, he felt an even greater outrage, but he'd had to squelch it. Seeing the kidnapped baby in his sister's arms had stripped him of any power or will to make things right. "What really hurt was having you turn on me. I understand your anger—I felt the same way—but the damage had already been done."

Ian slid open the door to the patio. The night was silent, other than the chorus of crickets in their backyard. The glint from a galaxy of stars shone down on them as they crossed the damp grass to the patio table. They pulled back a couple of chairs and turned to face each other.

"I know it wasn't your fault. There was nothing you could do. But Ian, do you understand how I felt, having a kidnapper in our home, with our children?"

Ian nodded, though he felt a pang of pity. Leslie spoke as if their brother-in-law were a dangerous criminal rather than a man desperate to bring happiness to his wife, the woman he loved. But Ian let it go; there were more important things to discuss. "Leslie, Mario has been in a serious accident."

Her eyes opened wide with alarm. "When? How serious is it? Why didn't you tell me?"

"I haven't had a chance. I didn't want to say anything in front of the girls before I had more facts." He told her everything the doctor had told him, then added, "Mario has not yet regained consciousness. I wasn't able to talk to him."

"Oh my God. Does Erica know?"

Ian shook his head. "I'm hoping she'll call soon. I have no idea where she and Mike are or how to reach her."

Leslie's misty eyes blinked back tears, and she inhaled a ragged breath. "What are you going to tell her if she calls?"

"God only knows. In a way, I'm glad she hasn't called yet. I don't know how I'm going to tell her."

"But she has to be told."

Ian shrugged, tossing his hands in the air. "I know. But what can we do? I have no way of reaching her. I don't even know how Mike routed the trip." He paused. Another thought occurred to him, and he shot to his feet. "She's probably been trying to get in touch with Mario at their new apartment. If that phone continues to go unanswered, she just might call St. Vincent's to catch him at work . . ." He broke off. "She'll be very concerned when she hears that he missed the first day at his new job."

Leslie's sigh was full of pity. "But she'll be devastated when she finds out why."

Erica's back ached. Her health still wasn't up to par, but she was getting stronger every day. They had made good time. Looking out her window, she saw a sign announcing that they were entering Lincoln, Nebraska. She glanced down at her watch. "Let's call it a day, Mike."

Mike gave her a big grin. "Hey, I'm good for another hundred miles or so."

Erica groaned. "Well, we aren't. It's time for Marnie to be fed, and seeing as we've stopped only once since lunch, she's likely to be wet clear up to her tiny little armpits."

Just off Interstate 80, she spotted a Days Inn and elbowed Mike. "How about stopping here for the night?"

"Your wish is my command, my lady." He loved to tease her, and she appreciated his good-natured humor. "How about grabbing a bite to eat first?"

Erica's expression must have telegraphed her thoughts because, in a flash, he said, "Never mind. Guess we'd better check into the motel first so you can properly take care of my little niece."

She nodded. "I'm really beat. For tonight, fast food will be just fine. Would you mind just picking up something for me?"

"Like a Big Mac and fries?"

"That would be great. I'd like to feed and bathe Marnie and try to reach Mario."

In less than ten minutes, Mike had checked them into the motel as Mr. and Mrs. Christonelli. He'd asked for twin beds.

In the room, he laid Erica's overnight bag on the luggage rack, dumped his on one of the twin beds, and set the cradle on the floor between the two beds.

"Be back in a jiffy," he said as he headed for the door.

"Take your time. Eat there, so you can enjoy some hot food?"

"Not a chance."

Erica's heart sank. Mike was so kind and thoughtful, but she really wanted some time to herself. "Please, Mike. I'm not really hungry right now, and I'd like to take a shower. I haven't been able to get in touch with Mario since we left, and . . ."

"You sure?"

She nodded, giving him a weary grin.

"In that case, I'll see you in about an hour."

As the door clicked shut behind him, Marnie pulled a strand of Erica's hair, stared up at her, and smiled. A real smile, not just gas—Erica was sure of it. She loved the soft, iridescent blue of Marnie's eyes. She knew it was much too soon to predict what color they would be when her daughter grew up, but she hoped they would remain that way forever.

Marnie began to squirm, breaking into her thoughts, and then let out a piercing wail. She had slept on and off throughout most of the day, so Erica knew she was in for another sleepless night. The newborn's non-stop crying the night before had worried her, and it still did. As the crying went on, hour after hour, Erica had found herself getting tense and even angry. Irrationally angry. She had wanted this baby for so long, and she loved her with all of her heart. *Why won't she stop crying?*

Intellectually, Erica knew that if Marnie was crying, there must be a reason. But what was it? She'd kept checking, but Marnie wasn't wet. She wouldn't take her bottle, so she must not have been hungry. And yet every time Erica had tried to lay her in her cradle, she cried. She wasn't satisfied with being rocked in the cradle or even just being held. She quieted down only when Erica walked with her.

In the car it was a totally different story. Only once had Marnie gone through one of her crying jags while on the road. Erica couldn't hold her in the car, but she'd discovered that shaking a rattle quieted her daughter, and so she had shook the rattle for miles and miles until she felt her hand might fall off and Marnie had finally fallen asleep.

She laid Marnie on the bed closest to the bathroom, on the small pad she kept in the diaper bag, and quickly unfastened the sopping-wet diaper. Soon she had her daughter in a dry diaper. While she cooed and sang to her fussing child, her thoughts turned to Mario. She hadn't been able to reach him for the past three nights. She didn't know his schedule, and she knew he had no way of reaching her, so she tried not to let her imagination run wild. If anything happened to Mario . . .

Stop, she chided herself, and she turned her attention back to Marnie, who was now wailing. Erica pulled the infant into her arms and plucked a bottle from the thermal warmer, sank down into the hotel armchair, and ever so gently wiggled the nipple between her daughter's lips. A few more wiggles and Marnie began sucking. Soon her eyelids began to droop.

Holding the sleeping baby in the crook of her left arm, Erica reached with her right hand for her handbag, pulled it up, and balanced it on her knees. Then she began rummaging for the phone number to their new apartment. She needed to call Mario—now. She needed to hear his voice. She needed to be sure he was alright. Balancing her daughter carefully so as not to disturb her, Erica pushed herself to her feet and slid into the chair behind the desk. Marnie's eyes sprang open, and for a moment she stopped sucking. *Not now*, Erica prayed. Immediately, her prayers were answered—the baby's eyes slowly closed, and her mouth again began to move rhythmically on the nipple.

Erica raised her eyes toward the ceiling and whispered, "Thank you." She picked up the receiver, laid it on the desk, and dialed 9 for an outside line. Then she punched in the numbers and drew the receiver to her ear. She let it ring more than twenty times. No answer.

She stared at the bedside clock. It flashed 7:47. *What time zone are we in?* She tried to think, then checked her own watch, which she had reset as they'd entered Mountain Time. It said 6:47. *So it must be eight forty-seven in New York.* Questions ran through her head as she tried not to panic. *Where is Mario? Is he working? Why hasn't he set up the answering machine?* She knew Mario would be worried about her and the baby, would want her to check in. She hadn't talked to her husband in days.

Something was definitely wrong.

With a sack of McDonald's food in one hand and a Pampers box in the other, Mike lightly tapped on the door to their motel room with the toe of his Nikes, for fear of waking the baby. His knock went unanswered. *Maybe that was too soft,* he thought. With a shrug of his shoulders, he set his parcels on the ground, fished for his room key, and let himself in.

Erica sat at the desk, holding the phone in one hand and cradling Marnie in her other arm. "New York, New York," he heard her say. Her eyes met his, but she went on speaking into the phone. "St. Vincent's Catholic Medical Center, please."

With a concerned frown, Mike whispered, "Should you be calling Mario at work?" *After all,* he thought, *this is his only first week on the job.*

Wordlessly, Erica tucked the receiver under her chin and raised Marnie to Mike's outstretched arms. Then she spoke to the operator. "One moment," she said, and pulled open the desk drawer and reached for the pad and pen.

Mike waited until she had written down the number and ended the call with directory assistance. "I take it you weren't able to reach Mario at the apartment."

She shook her head and looked down at the phone, the receiver still in her hand.

"Let's try him there again in the morning, first thing. If he doesn't answer, we can stop on the road and call him midday."

"It's been three days."

"He could be working nights," Mike reminded her.

"I know that's a possibility. He said he would probably draw some night duty. But there's no answering machine. That's the first thing he would unpack." She took a deep breath. "Something's wrong, Mike. Something has happened to my husband, and I'm not waiting till morning."

As Erica began dialing another number, Mike shifted Marnie to his other arm and tiptoed over to the cradle, lowering the baby into it without waking her. He rocked the child for a moment, then turned to Erica when he heard her hang up the phone. Her hand shook as she lifted it from the receiver. All the color had drained from her face, and her eyes had filled with tears, which were rolling down her cheeks.

"Mario hasn't reported to work."

In two steps Mike was beside his sister-in-law, who was now shaking uncontrollably. He wrapped his arms around her. "Let's call Ian—see if he's heard anything."

Since the first night on the road, when they'd been unable to reach Mario, he'd encouraged her to call her brother. Erica had refused, finally telling him that she didn't want to take the chance of Leslie picking up the phone. When he'd asked, "Why on earth not?" she'd been vague. He had the distinct impression that something had gone wrong between Erica and her sister-in-law, but he didn't know what it could be. It was clear that Erica didn't want to talk about it. Leslie had been a bit distant when they'd left Laguna Niguel, but she was always polite, and she'd seemed genuinely concerned about both mother and baby.

Erica shook her head now, pulled away from him, and ran into the hotel bathroom, shutting the door behind her.

Mike, his eyes riveted on the closed door, wondered, *What should I do?* Erica had been full of giggles that first night, when they'd first checked into the motel as Mr. and Mrs. Christonelli. Easing her initial unease, he pointed out, "We are indeed a Mr. and a Mrs. And we have the same last name. So what if I'm not the one you're married to?" That had sparked another round of giggles. But day by day her mood had deteriorated, and now it had hit bottom. *What can I do?*

Some time later, Erica emerged from the bathroom. "I'm sorry," she said, the box of Kleenex tucked under her arm. "You're right, Mike, I should've called Ian." She wiped her eyes once more and blew her nose. "I'll call him now."

Ten minutes later, Mike sank down into the armchair, waiting for Erica to fill him in. *What in the hell is happening?* He'd heard only her side of the conversation so far, but he knew that there had been an accident. Mario was in the hospital.

Erica jotted down a number, then hung up and tearfully related the other side of her conversation with her brother before calling the number of the hospital where Mario had been taken. Mike was in shock. *This can't be happening. Nothing bad can happen to Mario. He's the glue that holds us all together.*

One phone call led to another. It was after regular hours, but Erica managed to be put through to not one, but all three doctors who had been involved with Mario's case since the accident. She was holding it together, but Mike could tell she was totally unnerved. "They aren't telling me everything," she whispered. "I just know they aren't."

"Like . . . what?" he asked, bewildered.

"I don't know. But they're keeping something from me."

An hour passed. Realizing that neither of them could sleep, they checked out of the hotel. In the next twenty hours, they covered more than thirteen hundred miles. Erica offered to share the driving, but Mike was wired and well up to the task. Besides, he knew she was in no shape to get behind the wheel.

On Wednesday afternoon, before Mike had brought the car to a full stop at the entrance to St. Luke's–Roosevelt Hospital, Erica had her seatbelt unbuckled and was opening the door.

"Would you mind bringing Marnie and meeting me in ICU?" Erica asked, her eyes rimmed red, her uncombed blond hair a tangle of curls.

"Sure thing," Mike said in a daze. Erica slammed the car door, turning back to give him an apologetic glance. Then she raced up the hospital steps.

Mike found a parking space and sat for a few moments, praying that his brother had regained consciousness, that the accident was not too serious, that Mario would soon recover. *What will we all do if he doesn't?* He tried to push that thought out of his mind. Marnie was peacefully asleep in her car seat, and Erica would see to Mario in the hospital. There was no longer any need to hurry. His brother, still in ICU, would not be allowed more than one visitor at a time.

His thoughts turned to Jeff, who'd been a part of his life for the past seven years. Despite their recent breakup, Jeff had a right to know what was going on. He would know what to do right now, what to say. On the other hand, what could Mike really tell him about Mario's condition at this point? He knew he was probably just making an excuse to give his former partner a call. Everything—his whole world—just seemed so fragile right now. *What am I supposed to do if . . . ?*

Mike pressed the lever to recline his seat and leaned back. He might as well let his little niece sleep.

Lucky little Marnie, he thought. *So young, so innocent, so unaware.*

PART TWO: 1992

CHAPTER

27

"Nap time," Ashleigh announced. She smiled as she watched Callie scramble over to her bookshelf, gingerly pull herself up on tiptoes, then reach up to pull down her *Pat the Bunny* book. This March had been sunny and cool, and they'd enjoyed wonderful days in the park—just the two of them. Now that Callie had been fed and changed, Ashleigh was hoping her daughter would sleep for a couple of hours so that she would have some time to herself to get ready for Conrad's return.

Callie's room had turned out just as Ashleigh had envisioned it. It was decorated in soft shades of pinks and greens. Below the pale pink walls and delicate green wainscoting, the wallpaper displayed the nursery book characters of Ashleigh's childhood. She would introduce Callie to each and every one, as her grandmother had done for her. Taking the book from her daughter's outstretched hand, Ashleigh lifted the toddler high in the air, whirled her around, then brought her down and kissed her soft, rosy cheek. "You be a very good girl today and take a nice nap. Daddy will be home soon."

Conrad had gone straight from meetings in New York to Milan with the Michael Nason's divisional merchandise managers and their buyers. They had attended the fashion week that the world over referred to as *prêt-à-porter*; even though the phrase literally meant "ready to wear" in French, many of the modeled fashions were anything but. Featured on the showroom ramps were extremes in the world of fashion. Fortunately, behind the scenes there also existed couture for the real world, the new trends for the upcoming season that buyers would select for their stores.

For Ashleigh the past two weeks had felt like months, like an eternity. She had made many new friends in Dallas and had taken an active role in the community—that was expected of her, of course, as the CEO's wife. The city still didn't feel quite right to her, though, especially now that Paige had moved to New York. Time dragged by, and most nights she could hardly wait for Conrad to walk through the door. But Ashleigh was doing her best to turn their house into a home.

Before laying Callie in her crib, Ashleigh slipped into the rocking chair and opened *Pat the Bunny*. Though it was new to them both, Ashleigh knew that this wonderful touch-and-feel book had been around for more than fifty years. She no longer had to guide Callie's tiny fingers across the bunny fur; Callie herself held the book and felt all the fur pieces, not only with her hands but also with her cheek.

It was hard to believe that in another few months, she would be two. Where had the time gone? Still haunted by the disappearance of Callie's twin, Ashleigh did not allow herself to dwell on it often. But the ache was never far from her heart. How could she be detached when each day she watched Callie, the mirror image of her Cassie, grow and change—her personality already developing moment by moment? She said a little prayer for Cassie each day.

The Landes Agency still had not relegated the abduction to the closed-case files. But Ashleigh realized it could no longer be considered a top priority. Sixteen months before, Landes had refused to bill them, saying that with no new leads in three months, he could not in good conscience continue to take their money. Conrad had balked at first. However, Ashleigh's rationale—*If it's meant to be, Cassie will be returned to us*—along with his own common sense had convinced him that they had to get on with their lives. She had finally convinced Conrad that they had to leave it in more competent hands than even the Landes Agency's—they had to leave it up to God now.

On retainer or not, Ross Pocino had vowed that he would never bring the investigation to a close. "Not until I bring little Cassie home and the perp is behind bars," he'd told them. And every month or so, without fail, he'd turn up on their doorstep requesting a new picture of Callie. At first, Ashleigh had asked what he planned to do with the photos.

He'd said, "After all this time, it may be a long shot, but still, since she's an identical twin . . . What have we got to lose?" Shaking his head, he'd continued, "Wish I had a clue where the . . ." and stopped himself, cleaning up some descriptive language before continuing, ". . . where the lowlife took her. No idea if she's even in California. Could be damn well anywhere, but don't worry. We'll find her."

A thought struck Ashleigh before she'd handed over the first snapshot, bringing her heart to a dead stop. "Ross, you're not planning to hand out pictures of Callie, are you?"

"No way. Only me and our agents will have copies." Although diplomacy had never been Pocino's high card, he had carefully avoided getting the Taylors' hopes up while he pursued a lead, never revealing what he'd discovered until he knew all the facts. After the fact, he would tell them about those leads that had led nowhere. Ashleigh guessed it was his way of letting them know that he hadn't put the abduction on the back burner, and she was grateful for it, often reminding herself, *He knows how it feels to lose a child.*

"Once your little girl is no longer a baby . . ." But by the time Pocino got into the impossibility of concealing an identical twin, Ashleigh generally brought their conversation to an end, although the thought of her baby growing older with another set of parents was never far from her mind. The fact that Cassie had grown to love those parents and would not want to be taken from them tormented her.

This was yet another aspect that she was no longer able to discuss with Conrad. In the aftermath of their loss, Ashleigh had forced herself to take a good, hard look at her marriage. Keeping everything inside was not fair to the man whom she loved with all her heart, and it was creating a widening gulf between them, one she was determined to halt. She had done her best to open up to her husband, to no longer avoid this great tragedy in their lives. And over the past couple of years, although their talks didn't always end in agreement, sharing her thoughts and prayers for Cassie had brought them closer together at times, not eliminating but at least narrowing the gulf between them.

As Callie entertained herself with the new book she held in her tiny hands, Ashleigh thought about her last night with Conrad, before he had taken off for his business trip. She had confessed that she prayed not just for Cassie's return but, if a reunion was not to be, that she was being well taken care of by loving parents. Once again, Conrad's mind—usually open and receptive—had snapped shut. He had exploded. "How could the type of scum who would kidnap an infant be either good or loving?"

His words had wounded her to the core—she didn't want to imagine her daughter being mistreated. Her face must have registered her distress because he had immediately apologized. But he had apologized because he realized he had hurt her, not because he'd felt he was wrong about the kidnappers. Even so, she prayed he was.

Callie stirred on her lap, pulling Ashleigh's full attention back to her precious daughter, who was chewing on the corner of the book. Ashleigh gently lifted the book from her hands and lay it on the bedside table, then lowered her into her crib and rubbed her back while humming her favorite childhood lullaby. Soon the toddler nodded off to sleep.

With Conrad not yet home, Ashleigh showered and slipped into his favorite hostess gown. She checked on Callie, who was still fast asleep, then took a peek at the pot roast, which was one of her husband's favorite meals—one that she had made far too seldom lately. Now she had some time to herself.

She'd done a great deal of soul searching in his absence. She loved him with all of her heart, and she knew he loved her. She loved being Callie's mother, of course, and having time to spend with her, and other than a few hiccups, she adored being Conrad's wife and partner in the community. She could not ask for a better life. In time, once Callie was in school, maybe she would return to the world of retail, but for now she was content—as content as she could be. The only fly in the ointment was the frenzy she still felt in the pit of her stomach when references to Cassie's abduction surfaced. Although she had overcome her initial reluctance and opened up to Conrad, she knew she hadn't done all she could to be totally candid in these last eighteen months or so. Since the day their world had been turned upside down and torn apart, she had created an atmosphere in which the two of them could share their true feelings far too seldom.

Ashleigh's gaze dropped to the rings on her left finger. The solitary diamond glinted in the flickering glow from the candlelit dinner table, and her mind drifted back to the day she'd moved the engagement ring to her little finger so that Conrad could place the wedding ring closer to her heart. She remembered their commitment, their openness—all the promises they had made to each other. His anger over their stolen child had never been directed at her, and yet by forcing him to hide it, she'd helped build a wall between them. She hadn't lived up to her promises. She'd held back, and now she feared Conrad was doing the same.

If only Paige weren't so busy on the East Coast . . . She aborted that rationale the moment it surfaced, clearing her head with a mental shake. Avoiding issues had never been her style. In the business world, her expertise was communication, and she darn well better make it her number-one priority in her marriage.

Erica hobbled around on one shoe, frantically looking for the other. The clock read 7:15 already. Viviana De Mornay would blow a gasket if Erica were late for their morning meeting.

"Ma-ma. Up. Up." Marnie had pulled herself up on the crib rail.

Erica scooped up her daughter, kissed her on her soft baby cheek, and for a moment just held her tight. "Mommy loves you so very, very much, but she's got to get to work." Still searching about the room for her shoe, Erica called out, "Mike, I need your help."

"Yes, my lady?" he called back, appearing in the doorway in an instant.

"This morning I don't feel like anyone's lady," she said, gently handing Marnie over to him. Instantly, Marnie began to wail, "Ma-ma, Ma-ma!" She pulled away from her uncle, leaned toward Erica, and stretched out her arms. This familiar scene always tugged at Erica's heart. If only she could spend more time with her precious baby. But with the demands of her job, not to mention the daily visits to Crestwood Rehabilitation Facility on the way home, there just weren't enough hours in the day. Kissing the top of Marnie's head of silky blond hair, she said, "Mommy will be off on Tuesday. We'll go to see Daddy and then we'll go to the park."

Mike danced Marnie around the bedroom floor. "Hey, *mia bambina*, we don't have to wait till Tuesday for the park. Your Uncle Mike's taking you right after breakfast."

Marnie stopped crying and smiled. Maybe the dancing took her breath away, but Erica suspected that her daughter understood.

Oh my God, I've got to get a move on. "Have you seen my other Jimmy Choo?"

Mike rolled his eyes. "If you'd just—"

"I don't need a lecture. I just need to find . . . Oh, here it is." She plucked the other high heel from beneath Marnie's special blankie and smiled. "I've got to run, but thanks for everything, Mike. You're an absolute godsend."

He waved off her praise, as he always did.

Ever since Mario had been moved from St. Luke's to Crestwood a few months ago, having Mike here to help her had felt more and more natural. She still missed her husband every minute of every day, but after a long stint of constant waiting for Mario to come back to them, they were no longer in crisis mode. It was starting to feel comfortable—as comfortable as it could be, considering the circumstances.

The doctors claimed that there was nothing more they could do for him, that only time would tell. Erica still had hope that one day, the man they loved would emerge from that lousy coma and take his place by her side in raising the precious gift he had brought her over a year and a half ago. That's what kept her going. Mike was wonderful, and he loved her little girl with all his heart, but Mario was her father, and a young girl needed her father. Erica knew that Marnie's biological mother had wanted far more for her baby than she had been able to give. She had told Mario that she wanted the child to have two loving parents. And that was what Erica wanted too, more than anything.

Slipping on her shoe, she watched Mike lovingly change Marnie's diaper and realized how wrong she had been. She had balked when Mario had first suggested that his brother live with them while starting out in New York. Only the fact that they would have a built-in babysitter had turned the tide. *What on earth would I have done without him?* she thought now. She loved her job at De Mornay's, even though Viviana was a formidable taskmaster who felt that anyone working for her must make the success of De Mornay's not just the number-one priority but the only priority. Employees had to put in extra hours without question, whenever necessary—no excuses. It was something the instructors at the L.A. Fashion Institute had never covered in Erica's courses.

Blowing her makeshift family a kiss, Erica turned to leave.

"Your hair?" Mike grinned. "Remember, no stray strands."

"Oh, damn." She'd been in such a frenzy poking under the bed, the dresser, and the nightstand in search of her missing shoe that she'd forgotten to spray her hair. It hadn't been easy to master the art of twisting her wild, curly locks into the look of sophistication that Viviana demanded of anyone representing her boutique. But with the use of gel and a small aerosol hairspray stashed in her handbag, she'd managed to keep most criticism at bay. She dashed into the bathroom now, smoothed her hair, sprayed all the loose ends, and patted it in pace.

Nearly seven thirty. Unless she was able to run all the way to the subway in her Jimmy Choos, get directly on a train, and ride it to her stop on Fifth Avenue, there would be hell to pay.

Hearing the front door bang against the wall, Ashleigh rushed into the living room.

"Sorry." Conrad gave a warm smile. "Guess I don't know my own strength." He dumped his suitcase at his feet and held out his arms.

It doesn't matter, thought Ashleigh as she ran into them. All that mattered was that he was home safely.

"Where's my little love?" he asked.

"Still sleeping, I think." Hand in hand, they headed up the stairway to Callie's room. But she wasn't asleep. She had discovered her foot and, gurgling happy baby sounds, was attempting to bring it to her mouth. Looking at each other, they smiled, and Conrad scooped their daughter up and kissed her. Not showing any sign of jet lag, he sat cross-legged on the floor while Callie showed him her latest discovery. Knocking down the big plastic blocks, it seemed, was much more fun than stacking them up.

Ashleigh watched her husband and daughter at play. He seemed every bit at home romping on the floor with their little girl as he did sitting behind his executive desk or in a conference room, making important decisions for the continued growth and success of Michael Nason's.

How lucky I am, thought Ashleigh. *A happy, healthy daughter and a handsome, successful husband who adores us both.*

That night, after tucking Callie back into her crib and savoring a quick shower, Conrad found Ashleigh at the kitchen counter pouring two glasses of wine. *She looks so damn beautiful,* he thought. Tall and slim, she walked gracefully to the dinner table, her shimmering blond hair forming a silky frame around her face. What he wanted to do was take her straight upstairs to bed. But first, they must talk. There was so much he had to tell her.

Drawing her into his arms, he said, "God, I've missed you." Their kiss was passionate and it left him breathless, igniting a desire so strong that he forgot all about how badly they needed to talk about their future. A short silence fell between them as they looked into each other's eyes, then Conrad's arms tightened around Ashleigh's slim waist. "Let's go upstairs. I haven't made love to my wife in far too long."

Ashleigh smiled and set down her glass of wine. "That's the best suggestion you've had all evening." They laughed as he led her up the stairs. There was so much he wanted to say, but it could wait. At the top of the stairs, she paused and turned to face him, wrapping her arms around his neck, pulling him close. "I love you so much," she murmured.

Yes, it could most definitely wait. They were so close, he could almost feel the beat of her heart as he reached behind her to unzip her dress. The door to the master bedroom was open wide, and he saw that the bedspread was already turned down. Smiling, he swooped her off her feet and carried her to their bed.

Giggling, she tossed off her shoes and reached up to tug off his shirt. In seconds, with their clothes strewn across the floor, they were in bed and in each other's arms. Ashleigh was playful and seemed more carefree than she'd been in some time, perhaps since . . . since before their loss. Maybe the woman he had married, whom he loved with every beat of his heart, was returning to him at last.

He kissed her forehead, her mouth, her neck, and continued slowly down the length of her body, canvassing every inch. Her hands, which had been roaming his back, stopped exploring, and she pulled him tight against her and arched her back. "Now, love. I want you now."

Any real discussion would have to wait.

CHAPTER
30

Ashleigh floated down the stairs a few steps behind Conrad, her silky robe trailing behind her. *What a perfect homecoming.* She could still feel the touch of his hands—so strong and yet so gentle. Although aware that her husband had a lot on his mind, she had no doubt that they were once again the magical couple they had once been. *Everything is going to be alright. No, more than alright. Much, much more.*

Picking up the two glasses of wine Ashleigh had poured earlier, Conrad said, "How about taking these outside?" She smiled. "It's a terrific evening to enjoy our patio."

"Have you tried the new outdoor heaters?"

"Not yet," she said teasingly. "It wouldn't be any fun without you."

He handed her one of the glasses and flicked the switch on the outdoor heaters, bringing an instant romantic glow.

Settling into the patio chair he pulled out for her, Ashleigh began, "You haven't told me about the prêt-à-porter. What did I miss this year?" She recalled attending fashion week in Milan the year before the birth of the twins. She'd been mesmerized.

"As usual, many of the designers were showing their weird, 'artsy,' out-of-this-world lines of clothing."

"You mean the ones that, if people actually walked out on the streets wearing them, they'd appear deranged?"

"You've got it," he said, with a grin. "But of course there was also the prêt-à-porter designed with so-called normal people in mind, so overall it was a worthwhile trip."

He leaned forward, taking both of her hands in his. "I got a lot more than I bargained for on this trip."

"Like what?"

Stars twinkled above in a clear navy sky, and in the stillness of the night, with the exception of the occasional whoosh of the outdoor heater, only the sound of a few crickets could be heard. Conrad sank back in his chair, drew Ashleigh's hand to his mouth, and kissed it. Sensing he had something important to tell her, she leaned closer, gazing into his expressive blue eyes.

"When I was in Italy, I spent a bit of time with Mark." That came as no surprise to Ashleigh. "Without Toddman at the helm, you know, Consolidated might be headed for liquidation. But under his leadership, most of the creditors have been turned into investors. That's quite an achievement."

"Would you like to be working with him again?"

He was silent for what seemed a long time, then said, "No. At least, not now. But I'd say that within the year, Consolidated will not only emerge from bankruptcy but also expand."

"So when will Nason's become too small an arena?" Ashleigh knew him as well as he knew himself. She was no stranger to the retail industry, and reading between the lines had always been her special talent.

"Not now." He paused, squeezing her hand. "Not for at least a year or two. Michael Nason's is a vital organization with a lot more potential. I've just begun to tap into some of the resources and areas that I plan to expand. But you're right. Down the line, I will have accomplished all I set out to do here. That's when I'll want to move on to a much bigger arena, and I want to do it before Callie is in kindergarten."

The silence of the night was interrupted only by the occasional hiss of the outdoor heater. Ashleigh could almost read Conrad's silent thoughts. Reaching out, she slipped her hand into his. She loved this man with every fiber of her being, and she knew she always would. "Let's begin again," she said.

Conrad blinked and a dark brow lifted. "Begin again?" he parroted.

She rose from her chair, looked down at his puzzled expression, and lowered herself to his lap. "I think about Cassie every day, and I pray for her well-being. But I haven't been totally open with you."

Before he could respond, Ashleigh pressed her fingers against his lips. "You have every right to be angry, but your anger frightens me, so I avoid talking about . . ." His lips parted to speak, but she kissed them lightly. "Please, love. I want you to know that I've been wrong." Pausing, she searched for the words, then just plowed ahead. "Growing up in a very protective environment, dealing with anger was something I had to learn on the outside. The battlefields at Bentleys Royale gave me a crash course in confronting and defusing explosive executives. But none of that was personal."

Pressing back into the woven chair seat, Conrad gently took hold of her chin and raised it until her eyes met his. "Sweetheart, I've never been angry at you."

"I know that." Planting a kiss on his forehead, she said, "I've always known that." Returning to her own chair, she picked up her glass and took a sip of her wine, letting the silence linger between them for a moment or so. Then she took a long, restorative breath. "I've been doing a lot of thinking in your absence."

Conrad leaned forward again, with an expectant expression on his face.

"I know you would like for us to have another child and—"

"You know I would. But, Ashleigh, you can't do this for me. We must wait until you're ready."

Oh, how I love this man. "Watching Callie cut her first tooth, take her first step, say her first words, and all those other firsts—it's caused a new ache in my heart for Cassie. I want her back more than anything, so much I can barely breathe. But I no longer want to put our lives on hold. I love you, and I want to have your baby."

Conrad took the wine glass from her hand and set it on the small table beside her chair. He pulled her to her feet, a look of incredulity sweeping across his well-chiseled features. "Ashleigh! Are you sure? Are you really sure?"

Her heart flooded with love, and she said, "Yes. I don't want Callie growing up as an only child any more than you do." Then she winked, thinking about their recent romp in the bedroom. "Maybe our order has already been registered."

CHAPTER

31

Viviana De Mornay was seated at the French antique table in the center of her office, with sketches spread out in front of her. The garment models for each of the drawings were on the rolling rack on the far wall. She was so proud of this year's collection—and even more proud of the impact her name now had in the industry.

When Glenn Nelson stepped through the door and pulled up a chair beside her, she lifted her head briefly to greet him, then went back to studying the designs. "Did you catch the news about Mitchell Wainwright in *Women's Wear?*"

Viviana usually scanned *Women's Wear Daily,* the industry's fashion bible, from cover to cover before she even left home each day. "No," she replied. "I've been so busy with these designs, I haven't even picked up today's issue." She'd known Mitchell for many years, at one time had even set her sights on him. As a big player in the wave of leverage buyout in the early '80s, he had been the first to wage a hostile takeover in the retail arena on the West Coast and had been her former husband's most formidable rival.

Along with being the powerful owner of Wainwright Enterprises, he was a good-looking man with plenty of charm and charisma. But he'd met and been attracted to Ashleigh McDowell instead. Viviana had tried to warn him that Ashleigh was not only too young but also all wrong for him. But had he listened? No, indeed. He'd fallen hook, line, and sinker. As she'd predicted, their engagement was a short one—less than two months, as she recalled. Ashleigh was now the wife of the Michael Nason's CEO, Conrad Taylor. And then, damned if Wainwright didn't turn right around and marry Christine, his persnickety longtime assistant.

"The last I'd heard," Viviana continued, "Mitchell emerged from his self-imposed retirement a couple of months ago and has connected with the Jordon's management team." Mitchell was no doubt grappling with the financing for the troubled retail conglomerate. Love it or hate it, Jordon's was a department store brand that was known from coast to coast. In New York, it was a treasured icon, but in areas where beloved regional stores had been replaced by Jordon's, it was a different story.

Glenn's next words brought her abruptly out of her recollections. "Well, Wainwright will be out of commission for a while." He paused when she looked up suddenly. "Never cared much for the man's tactics, but you've got to respect his know-how—not to mention his chutzpah." He hesitated again. "A tragic story. A few days ago, it seems, his wife ran their car off one of the small bridges out in Greenwich. Reminds me of the Ted Kennedy debacle in Chappaquiddick. Wainwright survived, but his wife and nine-year-old son were killed."

Viviana gasped, her hand flying up to cover her mouth. "When? Where is he now?"

"A few days ago," Glenn repeated. "The article didn't say where they'd taken him, but I imagine it's Greenwich Hospital."

Viviana sprang from her chair and picked up her desk phone before it dawned on her that it was still before eight in the morning. Her expression of sympathy would wait just a bit. Replacing the receiver, she glanced at the Steuben clock and discovered she was wrong. "It's after eight. Where on earth is Erica? I told her how important this meeting was!"

"It's only three minutes past eight, Viviana darling," Glenn laughed. With a forty percent share of the business, he didn't take any flack. In fact, he was the only one who dared challenge her in any way. "That girl has a lot on her plate, and she's talented as hell, so give her a break."

"I have given her a break," Viviana protested. "I pay her well, and I expect her to show up on time, not keep us waiting."

Glenn shook his head at his partner, then turned his head toward the doorway at the sound of heels rapidly approaching the open door.

"Sorry," Erica said breathlessly as she dashed into the office, her hair dripping wet. "I hope you haven't been waiting for me." She didn't offer any excuses, knowing Viviana would not accept them. For that, Viviana was grateful; she could not tolerate excuses of any kind.

"You look like a drowned puppy, my dear. Don't you have an umbrella?"

"Yes, but I didn't realize it was raining till I got outside. By then it was too late to run back and get it. I thought it would be better to be wet and on time than late and, well, dry."

Shaking her head, Viviana said, "Well, take care of your hair and wipe off your shoes before you go out on the floor today. And Erica, you weren't actually on time. When I say a meeting is to begin at eight o'clock, that is precisely what I mean."

Erica nodded and said eagerly and excitedly, "I can't wait to get started." They were to select the items today for the fall catalog photo shoot, and Viviana knew that Erica was hoping for some recognition for her designs. Some of them were truly superb, and Viviana did plan to use them—but the girl worked for her, so De Mornay's would be the only name given.

And as far as she was concerned, that was as it should be.

CHAPTER

32

After finally getting Marnie to sleep, Mike had just slipped into his desk chair and was looking forward to at least one quiet hour of work when he heard the front door open and bang against the wall.

"I just can't believe it!" Erica cried out, tossing her handbag on the counter and stomping into his workspace.

"Shh!" he scolded. "I just got Marnie to bed, and I've got to work on this website or my ass is grass."

"Sorry," she said, lowering her voice to just above a whisper. When Mike looked up, he saw that her face was beet red and her hands were balled into fists. "That malicious, conniving bitch," she continued. "She thinks she's so hot and she can just use people, and they should be . . . should be honored to be used by her! Well, I'm not going to take it."

Mike glanced up from the computer screen, then rose and headed for the kitchen counter. He wouldn't get a speck of work done until she got whatever it was off her mind.

"I just made a fresh pot of coffee," he sighed. "Would you like some?"

"No. What I'd like is to slap Miss Fashion Goddess right across her perfectly made-up face, then take my designs and march straight out the door."

Mike poured himself a mug of coffee and, without asking, poured Erica a glass of cold water. Then he voiced the obligatory "What happened?"

"I found out that three of my dress designs have been made up and are being shot for the fall catalog."

"Well, that's what you were hoping for, wasn't it?"

"The thing is, no one will know they're mine. Everyone will think they're Miss Hoity-toity's." Lifting her brows in exaggeration, she mimicked, "Well, my dear, in *our industry,* the De Mornay's label is *prestigious.* You are *maturing* into a fine designer, but until you reach the level of excellence *required,* your name will *not* be on the label. It will be that of *De Mornay's,* which stands for quality and *fashion.*" She quickly gulped down some water, then hissed, "What . . . utter . . . bullshit. She's using my designs and putting her name on them! It's not my designs that aren't good enough—just my name!"

Before Mike could comment, she ranted on, "And, then the . . . the phony charlatan has the colossal nerve to tell me that I must *update my wardrobe* to *properly represent De Mornay's.*"

"My God, Erica," Mike said when he finally got a word in. "That's unconscionable. She doesn't pay you enough to make that kind of demand! Even at wholesale, the number of outfits she required for last season made a hell of a dent in our budget."

Erica was silent for a long, drawn-out moment. She took a small sip of water and, like a chameleon, changed her demeanor. The hard edge to her expression disappeared and the tension seemed to drain from her body. "Well, Mike," she said softly. "The ambiance of De Mornay's, it literally takes your breath away, and on the floor I must epitomize that. No way can I show up in last season's couture."

Mike blinked, regained focus, and asked, "So what do you plan to do about this? How are you going to get the recognition you deserve?" He knew his sister-in-law was a talented designer. Although it would present a hell of a hardship for them in the short run, he wondered if he should suggest that she look for another position—in an organization where her talent would be appreciated and rewarded.

Erica smiled sweetly. "Oh, Mike. Don't take me too seriously. I was just letting off steam. I am getting an opportunity of a lifetime at De Mornay's. While it's true that I designed three of the ensembles in the catalog, it was Viviana who selected the fabric and the special trim. Without them, the designs wouldn't make the same fashion statement. When I'm ready, I'm sure my name will be put on the label. Glenn will see to it."

Speechless, Mike heaved a breath, then said, "Alright, Erica. You know best." He hoped that was the right thing to say. *If only Mario were here* . . . "I really do have to get back to work."

Returning to his computer while Erica went to check on Marnie, he wondered about her sudden mood swing. Though she didn't seem to present any danger to herself or the baby, this wasn't the first time he'd seen it. *Maybe she's manic depressive.* Based on what he'd heard about that particular mental illness, Erica's highs and lows fit the profile—he'd noticed the clues often enough. And after living with her for more than eighteen months, maybe it was time to pay attention.

CHAPTER

33

Paige smiled at her nine-year-old daughter. She looked so grown up in her new fitted coat with its faux white fur collar and matching muff. The muff was April's favorite. She'd seen one in the American Girl series, which Paige had started reading to her before April herself could read. Her favorite, Samantha, had a muff, and now so did she. She could hardly wait to show off her new fashion statement; never mind that spring was just around the corner.

When they touched down at JFK Airport, the sun was shining and the weather only cool, not cold, but April was determined to wear her new outfit and show it off to Madison, her best friend in Greenwich. She had made sure that Paige called Madison's parents before she and her mom left Milan. She'd invited Madison for a sleepover tonight—their first night back home.

Overhearing Paige's call, Mark had raised an eyebrow, then shrugged his broad shoulders. Answering his unasked question, Paige said, "Well, maybe I am spoiling her a bit, but not in ways that will do her any harm." She didn't mention that it had been Mark's idea, not hers, to buy this extravagant couture outfit in miniature. He'd said it was April's reward for being such a trooper during their week at the prêt-à-porter, which had fallen at the same time as her spring break from school.

"It's good to be home," Mark and Paige said nearly simultaneously as the limo turned up the circular path to their suburban home. They turned to each other and laughed, then immediately turned their attention to April, who was tugging on the door handle before they'd come to a full stop.

Paige jumped in quickly before Mark had a chance. "April," she scolded, "wait." While her husband loved April as much as she did, she knew sometimes he could sound a bit on the harsh side.

When the limo came to a full stop, April said in her most polite manner, "May I be excused, please?" Paige knew it was all her daughter could do to keep from jumping out of the car. Madison was probably already here, her parents having dropped her off before heading to a party scheduled that afternoon.

"Get out of here," Mark teased.

April sprang from the car and raced up the steps, running smack into their butler, who had just stepped out through the front door.

"Whoa, missie," said Terrence, lifting her high above his shoulders, then setting her gently on the ground. He took a good look at her. "Aren't you a fashion plate? You take this old man's breath away." Terrence stood tall and straight and exhibited an amazing strength and agility for a man in his sixties. He and his wife, Wilma, had been with the Toddmans since their days in California and had moved with them first to Dallas and again two years ago to New York.

"Is Madison here?"

Before Terrence had a chance to open his mouth, a curly-haired, freckle-faced girl bounded out the front door. The two girls began talking at once, with Madison asking to touch the fur muff as they disappeared back into the house.

While Terrence and the limo driver unloaded the trunk and carried in the luggage, Mark headed for the garage. Paige dashed up the steps to fill Wilma in on the girls' plans for the evening: She and Mark would be going to Greenwich Hospital to visit a former colleague, but they would be back in a couple of hours, in time for dinner.

"My word, Miss Paige, I don't know where you two get all your energy. The last time my Terrence and I went back to England, it must have taken us a good two weeks to get over the jet lag."

"Well, Wilma, I may be dragging in a couple hours, but right now I'm okay. If I had my druthers, I'd be taking a nice, hot shower and curling up with the novel I started on the plane. But we learned that Mitchell Wainwright was in a horrible accident earlier this week. He's in critical condition." She took a breath and said quietly, "His wife and young son did not survive."

Wilma's gray eyes began to tear. "That's terrible. I remember him from years ago—that tall, good-looking man with the thick head of silver hair."

"Yes," Paige confirmed, "Mitchell was the one helping Mr. Toddman back when that crazy Australian was setting out to break up the Consolidated stores."

"There is no worse tragedy in life than losing a child," Wilma sympathized. "He must be devastated."

Paige heard the roar of the Cadillac's engine and simply nodded. *Nothing worse indeed.* The pain, she imagined, would be unbearable—she could hardly compare it to the dull, timeless ache of never knowing who your mother was, although this ache was still very difficult to live with. She ran up the winding staircase and gave April a kiss and a very tight hug. "You girls have a great time. We'll be back for dinner in less than two hours." Mark tooted the horn, and before rushing out to join him, Paige threw her little girl another kiss. For good measure.

CHAPTER

34

Blinding sunlight flooded Mitchell Wainwright's private hospital room. He awoke with a start. The young nurse who had opened the shade was humming "Oh, What a Beautiful Morning" softly—but not softly enough.

"You have visitors, Mr. Wainwright." That irritating singsong voice made him want to strangle her.

He glared down at his right leg, hoisted high in the air, then over to the intravenous tubing stuck into his arm. He didn't want visitors. Not now. Maybe not ever. But before he had an opportunity to voice his objection, Mark and Paige Toddman appeared in the doorway. *Why are they here?* He'd thought they were in Italy.

"We were in Milan when word of your accident reached us," Mark said as he approached the bed.

Accident . . . accident. The word rang in Wainwright's head. *It was no goddamned accident.*

"We came right over after dropping off April to see how you were doing and if there was anything we could do for you," Paige said, her eyes brimming with tears.

Wainwright neither wanted nor needed Paige Toddman's pity, her sympathy, or even her empathy. Not now, not ever. But he planted a phony smile on his face. "That was nice of you, but really, you didn't have to go out of your way."

A plump nurse, the perfect prototype for the grandmother in a child's storybook, appeared carrying a huge bouquet of red roses. "Here you go, Mr. Wainwright," she said. Then, without asking, she opened the tiny envelope and read: "To one of the most dynamic men in our industry. My heart goes out to you. Best wishes for a speedy recovery."

Wainwright frowned.

The nurse continued, "It's signed VIVIANA DE MORNAY." She paused and smiled. "Such a beautiful script."

Although his face was quite swollen, Paige was sure he rolled his hazel eyes before he thanked the nurse and asked for some water.

As far as she knew, he had no family other than his older son, Anthony, who had turned out to be the proverbial bad seed. She couldn't remember—was he in prison? Or maybe even dead? Although she had never been high on Mitchell Wainwright as a person, she respected his business acumen, if not his ruthlessness. And yet he'd done a complete turnabout when his young son was diagnosed with leukemia. Now the boy was gone, and her heart ached for Wainwright. She suspected he would not grieve for his wife, however, as he did for his son.

Turning toward Mark, Wainwright said, "Haven't had a chance to congratulate you on becoming the new darling of Wall Street. Not sure how you managed to pull it all together in such a short time. Lifting a bankruptcy is no small victory. Must have been tough to salvage that mess Sloane left behind."

Mark could hardly blame the man for wanting to shift the conversation. Without a moment's hesitation, he launched into his favorite topic. "Bounced back early this year. Our reorganization's running smoothly. Cut expenses to the bare bone, in the right places, and our legal eagles managed to convince most of our creditors to back us, so we're on a roll. In fact, with the recession coming to an end and the signs of a strengthening economy, we're looking toward future expansion."

Wainwright cocked his one unbandaged eyebrow.

"Not right now," Mark added in an instant. "We've got to get all our ducks in order and watch for solid signs of growth in the economy. But I see that happening soon, and we'll be ready for new challenges and opportunities that we can turn into bottom-line profit."

"And the new opportunities you have in mind . . . ?" The injured man's voice had lost the monotone quality of their initial conversation. In his element, he seemed to come back to life.

"We haven't—"

Wainwright hit the switch on the side of his bed, bringing himself to a semi-sitting position. "So you're not ready to disclose that Jordon's is your target?"

Paige inhaled but did not utter a word. It was not much of a leap for Wainwright to assume that Mark would set his sights on a merger with Jordon's. She just hadn't thought he'd make that jump so soon.

Although Ashleigh and Callie had arrived at Charles's tranquil Naples home a mere three days before, it seemed much longer. The timing for this trip couldn't have been more ideal, with Conrad scheduled to be away on business for the next few weeks, but Ashleigh missed him more than ever.

Ashleigh heard a light tap on her bedroom door. "Come in," she said, finishing the last brushstroke. She liked the way her hair shone in the bright sun that streamed through the guest room window.

It was Elizabeth, holding a grinning Callie in her arms. The toddler held an oval baby cookie in each hand and smelled of Johnson's Baby Powder. "Is Charles alright?" Ashleigh asked immediately. Elizabeth seldom came to her room.

"Your grandfather's in his room, right as rain. I came to tell you that Mr. Conrad is on the phone from Dallas."

Puzzled, Ashleigh said, "But I didn't hear the phone ring."

"Of course not. Don't you remember? I turned off all the upstairs ringers."

She nodded, recalling that Elizabeth hadn't wanted to awaken Charles. She stretched over to give Callie a kiss on her rosy cheek before dashing to the phone.

"Sweetheart! I knew I'd miss you, but I didn't realize just how much. It seems you've been gone forever," Conrad began.

Ashleigh laughed. "Exactly three days," she reminded him. "And I imagine you are all packed and ready to be picked up for the airport." He was on his way to New York for the next week, then on to the Asian markets with his divisional merchandise managers and buyers.

"You're right, I am. But it feels so strange to be rattling around in this house without both you and Callie. At least when I'm away, you have Callie."

"My poor husband. Are you feeling abandoned?"

Conrad's deep, throaty chuckle echoed over the phone line. "Sorry. Didn't mean to sound so pitiful. I just love being surrounded by my girls. I'm glad you're getting a chance to spend some time with Charles, and what you're doing for the Bentleys Royale group is important. I'm sure it's much appreciated by the remaining executives, if not by that colorful store manager."

"It's been great working with all the executives and with the sales and sales support staff. You know, I didn't know beans about outplacement, but with this talented group, I'm having a lot of success. The only real problem is that store manager. Elaine Ellis is her name. Remember when I told you on Tuesday that I felt like an outsider? Well, that's all changed. Ms. Ellis's personnel director quit a couple of days ago. Left without notice. I've filled in as best I can, but she seems to have forgotten that I'm a volunteer. She behaves as if I report directly to her."

"Hey, you don't have to take—"

"Hey, yourself," she said with a playful giggle. "If I survived David Jerome, I can survive anything." The former president of Bentleys Royale had been known as the "Benevolent Dictator." Sales associates had adored him, while executives had feared him. "Besides, I grew up in Bentleys Royale, and I love doing something really worthwhile."

"Everything you get involved with is worthwhile, sweetheart. You always give your all. I love that, and I'd never want to prevent you from following your own dreams. I'd never try to overshadow your talents and desires," Conrad affirmed.

"I know that." His confidence in her ability was something she never doubted—though between them it was understood that she would always be available at the drop of a hat when he needed her for Michael Nason's. "But right now I've got to get moving. I told Elaine—*Ms. Ellis*—I'd be in by eight for her morning management meeting."

"So now you're a member of her management team?" he said with a tone of incredulity.

"So it seems. I really do have to run. Love you." Ashleigh returned the phone to the hook and slipped into her shoes.

"Ma-ma. Ma-ma," Callie mouthed and then went back to munching her cookie, content to stay in Elizabeth's grandmotherly arms.

Giving her daughter another kiss, Ashleigh asked Elizabeth to tell Charles that she would not be late again tonight. She sensed that he was awake, but since he'd not yet come out of his bedroom, she didn't want to disturb him.

Taking a final glance in the mirror, she headed downstairs and turned her attention to the day ahead, wondering what it would bring and what the unpredictable general manager might have in store for her.

Unable to resist Marnie's outstretched arms, Mike scooped her into his. "Munchkin, I love you with all my heart," he murmured into the soft folds of the toddler's neck, giving her a playful raspberry. "But today, you've been a royal pain in the ass."

Marnie giggled and tugged on his ear.

"If Uncle Mikey doesn't get this website design for Carlingdon's put to bed, there'll be no more Gerber's cookies."

Today had been a tough one. Marnie was into everything, and her naps were getting shorter each day. Mike's only option was to make up for it at night—luckily, that's when he typically did his best work. Since his split with Jeff and the move to New York, his social life had been nearly non-existent anyway. Having Erica and Marnie in his life had turned out to be a godsend. But when the Carlingdon's website design had fallen into his lap thanks to Glenn's connections in the fashion and retail world, his window of time had grown too short.

Being the perfectionist that he was, Mike threw himself heart and soul into the task. As a result, last night—or rather, this morning—he'd had less than two hours' sleep. His back ached from being hunched over the computer, and he felt as if someone had pitched sand into his bloodshot eyes.

He adored being the one to watch over Marnie so that Erica could pursue her own dreams. No one deserved a break more than she did. But it seemed there just weren't enough hours at in the day—especially when Carlingdon's could be the pivotal point for his website business.

Oh God, I miss my big brother. But Mario was gone. He knew that, even if Erica didn't. The doctors had told them there was nothing more they could do for him, and he'd been moved again, to a long-term care facility. But Erica refused to terminate his life support; she insisted that one day he'd come back to them. Mike prayed for his brother, but in his heart he knew that Mario was no longer with them. All that was left was a shell.

He loved Marnie, and his heart ached for his sister-in-law, but he couldn't go on at this pace. He needed a break. The time had come to reconsider their arrangement. Now that they were both getting their careers off the ground, they needed a babysitter. *But how is that going to fit in our budget?* Just thinking about it had him worrying, until something occurred to him: Erica's brother. Ian had just about raised her. He would help. But before that idea was fully formed, he banished it from his mind. Since the birth of Marnie, Erica had seemed reluctant to call her brother. Mike didn't know what had happened between them, but he sensed it was something serious.

He put Marnie back on the floor with her playthings and sat at his desk, keeping a close eye on the little girl. Placing his cheeks in his hands, he strummed his fingertips on his forehead, willing another answer to come to him. *I'll have a heart-to-heart with Erica,* he thought. *There's got to be a solution.*

On Thursday morning, the thirtieth of April, Ashleigh descended the stairs of the associates' entrance at Bentleys Royale, wondering if the Personnel department would be bombarded with sick calls. No doubt, the verdict in the Rodney King police brutality case would be the major topic of discussion among those who did show up for work.

In the days leading up to the verdict, speculation about the consequences had been rampant. No matter which way it went, there was bound to be trouble. The charges were based on more than hearsay. A home video had been turned over to the media and was being played repeatedly on news stations around the world. The video clearly depicted Rodney King, a drug-addicted black man, as defenseless. It showed him on the ground, surrounded by police officers wielding clubs. This appeared to be a clear-cut case of police brutality, though it was up to the jury to determine the guilt or innocence of the officers involved.

At three fifteen the previous afternoon, the verdict had been announced. Splayed across the front page of the *Los Angeles Times* in bold capital letters, it stunned the nation:

NOT GUILTY . . .

NOT GUILTY . . .

NOT GUILTY . . .

NOT GUILTY . . .

By three forty-five, a crowd of more than three hundred people had appeared at the Los Angeles County Courthouse, protesting the verdict.

Last night, when Conrad had called Ashleigh, they'd talked about the unexpected verdict and the rioting that had started in the city's streets. He'd reasoned, "That's why we have juries. Obviously, they had more information than we could get from an eight-second-long videotape. We're in no position to second-guess . . ." Cutting off midsentence, he'd said suddenly, "Ashleigh, turn on your TV."

She'd picked up the remote from the guest room dresser and switched on the TV. The first channel was broadcasting the scene of a truck driver being dragged from the cab of his truck. She flipped the channel, not wanting to again see the man being beaten senseless. But channel after channel focused on gang-bangers attacking and looting local merchants in South Central Los Angeles. The situation was far worse than had been predicted, and the LAPD found that they were not only powerless to control it but also the main target of revenge. The police officers quickly backed off, attempting to cordon off sections of the city to confine the violence.

As she watched the TV screen in horror and disbelief, Ashleigh heard Conrad say, "The riots are escalating beyond local containment. Governor Wilson has requested the assistance of the National Guard. So for God's sake, Ashleigh, don't venture into L.A. till this is put to rest."

But when she awakened Thursday morning, she found herself unable to heed Conrad's warning. She had no intention of going anywhere near the heart of L.A., and she assured herself that the Royale corridor would be perfectly safe.

From the moment she arrived at Bentleys Royale, Ashleigh ran into clusters of associates rehashing the verdict. She was no stranger to most of these longtime employees, nor were they to her. But today was different—no one seemed quite themselves.

"The police," one housekeeping associate fumed, "run around with badges and think they have a right to do whatever they want." There were nods of agreement and the speaker, a young black woman, opened her mouth to continue until another associate spotted Ashleigh and placed his hand on the woman's arm. Raising his voice, he said, "Good morning, Miss McDowell," alerting the others to her arrival. Since she would only be here for a couple of weeks, Ashleigh did not correct his use of her maiden name. She would always be Miss McDowell to these employees.

Ashleigh smiled, returned their greeting, and went straight to her office—the same one that had been hers when she had actually been on the Bentleys Royale management team.

Around ten o'clock, she received a call from the head of security at the Bentley's downtown office building. "We've received reports that looters are headed this way. We're sending our employees home immediately; the downtown store is set to release theirs at twelve o'clock, and we just got word that another gang is heading in your direction. We recommend you also release your staff by noon."

She immediately spun into action. First she switched on the radio to keep abreast of further developments, turning it down low, and grabbed the telephone, punching in the general manager's extension. No answer. She dialed Pearl, the store operator, asking her to locate Ms. Ellis as soon as possible.

Next, Ashleigh called the store's security director to bring him up to date. When her other line blinked, it was Ms. Ellis, who had received a similar call from the downtown store. "We'll send the hourly associates home at twelve," she informed Ashleigh, "but I'd like to play it by ear for our management staff. Before we abandon this building, I want to secure as much as possible. Furs and fine jewelry will be locked into their vaults right away."

The clock ticked sluggishly following the dismissal of the nonexecutive staff. Management members kept abreast of the latest developments by checking the TV coverage in the associates' cafeteria or by keeping their ears glued to radios, which were housed in most of the offices.

At one fifteen, local news stations reported another fire set ablaze at the corner of Third and Vermont. Ashleigh visualized the looters, now less than half a mile away, heading in the direction of the flagship store.

Ms. Ellis's voice crackled over the loudspeaker. "We've done everything we can. The police have not responded, nor have we been able to engage our private security firm. Everyone is to vacate the building immediately. I repeat, vacate the building now."

Knowing that many of the back offices were out of earshot of the loudspeaker, Ashleigh swept through each floor to make sure no one was left behind. On the fourth floor, she heard a loud crash. She stood still, not sure exactly where the sound had come from. "Is anyone here?" she called out. She heard a moan, then a familiar voice speaking in an unfamiliar tremor.

"Back here." It was Dorothea Montgomery, the lingerie buyer.

Not wasting an instant, Ashleigh took off across the sales floor to the buyer's office, tucked in the far back corner. Hurrying through the aisles, she heard the loudspeaker blare, echoing off the walls of the sales floor. "Vacate the building immediately. The store will be locked down in ten minutes. I repeat, vacate the store immediately. Looters have been spotted and are headed our way."

Pushing her way through the stock room, Ashleigh spotted Dorothea and the source of the crash. The three-drawer steel file cabinet had fallen over, and Dorothea's foot appeared to be trapped beneath it. Ashleigh's heartbeat accelerated as she ran to the older woman.

Tears streamed down Dorothea's wrinkled face. "I can't get my foot out." Ashleigh knelt down beside her and squeezed her thin hand. "Hang in there," she said, attempting to convey confidence. "Just remain as still as possible while I get this off your foot."

Dorothea's leg was skinny—pencil thin—and it appeared that the slightest pressure would snap it in two. Dropping Dorothea's hand, Ashleigh stared at the file cabinet, trying to decide how she could lift it from the woman's foot without doing more damage. She searched the desk for something to wedge in beside the woman's ankle. Finding a thick black binder, she began to stuff it beneath the cabinet, when Dorothea let out another whimper.

"I'm so sorry," Ashleigh said, knowing this had to be traumatic for the older woman. If she didn't take care of this immediately, they could be locked in the store. She quickly determined that she would not be able to move the cabinet without risking Dorothea's frail ankle. Scrambling to her feet, she picked up the phone and dialed the operator. She let it ring three times before she disconnected. Pushing panic to the back of her mind, she dialed the security desk.

"Security. Clear this store ASAP," the head of security's voice barked, loud and impatiently.

"Tom, this is Ashleigh Taylor. I need help."

"Where in the hell are you?" He didn't pause for a single beat. "We have no time to spare. I just sent Sam in search of you. Fires are breaking out all along the Royale corridor. We can't delay lockdown."

"Dorothea Montgomery is trapped under a file cabinet. I need two men to lift the cabinet to keep from breaking Dorothea's ankle," she said, her words overlapping Tom's. The line fell silent. "Are you and Sam the only ones now in the store?" No answer. "Tom! Tom!" Ashleigh yelled into the phone.

"Ashleigh," Dorothea said. "You must go."

"Are you out of your mind?" The words flew out of her mouth before she knew it. Her gaze shot around the stockroom in search of something she could use for leverage. Catching sight of a dismantled rolling rack near the door that led to the sales floor, she scurried toward it, eying one of the loose metal poles. "Sorry to have yelled at you, Dorothea," she called back over her shoulder. "We're going to get this off your foot very soon."

As she ran for the pole, Ashleigh heard the blare of the intercom. "Sam to fourth-floor lingerie ASAP." There was a crackle of static; then, only silence. Ashleigh grabbed the pole and hurried back to Dorothea. The only sound was Dorothea's soft whimpers, which she was doing her best to conceal.

Heavy footfalls echoed through the stockroom and open office.

"Miss McDowell?" Tom's voice was loud and clear. When he finally appeared in the doorway, he stood stock-still, appraising the situation. Sam followed close behind him.

Ashleigh felt a flood of relief wash over her. With the two security men here, she and Dorothea no longer needed to fear being locked in the store overnight. "I tried to get the pressure off her foot," she explained, pointing to the binder propped beside Dorothea's foot.

"Lift from the top," Tom said, motioning with his head toward the horizontal cabinet, "while I lift the bottom." Ashleigh knelt down beside Dorothea, making sure the cabinet cleared her ankle. The two men locked eyes, and Tom said, "On the count of three. One. Two. Three." Both men lifted the cabinet.

Once her foot was free, Dorothea let out an earsplitting scream. Ashleigh grabbed a nearby cotton robe and gently wrapped it around Dorothea's foot. The lingerie buyer winced but did not make another sound. Ashleigh noted that, as usual, Dorothea had been wearing three-inch heels. She slipped the shoe off her injured foot and asked, "Are there any slippers in here?" Dorothea nodded and pointed to one of the shelves across from them.

"For the love of God!" Tom shouted. "She doesn't need slippers. We got to get a move on!" But pushing herself to a sitting position, Dorothea slipped off her other shoe and reached for the slippers Ashleigh handed her. The two security men made a cradle between them and lifted Dorothea into their arms.

"I'll drive you to the hospital," Ashleigh said.

"Think you better let me take care of that," Tom said. "Best you head out of town."

Ashleigh checked to see how Dorothea felt about that.

"I'll be fine," Dorothea said. "It's been a long time since I've had so many people making a fuss over me." She winced, then caught a breath and went on. "You get on home before Mr. Charles hears about the danger in this area."

Ashleigh didn't argue.

"My shoes, please?" Dorothea cried out, trying to look back over her shoulder.

"Holy mother of God," Tom roared. "Let's get the hell out of here before we get trampled or, even worse, become crispy critters."

With an amused grin in spite of herself, Ashleigh picked up the shoes and followed a few steps behind.

Ashleigh's pulse didn't return to normal until she was behind the wheel of the rented Buick and several blocks away from the store. She wished there was a phone in the car so she could call Elizabeth to let her know she was safe. *Calm down,* she scolded herself. *Charles probably has no idea the riots have spread to the Royale corridor.* She was thankful there weren't any reporters hanging around. *But who's reporting the fires and the routes of the looters?* Again she prayed, hoping she'd arrive at home before Charles realized the danger threatening her and his beloved cathedral of merchandising.

With no way of keeping the events of the day from Charles, and propelled by the fear he might be caught off guard by the heavy media coverage, Ashleigh went into the living room and sat down on the floor beside his armchair, as she'd done as a child.

She managed to give him the chronology of events in a steady, unemotional tone. She did not mention her greatest fears, only the facts. No doubt the rioters would ravage the store. But would the vengeance stop there, or would it lead to the store's total destruction? She told him only what she knew. She had no confirmation of whether Bentleys Royale had actually been hit—only that rioters were reportedly headed in that direction.

Once again—as when Cassie had been taken from them—she was amazed by the old man's ability to calmly take in stride situations beyond his control.

"Whatever will be, will be," he said. "I've done my grieving. Bentleys Royale began as a wonderful dream. I'm thankful for my good fortune in seeing that vision grow into a reality. But ever since I allowed Bentley's and Bentleys Royale to fall into the hands of a big corporation, I've been able to do little beyond watching it slip away, inch by inch."

Ashleigh looked up at her father figure, wanting to tell him he wasn't the one responsible for letting his empire fall to Consolidated, but he'd always taken blame, never mentioning the part his own daughter and son-in-law had played. Instead she said, her tone confident, "You did everything you could. If you hadn't been on the board, Bentleys Royale would not have remained a separate entity."

Charles held up his hand, not allowing her to go on. "Darling girl," he said, "that time has passed. It's time for you and me to let go." Then, almost to himself, he said, "Maybe in the long run, a quick death is better than the slow erosion of everything for which it stood."

She hadn't missed the subtle undertone. Without dignity, a life prolonged held no value. He desired no less for his historic monument than for himself. Ashleigh remembered only too well when Charles had showed her his living will, prohibiting the use of any type of life support. He restated his wishes now, in no uncertain terms. "I'm not being morbid, but when my time comes, I want you to make sure I'm allowed the same—a merciful death. On the inevitable day when I'm no longer able to enjoy a life of quality, I want the end to come as quickly as possible."

Later that evening, Charles asked Ashleigh to turn on the TV to see if there was any further coverage of the Royale corridor. As scene after scene of looters and protestors and massive destruction throughout the city flashed across the screen, Charles said, "It's hard to imagine how such vast numbers of people can take leave of their senses. Where are their moral values? Where is their humanity?" His eyes were partially closed, and he shook his head in sadness.

With the riots monopolizing every channel, Charles finally said, "I've had my fill; I think I'll turn in." He picked up the latest copy of *Business News*, kissed Ashleigh softly on the cheek, and headed for the staircase. She was glad that he didn't see the later news clips, clearly showing his magnificent store as one of the many victims of retaliation by enraged minorities.

At three o'clock the following morning, Ashleigh was wide awake. Though she'd switched off the TV hours before, the scenes captured onscreen ran nonstop in her head. Grotesque mental photographs of rampaging rioters flashed by, one after another.

Flinging the covers back, she slipped into her quilted robe and pushed her feet into furry slippers. Seconds later, perched on the edge of the bed, she dialed the Trump Tower in New York and asked for Conrad's room. Thrown off balance slightly that he picked up on the first ring, she asked, "Did I wake you?"

"Who can sleep? I wanted to call but was afraid I'd wake the entire household."

She let the silence hang in the air for an instant, then said, "Conrad, I'm sorry. But . . . I went to the store today. I know you asked me not—"

"When will you stop taking chances?" he interrupted. Then before giving her a chance to respond, he said, "Damn it, Ashleigh, I don't want to lose you, and Callie needs—"

"You're not about to," she broke in. Although she didn't regret going into the store, she did regret worrying him.

"Please stay clear of L.A., including the Royale corridor, until it's safe." Conrad's words echoed in her head. She would do almost anything for him, but she could not make a promise she wasn't sure she could keep. Though she was no longer an official member of the management team, the essence of Bentleys Royale would always be a part of her, and there remained a strong bond between her and the loyal long-term associates—a bond that did not exist with the new management. The rioting couldn't last forever. Right or wrong, Ashleigh felt that when management deemed it safe for the associates to come in, it would indeed be safe for her as well. But until she could assure her husband that it was safe, she must avoid causing him any more stress. Unintentionally, she'd put him through enough.

"I will," she finally said with total candor. "I have no intention of endangering our future. I love both you and Callie far too much to take any chances." It was the truth. Then before he could say more on the subject, she informed him, "Pocino called last night. He wants to get the 'skinny' on the 'happenings' at Bentleys Royale firsthand," she said, parroting Pocino's lingo. "He asked me to 'stay put' until I heard from him."

"Great," Conrad broke in. "Then promise me you won't go to L.A. until he says it's safe to do so."

Relieved, she promised with a clear conscience.

CHAPTER

39

Viviana patted concealer gently under each eye, looked at herself appraisingly in the mirror, and frowned. Philip Sloane, her soon to be ex-husband, had mentioned once that when she didn't smile, she appeared to be mad at the world. In the effort to be as sexy and appealing as possible, she'd smiled till her face seemed frozen in place. But all that damned smiling was forming a deep set of commas at the corner of each side of her mouth. The laser surgery had done little to improve those bothersome commas. Nor had it done the trick with those thin upward creases on her upper lip that always seemed to attract unwanted smears of lipstick.

Fortunately, she'd become a master with makeup, concealing nearly all of the age-telling flaws. Pulling the mirror out from the wall alongside her dressing table, Viviana leaned closer and went to work with more concealer, followed by a heavy layer of pancake makeup and just the right touch of blush. Then she flipped the mirror from the magnified view to normal. *Much better.* Relieved, she took out the can of hairspray and sprayed a light mist, smoothing each errant strand in place. For the final touch, she dabbed a smidgen of Joy—her favorite perfume, and the most expensive available—behind each ear, onto her wrists, and behind her knees. The final gesture brought a smile to her face. From all she'd been told, Mitchell Wainwright was not yet in any shape to take advantage of any feelings she might manage to stir within him.

It was a beautiful day, and she had been looking forward to making an appearance in his hospital room. She had planned for this day since Glenn first told her about the accident, weeks ago. Her confidence wavered only when certain memories flooded her mind—memories of how Mitchell had not given her a second look once Ashleigh McDowell had set her sights on him. *Well, Ashleigh is out of the picture. Besides, she hadn't managed to hold on to him. She wouldn't know the first thing about taking care of a man like Mitchell Wainwright.*

But Ashleigh sure was lucky. Mitchell had dumped her—at least, Viviana presumed he'd been the one to do the dumping—yet Ashleigh had landed on her feet without skipping a beat. Now she was the wife of the gorgeous Conrad Taylor—a good catch, though he would never wield the power of Viviana's ex. The old cliché *The mightier they are, the harder they fall* flitted across her mind. *Boy, did I learn that the hard way.*

Biting down on her lower lip and slipping into her Manolo Blahnik pumps, she tried imagining her visit with Mitchell. She checked her appearance in the full-length mirror. *Not bad,* she decided, turning to observe her legs from every angle. The four-inch heels definitely made her ankles look slimmer.

The limo driver arrived right on time, his black Lincoln limo clean and recently polished. After a polite greeting, he asked, "Where to, Ms. De Mornay?"

"Greenwich Hospital." She pulled out the sheet from her notepad. "The address is—"

"I know where it is, Ms. De Mornay," he cut in. "You just sit back and enjoy the ride. I know how busy you've been. We'll be there in under an hour, unless we run into unexpected traffic."

"Thanks . . . Lenny?" She thought that was his name.

She did as he suggested and, kicking off her shoes, turned her thoughts back to Mitchell. She would let him know that the minute she'd heard of his tragedy, she had wanted to drop everything and come to see if there was anything she could do for him. *If only he'd been allowed visitors before my Asian buying trip.* She didn't want to talk about the loss of his son or his haughty wife, and knowing Mitchell, he wouldn't want to talk about that either. She'd tell him she'd come as soon as she could, while at the same time letting him know how successful she was now and how hard it was for her to break away.

She could picture the entire scene. He'd tell her how wonderful she looked, and she'd tell him that the suit she wore was one of her own designs. She'd actually adapted it from one of Erica's sketches, but through her own talents as a top designer, she'd added the kind of excitement that had turned it into a true fashion statement—the twenty-four-carat gold buttons on the vivid red background of lightweight gabardine had given it the look she adored. Simple and elegant, that was her motto.

Exiting the highway at Greenwich, the limo passed several traffic circles and turned onto Perryridge Road. The hospital was to their right.

"I'm not sure how long I'll be," Viviana said when her door opened and a hand reached in to help her out of the limo.

"Take your time, Ms. De Mornay," the limo driver said, his eyes wandering to a group of attractive nurses who were cutting across the well-manicured lawn.

From the moment Viviana entered the sunlit three-story atrium, she realized she was in a unique hospital atmosphere—and why should someone as important as Mitchell suffer anything less? Every feature of the hospital was welcoming. She learned he even had a private room with large windows overlooking grassy lawns and trees. If ever she had to be hospitalized, this was her kind of place. *Nothing but the best.* That was her other motto.

Mitchell Wainwright raised the head of his narrow bed and turned up the volume on the TV. Scenes from the L.A. riots seemed surreal, particularly those last shots of looters clambering into Bentleys Royale through the broken display windows. If it were possible, he would have liked to hit the replay button for a second view—or to rewind to where the windows were being broken by looters.

"Riots have spread like wildfire across our nation," the newscaster exclaimed. "Disgruntled minorities . . ."

Wainwright flipped off the TV. Accounts of the riots, which had broken out from coast to coast in the aftermath of the shocking verdict in the Rodney King trial, were being continuously reported. For a few timeless moments, he gazed out the floor-to-ceiling window to the green belt beyond, while visions of the ransacking of Bentleys Royale cascaded though his head. Inadvertently, his thoughts turned to Ashleigh, the only woman he'd ever come close to loving. When he had lost her, it hadn't been to another man—that he might have been able to deal with—but to that goddamned store. It wasn't just bricks and mortar to her. Bentleys Royale was an icon representing quality, integrity—all that she truly valued. *A goddamned store.*

He wondered how Conrad Taylor felt about playing second fiddle to a specialty department store. Well, that was Conrad's problem, and perhaps he'd solved it by whisking Ashleigh off to Dallas, away from her precious Bentleys Royale. At some level, Wainwright wished that she'd actually been there this week. Witnessing the destruction of her beloved store would surely crack her calm, cool demeanor at last.

He continued to stare out the window, registering next to nothing, until he saw a black limo pull up. The hospital was known for attracting all types of high-profile celebrities, not that he much cared, but still, he kept his eye focused on the limo as the door opened. The first thing he saw was a glint of auburn hair, then the slim body of a fashionably dressed woman in very high heels. He recognized her immediately. *Now, what is she after?* He knew Viviana; she had to want something.

Most of the bandages on his face had been removed, but he was unshaven and had no idea what he looked like. He hadn't asked for a mirror because he really didn't give a damn. And he sure as hell wasn't expecting any visitors. To prevent future visits from the Toddmans, he told them he'd call once he was released. *That better be pretty soon.* Had it not been for the blasted infection, he'd be out of here. He craved a smoke, but it was not allowed in the hospital. He was trapped. With his leg still high above his head, he even had to pee in a goddamned urinal, not to mention use a bedpan.

He wanted to get the hell out of here and go home—but not to the Greenwich house. He didn't think he could bear to see little Mitch's empty room. He would never go back there. He'd have Stella, his secretary, go to the house to remove the contents of his home office and his personal items. Then he'd put it on the market and donate the entire remaining contents to one of Paige's organizations—Save the Children or whatever. He closed his eyes; images of his son flashed before him. *No, not the entire contents.* Mitch's favorite things must be boxed and placed into storage. Tomorrow he'd make a list of the things that must be kept.

His mind flashed back to Viviana, and he realized her visit might be just what he needed. He ran his fingers through his hair and adjusted his position in the bed.

After waiting for what seemed a very long time, finally he heard the click of stiletto heels tapping down the corridor. They stopped right outside his door. No one appeared, which brought a smile to his parched lips. He could picture the scene outside his door. Viviana would be pulling out her ubiquitous Chanel compact and making imperceptible repairs to her flawless appearance.

When she finally swept into the room, he saw that she was just as breathtaking as he remembered her. She hadn't seemed to age a day in the last four years. He was sure she'd had a great deal of cosmetic surgery, but what did it matter? As far as he was concerned, it was money well spent.

Viviana headed straight to Mitchell's bedside, forgetting all her well-rehearsed lines.

"Viviana." He gave her a crooked smile. His face was badly bruised, and a small bandage covered a portion of his bottom lip.

"I came as soon I could," she began. "I was devastated when I heard of your tragedy." *Oh my God.* That wasn't at all how she'd meant to begin. Overly dramatic, something strong men abhorred.

He held up his hand. "Rather not talk about the accident."

Despite his battered face and his plastered leg, Mitchell Wainwright was still a handsome man. The rakish look of his uncombed hair was not at all unattractive. But there seemed to be no life in his hazel eyes. She couldn't think of a word to say.

To break the tension, he joked, "I'd like to stand and greet you, but—"

Relieved, Viviana smiled. "Well, I can see that you're not quite up to par."

"But you, my dear, look absolutely smashing, as always."

After the first awkward minutes, they fell into comfortable conversation. "Have you been watching the news clips of the L.A. rioters?" he asked.

"Hmm, yes. As much as I was shocked by the four police officers being found innocent," she responded, "this whole rioting scenario is even more unbelievable. Even my neighbors on Fifth Avenue are holding their breath."

"I assume you know about Bentleys Royale." As he told her all he knew, Viviana's stomach did a flip-flop, and she felt the rhythm of her heartbeat soar. "Bentleys Royale! I can't believe it."

Mitchell decided to change the subject. "Well, my dear," he said, sounding just like Rhett Butler, "I'm not sure what brings you here—"

"Well, maybe I shouldn't have come," she said, straightening her back. His tone suggested she had ulterior motives. The fact that she did—well, that didn't make it any less insulting.

He grinned. "Don't get your knickers in a twist. It's good to see you." He nodded toward the cushioned chair beside the window. "Pull up a chair. There's a favor I'd like to ask of you."

She dragged the chair to his bedside and gracefully slid into it. Crossing her legs, she leaned forward. "Anything," she said. "Just tell me what you need."

"Anything?" he said in a mocking tone. But before she had a time to comment, he said, "I want to get out of this hospital, but I don't want to go back to the house in Greenwich."

Viviana took in a quick breath. *My extra bedroom? No, much too soon.* He needed time to grieve, if not for his wife, for his little son. Making that kind of gesture too soon would not be smart. *Besides, I have no intention of becoming anyone's nursemaid.*

"What I need is a condo in the city. As far from this damn hospital as possible."

She stared at the contraption holding his leg high in the air. "When can you be released?"

"I've been told that within the week I'll be able to get out of bed." He paused. "But I'm counting on the next few days. No point in staying here any longer than I have to. I'll need crutches, and one of these setups." He gestured to the pulley that lifted his leg above his heart. Noting her puzzled expression, he continued, "I have a compound fracture of the right tibia and several fractures of the fibula. They put a rod in my tibia and two screws." He chuckled ruefully. "Now, when I go through airport security, I'll set off bells. This contraption," he said, "is to keep the swelling down."

She hesitated before asking, "Will you be able to walk again?" *He just has to!*

"I'll walk with a cane, at least for a while. But for now, the pain is a real son of a bitch. I've been told it's something like childbirth." Pausing to look at Viviana, he said, "Well, I guess neither of us can really relate to that. But as long as they keep the Lortabs coming, it's tolerable."

Viviana smiled conspiratorially and a little sadly, even as her heart jumped into her throat. She said nothing. She *did* know about the pain of childbirth, but that was her secret.

CHAPTER

41

Ross Pocino arrived just before nine, pulling up in his Mustang beside a silver Buick parked in front of the Stuart residence's four-car garage.

His pissy mood hadn't improved one iota since the riots began. The craziness of the past two days had thrown everything out of kilter. And ever since Conrad's call—and their latest discussion about the lack of progress in tracking the elusive hospital abductor—Ross's thoughts had remained fixated on his failure to get a beat on the scumbag who had snatched the Taylors' day-old twin. All his leads had turned out to be dead ends, and he hadn't dug up anything worthwhile in months.

What grated on his nerves even more was Ashleigh's apparent understanding, making it ten times tougher to handle. If she'd just blow up and tell him to get off his dead ass and find her kid, he could turn his feelings of impotence into indignation. But that wasn't her style. Like a load of bricks, the missing whereabouts of the twin weighed on his mind, never far from the surface. He wasn't sure of his next step, but there sure as hell would be one. This kid could not suffer the same fate as his own son. As the matter involved an infant, that was unlikely. But over his dead body would this be relegated to a cold-case folder. No matter how long it took, he'd bring the kidnapper down. An identical twin would eventually be found. At least that's what he told himself, and that's what drove him to heave his sorry ass out of bed each morning.

He sucked in his gut, vowing to cut down on his beer intake, and hauled himself from behind the steering wheel of his Mustang. Today his mission was to make sure Ashleigh got to and from Bentleys Royale's headquarters store without incident.

He made it only halfway to the back door before Ashleigh dashed out to meet him. "Ciao," he greeted her. "Got here as soon as I could."

"Thanks, Ross. I really appreciate it," she said, extending her hand to him with a set of car keys. "Let's take my rental."

"Sure," he said, taking the keys and jogging around to open the passenger door. "Can't figure out why it's so darn important for you to be in the store today. From all reports, it's pretty much a disaster. The looters have taken every piece of merchandise and broken every single display case, at least on the first floor. They even took off with the mannequins."

As Ashleigh slid inside, Ross chuckled. "Sorry, I should have said first *level*," he said with a fair dose of mockery. The Bentleys Royale lingo amused him—*level, lift, patron, associate* . . . He climbed in the driver's side and quickly backed the car into the street, then turned onto The Toledo.

"To be honest, I want to be there for the associates." Not wanting to get into any kind of a debate, Ashleigh continued without pause, "I've made a few calls this morning. Elaine Ellis, in her own inimitable style, reported that reinforcements had been flown down from P. G. Marshal's, the San Francisco headquarters, and that the store is secure." She paused, then said, "Please assure Conrad that there is no danger."

"You wouldn't be en route if the vicinity wasn't secure. But I don't want you even stepping a toe outside the store. The cafeteria and tearoom won't be in operation, so if you want something to eat, I'll either take you over to Tiny Naylor's or pick something up for you. Understood?"

"Of course," Ashleigh said, her exasperation clear. "I appreciate you escorting me, Ross, but even if it weren't at Conrad's request, I would not like to venture into the Royale corridor on my own right now." Then in a softer tone, she asked, "Now can you bring me up to speed before we get to the store? All I know is what's been reported on TV and radio. Ellis didn't tell me much, only that she wanted me to get to the store ASAP."

Pocino shook his head. "What's the point? I can't imagine you'll be doing many outplacements with all the chaos." When Ashleigh didn't respond, he went on. "Okay, I'll give it to you the same way it was reported to me. The looters descended on Bentleys Royale at about three thirty." He paused, turning onto Studebaker, and then made eye contact with his passenger. "Just moments after you hightailed it out of there, right?"

"I guess so. I understand there were still looters in the store yesterday around seven in the morning?"

"Right. The police were nowhere to be found. You may hear about the doors being machine-gunned down, but that rumor has no legs. The rioters broke every display window and rammed either a truck or a van into those etched glass doors of the motor court. I also understand they wiped out the phone lines and the CRTs . . . ."

As Pocino told her everything he knew, Ashleigh wondered about the store's condition. She knew having the CRTs down would cause havoc with the merchants who had learned to rely on those computerized reports, but she was more worried about whether the looters had damaged the priceless murals, the Lalique chandeliers, the uniquely designed elevators . . .

She was surprised when Pocino slammed on the brakes, bringing the car to an abrupt stop in the upper parking structure. Traffic had been light, and they'd made the trip in less than forty minutes.

"No point in going down to the employees' lot," he said. "The store isn't likely to open anytime soon." He switched off the engine and climbed out of the Mustang. As he made his way around the car, Ashleigh sat riveted in her seat, hardly believing her eyes. She stared at the display windows; just two days ago, they were windows to the world of fashion. Now they were covered with plywood. Not just plain plywood, though. They were covered in colorful, childlike artwork, with large letters on each panel. The letters spelled out OUT OF SOMETHING BAD, LET'S MAKE SOMETHING GOOD. Ashleigh's usual optimism did not kick in, even as the significance of the words hit her. *What good could possibly come of this?*

Ross flung open her door. He followed her gaze toward the wood panels. "I'll be damned," he said, chuckling. "You suppose they made a midnight requisition in one of the nearby elementary schools?"

"Given the short time span, my guess would be that Susan Thomas pulled her sales promotion staff together and recruited a few kids to create some artwork." Finally, she smiled. "I like it." *Amazing what motivated people can come up with in such a small window of time.*

The minute they entered the lower level, Ashleigh was greeted with a buzz of activity. And as she made her way to the elevators, she saw groups of sales associates as well as sales support staff smiling and laughing as they worked on restoring order.

Ross said, "If you don't mind, I'll trot on over to security and see what I can find out."

Instead of going in search of the general manager, Ashleigh headed straight to the first level, where the greatest damage had been reported. The elevator doors opened and she stepped out, then stopped in her tracks. Every display case in the cosmetic aisle was shattered, the glass swept into piles along the Genevieve marble walls. To her right, in the salon shoe area, she saw hundreds of shoeboxes piled as high as she was tall. She also saw the devastation to the cases in the accessories area. But as she peered up at the murals, she saw that they had not been defaced, and the elevator doors were totally unharmed.

She turned and headed through sportswear and then beyond, to the crystal area. There, too, every case was shattered and void of merchandise, but mercifully the Lalique chandeliers were intact. Making her way to the men's department, Ashleigh saw that nothing of the store's structure seemed to have incurred any damage. Every one of the expensive hand-tailored Oxxford suits was gone; only the sculptured hangers remained. The media had been on target in labeling Bentleys Royale's rioters as "out on a shopping spree."

As Ashleigh looked around, she knew Pocino was right. She would be doing no outplacement for a while. So instead of going in search of Elaine Ellis, she wandered around the store, talking with the hourly associates. Miraculously, the employees' morale, which had hit bottom following the takeover a few years back, seemed to have climbed to new heights. Everyone was pulling together to restore Bentleys Royale to its former glory.

Out of something bad, something very good was indeed emerging.

CHAPTER

42

On Thursday, May seventh, at eight in the morning, Bentleys Royale's headquarters store reopened to the public.

From beneath the vibrant *porte cochère,* Ashleigh's eyes flicked from the plywood window fronts, still displaying children's artwork, to the motor court with its plush red carpet stretching from the curved drive to the double-door entrance. A steady stream of well-dressed patrons received a vibrant red rose from Burt, the elegantly tuxedoed maître d', who could usually be found charming the patrons as he seated them in the elegant tearoom.

The scene took on a semblance of the surreal for Ashleigh. Patrons were served coffee from elaborate silver urns set out on tables covered in Belgium lace, while contrasting pictures of the ravaging of Bentleys Royale flashed inside her head. But the planks of plywood still covering the shattered windows were the only visible remnants of the destruction.

She blinked, attempting to replace last week's nightmare with the reality of today and all that had been achieved. Out of something bad, something exceptionally good had happened. The sales promotion staff, along with hundreds of loyal associates, had once again pulled together. Revived by a common goal, they had set aside the indignities suffered in the takeover and allowed that unique Bentleys Royale team spirit to resurface. In round-the-clock shifts, they had accomplished the seemingly impossible. In one week's time, they had transformed the ravaged store from destructive chaos to something grand. While far from attaining the store's former glory, the transformation was nonetheless breathtaking and, in her opinion, miraculous.

During that week, Ashleigh had felt as if she was on an emotional see-saw. She'd visited and revisited every conceivable emotion, from shock, disbelief, fear, absolute horror, anger, and sadness to an overwhelming sense of relief and even trickles of hope. She'd experienced these emotions in a series of ups and downs, one tumbling haphazardly after another, in no clear or straightforward lines.

At the sound of her name now, she turned and saw her secretary. "Ms. Ellis just called," Betty said. "She'd like to see you as soon as possible."

"Tell her I'll be right there," Ashleigh replied. She made her way through the dwindling crowd. Waiting for the unmercifully slow elevator, she focused her thoughts on more positive aspects of the devastation. There was much to be thankful for.

As she continued to wait, she overheard snatches of conversation, mainly tales of what took place during the riots. She heard a great deal more fiction than actual fact. Had she been less emotionally involved, in fact, the entire experience could have proven a unique up-close study of human nature at its worst—and maybe its best. As unbelievable as it was to her—the concept of untold numbers of individuals running amuck throughout Los Angeles and across the nation—the aftermath seemed just as unreal.

The very day after the looting of Bentleys Royale, stolen merchandise began reappearing. Some was returned by repentant looters, even more by looters accompanied by grieving family members, and still more uprooted by police in their door-to-door searches throughout the neighborhood. Sadly, the majority of Bentleys Royale's looters had been the store's neighbors.

When the elevator doors finally slid open, she stepped inside and pushed the button for the fifth level.

She'd taken just a few steps out of the elevator when she heard the general manager's voice, loud and laced with profanities. Quickening her stride, Ashleigh saw that the double doors to the corridor, which led into Ms. Ellis's office suite, stood wide open, as did the inner office door itself. Slipping through the door, Ashleigh closed it firmly behind her, making no attempt to muffle the sound. She took a deep breath. It didn't help much; beneath the surface, she seethed.

Elaine Ellis aborted her tirade midsentence at the sound of the double doors banging shut. She wheeled around to face Ashleigh.

Chris Ferrari, the director of operations, and Susan Thomas, the sales promotion director, sat wordlessly in armchairs in front of the general manager's desk. They acknowledged Ashleigh's arrival with a nod.

Silence permeated the room.

Resentment burned inside Ashleigh. She had carefully held it in check since the takeover and this woman's appointment as general manager of the grand monument. To vent it now would be childish, as well as point-less. She was the first to break the silence. "Betty said you wanted to see me."

Erica pounded up the stairs. Flinging the door open, she saw Mike hunched over the computer. Marnie was nowhere in sight. She glanced at her wristwatch and saw that it was nearly nine. She wasn't going to think about not being home to tuck Marnie into bed. She was off tomorrow, and she would spend the day with her precious child. She was far too excited to let anything get her down tonight.

Mike barely looked up and motioned with his head toward the kitchen. "Dinner's in the oven."

"Please, Mike. Give me a few minutes of your time, then I'll be quiet as a mouse and leave you to your work."

Mike swiveled his chair toward her. "Just a few," he said, sighing. "This is my big opportunity. I can't afford to blow it."

"I know. And I don't want to get in your way. But I have really great news."

"I'm all ears." He gave her a broad smile, but still she noticed his bloodshot eyes.

The joy of her good news was diverted momentarily by her concern. "You've got to get some sleep, Mike."

"Okay, cupcake. Spit it out."

"Cupcake?" she said with a smile. "Well, for an Italian, that doesn't seem as out of tune as 'my lady.' Hmm, 'cupcake,' " she repeated. "I sort of like that."

They both laughed. It was always a relief and a pleasure to find something to laugh about, in spite of the strain Mario's condition cast over them.

"Well?"

"The catalog came out today. And look at the selections." She proudly handed him the sophisticated, glossy, four-color booklet and watched the expression on his face as he began turning the pages.

"Wow!" he exclaimed. "These look great." Then a frown settled over his brow. "Hey, six of these designs are yours, but I don't see any credit given to you. They all have the De Mornay's insignia." He threw out his hands, palms up, and asked, "What gives?"

"I know," Erica said, just a little deflated. "It would be better if I had some name recognition. But the important thing is, my designs were the ones Viviana and Glenn chose. There are even more of mine mixed in with all the top designers than there are of hers!"

"Obviously, it's because you are more talented than your boss. You can't let her steal your thunder."

"You don't understand," Erica began, but she didn't really understand either. Still, she felt that she must defend her boss. *Without Viviana, where would I be?* "I've learned so much from Viviana these last two years. Without her, my designs would be no more than sketches on paper. Even if I had the time to make the patterns and sew them into actual garments, there's no way I could afford the material. Without her selection of materials, these designs would be nothing."

"But Erica, if your name is nowhere on the garment, how will you ever be able to develop your own portfolio, or whatever it's called in the fashion industry? Maybe it's time you look into other opportunities, where your talents will be recognized and appreciated."

"We've gone over all this before, Mike. It's true, the job I have is far from ideal. But at least I am surrounded by the best fashions in the market, and Viviana is coming into her own as a top designer. I'm still learning, and De Mornay's is putting me in touch with the kind of people who enjoy and can afford the kind of clothes I want to design. I don't want to work my way up in the back rooms with some mediocre designer. I'd be no more than their errand girls, with no time to work on my own designs."

"In the meantime, you're putting all your energy and talents into creating remarkable fashion statements that end up with De Mornay's on the label."

Marnie's cry from the bedroom saved Erica from the need to reply.

That night, when Ashleigh hit the garage door opener, she saw that Charles's Rolls was back in the garage. There was so much she had to tell him, but first she wanted to hold Callie and tuck her in bed—if she wasn't too late.

The back door opened before she reached it, and Elizabeth, a crisp, white apron covering her dress, said, "Your grandfather delayed tea time for you. He's in the living room."

"Thank you." Her heart sunk. Without asking, she knew that Callie must already be in bed. Otherwise, when Elizabeth headed her way, she would've had Callie in tow. Ashleigh hurried inside, set her handbag and the plastic Super Crown bag full of books on the kitchen counter, and headed straight through to the living room.

Charles looked up from the *Los Angeles Times* as Ashleigh walked into the room, happy to see her safely home. But his elation was short-lived. By the slump of her slim shoulders, she looked as though she bore the weight of the past, present, and future. "A nice hot cup of tea should help you set things in perspective," he said.

Ashleigh sighed. "Am I so transparent?"

After Elizabeth had set the tray on the coffee table and poured the tea, retreating as silently as she'd come, he said, "Tell me about your day."

"Pretty grim," she said. "And I want to tell you all about it, but first I want to run upstairs and see Callie."

Charles was fairly certain that Callie was sound asleep, but he understood her mother's need to look in on her. The hours she had been putting in at Bentleys Royale were taking a toll on her. She left before Callie was up in the morning and often came home after her daughter was in bed. "If only I could be in two places at once," she had told him the night before, and knowing her as only he did, he realized she was trying to master that art.

When she returned from upstairs, her big, brown eyes literally glowed with love for her perfect little girl. Charles couldn't help but think about that missing baby now, as he always did when he watched Callie. It troubled him that Callie's twin had never been found. He wondered if Ashleigh could actually detach from those thoughts. She seemed happy, always concentrating on what was good and pushing the negative thoughts away. She was so like her grandmother, the only woman he'd ever loved.

"You would have been so proud today," Ashleigh said. "The reopening was miraculous, and it warmed my heart to see the throng of patrons. No matter what, people truly love and care about the future of Bentleys Royale." She beamed. "It's not just us. Your legacy to Los Angeles has become so much more than a store . . ."

She wasn't saying anything that hadn't been said time after time, particularly since the takeover. But beneath her pride, he saw that her glimmers of hope had turned to despair.

"Ashleigh," he broke in. She looked up, tears brimming in her eyes. "What's wrong? What is it you're not telling me?"

She dabbed the corners of her eyes with a tissue, then looked at him for a long moment before speaking. "I feel so helpless." He reached for her, but she held up her hands. "Please, let me finish. I've listened to what you've said about letting go, but it's no more possible for me than it is for you. I've tried to keep that stiff upper lip you've preached to me since I was a little girl. But how can I when, bit by bit, everything Bentleys Royale stands for is being stripped away?"

Charles wanted to talk reason to her, but forced himself to adopt an uncritical mode. All she wanted was for him to listen.

"Today I found myself downright resentful about the general manager's lack of insight . . ." She broke off. "I know it's not her fault. I realize she was a superstar at Jordon's. But a specialty store environment and its ideals—they're as alien to her as mass marketing is to me. All she cares about is the bottom line!"

"Darling," he interrupted, "that's the name of the game."

"I accept that," she said, "But Ms. Ellis even put a negative spin on the return of merchandise by rioters and their families." She paused as her more realistic sensibility set in. "I know that the returned merchandise can't be sold, but—"

"Enough," Charles said firmly. "Stop beating your head against those marble walls. The Bentleys Royale bottom line won't benefit one iota from those returns. And as miraculous as it may seem, the rioters' remorse came too late. Ms. Ellis is not running a charitable organization, and no matter how many good causes are helped by donations of the stolen merchandise, in the end, like it or not, it's the bottom line she's judged by." Ashleigh opened her mouth as if to speak, but he left no room for comment. "I don't like letting go any more than you do, but it's time to step back. Even if we had the power to reverse the trend, there's no point. Throwing your heart and soul into aspirations to restore the ideals that epitomized Bentleys Royale when it was a family-owned entity—it makes no sense. That sort of thing has no value in today's world of corporate retailing. You know as well as I do that, without an impressive bottom line, Jordon's will be further inclined to turn a deaf ear to the needs of their specialty store divisions. And with the change in demographics surrounding the Royale headquarters store, it's bound to be a major target for closure."

"If that's their intention," Ashleigh challenged, "why wouldn't Jordon's use the riots as an excuse to close it?" She went on, "The damage is estimated at $10 million, so why would they invest in new display cases, more purchases to replace stolen or damaged merchandise, and all the other expenses involved in today's reopening?"

Charles didn't answer immediately, instead waiting for logic to set in. She was far too bright not to have read the signs. They were as clear as if etched in the store's marble walls. Only her blind loyalty to him prevented Ashleigh from facing the inevitable fall of Bentleys Royale.

Somehow, he must make her understand that his grief was in the past. His comments the other night hadn't been empty platitudes, mouthed merely to make her feel better. Gone were the heydays when Bentleys Royale was frequented by the upper crust of Los Angeles society—patrons such as Marlene Dietrich, John Wayne, May West, Alfred Hitchcock, Greta Garbo, Clark Gable . . .

Taking her cold hands in his, he said, "Forgive me if I state the obvious, darling girl. The reopening not only has financial benefits in regard to insurance, but Jordon's management team is far too astute to close a historic monument without the appearance of an all-out attempt to save it. They are not fools. They already encountered the power of our loyal patrons and of the California Heritage Society when they tried to eliminate the Bentleys Royale signature from the headquarters store. Since the reputation of their P. G. Marshal's division is unalterably entwined with Bentleys Royale, it makes good business sense to phase out the Royale headquarters store gradually. That way, they can take advantage of the love and loyalty of our longtime patrons to sell merchandise and garner a great deal of free press in the process. But in the end, I wouldn't be at all surprised if the entire P. G. Marshal's division was phased out."

Ashleigh gasped, covering her mouth. But Charles knew that, in her heart, she must have come to the same ultimate conclusion. "My ideals have not altered a smidgen, nor should yours," he continued, "but times have changed, and Bentleys Royale must change with them." He held up his hand to ward off her inevitable challenge. "I've given this a great deal of thought," he said, "and there's nothing I'd like better than to see the city, or a local organization with high ideals, take Bentleys Royale out of the retail arena and turn it into a museum or perhaps a library, to be maintained as it was conceived and to be enjoyed by all who love it as we do."

Ashleigh threw up her hands in defeat. "You're right, Charles." Then, with a self-deprecating smile, she said, "Strange how you are the first to embrace today's business dynamics." Her eyes brightened and her erect posture returned. "I like the idea of a museum. Do you think there's any chance?"

He nodded. "But only time will tell," he said. "Without title to the land, Jordon's is not totally in the driver's seat. They can close the business and maintain the building for a while, making it available for motion picture and television filming, but you can be sure they wouldn't dare demolish it or let it fall into disrepair."

Since she was a young girl, Ashleigh had known of Charles's single act of revenge. He'd been able to stay one step ahead of his son-in-law's treachery by donating the land on which the headquarters store rested to California Technological University—a costly albatross for Consolidated and now for Jordon's, which was saddled with paying a percentage of sales to the university. As Consolidated had struggled to hold on to its empire, Charles had momentarily regretted his decision. But with the deterioration of the area along the Royale corridor, he knew he'd been wise to withhold total control from any corporate retailer.

Changing the subject at last, he said, "Now, let's talk about *your* long-range plans." But a cry suddenly emanated from the baby monitor across the room, and Ashleigh shot to her feet. Charles smiled. "Run along. We'll talk tomorrow."

Ashleigh returned his smile. "Tomorrow," she said, and dashed to the staircase.

In the quiet of the living room, it dawned on him that although Ashleigh and Callie had been with him for more than a week, he and Ashleigh had talked in depth only about Bentleys Royale and, of course, Callie. He'd known better than to delve into the topic of Cassie—one that Ashleigh always shied away from. But she'd shared little about either her husband or herself. Charles suspected that, not too far in the future, Michael Nason's would become too small an arena for a man with Conrad's talents, intelligence, and expertise. Now that Mark Toddman had led Consolidated out of bankruptcy, he wouldn't be at all surprised if Conrad joined his mentor and former partner in the rumored plans for expansion. They might recapture the West Coast stores from Jordon's. *That would be a smart move,* he thought. And Toddman might just be the man who was able to pull it off.

Erica's hand trembled. Visine dripped from the corners of her eye. It was no use; she couldn't hold the eyedropper steady. Being up nearly all night had taken its toll: the raging internal conflict, the lack of sleep, the off-and-on crying jags. It had left her eyes red and dry, burning like the scorching blaze of those infamous Southern California fires triggered by the dry, hot air of the Santa Ana winds.

Mario might never come back to me. It was a thought she could not vocalize, not even to Mike. Saying it out loud was like telegraphing her loss of faith to the world. And she had to keep believing.

The dreaded notice had been delivered yesterday. Just short of two years since Mario's accident. The coma it had left him in was a state one hundred times worse than if he had died. At least then, while she would have been heartbroken, she might have been on the mend by now. But Mario was neither dead nor truly alive.

Tiptoeing back into the bedroom, Erica stopped at the side of the crib and watched the gentle rise and fall of her baby's chest. She wanted to pick her up, to hold her close. But she must leave for work in the next ten minutes. If she woke her sleeping angel, Mike would not get the few hours of sleep he so desperately needed right now. Like her, the poor guy had been up most of the night.

Stepping back, Erica fixed her eyes on Marnie as she reached over to the bedside table and picked up her wedding photo. Mario's smiling face brought a new flood of tears to her eyes. Now she must face the cold, hard facts. She had to make a decision, one that might rob Marnie of ever knowing her father, a wonderful, loving man who would have idolized her and loved her with all his heart.

Last night, in a rage, Erica had torn up the notice informing her that Mario's medical insurance would no longer cover his long-term care. The letter expressed sympathy and regret, but stated that the rehabilitation facility had gone far beyond its obligation for Mario's coverage. Now that he'd been officially diagnosed as brain-dead, they could no longer justify the expense of keeping him artificially alive.

The word *brain-dead* rang in her head. When had it gone from suspected to official? Had she been told? Had she not been listening? This notice was clear. Mario's most recent electroencephalogram had been flat, and it was determined that he had suffered an irreversible loss of brain function. The choice to mechanically continue to keep his heart and lungs functioning, or not, was hers to make. *How can I give my permission to shut off my husband's lisfe support?*

And yet, she realized, how could she not?

Breathlessly, Erica dashed from the subway to De Mornay's. She paused a few feet before the entrance, to catch her breath. She must present herself in the professional manner demanded by her position. After checking her appearance in the glass of the display window, she strode purposefully through the ten-foot-high double doors.

Glenn greeted her warmly. "Viviana has a breakfast meeting," he said. "Should be in about ten thirty. Let's see . . ." He stopped midsentence. "Are you okay, Erica?"

She nodded, unable to squeeze out a single word. Turning away, she tried to rein in her emotions, praying she could stem the flood of tears that now threatened to spill over. She sobbed. *If only Glenn wasn't so kind.*

Glenn wrapped his arm around her shoulders and led her to the blue velvet love seat. Giving in to the weakness she felt in her unsteady legs, Erica sank down into the soft cushions. He disappeared for a moment and returned with a glass of water and a box of Kleenex. "Is there anything I can do?"

Although she didn't make a sound, her entire body quaked. Afraid to speak, she shook her head.

"Mario?" he asked. Glenn knew all about her husband's condition. After her first few months at De Mornay's, she had come to see him not only as her employer but as a friendly mentor. Then, several months ago, he and her brother-in-law had struck up an immediate friendship when Mike began setting up a website for De Mornay's. Ever the shrewd businesswoman, Viviana understood the importance of having a website to support their new venture into the catalog business. But the Web was foreign territory to her, and she had no desire to be involved. That bit of creativity she left entirely in the hands of her business partner, who discovered Mike's talent when Erica introduced the two of them.

For the past several months, Glenn had occasionally dropped by their cramped apartment. Mike would have dinner waiting, and afterward, the two men would work on the website well into the morning hours. Through that friendship, Glenn had learned a lot more about Erica's personal life than she ever would have thought of revealing. Despite her attempts to keep her personal and her professional lives separate, he had turned out to be empathetic, the kind of confidant she needed and could trust. And though there were things she could share only with Mike, such as her frustration over Viviana's demands on her time, she could talk with Glenn about certain personal things that she dared not discuss with Mario's younger brother.

As she sat trembling on the velvet couch, Erica let her mind travel back to her first days at De Mornay's. In the beginning, Viviana had seemed sympathetic when she'd heard what had happened to Mario, but that had been short-lived. She had been totally unsympathetic about Erica's desire to be at her husband's side during her first weekend in New York. Viviana's unfeeling words replayed in her head: *My heart goes out to you, my dear.* She recalled that her boss's tone lacked sincerity. *But we have a business to run. Since your husband is in a coma, he will not miss having you by his side. You may take tomorrow off, but I see no reason why you cannot report to work on Sunday as planned.*

"Silver dollar for your thoughts." Glenn moved the wastepaper basket closer and plunked down on the arm of the love seat.

Dropping the crumpled tissues in the trash, she looked up at Glenn. "I have to make a decision, and I do want to talk with you, but . . ." She glanced down at her wristwatch. "But," she repeated, "right now there's no time. We've got to get the store open." Glenn looked across to the Baccarat clock on the counter. "Right. Lunch at one thirty?"

The morning hours flew by. Viviana had breezed in just after half past ten with Sigtru, their freelance display director. Throughout the morning, off and on, when they weren't working with the clientele, all four of them worked on the display windows and on presentation throughout the store.

Just before one o'clock, two striking, beautifully put-together women walked into the store. The tall, willowy blond wore a Donna Karan dress and matching jacket in a warm cocoa, which accented her big brown eyes. The other woman with the sparkling green eyes had donned a classic Chanel signature suit in a vivid red. Chatting casually and laughing often, they clearly were good friends who enjoyed each other's company. Erica thought perhaps they were unable to see each other often and so were making the most of their time together on this shopping trip. She was surprised when Glenn rushed to embrace the two women.

"Ashleigh! Paige!"

Ashleigh surveyed the elegant store. De Mornay's seemed to capture the essence of Bentleys Royale, and yet it had its own distinctive ambiance. No doubt about it, Viviana De Mornay and Glenn Nelson were a dynamic duo in the world of fashion. Their personalities and lifestyles were as different as Los Angeles was to Manhattan, but they were both gifted with excellent taste and a flare for presentation.

Glenn gave her and Paige each a quick peck on the cheek and then stepped back with his arms outstretched and an appraising look on his face. Judging by his broad grin, they met with his approval. "Erica, I'd like you to meet two of the most savvy women on our planet—and the nicest, too. Paige Toddman." He nodded in her direction. Then, gesturing toward the younger woman, he continued, "And Ashleigh McDowell . . ." His face reddened. "Oh, I'm so sorry. That was Ashleigh's last name a few years ago, when I was a buyer for Bentleys Royale. Ashleigh's last name now is Taylor. Her husband, Conrad, is president and CEO of the Michael Nason stores."

Fully recovered from his faux pas, Glenn resumed his introductions. "And this is Erica Christonelli." He waited while the women greeted one another before filling in a bit more background. "Paige's husband, Mark, is CEO of Consolidated. You met him last month at the charity fund-raiser at Carlingdon's."

Erica nodded and smiled. "I did. I also remember seeing you, Mrs. Toddman, but I didn't have the opportunity—"

"Paige," she corrected. Paige gave Erica a warm smile, her eyes twinkling with vitality. "As I recall, you had your hands full that evening, but I'm pleased to finally meet you. Glenn has told me you are a very talented dress designer."

"She has designed some fantastic gowns and will soon be coming into her own," Glenn broke in. Erica's face reddened, but before she had a chance to respond, Viviana dashed toward them.

"Greetings," Viviana cried out. "I'm just finishing up on one of the window displays with Sigtru," she said. Looking directly at Ashleigh, she added, "You remember Sigtru, don't you?"

"Yes." Ashleigh remembered her well. It was Glenn who had discovered Sigtru while shopping the competition. Ashleigh had interviewed her upon his recommendation and had been responsible for hiring Sigtru away from Saks to become their display director.

Sigtru gave them a wave from the display window and went right back to work, unpinning the dress on the mannequin.

As this was Ashleigh's first visit to the store, Viviana showed her around the elegant boutique while Paige and Glenn caught up on each other's news. At the completion of the tour, Viviana pulled out some of her own designs as well as a couple that she'd adapted from Erica's sketches. Ashleigh commented on each of the designs that she found pleasing and simply nodded at those she was not particularly taken with.

Finally, Viviana said, "Did you hear about Mitchell Wainwright's accident?"

Ashleigh felt her heart slam against her rib cage. "I did. What a terrible tragedy," she commented. "Mitchell must be devastated. Mitch meant the world to him." She didn't trust herself to say more. His loss reminded her all too keenly of her own. And anyway, what else was there to say? Although things had not ended well between them, she did feel for him. She had wanted to send a card of condolence, but everything she considered saying seemed . . . wrong. She knew no words that could possibly bring him comfort, as she herself found little comfort in the condolences of others since the kidnapping. What she and Conrad had done instead was to make a contribution to leukemia research in the name of Wainwright's son.

As Viviana told her about her visit to Greenwich Hospital and about Wainwright asking her to help him find a condo, Ashleigh tuned out.

Does she already have her sights on Mitchell? she wondered. *Doesn't she realize it's much too soon?* The poor man's wife and son had just died tragically. And was Viviana's divorce from Philip Sloane even final yet?

Tuning back in, she heard Viviana say, "Pardon me, but I must finish up with Sigtru. Now that she's freelance, she's costing me an arm and a leg." She gave a false laugh. "So I'm afraid I must make the most of the time she's here. I'll just be a few moments."

Erica felt an instant rapport with the visiting women. Despite being so fashionably dressed and elegant, they seemed down-to-earth and were easy to talk with. Glenn filled them in on the store and recent happenings in the New York fashion world, and they all talked about mutual friends. Then, as if it had just occurred to him, he asked Ashleigh, "What brings you to our fair city?"

"We're visiting the Toddmans to celebrate their daughter April's ninth birthday," Ashleigh explained. "And our Callie's second. The girls' birthdays are just three days apart."

"Hey," Glenn said, "Erica also has a two-year-old. Cute as a button."

Erica smiled. "Yes, Marnie just turned two."

Glenn continued, "How sweet. Maybe you two can get the girls together for one of those . . ." His voice trailed off.

"A playdate?" Ashleigh filled in. She gave Erica a warm smile. "That would be great, but unfortunately we have a six forty-five flight back to Dallas tomorrow morning."

"Maybe next time," Erica suggested, thinking, *She seems so nice.*

Ashleigh agreed. "It really would be great fun to get our two toddlers together."

It was after two o'clock when Glenn and Erica were finally able to break away. The afternoon lull had set in on Fifth Avenue, Viviana was at the Mart, working with various upscale fashion vendors. Glenn felt comfortable leaving the boutique in the hands of one of the other sales associates, a mature, knowledgeable woman whom he'd brought with him when he left Bergdorf Goodman. "How hungry are you?" he asked.

"Not at all. But I know I should eat something."

"How about Carlingdon's coffee shop?"

"Sure. One of those bran muffins and a cappuccino would hit the spot."

Although coffee shop was as crowded as usual, they quickly picked up their order and made their way to an empty round table in the back. As soon as Erica slid in and situated herself, Glenn said, "I spoke with Mike last night—"

"Last night?" Erica leaned forward, her elbows on the table.

"Well, I guess it was actually early this morning."

Erica didn't say anything for a moment or two. "You and Mike seem to be hitting it off well."

Taken aback, he said, "I consider Mike a friend." He felt a grin spread across his face as he guessed what was on Erica's mind. "Just a friend. Nothing more." He paused for emphasis, not wanting her to misunderstand. "I like your brother-in-law a great deal, and I like you and Marnie. My friendship with Mike revolves around the website he's developing for us, and around you and your daughter. That's it. End of story."

Looking embarrassed, Erica said, "I didn't mean—"

"Forget it. I take no offense. Mike's a great guy, and I'm glad you have that kind of support. Under the circumstances, it appears to be a fantastic situation for the three of you."

Erica nodded. "So you know what we were discussing last night?" She was relieved. She wouldn't have to explain all the details about Mario.

"I think so," Glenn responded. "And I understand what a difficult decision it must be. But I'm confident that somehow you will work it out and do the right thing. Whatever that might be."

She nodded again, but uncertainty was written across her freckled face. "I keep asking myself what Mario would want, what he'd tell me to do."

"And what do you think that would be?"

She shook her head as if to dispel the conflicting thoughts swirling around in her head. "If I give my approval to shut off the life support, Mario will die." Taking a deep breath, she continued, "Before Marnie came into our lives, Mario was my whole world. I didn't think I could live in a world without him. He was all that kept me going through two miscarriages and three failed adoptions."

Glenn reached over and stroked her arm, the one now cradling her chin. Red-eyed, with dark circles etched in her skin, she looked so vulnerable. "You have so much to live for. Marnie is one of the sweetest little toddlers I've ever met, and you are extremely talented. Your talent will pay off in the world of fashion." He meant every word, though knew that any words at this point were inadequate. Then his mouth curled up at the corners. "As for your failed adoptions, I think maybe the man upstairs had better plans for you. Think about it. If you'd adopted, once Marnie came along you would have ended up with two babies just months apart."

Erica's breath caught in her throat, and she felt her blood run cold.

"I understand that's happened to a lot of couples who adopt," he continued. "It would have wreaked havoc on your budding career, and even as crazy as Mike is over little Marnie, I don't think he could have handled double trouble. That definitely would have curtailed his business plans."

Erica felt terrible about letting Glenn mistakenly think that Marnie was her biological child. Should she tell him the truth? After all, he'd been so kind to her. For a moment her thoughts teetered, but she quickly rejected the idea. She could not tell Glenn. No one must know that she had not given birth to Marnie—not even Mike. That's the way Mario had said it must be. Why should their daughter ever have to deal with that fact? Telling anyone, even Mario's brother, was too risky. Plus, even if he were no longer here in her world, she would never go against her loving husband's wishes.

Glenn cleared his throat and said, "You haven't eaten a bite. Come now, you need your strength." He studied her closely, as if trying to find the right words to comfort her. "Whatever decision you make, Erica, I'm in your court."

She looked down to the tile floor. Her eyes widened. Suddenly she knew what she had to do. She knew what Mario would have told her to do. "Mario is a proud man. He would not want to live like a vegetable. He always loved taking care of others. That's why he became a nurse practitioner. He would hate if he were the one in need of round-the-clock assistance."

Glenn nodded. "I never got a chance to meet your husband, but from all you and Mike have shared with me, I think perhaps that is the very best decision you can make. If I were in Mario's place, that's the kind of decision I'd want my loved ones to make on my behalf."

She wondered if he and Mike had discussed how they felt about keeping Mario on life support. "You never shared those thoughts before."

"It's your decision to make, and since you are the one who must live with that decision, it must be right for you. It would be wrong for me or even for Mike to interfere." He reached across the table and took her hand. "If you need a few days off, just let me know."

"Not a few days, but if you don't mind, I'd like to leave early today."

"No problem. Just finish your muffin, and then you can take the rest of the day off."

Picking up the muffin, she took a nibble and wiped her mouth, deciding to change the subject. "Those two women who dropped in today were very nice. They both seem to have everything going for them—successful husbands, happy families, plenty of money. Yet they took the time to talk with me and seemed genuinely interested in what I was doing."

"Paige and Ashleigh are very classy ladies. But don't let their outward appearances deceive you. They've both traveled some pretty bumpy roads."

"What do you mean?"

"Back in 1987, Paige's world was turned upside down by the hostile takeover of Consolidated. Her husband was CEO of the largest West Coast division . . ."

Erica was aware that Mark Toddman was responsible for restructuring Consolidated, but before she had a chance to comment, she heard Glenn saying, "And a couple of years ago, Ashleigh experienced the kind of tragedy that will haunt her for the rest of her life."

"Oh, that's a shame." She hated to hear about bad things happening to good people. "Well, don't stop there."

"Just trying to recall the details," Glenn said. "Her daughter—the one who was celebrating her second birthday—was actually an identical twin."

"A twin? What happened to the other girl?" Erica asked, hoping he wasn't going to tell her the child had died.

"She was abducted from the bassinet in Ashleigh's hospital room the day she was born."

Erica gasped.

"From what I understand, to date neither the police nor the private investigators hired by the Taylors have turned up anything. The infant seems to have vanished without a trace. Ashleigh has done an admirable job of concealing her heartache and getting on with her life. But as a mother, you must know that when a baby is kidnapped—well, needless to say, their lives were forever changed."

"How horrible." If anything were ever to happen to Marnie, Erica knew that she would find it impossible to get on with her life. She found it easy to sympathize. In fact, she vaguely remembered something about the kidnapping of an infant twin from a hospital—remembered how easy it was to put herself in that mother's shoes. It was close to the time she'd lost her own in vitro baby. Of course, she hadn't been all that tuned in to the outside world at the time, but she remembered overhearing Leslie talking about the tragedy. But it couldn't be the same case. "They live in Dallas, right?"

"Right. But they were in California at the time. As a matter of fact, that's where the twins were born."

"She was away from home when her babies were due?" Erica was incredulous.

"As I understand, the babies were born about three weeks prematurely. Ashleigh was actually in Long Beach, at her grandfather's ninetieth birthday party."

"Long Beach," Erica echoed. Then, with a sinking feeling in her stomach and a burning sensation in her chest, she asked a question she didn't really want Glenn to answer: "What hospital?"

CHAPTER

48

For Erica, the next hours passed in a blinding blur. Temperatures had risen to the low nineties, and the humidity was a killer. She vaguely remembered leaving Glenn at the store. The crowded subway ride home and the climb up the stairs to their third-floor apartment left her hot and miserable. Without a good night's sleep, she was coming apart at the seams. But here she was, standing in the doorway to Mike's home office.

Since they seldom had company, and the kitchen counter was where they ate most of their meals, Mike had converted the dining space into his headquarters. A large desk and working area now covered the entire wall. Mike gave her a distracted wave, remaining hunched over the computer. Then he abruptly swiveled his chair in her direction and raised his wristwatch to eye level. "What brings you home at such a reasonable hour?"

"We need to talk."

"Isn't that what we were doing all night long?"

She nodded. "That's true, but I've made a decision. And I need to talk to you."

He looked back to the computer and studied his watch for what seemed a long time. "Can you give me about thirty minutes to finish up?" He told her that Marnie was taking a nap, then vanished into his computer once more, immediately tapping keys and clicking the new-fangled cordless mouse.

Like an automaton, Erica made her way to the bedroom she shared with her daughter. She tossed her Chanel shoulder bag on the bed and began undoing her French twist, flinging the hairpins onto the oak dresser. As she ran her fingers through her hair, she was not in the least bit surprised to find it damp at the roots, particularly at the base of her neck.

Tiptoeing to Marnie's crib, she took in the sweet baby scent, studying every feature of her precious child. Marnie's tiny fingers clutched a piece of her favorite blanket, which was worn thin from her dragging it everywhere and chewing on the corners. Her silky blond locks were damp, too, and clinging to her scalp. After the shock of the prior month's electric bill, Erica and Mike had agreed to cut down on the use of the air-conditioner, but she was afraid they might have to break down tonight so they could get some much-needed sleep. For now, she directed the large upright fan toward Marnie's crib.

Earlier, when Glenn had dropped the bombshell that the Taylor twin had been abducted from Long Beach Memorial Hospital, she'd felt the universe shift beneath her chair. She wasn't a great believer in coincidence. *Is it possible?* It couldn't be. But then again . . . *Could my Marnie be the abducted Taylor twin?* It was too horrific to contemplate. But if it were true, what would she do? The answer was easy. One thing she knew for sure was that she would never let anyone take her daughter from her.

Sinking down into the rocking chair beside the crib, Erica covered her face with her hands. *No, no, no, this can't be happening.* Lifting her eyes to the ceiling, she whispered out loud, to whomever might be listening, "Don't let this be true." Then her thoughts turned to Mario and to Rose, the teenager whom she'd never met but felt as if she had. She owed so much to the faceless young girl. Mario couldn't have made up that story about Rose. He would never lie to her; he loved her, of that she was absolutely sure.

With as much conviction as she could muster, she told herself that she had nothing to worry about. Rose, not Ashleigh Taylor, had given birth to Marnie. Besides, she reassured herself, Marnie looked nothing like the beautiful blond woman she'd met earlier. In fact, people were always telling Erica that the baby looked just like her. *I'm Marnie's mother, not Rose, and certainly not Ashleigh Taylor.* This gave her a sense of relief. And yet that annoying *What if?* remained entrenched in a tiny corner of her mind.

Wearily, Erica heaved herself from the chair and headed for the kitchen. It was well past the half hour that Mike had requested for finishing up when she padded out in her stocking-feet to meet him.

"I was just pouring us some iced tea," Mike said as he placed the tall glasses on the kitchen counter. Looking up, he wondered when her face had become so pale. Pulling out one of the bar stools, he added, "Can I get you anything else?"

She shook her head. Her eyes pleading for understanding, she said, "I'm going to sign the papers to withdraw Mario's life support."

For a long thirty seconds, neither of them spoke. Mike didn't know what to say. The room was so silent, they heard the whir of the refrigerator, the traffic below, and the small fan on the kitchen sink.

Erica's interlocked fingers twisted in agitated circles. "Mike?" After another few seconds, she began again. "Say something, please. Tell me what you think. Do you think I've made the wrong decision?" She hesitated. "It's not cast in stone."

Finally, Mike forced some words past the lump in his throat. "No, I don't think you made the wrong decision; it's just one I hadn't expected. Last night you were in a very different place."

Erica's eyes dropped. They were filled with tears. "I know. I thought that if I gave my permission to turn off the life support, I would be responsible for killing the only man I'll ever love." After a moment's hesitation, she continued, "But after talking with Glenn today, I knew that—"

"Did Glenn advise you to do this?"

"No. He didn't offer any suggestions. But as I was telling him that I couldn't make the decision, everything crystallized, and I knew that this is exactly what Mario would want me to do. Do you think I'm wrong?"

Thank God, I don't have to be the one to make the decision. Slipping off the bar stool, he reached out for his sister-in-law and gave her a huge hug. "We'll both miss him, maybe more than we already do. But it's for the best." His voice unsteady, he pulled out a tissue from the box on the counter and handed it to Erica. Somehow he managed to hold back his own tears. "I truly believe that."

When her tears subsided, Erica said, "I know that if the life support is withdrawn, Mario will die. But really, he died nearly two years ago. Now that he has officially been declared brain-dead, we have to accept the fact that it's irreversible. It's time that I accept the unacceptable. That the man we love can never be Mario again. I wouldn't want to live like that. Would you?"

Mike shook his head. *I wonder what Father O'Reilly would say.* As for himself, he had no idea of what was right or what was wrong. But he knew his brother believed in God and had earned his place in heaven. Unconsciously, he made the sign of the cross. Then he refilled their glasses. He made no move to get back to his computer. He just listened, knowing that Erica had to talk, that she needed reassurance that she was doing the right thing.

"Am I interfering with God's will? By terminating the life-support system that has kept Mario's heart beating and his lungs pumping, after being told that he has suffered the irreversible end to all his brain activity?" She said it so softly, she might have been talking to herself. "Or have I been interfering with God's will all along, by allowing Mario to be kept alive by these artificial means for nearly two years? What is God's will? How am I supposed to know?"

Mike could only look at her sadly and wish he had the answers.

Funeral arrangements were made. People were called. Ever since she had said her good-byes to Mario, the week had passed in a flurry of activity. Erica didn't know what she would have done without Glenn. The director of the Frank E. Campbell Funeral Chapel was a personal friend of Glenn's, and he'd shepherded her through the arrangements and given her a sizeable discount on Mario's casket. Erica put in as many hours as she could at De Mornay's, and thank God that although Viviana was unable to attend Mario's funeral service—due to an important meeting with Mitchell Wainwright and a potential investor—she had been understanding and had not challenged Erica's need to take off the hours required to make all the necessary arrangements.

Even so, Erica was running late. Mario's father had called a few minutes before. He and his wife had taken the red-eye from Florida the previous night. With no preamble, he'd asked for directions to the funeral parlor. His stilted conversation had left Erica with a queasy feeling in the pit of her stomach. She had never figured out why Nico and Carmella seemed so indifferent toward her. With no time to dwell on it, though, she scurried to the mirror on her dressing table and attempted to repair the damage from another sleepless night.

Marnie tottered precariously across the bedroom carpet, carrying her plastic bib. She stopped within inches of her mother, who was doing her best to make sure that nothing would be forgotten on this day. Although the funeral service would be small, the preparations had been more daunting than Erica had imagined. Now she had just a few more minutes to get ready herself.

She'd decided to wear a simple Anne Klein suit, and her hair hung in loose curls, the way Mario had liked it best. Clutching the hem of Erica's skirt for balance, the child thrust the bib toward her mother. The action brought a smile to Erica's lips, and she said, "You are one smart cookie." She hugged her daughter to her.

Just a few moments earlier, as Erica had finished dressing her, Marnie had looked up at her and said, "Cookie, Mama." Erica had told her to wait, saying, "We can't get your pretty new dress dirty." The lightweight, royal blue dress and black patent leather Mary Janes that Mike had bought for her to wear at her father's funeral were perfect. Erica had agreed with him that Marnie was not to be dressed in black. Though the toddler had parroted the phrase, "Have to wait!"—she didn't want to wait. But she hadn't cried; instead, she had gone about finding a solution.

"Cookie," Marnie repeated now, still holding the bib toward her mother.

Erica scooped her up in her arms and took her to the kitchen. Setting her on the counter for a moment, she tied the bib. Then she slipped Marnie into her high chair, locked the tray in place, and gave her a cookie. "Now, you be a good girl while Mommy finishes getting ready."

The phone began to ring again. Mike was still in the shower, so Erica dashed back to the counter and picked it up.

"Yes, Ian," she said. When Ian, Leslie, and her nieces had left the apartment the night before, Erica noticed that Ian had left behind the paper with the directions she'd written out for him. Now, as she repeated the name of the funeral parlor and gave him directions, she thought about the previous evening. She couldn't put her finger on anything specific, but something was wrong. Leslie had greeted her with a hug, but there was no warmth in it. It was like receiving a hug from one of the Stepford wives. *But why?* She caught a glimpse of Marnie, who sat contentedly in her high chair, soggy cookie all over her face. Fortunately, the bib was keeping the muck away from her clothing. "Sorry, Ian, I'll talk with you when we're all at the funeral home. I've really got to run."

Mike strode into the kitchen, his hair still damp from the shower. He wore his only suit, a charcoal gray one that was slightly short in the sleeves. He looked quite presentable, nevertheless, with his face freshly shaved and his hair neatly combed.

"You clean up real good," Erica teased him. "Your brother would've been proud."

Mike gave her an understanding grin and stood still for a moment, thinking of his big brother. Then he took one look at his niece's cookie-smeared face, made a dramatic squeal, and dashed over to the sink to grab a washcloth. "I'll take care of the princess. It's ten past nine, and the livery cab is coming at nine fifteen, so best you slide into your shoes and we get going."

On the way over to the funeral home, Erica had time to think—time to worry. She had shed so many tears over the past week, she was sure there were none left to shed. They were all dried up. There was nothing she could do about her red eyes or the dark circles beneath them, which concealer did little to hide. She'd done the best she could.

Nico and Carmella. Each time their names popped into her exhausted mind, her body began to tremble and her hands became damp and clammy. With all the things on her mind, she kept conveniently forgetting that she would have to face Mario and Mike's parents. But the time was growing nearer. No longer able to keep her fears to herself, she turned to Mike. When she spoke, her voice was unsteady.

"I've tried so hard to get close to your parents over the years. I want Marnie to have grandparents, but they . . . they just seem so much more distant than even the miles between us. And now . . . I'm sure they'll never forgive me for withdrawing Mario's life support. They think I was wrong, don't they?" It wasn't really a question.

Mike squeezed her hand and said, "You were forced to make a difficult and heart-wrenching decision. What's important is that *you* know you did what was best. What Mario would have wanted you to do."

The cab had pulled up to the curb in front of the funeral home. Erica kissed her daughter on the cheek and turned to Mike. "Would you meet me in the chapel with Marnie in a few minutes? I'd like to spend some time with Mario before the ceremony." Mike nodded as he unbuckled the little girl's car seat.

Erica felt as though she needed a few moments to be alone with Mario before facing his parents. She would say her final good-bye while looking at his face, with the casket open. After that, the lid would be closed, and the casket would be moved into the chapel. She felt strongly that the handful of people at the funeral should remember Mario as he was.

Erica walked to the viewing room and took in a few short breaths before she slowly opened the door. The steel-blue casket stood in the center of the room. Mario's face was not as pale as she'd expected. His profile appeared strong and handsome against the light blue satin. Goosebumps rose on her arms. *Why my Mario? He was such a kind and good man.* He'd taught her to believe that all things happen for the best. But his being taken from them, how could that be rationalized? He'd never heard Marnie say her first words, hadn't seen her take her first step. He'd never know her laughter or feel her wet kiss upon his cheek. *It isn't fair.* Mario had never done anything to hurt anyone, and yet he'd never know the joy of the precious child he had brought into their lives.

The scent of the few floral arrangements wafted through the air, subtle and sweet. Erica felt desperately sad. Today would be the end of her very long good-bye to the man who held her heart. She would never love another man as she had loved Mario. *I'll never love another man, period.* The words from their wedding vows—*until death do us part*—drifted across her mind, and she leaned over and kissed her husband for the last time. She closed the lid to the coffin and heard the locks click into place.

When Ian McDonald pulled into the parking lot of the Frank E. Campbell Funeral Chapel, it was about twenty minutes to eleven. Ilise and Laura scrambled out of the backseat before he even had Leslie's door open. He noticed that there were only three cars in the lot.

Opening the passenger door for Leslie, he saw a tall, lean, immaculately dressed man with thick blond hair emerging from a sporty gold Porsche Boxster. He glanced over at Ian's rental car and headed in their direction.

"Glenn Nelson," the man said, thrusting out his hand. "I work with your sister."

Puzzled, Ian said, "Erica?"

Glenn nodded. "She asked me to introduce myself." Erica had been expecting her brother and his family, and it didn't take any supernatural intellect to pick them out. "Other than a couple of people from the hospital—and Mario's parents and his sister and brother, along with Mike's friend Bill, I don't believe anyone else is expected."

The memorial service was brief but poignant and personal. Erica found she was holding up well despite her grief. During the service, she'd held Marnie close to her heart. Somehow her little daughter seemed to sense that this was a time to exercise her ability to entertain herself, and thankfully, she had managed to get though the entire ceremony without making a peep. *Without this precious child,* Erica realized, *Mario's death would have been my undoing.*

After the service, everyone returned to the apartment Mario had chosen for his family two years before. Mike had organized for the small reception to be catered. It didn't take long before the first glitch of the evening arose, when Marnie's grandparents suggested they take her away from the noisy apartment to their hotel room so they could put her to bed. Erica flatly told them no. "Marnie will stay with us. If she's tired, she'll fall asleep. And if she misses a few hours' sleep today, it's not the end of the world."

Jean Christonelli gave Erica a supportive grin, then turned to her parents. "I think it's important that the whole family be here. Besides, this is the first time I've seen my precious little niece." Neither Nico nor Carmella looked pleased, but they made no further suggestions.

Ilise and Laura adored their little cousin, but they had a hard time getting near her with Carmella constantly hovering. When Erica was no longer able to tolerate her mother-in-law's monopoly on her daughter's attention, she took the necessary steps to free Marnie from her clutches. With no fuss, she plucked the child from Carmella's lap. "Time for a diaper change."

Turning to her nieces, Erica said, "Come and give me a hand." Eight-year-old Ilise, with the fiery red hair of her mother, sprang up from the floor beside Marnie's empty cradle, a wide grin spreading across her freckled face. Laura, whose darker hair was more like her father's, had just celebrated her twelfth birthday and was much more restrained, but Erica could tell she was pleased and eager to spend some time with the baby. They followed their aunt into the bedroom. After she had changed Marnie and slipped her into her pajamas, she placed the baby in Laura's arms and handed her the baby's bottle. "You can give your cousin the first half of her bottle, and then let Ilise finish up after you burp her."

When Erica came back from the bedroom, Carmella asked, "Where's Marnie?"

"Time for a nap," Erica told her. "The girls are feeding her."

Carmella looked pointedly at her husband. Nico turned to Mike, who was engrossed in conversation with his sister, Glenn, and Ian, and said, "Could we have a few moments in private with you and Erica?" Leslie used the occasion to join the girls in Erica's bedroom.

Did they set up some sort of signal? Erica wondered.

Mike looked to Erica and shrugged his shoulders. "How about my room?" He hesitated and then looked back toward the others. "Excuse us. We'll just be a few minutes."

Once inside Mike's room, Nico made direct eye contact with his son, ignoring Erica's presence. Even though he'd said they wanted to talk with the two of them, Carmella stood beside her husband. They all remained standing. As Erica closed the bedroom door behind them, Nico cleared his throat and began, "Your mother and I have been concerned over your living situation for quite some time. It was bad enough while your brother was—"

"Whoa!" Mike broke in. His father's tone was hushed, but there was no mistaking his intent. "Dad, you're out of line."

"Don't talk to your father in that tone," Carmella interjected. "If you're not concerned for your own sake, you must at least think about Marnie."

"Sit down," Mike said with an unmistakable air of authority.

Nico and Carmella looked at each other as if they meant to challenge their son, but instead, they lowered themselves to the edge of his bed. "Hear your father out," Carmella said.

Erica's stomach churned. She could hardly believe that they would choose today, of all days, to spew their preconceived ill judgment of their son and daughter-in-law's lifestyle.

"I've heard enough," Mike fired back.

"Not nearly enough," Nico said. "Have you totally taken leave of your senses?"

"It's *you* who doesn't have things straight. Erica and I loved Mario and prayed for his recovery, but apparently that was not God's will. Circumstances threw us together after Mario's accident, and we learned to love each other." Before either of his parents could interrupt, he raised the palm of his hand toward them and repeated. "We love each other like the brother and sister we are, and we are making a good home for Marnie."

"Like brother and sister?" His mother's tone was incredulous and demeaning.

"Yes. Like brother and sister. We have a win-win situation. The only impropriety that exists is in your minds. If you'll remember, it was Mario who arranged for us to all live together for our mutual benefit." The idea that anything was going on between them was ludicrous. Mike's parents had never met his former partner, Jeff, and they'd been introduced to Bill Reynolds today as just a "friend." But even though Mike's parents couldn't know about that part of his life, Mike had thought they'd known enough about their son to realize that he would never have betrayed his brother in that way.

Nico leapt to his feet. "You know damn well that Mario never expected you to set up housekeeping with his wife and their daughter."

Erica was about to explode. She could hold her tongue no longer. "You know damn well that was no more our intention than it was his. You have dirty, evil minds, and to surface this on the day of your son's funeral . . . It's simply unspeakable!"

"Don't speak to me about evil!" Carmella spat out the words. "How do you think it looks, to openly live with your brother-in-law in this way? And then to make a decision to shut off your husband's life support—my son's life support—while you continue your sordid lifestyle?"

Erica felt the air leave her lungs. She couldn't believe what she was hearing. These were Marnie's grandparents. With no parents of her own, she had so desperately wanted Mario's parents to accept her and become a part of their lives, but she knew now that she would never allow their venom to touch the life of her baby. She stood beside her brother-in-law, totally speechless. Mike, Nico, and Carmella—they were all talking at once. Their voices had risen to a feverish pitch. She wanted to place her hands over her ears to drown out the sound.

Then, suddenly, the room became deadly silent. Mike had both his mother's and his father's undivided attention. His voice was barely above a whisper when he said, "It's time you left our apartment. You are no longer welcome here."

Once again, they were all talking at the same time. The words floated over Erica's head like a heavy, gray cloud. She caught only a phrase now and them, the word *slut* and something like *with the respect she deserves*. But each of the words and phrases she heard were just pieces, and she couldn't seem to put them together. She knew she didn't belong here. Saying not a single word, she pushed open the door and left. Instead of rejoining Ian, Glenn, and her sister-in-law, she turned down the corridor to her own room.

Ian was finding out a great deal about Erica's life since she'd moved to New York. Glenn praised her as an up-and-coming dress designer. Ian was relieved and pleased for his sister. Maybe, after all the trouble and the pain, she was finally coming into her own.

Once Glenn learned that Ian had lived all his life in Southern California, they began to discover many more areas of conversation. "Actually, my business partner, Viviana De Mornay, and I began our retail careers at Bentleys Royale." As his sister's employer continued to tell him about his early career in retail, Ian found his thoughts wandering in another direction. *Bentleys Royale, Bentleys Royale*—the words rolled around in his head as if on a loop. The old cliché *It's a small world* never seemed so real. He'd thought Erica's secret, the one even she didn't know she was carrying, was safe here in New York. But now he wasn't at all sure.

Viviana retreated to her office, leaving the cleaning up to the catering staff. Kicking off her stilettos, she gave an audible sigh of relief.

She retrieved the makeup mirror from her bottom desk drawer and leaned in close. The smile she'd planted on her face for the evening was definitely deepening those damnable commas rising from each corner of her mouth. If she wasn't careful, she'd be applying concealer with a putty knife. But the employees' Christmas party had been sensational. The food had been scrumptious, the wines superb, and the floral arrangements extraordinary. Throughout the holiday season ahead, her staff would be talking about this party and the bonuses she'd handed out. *Money well invested.*

For her, the evening would have been a perfect if only Mitchell had shown up. But once again, he'd disappointed her.

In hindsight, Viviana never should have mentioned to him that Erica might bring her little girl. She could kick herself. *Maybe that's why Mitchell didn't show up.* Ever since his own tragedy, he could hardly stand the sight of children.

Shaking her head, though, she had to face reality. *Who am I kidding?* The truth was, Mitchell Wainwright the goddamned Third was an enigma. She couldn't break through that impenetrable wall he'd built around himself since the death of his little boy. He was now walking with a cane and had moved into a condo at the Tuscany Arms in Manhattan, just two floors above hers. As of yet, though, he had never invited her to accompany him to either a social or a business affair.

Oh, he'd been her escort a few times, but she'd always been the one to extend the invitation. She sure wasn't used to being the one who did the asking, and she hated it. It was even more unnerving that Mitchell never batted an eye when he ran into her as she left the building with an admiring young man or even a distinguished older one. And none of her recent romps in the hay had been with him, although he was the one man she longed for—the man she intended to win over, one way or the other. Four months had passed, and he showed no signs of snapping out of it. He had never tried to kiss her the way she longed to be kissed, nor had he made any attempt to get her into his bed. She heaved a sigh. *Well, that's going to change—maybe even tonight.*

As it had turned out, Erica had not brought her toddler to the Christmas party. In fact, she and her brother-in-law had stayed less than an hour, saying they had to get back to the child—supposedly to a babysitter who had plans of her own for the evening.

There was something elusive about that woman, but Viviana couldn't quite put her finger on it. Erica had proven to be reliable, not like some of those young mothers who were always coming up with some emergency. She was also talented and a quick study, absorbing like a sponge all that Viviana had to teach her. She still seemed so sad, though, and she was often edgy and distracted. It must have been difficult to pull the plug on her husband, so to speak, but by now Viviana figured she should be feeling a huge sense of relief. Those nightly trips to the hospital and, later, the long-term care facility were well behind her, so why wasn't she ready to snap out of it?

Viviana had silently gone through her own period of hell. No one would believe what Philip had put her through during the divorce settlement. It was humiliating to discover that he'd hidden so many assets in his ex-wife's name—and even more so that he had taken Helga with him on his new venture in Germany. Although Viviana had been accused of being self-indulgent, she was getting on with her life. Unlike Erica, she was not the one wallowing in her own pain. Even the greatest tragedy of her young life she hadn't dwelled on or shared—not with Philip, not with anyone.

Opening her Chanel handbag, she took out her lipstick and a small comb. After applying a fresh coat of lipstick, she flipped the mirror from the magnified side and unclamped the bow at the base of her neck. She ran a comb through her hair and reclamped it securely in place, leaving a wispy, curled strand loose on each side of her face. Satisfied, she strode to the full-length mirror. Her midnight blue Yves Saint Laurent gown fit to perfection, and Mitchell Wainwright was tall enough that she didn't have to worry about the ankle-slimming stilettos making her tower over him. She prayed that he was home.

Tonight she would make him forget about his losses and begin to live again.

CHAPTER

52

Wainwright sank down, letting his body compress into the plush leather armchair. Pouring another Scotch, he set the nearly empty bottle on the hardwood floor beside him and gazed out the floor-to-ceiling window, through the intermittent snowfall, toward Central Park. The only light from inside his spacious condo came from the stereo. The only sound, his favorite selection of jazz, played sotto voce.

He held up his half-empty glass and stared at it for long seconds. He knew he had to cut down. The Scotch dulled the throbbing ache in his right leg—at least, that's what he told himself—but it did nothing to ease the pain in his heart. Maybe it intensified it.

Lifting his eyes to the high ceiling, he murmured, "Why? If there really is someone up there, give me an answer! Why did you take Mitch? He had his whole life ahead of him. He fought so hard, and he was winning the battle. Why him? Why not me?"

He heard a distant tapping sound and strained to listen. It came again. It was his front door knocker. A quick glance at the wall clock told him it was after eleven. Who could be at his door at this time of night? And why hadn't security called? Straining against the gravity that seemed to be anchoring him to the chair, he grabbed his cane and heaved himself up.

Not bothering to look out the small peephole at eye level, he flung open the door.

"Merry Christmas."

"Viviana!" As usual, she was breathtaking. Every hair in place, warm inviting lips, and dressed to perfection. In one hand she gripped a tote bag bearing the De Mornay's insignia, which, judging by the palatable aromas, appeared to be crammed full of food; in the other hand she held a gift box wrapped in red satin paper and tied with a fancy gold bow. But what was she doing here? He had no interest in Christmas this year. Worse than no interest, in fact—he hated every reminder of what was supposed to be the happiest season of all.

"Aren't you going to invite me in?"

"Sure." Wainwright stepped back, leaning heavily on his cane. "I didn't mean to be in-hosh-pi-table." He realized he was slurring his words and tried to get a grip. "Hadn't been expecting company."

"And do you mind?" Viviana retreated a step, looking hurt and insecure. Quite out of character for the fashion maven.

"Come on in," he said, opening the door wide. "Sorry, I'm not at my best."

"I didn't mean to barge in on you, but when you didn't show up at my party, I was afraid you might not be feeling well, so I brought you a little Christmas cheer." With a bit of a frown as she stepped over the threshold, she added, "But it appears that you've been celebrating on your own." Leaning toward him, she gave him a peck on the cheek, and with another *Merry Christmas,* she handed him the box.

For a few awkward seconds, he said nothing; finally, he managed to speak. "Thank you, Viviana. You shouldn't have—"

"Of course I should. It's Christmas, and I want to share with all my friends. And don't worry, Mitchell. I don't expect anything in return." Lowering the tote bag to the floor, she slipped out of her full-length sable coat. She started to hand it to him. He could almost visualize the wheels turning in her brain when she paused and then headed to the coat tree beside the double doors leading to his bedroom.

Before he had a chance to say more, she gushed, "We had so much extra food tonight." She took in the glass of Scotch beside his chair. "And I'd be willing to bet you haven't had a thing to eat."

"Not hungry," he said.

She seemed to be studying him, and he was sure he didn't measure up. *Unshaven, three sheets to the wind, and I can't even walk without the aid of this blasted cane.* But he didn't really give a damn what she thought. Not much, at least.

"You really should eat something, Mitchell," Viviana said, picking up the tote bag and heading toward the granite countertop and stainless steel appliances that served as the kitchen area and fit in perfectly with his modern living room decor. "I'll just put a few of these things on a plate, and you can eat what you want."

It was awkward, her giving him a gift. He had nothing for her, nothing for anyone, and he had no intention of buying any damn Christmas presents. Not this year; maybe never. He had nothing to celebrate. As Viviana busied herself in the kitchen, he tried to think of some way to excuse himself that would not be offensive. *Oh, hell. I'll just say it like it is.*

"It's awfully nice of you to stop by, but I'm afraid I'm rotten company. I wish Christmas would evaporate. I am in no mood to celebrate."

Viviana stopped spreading the assortments on the plate. She looked stricken. "I know you have suffered a horrible tragedy, Mitchell, but you must go on. Life is for the living. Try to focus on all the good things around you. The longer you allow yourself to remain maudlin, the harder it will be for you to come back and be the dynamic man I've always believed you to be. Christmas can be one of the happiest times of the year."

"Yeah, right. It's also the time of year that posts a record numbers of suicides." He wanted to add, *What do you know about tragedy?* "I don't need any goddamned perky platitudes, Viviana." Her biggest tragedy, if it could even be considered a tragedy, was her recent divorce from a man he was sure she'd never loved. That was no comparison to the loss of a child.

And anyway, she'd landed squarely on her pretty, strappy stilettos.

CHAPTER
53

Viviana stormed out of the kitchen. *What have I been thinking?* Mitchell Wainwright is no longer any prize. He's weak—he's not that ruthless, powerful man he was just a few years ago. When she'd leaned over to lightly kiss his cheek, he'd smelled like one of those lingering barroom losers in some low-class dive at closing time. To think that she'd been agonizing over him! It made her want to puke.

He stood looking at her, leaning heavily on his cane, a mystified expression shadowing his face.

She glared back at him. There were no longer any traces of the accident on his face, no scars—nothing. He was as handsome as ever, even with the stubble, which she was sure was at least a couple of days old. His thick silver hair, though uncombed, did nothing to distract from his good looks. He could still be considered "eye candy." Even his injured leg and need for a cane did not faze her, nor did the disability distract from his spectacular appeal. But she simply could not respect a man who was weak of character, who allowed himself to wallow in self-pity. It was intolerable in a man—intolerable in anyone.

Kicking off her shoes, she walked up to within inches of her host. "Sit down, Mitchell. We need to talk."

He blinked. "I'm really not in the mood."

"The hell with your mood. We've known each other for a long time, but suddenly you've become a morose stranger. I have no lack of empathy for your loss, but it's time you started getting it together." As she spoke, she took hold of his arm and gently led him to his armchair, where he'd obviously spent most of the evening. He didn't resist, but looked at her as if she were from another planet.

He rested his cane beside the chair and lowered himself into it, his eyes never leaving hers. He did not appear compliant, only curious.

Viviana plunked down on the couch across from the armchair and leaned forward. "It's been nine months since the accident. While most of your injuries—"

"I know exactly how long it's been."

"Well, instead of keeping track of the past, how about making plans for the future? Do you plan to station yourself in this . . ." She swept her eyes around the elegant but messy condo and began again. "How long do you plan to leave the running of your business in the hands of your CFO?"

He braced himself, holding on to both arms of his chair, and leaned toward her. "I don't see that Ron Dean or any other part of this is any of your goddamned affair."

She realized that she was overstepping her bounds, but at this point she couldn't care less. At least she'd gotten a rise out of him. "You're right, but I consider you a friend, and I can't just sit by while you—"

Wainwright cut in. "Who asked you to play nursemaid, Viviana? I can take care of myself." Heaving himself up with the aid of his cane, he took a step toward her, accidentally knocking over the bottle of Scotch beside his chair. Distracted, they both watched the remaining contents dribble from the bottle onto the hardwood floor. Viviana did not respond. It seemed as if they were actors in a B-grade movie with the reel being played in slow motion.

After what seemed an eternity, he sighed and said, "You're right. I'm not myself lately. I've been self-indulgent." He hesitated. "And yes, it's time I got it together. You've been a real trooper, and I haven't done much to show my appreciation."

Taken aback, Viviana wanted to stand, but now he was towering over her. "I'm sorry, too, Mitchell. Here, let me clean that up," she said, looking down at the floor, "and fix you something to eat."

He stepped back and nodded. "Truce?" He looked back down at the puddle of Scotch. "Forget about that. But I will eat something. How about bringing it out here?"

"Fine," Viviana responded. "But that spill stinks to high heaven." To emphasize the point, she held her nose.

He laughed. "Guess it does."

As Viviana busied herself in the kitchen, he made his way to the wet bar at the far corner of the room. "How about a glass of pinot noir?"

At least the man isn't oblivious to my choice of wine. "I'd love one." The moment the words were out of her mouth, though, she regretted them. Mitchell shouldn't have any more to drink. She picked up a sponge and a towel. *Well, I'm not his mother, and he just told me he didn't want a nursemaid.*

As she wiped up the Scotch from the floor, out of the corner of her eye she caught a glimpse of him reaching up to retrieve another bottle. Biting her tongue, she returned to the kitchen and threw the sponge and towel into the sink. Then she brought the plate of assorted hors d'oeuvres to the living room and set it on the white lacquer coffee table, between the sofa and his armchair.

For a while they kept the conversation light, but when Viviana could no longer tolerate the idle chatter, she said, "Earlier, you mentioned that there were more suicides at this time of year than any other. I realize that's true, but seriously, Mitchell, your mind is not going in that direction . . . is it?" As she waited for him to respond, her heart pounded against her chest so violently, she feared he could hear it.

"Me? Suicide?" A frown crossed his brow. "Can't say that I never thought of it in passing, but suicide is a coward's way out. Not that I have anyone who'd give a damn."

"I'd care," Viviana said. And she meant it, even though her thoughts and feelings toward him were vacillating. She found herself leaning first one way and then the other, but she had to admit, he remained an enigma.

Either he hadn't heard her, or his mind was elsewhere. After a long moment, he said, "Nine months ago, when we returned from Europe, I was on top of the world. Mitch was in remission, my business was healthy, and the future looked bright. Now . . . now it's all gone."

Ignoring the personal revelation, she said, "Your organization is still representing Jordon's, isn't it?"

"More or less. It needs more hands-on by me, but I can't seem to muster the motivation." Before Viviana could respond, he dropped his eyes to the floor. "I killed the one person in my life that meant the world to me."

Every nerve in Viviana's body snapped to attention. What he was saying was crazy. He hadn't even been driving the night of the fatal accident. The death of his wife and son—it wasn't his fault.

At least, that's what *Women's Wear Daily* had told the world.

CHAPTER

54

Wainwright slumped down, his elbows resting on the arms of the chair, his hands holding the weight of his head. Viviana's voice seemed far away; he couldn't make out her words. *She doesn't know the truth.* No one knew that he was responsible for Christine driving off the bridge.

He lifted his head, looking into her troubled eyes. "It's true that I wasn't driving. But I was responsible for the accident that killed my son." Her eyes widened, but she remained silent. *How pathetic,* he thought. *I'm fifty-five years old, and I have only Viviana De Mornay to tell my troubles to.* Hardly his idea of a confidante, but . . . what the hell.

"As you know, my son was in remission, but there was always a chance that he'd slip out. That had already happened once, while we were in England."

Viviana nodded, but did not comment.

"If he slipped out of remission again, the doctors said he would need a bone marrow transplant. As you may or may not know, those are hard to come by. Neither Christine nor I was a match. The only way to be absolutely sure that we had that match was to have another child."

"Another child?"

"Yes," he said, ignoring the skepticism in her voice. "But Christine refused to even think about it. She said we were too old."

Without another word, Viviana sank back into the couch and waited for him to go on.

"That was a crock of shit. She was only forty-two, for Christ's sake!" He swallowed hard. "Sorry. But they have ways of testing now, and the age factor is not such a risk. Hell, Anthony Quinn and Strom Thurmond fathered children when they were in their eighties—or pretty damn close.

With women putting off childbirth today while they establish their own careers, it's not unusual for a woman in her late thirties or early forties to want children—and to give birth to healthy children." When Viviana picked up her wine glass and took a sip without comment, he sank back in the chair. Judging from the look she gave him, he realized that she could not relate. She must think he was totally off the wall. He scratched his head, which was starting to ache.

Uncurling her legs on the couch, Viviana swung them to the floor. "Mitchell, I want to continue our talk, but if you will excuse me for just a moment . . . ," she said, and headed out of the room.

Visions of the fateful night returned to Wainwright like a movie filmed through a gauze-covered lens. He had been in meetings with the Jordon's principals until the wee hours of the morning and had gotten less than two hours' sleep the night before. But the school theater performance was one that Mitch had been looking forward to for months. He was in charge of the spotlight, and he'd been practicing in the rehearsals for the past week. The performance had gone off without a hitch. Mitch had done a great job, and to celebrate, they had taken him to Putnam's for a hamburger and milkshake. It was late when his mother drove the three of them home, and Mitch had fallen asleep in the backseat.

Keeping their voices low so as not to awaken their son, they had started in on the same old discussion. Christine's voice was woven with venom when she said, "Neither of us is young. I will not turn my body into a baby machine to produce spare parts for our son. You know how much I love little Mitch, but—"

"Love? Give me a break, Christine. Your protestations of love for our son—you know they don't ring true! You've never shown any real affection for Mitch." He paused. "And stop using the diminutive when you talk about him; he's no goddamned Lilliputian. Give him the dignity he deserves."

Wainwright had been too angry to curb his deep-rooted disgust. He could never fathom how a mother could be so devoid of maternal instincts. Most men complained that they were the ones who felt like the third wheel after they had begun a family. That their wives seemed to give all their love and affection to their offspring, and the husband-fathers had to get in line to get a bit of attention. Well, that was not his experience—not even close. It was Christine who seemed to resent his attention to their son. "You are the most unnatural mother I've ever known."

"That's unfair. I've always been there for lit . . . for Mitch. I've been right beside him for every one of his transfusions and—"

"Of course you have. It wouldn't look right for a child's mother to be missing at those times. But who is it that Mitch calls out to when he needs comfort?"

"Well, can I help it if you've become his hero?"

"It's more than that, my dear." His voice had been laced with sarcasm. "When I have to be away from home, he doesn't call out for his ever-loving mother. He calls out for his nanny or nurse. Never you, my dear." He knew how much the term *my dear* irritated her.

"You son of a bitch." Christine's voice had risen an octave.

"Shhh! You'll wake Mitch," he hissed, and he twisted around to check on his son, who was still sleeping soundly in the backseat. He sure as hell didn't want Mitch to hear any of the conflict. As he turned frontwards, he saw tears running down Christine's cheeks, but he didn't give a damn.

When she spoke again, her voice was almost a whisper. "I've done everything I know how to do to make you happy, but you don't love me. You never loved me. We've seldom even made love since Mitch was diagnosed with leukemia. And yet you want me to manufacture spare parts for him, not because he needs a bone marrow transplant but because he might. You care nothing about the future of the child you want to bring into our lives—or about me."

"Shut the fuck up!" he spat at her. But it was true—he'd stayed with Christine only because she was Mitch's mother. She was his only chance to save his son if, someday, he should need a bone marrow transplant. But the selfish bitch was refusing.

"We don't even know if Mitch will ever require bone marrow," she sniffed. "He's in remission, and for all we know he may be out of the woods. Dr. Wong told us that children are the most resilient for Mitch's type of leukemia."

"I'm not willing to leave it to a hope and a prayer. Apparently you are."

"Mitch is the only one you have ever loved," Christine wailed.

"You've got that right!" When she'd married him, he'd told her that he was incapable of that deep feeling that everyone referred to as "love." And that had been true, until Mitch came along and captured his heart, his soul, and his dreams for the future.

She turned her head to stare at him, tears dripping off her chin. Then, as if in slow motion, his wife had twisted the steering wheel sharply to the left. Wainwright heard the car slam into the rail and felt it roll to the side, and then everything had become dark.

He didn't remember anything from that point onward. He didn't remember going off the low bridge, didn't remember being in the water, didn't remember anything until he'd woken up in the emergency room at Greenwich Hospital. What he did remember, and what would be etched in his memory for all eternity, was the grim face of the doctor who walked in and told him there was nothing he could do for Mrs. Wainwright.

Before he finished that sentence, Wainwright had said through his bloodied face, his teeth clenched in pain, "My . . . son. What about . . . my son?"

"I'm sorry, Mr. Wainwright. There was nothing we could do. Your wife and son both drowned. They were already dead when the truck driver discovered your car."

Mitch and Christine were dead. He was alive. *Why?* "I don't understand. We were all together." *Why was I spared?*

"You were on the opposite side of the car from your wife and son. Apparently, Mr. Wainwright, when the car rolled off the bridge, you were not fully immersed in water right away. Had the truck driver not found you when he did, however, you might also have drowned."

Wainwright wished with all his heart that he had.

Viviana walked back into the living room with a cup of hot coffee for Wainwright, who was still slumped in his chair. *Was he even aware that I left the room?* She refused to discuss what she thought of his desire for Christine to produce another child. *My God, the woman was in her early forties.* Thank God, Philip had not wanted children with her—it had never been an issue between them. The two boys he'd had with his former wife had never been a part of Viviana's life with Philip, and he'd seemed content with their childless life together. If he had wanted her to have children, she would have flatly refused.

Kneeling down in front of Wainwright's chair, Viviana placed a hand on his knee. "Here, drink this." His head shot up. *No doubt about it,* she thought, *he'd forgotten I was even here.*

For a moment or two, it seemed as if he were fighting some unseen demons within him. He said nothing. Finally his eyes focused on her. "Sorry. I was just thinking." He took the coffee. The cup rattled in the saucer, but he picked it up and took a sip, then set it on the floor. "I just can't get past—"

Viviana cut in, not wanting him to go on. "Stop beating yourself up. You were not the cause of your son's death. It was an accident."

"One that I was responsible for, and one I will have to live with for the rest of my life. I should have been the one to die. Not Mitch."

Viviana looked down at the broken man. She was vacillating again, but not for long. She'd had enough of his foolishness. "You're absolutely right. Your son should not have died. But he did." She waited until the impact of those words registered. "That doesn't mean *you* should have died, nor does it entitle you to continue to wallow in self-pity."

Wainwright didn't utter a sound; he just glared at her. Had she slapped him across the face, she would not have been met with a more startled gaze. Before he had a chance to regroup, Viviana continued, "I don't doubt your pain. What you've been through is shattering, but it's been nearly a year. By now you should find comfort in the happy memories your son left behind. From all you tell me, he was a happy, loving son. One who looked up to you, one whom you were able to hold in your arms and who responded to your touch. I bet you even remember his first words and the first time he called you Daddy."

She'd give the universe to have any of those memories of her own son—the son who must remain her secret.

Wainwright continued to stare at her, a flash of anger in his steel-blue eyes. He grabbed his cane and heaved himself to his feet. "What in the hell do you know about losing a child?"

"A lot more than you think," she fired back. "I didn't sprout up in a vegetable garden, you know. I have a family, and I know what's it like to have a child who is unable to communicate or respond to you in any way. There are things that are a helluva lot worse than an instant death."

"You have no idea whatsoever . . ." He stopped midsentence, his eyes following the descent of a small, amber bottle that had spilled from his pocket. It bounced on the floor, landing beside Viviana in her stocking feet. By now she was so angry, her hand shook. She bent down to retrieve the plastic container. Wainwright watched as she raised it, holding it under the dim light of the table lamp beside the couch. Though defiant, he felt a sheepish expression spread across his face.

"First Lortab, now Percocet?" Looking up into his eyes, she spat, "Are you downright suicidal?"

"No, Ms. De Mornay," he said. His voice oozed with sarcasm. "In case I forgot to tell you, I was in a near-fatal accident in which I broke several bones in my right leg. The steel rod in that leg hurts like an S.O.B., especially in this cold weather."

Viviana sucked on her bottom lip, not taking her eyes from his. *Why don't I admit that this visit was a rotten idea? Why don't I just trot right down to my own condo and leave him to his own devices? I'm not Mitchell Wainwright's mother.* But before she finished her thought, she looked down at his outstretched hand and realized something: She'd been trying to reason with a man who was beyond the point of being open to reason. She stepped back, keeping the bottle out of his reach. "Don't you know that the combination of Percocet and booze is deadly?"

"That's really not any of your business. Now give me my goddamn medication. I need it . . . for pain control."

His rationalizations sounded as pathetic as her own must have sounded to Philip after he'd discovered that she hadn't given up amphetamines and quaaludes. *Thank God, I'm no longer dependent on those uppers and downers.* She still had an ample supply, of course, but they were only for the times when she *really* needed them.

She handed Wainwright the bottle. "It's your life. You don't want a nursemaid, and I don't intend to become one—not for you, not for anyone. So, go to it." She marched over to the coat tree and pulled down her sable coat, for a moment mesmerized by the teetering base. Throwing her coat over her arm, without another word, she stormed out.

And a very Merry Christmas to you!

PART THREE: 1994

56

The shrewd, gray eyes of Jordon's CEO Cyril Stein locked momentarily on Mitchell Wainwright, then moved slowly around the management table and rested on his CFO, Brendan Harvey. Stein grabbed his water glass and downed the remaining liquid. "Seven years ago when we sat around this table, we were one hundred percent in tune. Our own in-house buyout was the right action then. Remaining independent is the only prudent action now."

The room fell silent. Stein reached for the pitcher of ice water and refilled his glass. Never before had Wainwright witnessed this outspoken group of savvy merchants and businessmen fail to jump in to fill the silence. Finally Harvey leaned forward, resting his elbows on the table, and appeared ready to respond—but he wasn't quick enough.

Stein slammed down the pitcher. "We all know and respect Mark Toddman. In 1987, his friendship and support paved the way for our victory in snatching Consolidated's West Coast divisions from the clutches of Philip Sloane. But I'll be damned if our repayment for that favor will be surrendering the whole of Jordon's. Toddman's proposal is no more a merger than Sloan's takeover of Consolidated was a healthy downsizing. Don't let the semantics delude you. This so-called merger would be the end of the Jordon's we've dedicated our lives to building."

Clearing his throat, Stein continued. "And I don't mean to downplay Toddman's accomplishments. We can't dismiss the fact that he's set what remains of Consolidated back on track—but that's just one achievement. Collectively, those of us sitting around this table have a hell of a lot more retail expertise. Most of us were part of the retail evolution while Toddman was still in diapers. We can't allow him to call the shots. The collective intelligence in this room is the best barometer for measuring what is in the best interest of Jordon's."

Taking advantage of Stein's momentary silence, Harvey broke in. "We may not have a lot of choice if Consolidated buys up much more of Jordon's outstanding debt."

Stein looked at the CFO as if he'd stabbed him clean through his heart.

Wainwright's mind was in overdrive as he strode unevenly from the conference room. When he used his cane, his limp was less pronounced, but still, it was troublesome. This week's meetings with the Jordon's creditors had not gone well. Instead of running smoothly, as in their initial rounds, they were running into one dead end after another. He was prepared to call in a few favors, but despite his claims back there in the meeting, Cyril Stein, though an experienced and well-respected merchant as well as a competent businessman, was no Mark Toddman.

Now that it was out in the open—that Consolidated's CFO, who had been successful in restructuring and reorganizing some $8 billion of the company's debt, had a plan in motion to buy into Jordon's own considerable debt—Wainwright feared that this was not a game in which the Jordon's executives had what it took to win. Not even if they managed to entice Conrad Taylor to head their West Coast division. Chapter 11 for Jordon's was a blow they were unlikely to survive.

Wainwright nodded to Stein's assistant, who was on the telephone, as he passed her desk on the way to the elevators. She gave him a wave.

The statistics from the *Wall Street Journal* washed across his mind. The lengthy article recapped the results of the mergers, acquisition, and takeover of the 1980s in which, of the fifteen-thousand-plus companies that changed hands, worth about half a trillion dollars in total, a large percentage had not worked out for the workforce, the community, or the shareholders. The article went on to state that more than half had failed, resulting in bankruptcy or liquidation. None of this came as a surprise to Wainwright, of course.

The security guard glanced up from his clipboard as Wainwright approached, and the man climbed down from his high stool to press the elevator button. They exchanged a few words, but his head was filled with thoughts of Cyril Stein and his management group. All had been dedicated and loyal members of the Jordon's team for many years— maybe too many years. When Stein had informed Wainwright that he'd been hot and heavy about pursuing his nemesis, Conrad Taylor, Wainwright had to admit that it was a smart move. It was no secret that Taylor, Toddman's protégée, had earned himself a well-respected place in the retail world. After running his father's investment company for a stint in the late '80s, he had a superior handle on the financial aspects of a leveraged business. Though not yet up to the standards of his mentor, Taylor had become one hell of a merchant.

The elevator doors swished open, and Wainwright stepped in, his mind still filled with the fact that he'd signed on for a battle he had little chance of winning.

Keeping an eye on Callie, Ashleigh spread her blanket between the brookside bench and the elaborate playhouse that stood beneath the giant oak tree on the Toddmans' five-acre estate.

Yesterday April had been quite forthright in letting Ashleigh know that she and her friends had outgrown the playhouse long ago. But today, as Callie's self-appointed babysitter, eleven-year-old April had energetically gathered her old tea set and other paraphernalia and asked if she could take Callie to the playhouse—"The one on the ground," she'd assured Ashleigh. Although April was mature for her age and would begin middle school in September, Ashleigh did not feel comfortable leaving her spunky four-year-old totally in the care of the bright-eyed child, no matter how responsible she was. The rope ladder, with its narrow stepping planks reaching up to the tree house high in the towering oak tree, was just too big a temptation for her curious daughter.

Earlier this morning when Ashleigh had drifted downstairs from her guest room into the kitchen, Wilma had greeted her warmly and offered her a steaming cup of coffee. "Miss Paige told me to tell you that she had to go a meeting this morning, but that she'd return before Mr. Mark and Mr. Conrad finished their game of golf."

Strange, Ashleigh had thought. Paige hadn't mentioned anything about a meeting the night before. But a little alone time sitting in the fresh country air had given her a chance to sort things out in her mind. *Just what the doctor ordered,* she thought now.

An old tune of her grandmother's played through Ashleigh's head as it had so many times since Gran's passing. "What a difference a day makes! Twenty-four little hours . . ." *The story of my life.*

Just two days ago, she and Conrad were discussing a possible move to San Francisco. Now that Conrad had accomplished most of what he'd set out to do for Michael Nason's, he was ready for a larger challenge. He had made a huge ripple in the world of fashion over the last four years, and he was highly visible in the retail community. Known for his level-headed management style and his ability to motivate, as well as to bring profit to the bottom line, he had been wined and dined by one large retailer after another. But the organization that he'd had his eye on was Jordon's—the prestigious retailer that had taken over Consolidated's West Coast stores, where he'd begun his career.

After a few intensive talks with CEO Cyril Stein and various members of his management team, Conrad was entertaining the idea of joining the firm as head of Jordon's West. The contract they offered was enticing, but before accepting, he'd bounced his future plans off Mark. After less than half an hour on the phone with his respected friend and mentor, Conrad had brought his talks with Jordon's to a screeching halt.

The timing couldn't have been better. The Taylors and the Toddmans had made a tradition of getting together for their daughters' August birthdays, and this year, due to a conflict with April's dance team, they were celebrating a week early, so their flight to New York had already been booked for the very next day. Mark had advised Conrad not to take the job with Jordon's until they could meet in person to discuss things. Conrad hadn't known exactly what Mark had in mind, but since his early days in retail, the older man had never misled him. "There is no one more savvy in the world of retail, nor anyone whom I trust more," he'd told Ashleigh. "If he says taking the job with Jordon's would be a big mistake, my gut says to put on the brakes and hear him out."

While she didn't know all the specifics just yet, Ashleigh knew her husband would fill her in as soon as he had the total picture. What was clear to her now, just twenty-four hours later, was that their next destination would not be San Francisco but New York.

Ashleigh was excited about the opportunity to once again be close to Paige, her dearest friend—not least of all so she could host next year's birthday party for once. But the added distance from Charles was a bit of a concern. He was doing quite well for a man of ninety-four, but he was not as steady on his feet, and he complained that his memory was not as good as it once was. She didn't know how much longer this wonderful man might be in her life. If only it were possible to have Charles come to live with them. But she knew there was no point in pursuing that thought—it simply was not an option. Even though most of his close friends had passed away, he would never consider leaving his daughter, Caroline. Diagnosed as paranoid schizophrenic many years before, she had made tremendous progress, having found some meaning in her life through oil painting. But she would live the rest of her days at New Beginnings, a private mental facility in Southern California. Now that Caroline had made peace with her father, Charles would neither abandon her nor risk upsetting her progress by moving her to another facility on the East Coast.

Thundering footfalls, pounding across the bridge a few yards away, pulled Ashleigh from her meandering thoughts. April's friend Madison, breathless from her sprint from the Toddmans' private road beside the house, stopped in front of Ashleigh and flopped down on the blanket. Her cheeks were beet red and her freckles prominent. Ashleigh had become quite fond of April's best friend over the past two years. Callie, of course, was head over heels for both girls.

Like April, Madison greeted her with her honorary name. "Auntie Ashleigh! Where's April?"

"In here, Madison," April called out from the playhouse. After a quick hug for her "aunt," Madison sprang from the ground and joined the girls.

Though she knew Callie loved being the center of attention, Ashleigh wanted the older girls to have time to themselves. She rose to her feet, but before she had a chance to distract her daughter, she heard Paige's high heels clattering over the bridge. She hadn't noticed the Jaguar pull up in the driveway.

"Ashleigh!" Paige cried out as she rushed toward her friend, stopping just inches in front of her. Her face was flushed and her mascara running.

Alarmed, Ashleigh waited for her friend to speak.

"My mother," Paige said breathlessly. "I've found her! I've found my mother!"

Paige drew in a quick breath and sank down on the blanket beside her friend.

Ashleigh said nothing, but tilted her head quizzically.

"No more hiding behind those fictional tales about my youth," Paige said triumphantly. "It's over. Those damnable lies almost destroyed my marriage. Never again."

Ashleigh looked up, shielding her eyes from the glare of the sun. "I've never heard you mention your mother." Although the two women had become very close during their time together in Dallas, Paige's past was something they had never discussed. Through the never-ending retail grapevine, Paige had learned about the plane crash that had killed Ashleigh's parents when she was just a baby. She knew, of course, that her grandmother and Charles Stuart had raised her. Paige had just assumed that her own life story—fictional though it was—must somehow have reached Ashleigh's ears, too. Apparently it had not.

"I told you a few years back that we would get into my 'personal drama' one of these days. Well, no time like the present. I am bursting at the seams. If you hadn't been here, I think I might have boarded the next plane to Dallas!" Other than Mark, Paige could think of no one she'd rather share her news with than Ashleigh. If only the vivacious Sonny were there, instead of off on a fifteen-day Caribbean cruise with Brad, her happiness would be complete.

Ashleigh uncrossed her legs and leaned forward. "Please, Paige, tell me! You seem so excited, I can't wait to hear about it."

"Most likely, you thought my mother was dead."

Ashleigh nodded. "I'm not sure why. I've just never heard you mention anyone other than Mark's mom."

"Well, there's a whole lot you don't know—and not just because we seldom talk about the past." Locking eyes with Ashleigh, she continued, "I've been doing a lot of thinking lately, and as different as you and I are in many respects, I believe we are very much the same in others."

Again, Ashleigh nodded.

"Everything you may know about my life before I met Mark—it's pure fiction." She paused, letting her words sink in. "Fiction of my own making."

Ashleigh's brow was creased in bewilderment, but she said nothing.

"The truth is, I have no idea who my father is, and I was abandoned by my mother. I grew up in one foster home after another, and ended up as a runaway before I turned sixteen." With those words, Paige felt as though a weight was lifted from her soul. She was suddenly free of the burden of guilt that remained from a childhood over which she'd had no control.

"I had no idea." Ashleigh said simply. Her statement expressed surprise but no judgment.

A rush of love for her friend came over Paige. She was so grateful for their mutual trust and the true friendship between them. She laughed when the stunning news at last seemed to hit.

Ashleigh began firing one question after another. "And now you've found your mother? How? Where is she? Have you seen her?"

The questions just kept coming, but Paige didn't mind. She felt nothing but relief. She was finally going to find answers to the questions which had haunted her since she had been abandoned and woken up in a foster home.

Mark dropped his putter back in the bag and climbed into the driver's side of his custom-designed golf cart.

Conrad sat in the passenger seat, lost in thought.

"I realize it's a lot to take in," Mark said, "but we've got our ducks in order. The purchase of Jordon's, with its one hundred twenty-three high-end department stores, will position Consolidated as the largest retailer in the U.S."

A lot to take in! That understatement was like saying that King Kong was a big gorilla. Conrad's brain shifted into high gear even as he sank back in the plush leather seat. He studied Mark, who revved up the motor of the golf cart, and they headed for the locker room.

"Timing couldn't be better," Conrad thought out loud. "A brilliant move in this booming economy." Mark was moving Consolidated in the right direction. Under his leadership, Jordon's was bound to be a profitable addition. Absorbing all the information his friend had made him privy to over the past few days, Conrad shuddered at the thought of how close he'd come to climbing on board Jordon's sinking ship.

"Granted, moving from Michael Nason's in Dallas to join us here in New York—it's a gigantic step," Mark confirmed, slipping the cart into overdrive as they crested a manicured hill. "If I didn't know you were up for the challenge, the offer wouldn't be on the table."

"I appreciate that."

Mark nodded. "You are the right man for the job. And it's the right move for you. One that will position you for the future."

Conrad nodded in return. *No point in hiding my interest. If Mark feels this is the right move, it's the right move.* "So what's the next step?"

Mark pulled into the parking spot in front of the locker room door and turned off the motor. As they unloaded their clubs and walked inside, Mark responded, "Well, are you working with the same group of attorneys?"

Conrad nodded again. He'd learned early in his career that it was unwise to sign any contract without passing it by a trusted team of lawyers.

With complete candor, Mark continued, "Wouldn't expect your attorneys to be any less diligent than my own. They'll ensure that the proper safeguards are in place before you sign a contract. Give me a window of time, and I'll set up a meeting between you and our CFO, Jim Short, to spell out your compensation and all the minutia of the five-year contract. You should have plenty of time to run it by your attorneys."

Conrad was starting to remember how confident he was in the more experienced man's abilities and business sense. Working in tandem again with Mark Toddman was bound to be the smart move. He was comfortable with having his compensation tied to his results. Mark's entrepreneurial environment suited him. That's how he worked best and how he'd always garnered the most from the executives who reported to him. However, there were a lot of details to be hammered out and agreed upon before he signed on the dotted line.

Not least among them were the remaining seven months on his contract with Michael Nason's.

Paige dashed to her room for a quick change of clothes while Ashleigh took Callie to her usual guest room for a nap. Downstairs, Wilma was busily preparing a picnic basket for April and Madison to take out to the treehouse, and a lunch tray for the women to take out to the gazebo.

If only Sonny were here, Paige thought again. Slipping into a lightweight sundress and a pair of sandals, she smiled, thinking of how Sonny's dazzling Irish eyes would twinkle. She could picture him pushing that stubborn lock of flaming red hair from his eyes, sweeping her off her feet and dancing her around the room. *Aye, colleen,* he would say. *That warms the cockles of my heart. So what's the plan? And how can I help?*

Before Ashleigh, Sonny had been her only confident and had seen her through her most trying days. *Thank God, Ashleigh is here and not in Dallas. How wonderful it will be if Mark can convince Conrad to come to New York so they can work together again . . .* Pushing that thought from her mind for the time being, she grabbed her sunglasses and tore down the stairs.

Ashleigh was already in the kitchen with April and Madison, who had picked up the picnic basket and were heading for the door. "Bye," the girls sang out like a duo, swinging the basket between them. Eager to talk with her friend, Paige told Wilma they could manage carrying the tray of sandwiches and iced tea out to the gazebo. Soon the two women followed their daughters out the door with their own lunch.

Once settled in the gazebo, Paige didn't waste a moment. "There is so much I want to tell you." She leaned back into the slant of her Adirondack chair. "Now that I've discovered my mother's whereabouts, I'm not sure what to do. I haven't yet made any contact." She ran her tongue along her lower lip. "Someday I'll tell you all about my own precarious upbringing and being in foster care and how it affected my attitude toward children. Toward having children of my own, that is. But that can wait." *Where to begin?* Paige took a slow drink from her glass of iced tea.

"I guess the best way to bring you into the picture is to tell you that, for as long as I can remember, I wasn't able to conjure up any sort of memory of my mother. But after I met April and her nineteen-year-old mother, my own childhood, which I'd done anything and everything to conceal, began coming back to me like a series of blurred photos. I'd believed that my mother had abandoned me because she didn't want me, that I must have been a horrible, unlovable child. But Patti—April's biological mother—changed my perspective." She hesitated, then clarified. "Patti's love for her child shone in her eyes, which were otherwise . . . just vacant. She loved her daughter and wanted a better life for her than the one she could provide. I hadn't remembered my own mother—couldn't surface a single image.

"But while I was volunteering at the shelter, I began to remember. Little by little, one image and then the next played in my head. Finally my own mother's face materialized in my mind. It wasn't like in the movies, when everything comes back in a blinding flash. It was a slow, agonizing process."

Paige leaned down, absently picked up one of the leaves from a nearby maple tree that had already started to litter the floor of the gazebo, and twirled it by the stem. "Ever since then, I've wondered about her. Wondered if she was still alive . . . if she was married . . . if she had any other children. I wondered . . . if she ever thought about me." She looked down at her uneaten sandwich, but she wasn't hungry, and anyway, she couldn't go on with a full mouth.

"Following the death of Mark's mother and Martha Winslow, what I felt became more than curiosity," she continued. "I don't want April to grow up without a grandmother. I want to give her what I longed for when I was her age. So, since coming back to New York, I began my search in earnest." She took another sip of tea. "Am I boring you out of your skull?" she asked, afraid Ashleigh might tire of her long monologue. But how else could she be sure her friend understood? Ashleigh had to know where Paige was coming from.

"Not at all. Paige, I can't know what you're going through. But I know if . . . if my Cassie ever had a chance to find me, I . . . I would welcome her with open arms, and I would never, *ever* let her go." Ashleigh leaned closer, her eyes full of sincerity. "Please go on."

Needing no more assurance, Paige continued. "After April lost both her real and surrogate grandmothers, my need became an obsession. But I found I had neither the expertise nor the time necessary to track down my missing mother. I ran into nothing but blank walls, so I finally turned to the Landes Agency." Paige shifted in her seat, then explained. "Even though there are plenty of agencies headquartered in New York, I knew Landes had agents here, and I felt more comfortable working—"

"I understand," Ashleigh broke in. "I would have done the same. Conrad has worked with Landes in New York, and they're first-rate. Besides, Landes is on top of every case he takes on."

With no further explanation needed, Paige skipped straight to that morning's meeting. "Well, actually, I haven't been working with his New York crew. Your old teddy bear was dispatched to help me out."

Ashleigh giggled. "Pocino? He's here in New York?"

"He is," Paige confirmed. "He called late last night from Albany and asked me to meet him in the courthouse. What that man lacks in class, he makes up for in spades when it comes to getting the job done. That's who I was meeting with this morning."

"In the city?"

"No, at the Greenwich Courthouse on Field Point Road." But they were getting off track, so Paige leaped ahead in her story to tell Ashleigh about the records he had faxed from the courthouse in Albany. "*He found* her! He actually found my mother. Her name is Helen Sheldon. She's sixty-two years old. Her husband's name is Rupert, and they live in Queens. I have the address and a phone number."

"Are you going to call, or are you going to meet them in person?"

"Yes." Paige felt her heart thudding clear up to her throat. Ashleigh looked at her, puzzled, which made her smile. "I must admit, I have no idea what to do with this information. I don't want to just show up on my mother's doorstep, but I'm afraid that if I call, there's a chance she would either hang up or refuse to see me."

A series of faint lines crossed Ashleigh's forehead. "I understand. You say you don't remember your father, so she must have married or remarried after you were sent to foster care. Are you afraid her husband might not know she had a child before they married?"

She nodded. "Along with the fear of getting the door slammed in my face." She stopped and took a deep breath, nervous about her next words. "Ashleigh, I have something I'd like to ask of you." Unaccustomed as she was to reaching out for help, especially considering the step she was about to take, Paige needed moral support. She could not turn to Mark—not because he was too busy or would be unwilling, but because she knew, in his heart of hearts, he felt she was borrowing trouble and should leave well enough alone. "I'd ask Mark, but . . ." Biting down on her lower lip, she took in a sharp breath, then plunged in. "Would you go with me to Queens?"

"Of course I will, Paige. When are you thinking of going?" Ashleigh said without hesitation.

"Yesterday." Paige grinned. A wave of relief washed over her.

"That's my line. I always want things done yesterday," Ashleigh responded. "Oops! Here comes trouble."

Paige turned to look in the direction of her friend's gaze. Wilma was trudging across the grass, Callie grasping her index finger.

Ashleigh jumped up and hurried across the lawn to her daughter. Just then the hum of Mark's Porsche reached Paige's ears; a moment later, it rounded the curve of their driveway. She strode purposefully toward the car, wondering if Mark had made the job offer official and if Conrad had accepted. Observing their smiling faces as they emerged from the convertible, she assumed all had gone according to plan.

By the time Paige had finished telling her news to Mark, who seemed happy for her despite his own misgivings, Ashleigh had joined Conrad, too. Looking as if he'd won the lottery, he hoisted Callie up on his shoulders and wrapped his arm around his wife's slender waist.

Turning to Paige, Ashleigh said, "It appears that we will be in the market for a new home here in New York quite soon. Any suggestions?"

The delivery truck pulled out from the alley behind De Mornay's just before eight in the morning. Breathless and giddy with excitement, Erica hurriedly unlocked the back door and entered the back room, which was filled with the familiar brown garment boxes. Today she could not wait for the sales support staff to assist her. She grabbed the heavy-duty cutter and dropped down to open the first box. After carefully cutting down the crease beneath the brown package tape, she attempted to pry the box open. Making no headway, she noticed that each end was also taped crosswise. Before slashing impatiently through the remaining tape, she heard heavy footfalls behind her and looked up. Glenn Nelson smiled down on her.

"Just couldn't wait, could you?"

"You knew I couldn't." She checked her watch. "Guess you couldn't either."

Glenn knelt down to help, pulling all four flaps of the box open wide.

Erica began throwing out layers of bubble wrap and tissue. At last she came to her first creation, a gorgeous four-piece suit in an electric blue, which she had designed with trousers as well as a skirt to be worn beneath the hip-length jacket and pale blue silk blouse. The lightweight gabardine that Viviana had suggested was perfect.

Erica inspected the label. Under the sweeping script of the De Mornay's label were her initials. Although minuscule, in lowercase letters, the *ec* nevertheless appeared in gold. A frown clouded Glenn's handsome face as he slipped the jacket onto one of the embossed mahogany hangers that bore the De Mornay's signature. "You don't like it?" she asked in surprise. He had approved the design; otherwise, it would not have made it to production.

"Sensational," he said.

"But . . . ?"

"But nothing. Love it. The color, the design, the fabric. A winning combination."

Looking again at the small initials on the final product, she sensed he was disappointed on her behalf. After all, if not for Glenn, Erica might no longer be at the Fifth Avenue boutique. She'd had been fed up with Viviana taking credit for her designs, and with Mike's encouragement, she'd finally stood up for herself a few weeks back. When she'd confronted Viviana, though, her boss had become irate.

"The De Mornay's label *means something* in the world of fashion." she'd said. "You can't expect to make a name for yourself overnight. You are a talented designer, but until you have a better feel for the fabric and color, your name does not belong on my label."

That night, standing at the door to Viviana's office with her letter of resignation in hand, Erica had heard a cacophony of expletives issued between her two employers as they went head-to-head. She did not hear complete sentences, only snippets—*not ready . . . unknown . . . fabric . . . using her . . . experience . . . rare talent . . . my name on the door . . . find a new partner*—but it was enough for Erica to know that Glenn had taken her side.

She'd left that night without resigning.

The next day, Viviana had called her into her office. "I've been thinking things over," she said. "You are developing nicely, and I'd like to encourage you." That was high praise coming from Viviana. Erica had waited for the other shoe to thud to the floor, but Viviana's codicil was not what she expected or feared.

"Even though you still have a lot to learn, I've decided to add your initials to *my* label. You understand that the De Mornay's label, which is well respected in the industry, will be on all garments that are designed by anyone under this roof. However, your initials will be added to the fashions designed by you." Erica had been stunned into silence.

Taking a break from riffling through the new arrivals, Glenn waved a hand in front of Erica. "Earth to Erica," he joked, then told her, "I spoke with Melissa at Carlingdon's yesterday."

"Yes?" she said expectantly. Glenn had managed to get a few of their designs into the Carlingdon's multidesigner boutique with the approval of Melissa, the buyer. Although he and Viviana were negotiating for their own separate boutique, this was an encouraging beginning.

"She showed me her selections for the Christmas catalog. Two of them are your creations." He arched a blond eyebrow, and with a playful grin he added, "Before having them shipped, maybe you can sew in a small magnifying glass."

Giving him a light swat, Erica sang, "I've only just begun." Though small, her initials now appeared on a very classy label. It was a start. And if Carlingdon's added a De Mornay's boutique, her world would surely expand.

Terrence laboriously made his way through the bumper-to-bumper traffic on the Avenue of the Americas. Easing the limo to the curb in front of Consolidated's merchandising offices, he ignored the usual cacophony of idling engines and blasting car horns.

Mark Toddman leaned forward. "After you pick up the dry cleaning, please, wait for Mr. Taylor's call early this afternoon, and then pick me up at five thirty. We'll both be returning to Greenwich tonight."

"Yes, sir," Terrence said.

Conrad broke in. "No need to return for me before then, Terrence. I have plenty to keep me busy—if Mark can simply lend me a spare corner and a phone line . . . ?"

"Not a problem." As Conrad opened the door and stepped onto the sidewalk, Mark turned his attention back to Terrence. "We'll both be ready at five thirty, then. Thanks." He swung the door shut and followed the newest Consolidated executive into the merchandising offices.

Passing the reception desk, Mark stopped to introduce Conrad to the portly security guard. "Jack, this is Conrad Taylor. He'll be coming on board in a few weeks as our vice president of merchandising." Jack extended his beefy hand, his sausage-shaped fingers grasping Conrad's uncalloused ones with the force of a steel vise. "Jack has been with this organization since I was a trainee."

After the men exchanged greetings, Mark and Conrad headed for the elevators. Mark pushed the UP button before turning in the direction of rapidly pounding footfalls. Jim Short was dashing toward them. The elevator doors slid open and the three men stepped inside.

"Good timing." Mark said. "Conrad Taylor, this is our CFO, Jim Short." The two men shook hands, and Mark continued, "My assistant scheduled a time for you to go over the preliminary details of Conrad's contract, following our brief staff meeting this morning. You can schedule a mutually convenient time as soon as possible to meet with the attorneys to hammer out the specifics."

Jim and Conrad fell into easy conversation, further convincing Mark that he'd made the right choice. When his own five-year contract came to an end, he would be up for a new challenge, and Conrad would again be ready to step in—heir apparent to the Consolidated empire.

Like clockwork, the executives filed into the conference room a good five minutes before the scheduled meeting.

Conrad glanced around the table. He knew all the merchants and would make it his business to get to know the others. If they sat around this table, the individuals in charge of sales promotion, fashion merchandising, operations, and personnel were bound to be first-class. He knew this without a shadow of a doubt. Mark always surrounded himself with the best executives he could find in the retail community and beyond. Then, unlike many top executives, he allowed those he'd chosen to do their jobs in their own style. He was no micromanager. His staff had a great deal of freedom, yet they also had accountability. Conrad liked that about working with Mark.

As the door closed behind them, Mark began his introduction. "The purpose of today's meeting is twofold. First, for those of you who do not already know him, I'd like you to meet Conrad Taylor. Conrad will fill a newly created and much-needed hole in our organization as vice president of merchandising. He is no stranger to the retail industry. He's well grounded and has excellent credentials. As many of you already know, Conrad began as a trainee at Bentley's and rose to the position of president of the department store division, with twenty-six locations. I served as CEO during that same period, and I couldn't have asked for a more intuitive merchant and business partner than Conrad." Mark clapped a hand on his friend's shoulder. "He currently serves as CEO and president of Michael Nason's. However, he will be coming on board with Consolidated in mid-September. He comes to us with the entrepreneurial approach to business that I admire in each and every one of you seated at this table."

One by one, Mark went around the table, introducing each of his key executives. Conrad did his best to remember all the names. Not until all the introductions had been made did Mark slip into the chair at the head of the table. He poured himself a glass of water, took a quick swig, and then began the second part of the meeting with a question.

"What's wrong with the retail business?" He did not wait for a response to his rhetorical question. "Everyone's got a theory. A survey of American buyers published in yesterday's *Wall Street Journal* is something every retailer should take note of. It seems that shopping has become such an unpleasant experience that people hate browsing in stores more than doing household chores. They complain of the ordeal of making a purchase, of poor sales help, low-quality merchandise, sky-high prices. Our consumers are too stressed to enjoy shopping. Instead of helping customers escape from these pressures, department stores have made things even harder. When our customers must endure clogged elevators and encounters with an uninformed and unmotivated sales staff, the magic evaporates."

Making direct eye contact with each of his executives, the CEO continued, "It wasn't so long ago that the great department stores of our nation offered a unique experience. Now they are vulnerable." Holding up the fingers of one hand, he began ticking off the casualties with the index finger of the other. "B. Altman's is gone. Buffum's is gone. Gimbel's is gone. Saks was sold. Bonwit's has closed most of its stores . . ."

Conrad had heard Mark discuss his retail philosophy countless times over the years, but he never failed to learn something new.

"As we all know, after their management-led leverage buyout, Jordon's became engulfed in debt. Jim Short's plan to buy into their debt is not only good for us; it will be the salvation of Jordon's, one of the nation's most beloved retail entities. We are now in the driver's seat and have overcome the initial objections of Jordon's board. You heard it here first: Cyril Stein, who remains unconvinced of the wisdom of this merger, has tendered his resignation. It's now a go, a win-win situation for Consolidated and Jordon's." Mark smiled as the room exploded in applause.

And it's about time, he added to himself.

The morning passed in a haze of activity. All the extra time Ashleigh had thought she had was gone now. It was nearly ten, and with Paige keyed up for their trip to Queens, she knew she had to get going. She slipped on a pair of sandals, ran the brush through her hair, and then dashed down the stairs in search of Callie.

At the door to the kitchen, she ran straight into Wilma, who was balancing a white lacquered tray on which sat two glasses of milk and two sliced apples. Answering Ashleigh's unasked question, Wilma pointed with her head to the side door. "April and Callie are out on the veranda. And Miss Paige has gone to get the car."

After giving the girls a parting hug, Ashleigh slid into the passenger seat of the Jaguar. Paige waved good-bye to their daughters, who now stood beside Wilma on the lawn. Ashleigh sat back, wondering what was going though Paige's head as she drove down the sloping path and nosed onto Bedford Road, heading south. Most likely, she was rehearsing what she planned to say to her mother. Ashleigh tried to put herself in her friend's shoes. *What must it have been like to have been abandoned when she was no older than Callie's tender age?* The thought saddened her, and she thought again of her own missing daughter.

Catching her totally off guard, Paige said, "Now that there's nothing left to tell you about my life—past, present, or future—I believe it's my turn to be on the listening end."

Ashleigh shrugged. "There's really not much you don't know."

Paige turned right onto King Street, then gave her passenger a penetrating stare. "How about your plans for a large family?" She reached over to squeeze Ashleigh's hand. "I've been walking on eggshells about that question since the kidnapping, but . . ."

Ashleigh leaned her head back against the headrest. "Callie was never meant to be an only child, and I don't want her to be one. Neither does Conrad. But as you know, right after Cassie was taken from us, I wasn't ready. It felt like I'd be giving up on her ever being returned to us. But now . . . That was a long time ago." She sighed before continuing, "For months now, we've been going through all the suggested routines, followed all the advice for conception, but I haven't gotten pregnant again. I'm ready to explore adoption." She paused. "As you say, biological birth is overrated, and I only have to look at you and April for validation. But Conrad feels it's too soon to consider that route, and he has a good point. Our doctors have found no medical reason that either of us is unable to have another child. Conrad wants to keep trying."

"Well, that's not all bad." Paige gave a raised eyebrow and ran her tongue across her top lip.

Ashleigh returned her smile and added, "I'm afraid it's taken a lot of the spontaneity out of our lovemaking."

Paige didn't respond right away; instead, she concentrated on merging onto the highway. She drove along for a while as the two friends caught up on this and that. At the Hutchinson River Parkway exit, a grin spread across her face. "On the way back home, let's take a detour into Manhattan and slip into the lingerie department at Carlingdon's. Their buyer came from Bergdorf's and has a knack for selecting sexy pieces—tasteful, though!—to spice up any bedroom."

Ashleigh laughed. "Leave it to you to be thinking about my predicament rather than your own." Noticing her friend's flushed cheeks, she asked the question she knew had been hanging between them all morning: "Paige, do you know what you're going to say when your mother comes to the door?"

Paige had been asking herself the same question all morning.

Paige turned onto Sixty-eighth Avenue and looked to the right and left, trying to see the numbers along the row of modest houses. The first one to her right was number 130.

"Next block," Ashleigh said. "It should be on that side." She pointed to the left.

On the corner of the next block, Paige spotted 141 and pulled up to the curb directly across the street. Her heartbeat felt erratic, and she found herself holding her breath. Traffic hadn't been heavy, and they were here ahead of the predicted schedule. *Now what?*

Paige realized that she hadn't heard a single word that Ashleigh had just spoken. "Sorry. What did you say?"

"Would you like me to wait in the car or to go up to the door with you?"

For a few awkward seconds, silence settled between them. Paige couldn't believe that she hadn't thought this part through. She wanted Ashleigh with her, and yet she sensed that this was something she must do alone.

Ashleigh was the first to break the silence. "I think it's best for you to meet your mother on your own."

With nails biting into the palms of her hands, Paige nodded and threw open the door. The unpretentious, Tudor-style house appeared neat and clean. The flower beds in front were filled with a variety of colorful flowers. On her way up the walk, Paige rehearsed her lines, praying that she would not be rejected—again—by the woman who'd given birth to her.

The dark mahogany door had a semicircle of beveled glass above a big brass knocker in the shape of an eagle. To her right was a small brass ring with a white button doorbell. Paige pushed the button and waited.

The door cracked open for an instant, then swung wide. A slender, balding man with rounded shoulders stared out at her. He was no more than five-foot-eight. Despite the heat, he wore wool trousers, along with a white button-down shirt and a pair of brown Florsheim shoes. But even more than his attire, Paige noticed the expression on his face.

His mouth had literally dropped open.

"Is this the home of Helen Sheldon?" Paige asked.

The man nodded and stepped back. "Oh my God. Oh my God," he repeated.

Baffled, all Paige could manage was to stare back at the man. He looked as if he'd seen a ghost.

"Debbie?" he asked.

Paige froze in stunned silence. She'd been called by that name when she was a child. At sixteen she had run away from her last foster home. Mature for her age, she had renamed herself and claimed to be eighteen in order to escape being found and returned to foster care.

"I remember being called Debbie when I was a little girl and in foster care."

"Oh my God," he said again. "You're Helen's daughter."

For an airless few seconds, Paige felt weightless. He hadn't asked who she was. He knew. *But how?*

The man blinked, and as if he'd just been awakened from a deep sleep, he lifted his hands to his cheeks and shook his head slowly back and forth. Eventually pulling himself together, he said, "I am Rupert Sheldon. Please forgive me." He took a deep breath. "It was such a shock when I opened that door. My mind tumbled backwards to the first time I saw Hel—your mother. You look . . . just like her."

"Is she here?"

He nodded, his brow a mass of corrugated lines. "She's asleep upstairs. But please, come in and sit down. We need to talk."

Paige surreptitiously glanced down at her watch. It wasn't quite noon. "Is she . . . ill?"

"Please sit down, Deb—" He broke off. "No, that's wrong. What should I call you?"

Paige stretched out her hand. "Paige Toddman." As Rupert Sheldon took her hand and gave it a squeeze, she felt foolish for being so formal.

"Please come in and sit down," he repeated.

Paige's mind shot to Ashleigh, who was outside in the car. "I have a friend who is waiting in the car."

"By all means, invite her in. It's supposed to reach the high eighties or even ninety today, and this humidity is a killer."

Paige thanked the man, who obviously knew a lot more about her than she would have imagined. She turned and ran down the steps and across to the car.

Ashleigh had left the door open, hoping to catch a bit of the nonexistent breeze. Knowing that she'd have some time on her own, she had brought a novel with her. But in this heat, even Barbara Taylor Bradford's *Woman of Substance,* in which she'd been totally engrossed the night before, couldn't distract her. She looked up at the sound of Paige's rapid footsteps.

"Come in the house."

Ashleigh protested. As hot as it was out in the car, she didn't think she belonged inside during this reunion.

"Ashleigh, please. I don't know what to think. Apparently, Rupert, my mother's husband, knew all about me. Said I looked just like her."

"And your mother?"

"I haven't seen her yet. Rupert said she's asleep, and he wants to talk to me. I think she may be sick. Possibly very sick."

"Why don't I wait in the car then, Paige?"

Paige shook her head, her short locks bouncing easily back into place. "It may take a while, and Rupert seems very friendly. He's got to be a lot older than my mother. He's sort of wizened and quite bent over— but not in the least bit intimidating. Anyway, he invited you to come in. Besides, it's hotter than Hades out here, and I don't want to be accused of manslaughter."

Ashleigh followed Paige inside, and after a brief introduction, Rupert led them through the kitchen to the breakfast nook in the far corner at the back of the house. There was a musty odor that Ashleigh associated with the nursing homes she'd visited while doing community service in college. Rupert gestured them toward the rectangular oak table that had built-in seats in an L shape against the walls.

As they took their places on the bench seat, Ashleigh noticed that the inside of the house was not nearly as pristine as the outside. The older gentleman must have just wiped off the table, because it was still damp.

On the kitchen counter, there were three tall glasses filled with ice. A pitcher stood beside a vase filled with half a dozen red roses. She caught no scent of roses, only a stale odor of food, which came from the open trashcan at the end of the counter. Without asking, Rupert poured the tea and brought the first two glasses to the table, before returning for his own and a plate of Oreo cookies. The glasses and the plate appeared clean, and so did the kitchen counter, but everything else seemed to be covered in a layer of dust.

Rupert pulled up a chair to the end of the table. "Bon appétit," he said kindly.

Paige didn't waste any time. "Is my mother sick?"

Rupert slumped back in his chair. He began chewing on his bottom lip. Paige leaned forward, but the old man just stared up at the ceiling for an agonizing moment. "Yes, Paige, your mother is ill." His face was etched in sorrow, and his voice was unsteady. "I'm sorry to have to tell you that a couple of years ago, Helen was diagnosed with Alzheimer's."

No, that can't be true. Paige's brain was churning. She couldn't wrap her mind around the word *Alzheimer's*. That was something to fear in old age. A couple of years ago her mother would have barely reached sixty.

The frail old man reached out for Paige's hand and gave it a gentle squeeze. "I know," he said, reading her thoughts. "It is rare at her age, but not unprecedented."

Paige gripped the edge of the table as the old man's words washed over her.

"In my support group," Rupert went on, "there is a young woman with three children whose husband is only forty-five. He became afflicted with Alzheimer's when he was only thirty-nine." Rupert took a long swig of his iced tea. "But it is rare in those under seventy, although not as rare as the uninformed think."

"How bad is it?" Paige's eyes held steady on Rupert, who seemed to be folding in on himself. She reached out and touched his shoulder.

Rupert sat up taller, lifted his chin, and did the best he could to straighten his shoulders. His eyes were brimming with tears. He wiped them away with the back of his hand. Then, after taking in a deep breath, he spoke in a strong voice. "She still has some very good days."

"Does she recognize you?"

"Oh, yes. Always." He paused, then with a wistful look, he said, "It should have been me. Oh God, how I wish that I'd been the one! That Helen had been spared."

Paige didn't know what to say. She had been thinking the same thing. The man must be nearly eighty—but maybe those stooped shoulders and thin body just made him appear older.

"I'm nearly ten years older than your mother," he said in answer to her unspoken question. Shaking his head, he repeated, "It shouldn't have been Helen."

Paige quickly did the math. Rupert was only seventy-two. "How long have you and my mother been married?" But before he had a chance to answer, she asked, "Do you have any children?"

"Our thirtieth anniversary was yesterday." He gestured to the red roses on the kitchen counter. "Your mother loves roses." He inhaled and then continued. "And no, Helen and I did not have any children. We wanted them, but it just didn't happen. You are Helen's only child." He paused as if to let that sink in. Paige was grateful. "I'm curious how you managed to locate us after all these years, and I will tell you whatever it is you want to know about your mother." He locked his eyes with hers. "She felt that losing you was the biggest mistake of her entire life."

Paige straightened, her posture ramrod-straight. "Mr. Sheldon," she said with authority, "my mother did not *lose* me. She gave me away."

Rupert took his time before answering. He crossed his arms in front of him, rested them on the table, and leaned toward Paige.

Paige wanted to ease away, gain a bit of her own space, but she did not.

Her mother's husband cleared his throat, and then cleared it again. "You appear to be a bright young lady," he said, his voice now barely above a whisper. "You must know that things are not always as they appear. Your mother was not even fifteen years old when you were born. She loved you with all of her young heart, and the last thing in the world she desired was to lose you. But she was terribly young and unable to take care of you." Again, the gravelly-voiced man cleared his throat.

Paige shook her head slowly, thinking impatiently, *I didn't come here for platitudes.* She knew how young her mother had been. It was all in the records Pocino had uncovered. Next Rupert would tell her that her mother had wanted a better life for her than the one she could provide. Wasn't that what they all claimed? A thought skipped through her mind. *That's what Patti had wanted for April.* And yet, couldn't it also be the God's honest truth?

"Paige, I understand your feelings," said Rupert. "Truly, I do. But please hear me out. Let me take you back to the Halloween night of 1946. Your mother, as well as you, became the victims of that fateful night."

Adjusting her position on the bench, Paige sat back, ready to listen to what Rupert had to say. As long as it didn't begin with *It was a dark and stormy night,* she'd try to be a good listener. She had no choice but to pay attention. It seemed that Rupert Sheldon might be her only window into the past.

"Helen was in her first year of high school. At that time, high school began in the tenth grade, not the ninth as it does now in most states." He shook his head. "Your mom told me she had her first boyfriend that year, but your grandparents didn't approve of them spending time alone."

And rightly so, Paige thought, as April and her birth mother shot to mind.

"Anyway, to make a long story short, your mother lied to her parents and told them she was going out trick-or-treating with her girlfriends. Instead, she snuck off to meet this boy, Bobby, who had asked her to go with him to a Halloween party with a group of his friends. He was a football star and one of the most popular guys at school. She said she was not only thrilled but also flattered that she was the one he asked. 'I was young and dumb,' she told me.

"So, against her parent's wishes, she met up with the boy a block from her house. Instead of taking her to a party, he took her to the neighborhood park. He'd brought along a couple of bottles of soda and some chips and suggested they have their own party. Your mom got scared and said she had to go home, but Bobby wouldn't let her go. As she told me, the story went like this: 'He jerked me off my feet, and I fell down to the ground. I must have passed out, because the next thing I remembered was waking up in the park all by myself, with my . . . my panties around my ankles. I felt a big knot on the side of my head, so I must have hit my head on something when I fell, or maybe he hit me. I don't really know, but I remember there was a broken Coke bottle behind me when I finally staggered to my feet.' "

As Rupert continued his tale, all Paige could think of were those vulnerable teenage years. How helpless her mother must have been! She too had been vulnerable at that age. She thought of how rapidly April was approaching her teen years.

Again doing the math, Paige calculated that her mother must have given her up when she was about eighteen. But she hadn't married Rupert until she was much older. "When did you come into my mother's life?"

"I was a professor of business law at LaGuardia Community College when I first met Helen."

Paige was taken aback. "My mother went to college?"

Following the brief staff meeting, Mark spent the better part of the morning strolling through Carlingdon's. He loved talking with sales associates and area managers, loved listening to customer comments. More could be learned through observing the heartbeat of the store than from any of those damned statistical printouts, no matter how sophisticated.

When Mark saw Mitchell Wainwright, he was approaching at a rapid pace, his cane tapping lightly on the marble floor. He'd been expecting a call from Wainwright now that the merger with Jordon's had been set in motion.

The two men greeted each other cordially. Mark noticed that Wainwright was casting an appraising eye around the store.

"Nice to see Carlingdon's returning to its former glory," Wainwright said, moving his cane in a circular motion in a gesture that encompassed their surroundings.

Mark nodded, but made no comment. He was weighing the plusses and minuses of bringing Wainwright onto his team. The man was smart as hell and well connected in the world of finance, but rumors of his drinking and drug use troubled Mark. Yet the Jordon's outfit still thought highly of his expertise, so perhaps those rumors were gross exaggerations.

Wainwright asked, "Is it true that you plan to enter Jordon's and Carlingdon's into the Mall of America in Minneapolis?"

"Don't believe everything you hear. We're a long way from making that kind of decision." Although the seeds had been sown for a $100 million expansion in North America, Mark was not about to go forward before slating renovations for existing stores that had fallen into disrepair in the wake of the cost-cutting effects of Chapter 11. Wrapping up their conversation, he said, "Give my best to Viviana."

Wainwright grinned. "Will do."

As Mark headed over to the handbags department, he registered surprise that Wainwright hadn't asked for a meeting. A puzzled frown crossed his face. *Maybe he isn't interested in jumping onto my team again.*

Wainwright's liaison with Viviana De Mornay was even more puzzling. Generally, in Mark's estimate, men fell for the same kind of woman time and time again. Apparently, Mitchell Wainwright was the exception. Although Mark hadn't known Wainwright during his brief engagement to Ashleigh, he did know that she was the polar opposite of Viviana. Both were beautiful women who turned heads whenever they entered a room, but the similarity stopped there. He had no idea what Wainwright's first wife had been like, but Mark had met his second, Christine. Not to speak ill of the dead, but she'd appeared cold and somewhat officious with anyone but her husband. And although Christine could be attractive, she couldn't hold a candle to either Ashleigh or Viviana.

Passing through shelf after shelf of designer purses and shoulder bags in suede, leather, and luxurious fabrics, Mark continued to toss the issue back and forth in his mind. Wainwright remained an enigma. *But if those rumors of his instability prove false, maybe I'll set up a meeting after all.*

But what if those rumors proved true? Mark stopped dead in his tracks. *Could Wainwright be behind the abduction of the Taylors' twin? Could he have been seeking revenge for Ashleigh's desertion by turning her life upside down?*

CHAPTER
67

Rupert seemed pleased and proud when he said, "Yes, your mother worked very hard to get herself an education. And lucky for me, because LaGuardia is indeed where we met. But we are jumping too far ahead. To really understand your mother and the frightened young girl she was back then, I need to tell you more about what happened to her after she was raped in that park." He picked up the pitcher and refilled all three glasses, then said, "You girls must be hungry. Can I fix you a sandwich?"

Both Ashleigh and Paige declined. They spoke in unison, sounding like an out-of-tune duet.

"I'm not much in the kitchen, but I have some tuna salad that I mixed right before you got here. I'm ready to eat and would love to have you join me."

Paige did not want him to interrupt his story, but it was after noon and she could hardly ask him to put off his own lunch any longer.

"Okay, I'll take half a sandwich, thank you."

Ashleigh repositioned herself on the bench and made eye contact with Paige. "Actually, Paige, would you mind if I left you two alone for a bit? I saw a drugstore before we turned into the neighborhood, and there are a few things I'd like to pick up—if you don't mind me taking the car."

"Of course," Paige said, knowing that Ashleigh had no urgent business in the drugstore. Perhaps the thought of witnessing a mother-and-child reunion was just too much for her, considering her own loss.

"Would you like to take a sandwich with you?" Rupert offered.

"Thank you," Ashleigh said. "If you don't mind, I'll take Paige's other half."

The two women gave each other a hug. Ashleigh thanked Rupert, and she was on her way.

"Seems like a nice young woman," Rupert remarked as Ashleigh made her way to the front door. Almost simultaneously, the cat door leading to the small backyard opened, and a white, long-haired cat crept silently into the kitchen.

Paige smiled and dropped back down on the bench. "I couldn't ask for a better friend."

Rupert picked up the cat. "I'm afraid your friend felt a bit like a voyeur, but I understand you needing a bit of moral support, stepping into the unknown as you've done today."

Paige nodded. "I regret putting her in that position, but I must admit that this is one of those rare occasions when I was a bit of a coward. I knew my mother had a husband, but I had no idea what you might be like or if you even knew about me."

Momentarily embarrassed that the conversation was focused on him, Rupert said, "This is Opal, by the way. She has been with us since before your mother was diagnosed, and she is a great comfort to both of us." He stroked the cat before setting her on the floor again.

Opal looked up at Paige with huge, crystal blue eyes. She seemed to be appraising the woman, and then she settled herself at the foot of her master's straight-back chair.

"Let's see. Where was I?" Rupert began. Then, without hesitation, he resumed his story. "Oh, yes. After the . . . the rape. That Halloween night, when your mother returned home, she told no one what had happened to her. It was still quite early when she slipped in the house through the back door. No one heard her come in. She told me she went to her bedroom and took off her clothes, then went straight to the adjoining washroom and scrubbed her body over and over again. It wasn't long before Helen's parents discovered that she had returned home very early, before Halloween night had even really begun. She told them she was sick, and she went immediately to bed. After that night, Helen told me, she never had a full night's sleep."

An involuntary shiver crawled up Paige's arms. She had not had a full night's sleep for years after her mother had abandoned her.

"Evidently school became hell for her after that night. That bastard Bobby—" He broke off. "Sorry for the profanity, but Bobby, the big football hero, was a real shit. He began spreading rumors about your mother. Posted her name and phone number in all the men's johns. It didn't take long before your mother's reputation was ruined. Then she found out she was pregnant.

"By then, she felt she couldn't tell her parents the truth. She had buried herself in one lie after another. Your grandparents were the strictest of Baptists and had no tolerance for an unwed mother's lies and even less for a liar." An enormous cloud of déjà vu descended upon Paige. "Oh my God. I guess the apple doesn't fall far from the tree," she said.

Rupert's bushy eyebrows rose above his heavily lidded eyes. "What was that?"

Until she saw his expression, Paige hadn't realized she'd spoken the old idiom out loud—it must have just popped out. In answer to his expectant look, she said, "I just realized that I'd unknowingly followed in my mother's footsteps."

"Meaning . . . ?"

Paige shrugged. "It's not important. At least, not now. I want to know all you can tell me about my mother." She didn't want him to get sidetracked. He didn't need to know about the unending stream of lies she'd woven together to create the fiction of her childhood—lies that had nearly unraveled the fabric of her life.

Rupert picked up Opal and began stroking her as he told how the teenaged Helen's parents had cast her out of their home when her pregnancy began to show. As his tale unfolded, Paige longed to see her mother, to speak with her, to be recognized by her. She hoped she wasn't too late.

"Don't think for one minute that you were ever forgotten. That's just not true. Finding you and getting you back was your mother's obsession. Every step she took was with that goal in mind."

To Paige, however, those words did not ring true. "Until recently, I might not have understood the circumstances that led my mother to place me in a foster home. But a few years ago, I had an eye-opening experience." She leaned forward. "You see, I have an adopted daughter. Her name is April. I worked with her biological mother, and I know how much that woman loved her little girl. But she found herself in a similar situation to the one you describe." Her voice hardened. "What I can't understand is, if my mother was so desperate to get me back, why she didn't do so."

"Paige." Rupert's voice was taut, his eyes pleading. "Please try to understand. Things were different at that time. Helen did not want to put you in foster care, but she was without means to provide for you. She was a beautiful woman, and there was no shortage of men offering to take care of her, but she'd had a couple of bad experiences . . ."

When the old man's voice began to fade, Paige did not hesitate. "Did one of them try to . . . molest me?" It wasn't really a question. She wondered how much Rupert knew. Could he confirm what she'd tried to string together, her vague memories of the time leading up to her placement in foster care?

He nodded slowly, his head dropping into his bony hands.

Unconsciously, Paige traced the thin scars that circled her wrists. Her stomach turned in a slow-motion cartwheel.

Quickly regaining his composure, Rupert looked up and continued. "There were very few programs that Helen could turn to in those days for help, and knowing how proud she is, she probably would have refused them anyway. She was bright and determined, but she had no money and no support of any kind. She got two jobs, one at the local cleaners and the other at a convenience store, and lived in a room at the YMCA while she got her GED, which thankfully was a new option available at the time. Then she set out to get a college education. She saved every penny that was not needed for necessities. She worked for the day that she could get you back and support the two of you without having to rely on any man.

"I met your mom when she enrolled in my business and general law classes during her first year at LaGuardia. She was eager to learn and asked all kinds of questions. She focused on her rights as a mother of a child who had been taken into foster care. I was drawn to your mother from the first day I laid eyes upon her." Rupert licked his dry lips as he arranged and rearranged the salt and pepper shakers around the napkin holder. With a faraway look in his eyes, he appeared almost to have gone back in time. Opal pawed at his sleeve, and once again he began to stroke her.

Paige heard the hum of the refrigerator in tune with the purr of the cat as she waited for Rupert to go on. After what seemed like an eternity, he said, "Helen was in her early twenties, and I was thirty-two. At first our relationship was strictly that of teacher and student, and I think that's what made her feel safe. But we soon became close friends, and I became her confidant. She told me all about you. She missed you so much and was so proud of you. Said she loved to color with you and boasted that you could color within the lines and that you were talking in whole sentences before you were even two years old."

Coloring within the lines, coloring within the lines. Images of Snow White and the Seven Dwarfs flashed before Paige's eyes. The memory was so vivid, she felt as though she could reach out and touch it. "I remember," she said, her voice a whisper.

Rupert's face lit up. There were flecks of gold in his hazel eyes and his body seemed to relax. "I can hardly wait for Helen to wake up. You might be just what the doctor ordered."

Paige's mind churned. Taking a deep breath, she began peppering him with questions. "What kind of things does she remember? Do you think she'll remember she had a daughter? Won't seeing a grown woman claiming to be her daughter be a shock to her?"

"I think perhaps I need to explain your mother's condition. Helen was a very bright woman. She hasn't suddenly lost all that intelligence. Alzheimer's doesn't fit under one overall umbrella. Short-term memory is the first thing to go, but long-term memories are retained for a very long time with some of the victims of this atrocious disease."

With the sudden sound of footfalls overhead, Opal leapt from the old man's lap and headed for the staircase. Rupert followed the cat with his eyes and patted Paige's arm with a thin, shaky hand.

Rising, he told her, "Be back in just a few moments. I'd like to prepare your mother."

Paige felt as if her heart had stopped beating. One of Mark's common phrases played in her head: *Be careful what you wish for.*

Rupert held on to the banister, careful not to trip over Opal, who clung close to his pant legs. Breathing hard, he wondered how long he'd be able to manage these stairs.

"Rupert," his wife called. He quickened his pace.

Helen sat on the side of the bed, her eyes brimming with tears. "Oh, Rupert," she wailed. "I've had an accident." She swiped at the tears as they streaked her cheeks.

Rupert bent down and wrapped his arms around Helen's trembling body. The bed was soaked and so was she. The room reeked of urine.

"It's okay, pet. Accidents happen to all of us." Only last week at her doctor's office, he'd been given a referral to a urologist. There might be a physical cause for Helen's incontinence. He hoped that was the case. It would be wonderful if a simple operation could free her of this indignity.

She stared back at him with those still-brilliant green eyes. The deep green, now damp with fresh tears, touched him clear to his soul. Until today, he'd never seen another set of eyes to equal them. But downstairs, the woman who was the spitting image of his wife in her younger days shared an identical pair, and they too sparkled like emeralds.

With her head bent, her eyes focused on the floor, Helen said, "This is so humiliating. I hate being such a burden."

"You could never be a burden to me," he said kindly. But the truth was, as much as he adored his wife, he feared that the day when he'd no longer have the strength to take care of her might not be too far in the future. He worried about what would happen to her when he was no longer around. She was younger than most Alzheimer's patients, and much of her mind was still intact. She would hate being in one of those long-term facilities.

There were days when she was like she'd been years before. While those times were occurring further and further apart, Helen was still a remarkable lady. She was not in denial about her illness, as so many were, but she hated her inability to take care of herself. She knew that she was slipping, and that was the real hell of it. With so many Alzheimer's patients, denial and lack of awareness served as a protection.

Meanwhile, Helen felt every loss: the loss of her memories and, each day, the loss of a little more of her dignity.

Downstairs, needing to keep busy, Paige had cleared the table and washed the few lunch dishes, and she was wiping off the counters when she heard the light tread descending the staircase. She dashed across the room and slid into the bench seat. Her heart raced. *What has Rupert told my mother? How does she feel about me finding her? Is she in any condition to understand?* Those and countless other questions swam in her brain.

Helen Sheldon was a petite woman. She wore a bright aqua dress that zipped up the front. Her salt-and-pepper hair was short and wavy. Her eyes, the mirror images of Paige's own, held an inner glow. They did not possess that dull, vacant aura that Paige had expected.

Rather than introducing the two women to each other, Rupert stood still, nervously observing them. Paige didn't know how to begin, and she prayed that the old man would pop out of his trance. The woman who was her mother stood less than two yards away, staring at her, a benevolent smile on her unlined face.

Slipping his arm around Helen's waist, finally Rupert addressed Paige. "I've told Helen that I have a wonderful surprise for her."

Paige's heart thudded to her toes, and she felt heat rise throughout her entire body. Hadn't he prepared her for their meeting while he was upstairs? He had certainly been up there long enough. *But what was*

*he thinking? How could he just spring a long-lost daughter on this ill
woman with no preparation?*

"When I told Helen that you had found us, she gave me that special
smile she has, the kind of smile that comes from her heart. One that I
haven't seen in a long time."

"Rupert," Helen said firmly, though she looked baffled, "I'm right
here. Please don't speak about me like I'm in another room." Then, turning to Paige, she said, "Rupert said that you were Debbie, but I don't see
how you can be."

Paige was blown off course. The woman seemed quite rational,
though perhaps her illness had led her to expect the little girl she'd been
forced to give up. "Well, that was my name when I was a child. That's
what all my foster families called me. When I grew older, I took the
name Paige."

Helen looked to Rupert for support. "I don't understand. We tried to
find my little girl, but the records had been destroyed. A fire had burned
down the entire block where the social services building stood." Helen
slid into the far end of the booth.

Paige felt as if she were on a roller coaster. The highs and lows of the
day boggled her mind. This woman seemed no more a victim of Alzheimer's than she herself was. She didn't know what to call this woman whom
she knew to be her mother, so she just plunged in.

"I have done a great deal of research," she said, "and you are the
mother I have been searching for. When I discovered that the social services building had burned down, I almost gave up. But I hired an investigator, and he found out that duplicate records were kept in the state
capital, in Albany."

Rupert took hold of both of Helen's hands. She looked dazed, blinking as she tried to take it in. "Just look at her, pet. She looks just like
you. She even has your heart-breaker eyes."

Helen slid closer to Paige and ran her finger across her cheek. Tears
filled her eyes, and when she spoke her voice shook. "Dear God," she
said, "if this is a dream, don't let me wake up."

After spending an hour or so at the local Barnes & Noble, Ashleigh returned to Helen Sheldon's neighborhood. Pulling up to the curb, she shifted the Jaguar into park, flicked off the ignition, then reached for the car phone and dialed the Greenwich number.

Paige's personal secretary answered the phone. Before Ashleigh could ask about Callie, Anna said, "I'm so glad you called. We tried the car phone but couldn't reach you."

Ashleigh's heart pounded against her chest. "Is Callie—"

"Callie is fine. Ashleigh, I'm afraid it's . . . it's your grandfather."

Oh, no, not Charles, her heart cried out. "What's wrong? Is he alright?" *Is he alive?* Closing her eyes momentarily, she prayed that whatever was wrong, it wasn't serious.

"I'm afraid he has pneumonia."

"Is he in the hospital?"

"I don't think so. Conrad asked that you call him on the car phone in the Lincoln." She gave Ashleigh the number.

Before calling Conrad, she dialed the Stuart resident to check on Charles's condition, but all she got was a busy tone humming in her ear. Next she called the number Anna had given her.

Conrad answered on the first ring. Before Ashleigh could say more than a few words, he told her how sorry he was about this turn of events and explained that plans to get them to Long Beach were currently being made. His voice crackling above background noise, he said, "Mark's assistant is checking on flights. Get back to you within the next fifteen minutes, sweetheart."

Next Ashleigh again dialed the Stuart residence. Elizabeth picked up on the first ring.

Without any greeting, Ashleigh said, "Has Charles been taken to the hospital?"

"Oh, Ashleigh. I was so worried when I wasn't able to reach you." After a shallow intake of breath, she continued, "No. Mr. Charles is here in the house, with twenty-four-hour care."

Ashleigh sighed with relief. *Thank God, he hasn't been taken to the hospital. He would hate that.* "How is he?"

"He's very weak. He told me not to bother you, but—"

"You did the right thing, Elizabeth, and I appreciate it. We will be there as soon as we can arrange a flight."

After chatting briefly with Elizabeth about what had brought on Charles's condition and what the doctor's prognosis was, Ashleigh bade her good-bye. Not knowing if her husband had tried to call while she was on the phone, she called him again. Conrad picked up and went straight into their agenda. "We have a flight direct to Long Beach at four fifteen. I'm on my way back to Greenwich now with Terrence. Wilma is packing our bags and getting Callie ready. We'll meet you at the airport."

Ashleigh's head spun. "What time is it?"

"It's just after one. You have plenty of time. Would you like me to have a car sent, or could Paige take you?" Then without a pause, he told her, "JFK is probably less than half an hour away depending on where you are in Queens, and provided you don't hit traffic."

"I'll call you back after I talk with Paige."

70

Charles awoke with a start. His room was dark, and he was in a narrow hospital bed. It took a few minutes before he was able to reorient himself.

"May I get you anything, Mr. Stuart?" said a voice from across the room.

Charles turned his head and squinted his eyes. He saw that sunlight was trying to get in through the slim parting of the drapes. He took in the shape of a heavyset woman in a white nurse's uniform.

"Yes. Please open the drapes. What time is it?"

She began opening the drapes, then looked down at her watch. "It's nine twenty."

The bright sun was blinding, and it took a few minutes for his eyes to adjust. He looked around, relieved to find that he was in his master bedroom and not some hospital room. Other than his usual king-size bed, everything seemed to be the same. But it was well past the time he should be up and dressed.

Charles fumbled for the button on the side of the narrow bed, then pressed it until he was upright. Slowly, he shifted his legs over the side.

In an instant, the nurse was beside him, breathing heavily. "Mr. Stuart. You can't get out of bed."

He looked at her intently. "Excuse me?"

"It's doctor's orders."

Charles smiled. "Miss . . ." He paused, looking at her nameplate. "Miss Johnson. I would like to thank you for your services, but you can let the doctor know that I will no longer be in need of extra nursing care."

"But Mr. Stuart . . ."

"Please get Elizabeth." His voice was soft but commanding.

But Elizabeth, whose sixth sense was strong when it came to Charles, was already at the bedroom door. "Mr. Charles?" She stepped inside.

Charles smiled. "Just who I wanted to see. Would you please tell the staff of nurses who have been floating in and out of here that we will no longer be needing them?"

"Are you sure?" Her expression was filled with concern.

"Yes." *God bless her.* How he appreciated the fact that while Elizabeth occasionally made suggestions, she never actually challenged his decisions. While she walked the nurse downstairs, he slipped off the bed and pushed his feet into his soft leather slippers. His legs felt unstable, and he found he had to hold on to the end table to steady himself. Inch by inch, he made his way into the walk-in closet.

"Mr. Charles?" Elizabeth called out once more.

"In here."

She came to the closet door and shook her head in wonder. "How are you feeling?"

"Good," he lied, knowing that she would see through his bravado. He smiled at her and amended his statement. "Better."

She smiled back. "Would you like me to lay out your clothes?"

"Yes, please," he said, making his way back to the side of his bed.

After Elizabeth left, he set about dressing himself. Today he found the task a formidable one. He was as fragile as a newborn kitten. *But as long as I remain here on this Earth, I will not lie in bed or slop around in slippers and a robe,* he told himself as he pushed his feet into his shoes. He'd had a good life. He did not fear death; what he feared was illness. Disablement. Indignity.

He looked up and saw Elizabeth walk into the room with a hot cup of tea. "Elizabeth, I know I asked you not to call Ashleigh, but—"

"She's already on her way."

Paige waited impatiently outside the car, anxious to have her best friend meet her mother. Perhaps she would think, as Paige did, the diagnosis of Alzheimer's could be a mistake. But when Ashleigh finally returned the phone to the console and threw open the car door, her pained expression put Paige on full alert.

"What's wrong?"

"It's Charles. He has pneumonia. We have a four fifteen flight out of JFK to Long Beach. Conrad can send a car for me." The staccato rhythm of her statements did not mask the tremor in her voice.

A vision of Charles Stuart at his ninetieth birthday celebration—four years ago, just before the twins had been born—flashed in Paige's head. The stately nonagenarian defied his age. He stood straight and tall, in full possession of all the considerable mental astuteness that had made him somewhat of a legend in the world of retail. "I'm so very sorry, Ashleigh. Is he in the hospital?"

Ashleigh shook her head.

"I pray with all my heart that he will recover." Paige glanced down at her Piaget watch. "We have a good three hours, which is more than enough time even if we run into traffic. I'll drive you to the airport, but first I'd like you to meet my . . . to meet Helen." She just couldn't say *mother*. It was all so new.

"You're sure you don't mind?"

"Of course not. Besides, it will give us time to talk."

Ashleigh followed Paige up the walk beside the neatly manicured flower beds. Rupert stood just inside the open door, a broad smile lighting up his thin face. "Please come in, Ashleigh. Helen is in the living room."

"I'm afraid we can't stay," Paige apologized. "Ashleigh has a family emergency, but I wanted her to meet Helen."

A series of deep wrinkles spread across his forehead, and his eyes flickered to Ashleigh. "I hope it's nothing too serious." Then his eyes returned to Paige nervously. "You will come back, won't you?" His voice was etched in uncertainty. Instead of waiting for a response, he continued to make his case. "Your visit has done Helen so much good. I haven't seen her this happy for months." He glanced toward the living room and added, "Actually, not for many years—maybe not ever."

Paige spoke in a comforting tone. "Of course I will come back, but we really can't stay more than a few more moments now." She had taken just one step toward the living room when Rupert's hand shot out and grasped her forearm. "Paige. Do you think you could . . . call her 'Mother'?" There was such an air of pleading in his voice that she couldn't refuse.

In the living room, Helen sat on the well-worn print sofa, Opal purring contentedly on her lap. Gripping Ashleigh's hand, Paige stepped up to the sofa and cleared her throat. "Mother," she said, "I'd like you to meet my good friend, Ashleigh Taylor."

Ashleigh was taken aback by the eyes that met hers. There was no mistaking that Paige had indeed found her mother.

"I'm delighted to meet you." Helen said, the cat spilling to the floor as she scrambled to her feet and walked toward Ashleigh.

They chatted for a few moments. Helen Sheldon was utterly charming. Her conversation was not in the least bit repetitious. As far as Ashleigh could see, Helen showed no signs of dementia.

Paige finally drew their first encounter to a close. "We really must go, but I'll come back next week if you'd like."

"Very much," Helen and Rupert said simultaneously.

"You've made me so happy," Helen continued, pulling Paige into a hug. "I had given up hope that we would ever find you." Her eyes sparkled brightly, and her voice was filled with so much emotion, it brought tears to Ashleigh's eyes.

Helen released Paige and stepped back, including Ashleigh in her gaze. "I'd like to invite you both to dinner, but I just can't seem to manage in the kitchen anymore. There are so many things to remember, and my memory is no longer very good."

Paige smiled and said she understood. As they walked away from the Sheldons' house, Ashleigh knew that—dinner or no—Paige and her mother would now have the chance to make new memories together. And she knew her friend deserved that chance.

Charles sat at the rolltop desk in his master bedroom. A *Barron's* magazine was spread open before him. When the words began to blur, he rubbed his eyes and tried to refocus. But his interest had waned, and he found he no longer had any desire whatsoever to read.

Through the bay window, he focused on the rising sun in the distance, the radiance of the orange sky nearly blinding him. With an overwhelming feeling that he was not alone, he turned his head quickly and looked toward the open doorway, expecting to see Elizabeth. But no one was there.

"I must be imagining things," Charles said out loud, then laughed. "I'm also talking to myself." He lifted his eyes skyward. *I pray to God I'm not getting senile now that I'm nearing the end.* He peered at the clock on the bedside table; his family would soon be here. Ashleigh, little Callie, and Conrad. And Caroline. *God bless her and keep her safe and well.* He paused as the sadness washed over him. *And our little Cassie, too.*

At the thought of his loving family, a smile of great pleasure softened the corners of his mouth. Rising, he hobbled on unsteady legs over to his bed, sank down, and slowly lifted one leg and then the other on top of the covers. Laying his head back against the pillows, he closed his eyes and imagined he felt his precious Louise beside him. He tried to shut the rest of the world out, but a radiant light penetrated through the thin skin of his old eyelids. Shielding his eyes with his arm, he turned from the brightness.

When he again opened his eyes, they rested on the framed photographs on the cherrywood dresser across from him. In sterling silver and gold frames sitting side by side, all the well-loved faces stared back at him. Lately, they'd haunted his dreams and remained with him during his waking hours, their voices strong and vibrant. They were as real to him now as when they were alive and he could reach out and touch them. He knew he was now ready. It was time for him to join those loved ones for eternity, those who had gone before him. *My beloved Louise. My brothers, Jim and David. Dear, sweet Mary. John Bentley. Walter Winslow* . . .

Memories of years gone by rushed at him with a force and clarity that stunned him. Engulfed in nostalgia, he reached for the framed picture of Louise on his bedside table. *Louise, my one true love.* Smiling to himself, he looked down into her lovely face and pressed the picture to his heart. *I'm ready. We'll soon be together again, my love.*

After a few moments of gazing at her photograph, he set it beside him on the bed, leaned his head back against the pillow, and allowed his eyes to again close. A feeling of warmth spread through his body, and he was filled with a sense of peace and happiness like he had never known before—had never even known existed.

He felt drowsy and enervated, and yet he also felt stronger than ever before. Gradually, he became aware that Louise was there in the room beside him. *She* was the presence he had felt earlier. Now she walked toward him, growing nearer and nearer. She was young, so very young. Her angelic face smiled down at him, her soft, brown eyes wide and translucent, dancing, spilling over with love.

Her arms opened and reached out to him, and he knew his time on Earth was nearly done. It was time for him to be with the love of his life. They had waited such a long, long time. He longed to be with her for now and forever. But first he must say good-bye to his loved ones still here on Earth. To Ashleigh, to Callie, to . . .

That night, when the Taylors arrived at the Stuart residence, they were greeted by Elizabeth, who was dressed in a lightweight jacket and held a set of car keys in her hand.

After a round of hugs, Elizabeth informed them, "I think Mr. Charles is resting, but go right on up. Miss Caroline is in the living room, and I have to run down to the drugstore, but I'll be right back."

Conrad unbuckled Callie's seat belt and told Elizabeth that he'd go to the drugstore for her, if she could keep an eye on Callie.

"You're sure you don't mind?" Elizabeth said, a warm smile on her worried face as she already started to reach for Callie's hand.

"Not at all. Just tell me what you need."

She told him, then accompanied Ashleigh and Callie into the house. Stopping in the kitchen, she said to them, "I'll be right with you."

Caroline, seated in one of the armchairs and sipping a cup of tea, looked up and greeted Ashleigh and Callie as they drifted into the living room.

Ashleigh went straight to Charles's daughter and gave her a hug, but Callie hung back, always a bit shy with those whom she didn't know well. Ashleigh was about to ask Caroline about her father when they heard a sudden *thump*! from above. For a moment, Ashleigh and Caroline stood frozen in place. They first looked at each other, then dashed up the stairs toward the master bedroom. Callie, on her short little legs, trailed not far behind.

Ashleigh looked at Charles, who lay motionless against the pillows. Then her eyes were drawn to the photograph of her grandmother, the one he most treasured. The frame lay on the hardwood floor beside his bed, the glass shattered into numerous shards. She placed a calming hand on Caroline's arm, then gazed down at Charles's peaceful face with apprehension. *This man has given me so much. My appreciation of beauty, my values, my entire moral fiber.*

Callie tugged at her mother's skirt, making her presence known. "Why is Grandpa sleeping?"

Scooping her daughter up in her arms, Ashleigh whispered, "Grandpa is very tired. He needs to rest."

Caroline sighed with relief at her words. "He's just napping. He's going to be alright, isn't he?"

Ashleigh bent down, picked up her grandmother's photograph, and returned it to the bedside table, where it had been for the past ten years. With her foot, she swiped the glass into a pile before turning her attention back to Charles.

She watched the shallowness of his breath and noted his pale lips and the chalky pallor of his skin. Uncontrollably, her mouth began to tremble.

She wasn't certain how much she should share with Caroline, and wondered if she were really as stable as Charles and Elizabeth believed she was. Was Charles's daughter strong enough to know the truth? But in a blink, Ashleigh realized that she did not have the strength to lie, and she couldn't give Caroline false hope.

"I'm afraid not, Caroline."

Caroline's face went rigid, and Ashleigh caught a glimmer of something that might be anger flash across her face an instant before her eyes welled with tears. "No, no! I can't lose him now. Not now. He's all I have! I was a rotten, evil daughter. I took from him what meant the most to him in the whole, wide world." Her remorse was genuine over the part she and her malevolent husband had played in Charles losing Bentley's and Bentleys Royale to Consolidated all those years ago. "I'm just beginning to make up to him for all the wicked things I did. Please, call his doctor! You can't let him die." Her voice was just above a whisper.

Ashleigh's throat constricted and tears rolled down her cheeks. She dabbed them away with an unsteady hand. "It's too late, Caroline. I'm afraid he doesn't have long."

Elizabeth dashed into the kitchen at the sound of Conrad's voice calling his wife's name softly. He was closing the back door as silently as possible.

"She's upstairs with Mr. Charles. Miss Caroline and Callie are with her," Elizabeth told him in a hushed tone.

He handed her the bag of prescription bottles he'd picked up from the nearby Naples Pharmacy and asked, "Any change?"

Before Elizabeth could respond, Callie ran in and said in a serious voice, "Mommy wants you to come upstairs."

Ashleigh knelt down beside the bed. "Charles. It's me, Ashleigh," she said softly, taking his cold, damp hand in hers. "Caroline is here too."

With effort, Charles lifted his eyelids. Instantly, his face lit up. "I waited for you, darling girl. And Callie. Where is she?" His voice was frail, fading.

Ashleigh sensed Caroline stiffening. She looked up.

Caroline's glance fell on her for just a moment before she walked to the other side of the bed and took hold of Charles's other hand. "I'm here, Daddy. It's me, your daughter, Caroline."

Conrad walked through the doorway with Callie in his arms, Elizabeth a step behind them.

"Hi, Grandpa," Callie called out, her voice soft and sweet. Conrad placed her on the narrow bed beside Charles, whose eyes had once again closed. At the sound of the little voice, he opened them instantly and straightened up with a small burst of energy.

He stared directly into Ashleigh's tear-stained face. His voice was weak but crystal clear. "Don't weep for me. I've had a wonderful life and I love you all so very much." His eyes touched on each of them. "No one could have been more blessed. Do not let your hearts ache for me. You have made my life full and worthwhile. Love and take care of each other, and be happy for me. Now I'm free. I will be with my sweet Louise and the others—the loved ones who are waiting for me."

Callie leaned over and kissed Charles on his pale cheek.

Conrad stood behind Ashleigh. He lay his hand gently on her shoulder, and Ashleigh released Charles's hand to reach up and touch her husband's.

Charles's mouth turned up in a radiant smile. He ran his finger across Callie's baby-soft cheek and gave Caroline's hand a gentle squeeze. Then, exhausted, he sank back against the pillow. His eyelids drooped closed.

The grief-filled room was silent. Conrad scooped his daughter into his arms, and she threw her arms around his neck and buried her face, sensing that something bad was about to happen.

Suddenly, Charles opened his eyes again. He smiled at Ashleigh and then at Callie and Caroline and mouthed a kiss to them all. His eyes swept around the room, taking in Conrad and Elizabeth as well, and his face glowed with a warm luster. His hazel eyes were bright and shining, and he seemed somehow youthful, shining with an inner light as he stared off into the distance, to someplace and someone only he could see. "Yes," he said. "It's time."

As he closed his eyes, Charles's expression was one of pure rapture. His hands went limp.

"Daddy, Daddy! Don't go! I love you so much," Caroline sobbed as if her heart would break. Her body shook as she leaned over and began kissing her father's face, squeezing his lifeless hand.

Elizabeth stepped forward and helped Caroline to her feet.

With tears trickling down her face, Ashleigh whispered, "He's at peace." She leaned down over her grandfather, kissing him on his forehead and his cheek. "I'll never forget you. As long as I am alive, you will live on in my heart."

Later that night, after they had tucked Callie in, Ashleigh sat down on the sofa beside Conrad. An enormous feeling of relief washed over him. He wrapped his arms around her and felt her relax and lean against him. She made no sound, but he knew she had finally let go when he felt her tremble with silent sobs. As they sat in companionable silence, he thought of all she had been through and wished he could do something—anything—to ease her pain. She had been a tower of strength as they'd witnessed Charles's passing, holding everything back so she could support the rest of the family. The only evidence of her great sorrow had been her tear-stained face.

Knowing how deeply she felt about this wonderful man, Conrad did his best to control his own frustration. It had taken every ounce of his will. If only she would allow him to share some of the load! But it seemed that Ashleigh felt compelled to attend to each and every detail herself. She had gone from one thing to the next like an automaton, doing what little she could tonight and making copious notes on what she must attend to in the morning.

Earlier, as Ashleigh was putting Callie to bed, he was almost brought to tears himself. Ashleigh had sat on the bed beside their little daughter, attempting to tell her about heaven, but it was beyond the little girl's understanding. "Why was Grandpa so tired?" she'd asked, followed quickly by a curious tilt of her head. "Did he stay up past his bedtime?"

He saw Ashleigh's abrupt intake of breath, her full lower lip quivering as she sucked it in, but when she answered, her voice was rock-steady. "No, darling. Grandpa did not stay up too late, but you are right. He was very, very tired. He loves you very much, but he had to leave us."

"He can't go to the park with us tomorrow?" Callie asked, with the hallmark innocence of childhood.

Ashleigh blinked and looked away for just a second or so, then said, "No, precious. He is in heaven now with your great-grandmother and all his other loved ones."

"But why can't he be with us? We have fun together, and he likes to play with me." She stopped short.

Ashleigh wrapped her arms around Callie and whispered into her hair, "He stayed with us as long as he could, and now it is time for him to go to heaven. Although we will all miss Grandpa very much, we must feel happy for him. He has left us with so many wonderful memories of our time together. He will always be in our hearts. He has gone to a place where he will be forever young, and he will never feel pain or be tired again."

Callie's expression revealed that she was deep in thought. "Grandpa likes playing blocks. Do they have blocks in heaven?"

"I'm sure they do, my precious girl."

Conrad's gaze did not drift from the scene between mother and child. He noticed the instant that Callie, who had been fighting sleep for the last several minutes, lost her battle. He'd stepped forward when he saw her eyelids close one last time and kissed her gently on the cheek. Then he tucked her into bed and wrapped his arm around his wife.

Ashleigh wiped her eyes with the tissues bunched in her hand and shifted on the sofa. With an almost imperceptible breath, she seemed once again to take control of her emotions. She looked up at her husband with moist, brown eyes and asked, "What would you think about having Caroline leave New Beginnings and coming to live here?"

Conrad stared at her in stunned silence.

"Please, love. Hear me out. This isn't something that just popped into my head."

"But Caroline—"

"Please." Ashleigh squeezed his hand. "I've been thinking about it for a long time. I love this house, but without Charles . . ." She swallowed, waited for a moment, and began again. "We have no need of this house, and Caroline has been doing so well for the past four years. . ." She felt Conrad stiffen beside her, but he held his tongue, so she went on. "I'm thinking of Elizabeth as well as Caroline. This could be an deal situation for both of them. Caroline would be able to enjoy her father's home rather than being confined to an institution, and she would have Elizabeth—"

Conrad gripped both of her hands and broke in. "Darling, you aren't thinking straight right now." Quickly, he added, "And that is understandable. But while she may be doing considerably better, Caroline was diagnosed as a paranoid schizophrenic."

"I understand that, but haven't you seen how—"

Again, Conrad cut in. "Tonight, what I saw upstairs . . . She is barely in control of her emotions. At one point I saw a flicker of something, something very like pure malevolence, cast in your direction."

She too had seen that flash of anger. But she was also aware of how close Caroline had finally become to her father and how devastating it must be for her to lose him. "The fact that she's jealous of my relationship with her father is hardly abnormal."

"She might be related by blood, but you were the light of Charles's life. You have been the one who—"

"As you said, Caroline was a paranoid schizophrenic for most of her adult life. She was not responsible for her actions. But talk about malevolence! Morris Sandler was evil personified." Although she had met Caroline's husband only once, she'd recognized him for what he was—a sociopath if she'd ever seen one. "His influence turned her against her father. And her embittered, alcoholic mother greatly exacerbated Caroline's problems.

"I realize that Caroline is no John Forbes Nash, Jr., but she has come such a long way. With great passion and the support of a loved one, Nash proved that it was possible to overcome the symptoms of paranoid schizophrenia. Caroline's passion is her art, and with the success of her oil paintings, she seems to have found meaning in her life. Of course, she would need to continue with her psychologist, but Elizabeth is very responsible and could see to that."

Conrad rose. "I don't know. It's one hell of a risk." Then her husband was silent for what seemed an eternity. He stood statue still, his jaw rigid and his fists balled.

"What is it?"

"Caroline . . . her jealousy . . . She may be paranoid, but she's not lacking in intelligence. She knew of your premature delivery . . . What better motive could anyone have for kidnapping a child?"

Curled in Conrad's arms early that morning, Ashleigh had miraculously drifted into a deep sleep—one that unfortunately lasted less than two hours. With so many thoughts churning in her head, it was impossible to get back to sleep. *Can Caroline be behind our baby's abduction? But how?* She might have had the motive, but as far as Ashleigh knew, Caroline never had the means. She would have had to pay someone to commit this sort of crime, and Ashleigh knew she didn't have those kind of finances available. No, Caroline might be troubled, but she was not a criminal.

After another hour or so of tossing and turning, she felt utterly wiped out. She slid out of bed, careful not to awaken her husband. Picking up her slippers, she silently padded to the bathroom to retrieve her lightweight cotton robe from the hook on the inside of the door.

It was only eight fifteen. Too early to call Forest Lawn to schedule an appointment.

She wandered into Callie's room and found her rosy-cheeked daughter sound asleep, her blond hair splayed across her pink pillowcase. She leaned down, giving Callie a light kiss on her plump cheek. Callie shifted on the bed but did not awaken.

Ashleigh heard the rush of water, followed by light footsteps moving across the tiled kitchen floor. But despite the signs of Elizabeth bustling about below, she felt totally alone. Charles was no longer here. She felt the pain of losing him as she stood in the open doorway of his bedroom. For just an instant, she thought of going downstairs for a cup of coffee, but something drew her inside Charles's bedroom instead.

She looked around the room, murmuring a private farewell. The only sounds to be heard in the quiet Naples cul-de-sac were the gentle chirping of the birds right outside his windows, perched on the bird feeder in the planter box. Her eye fell on the photographs lined up along his dresser. She picked up the picture she loved most, the one of Gran and Charles in the center of the dance floor, with the Les Brown orchestra in the background. *Charles and Gran are in loving company. Be happy,* she told herself, blinking back tears. Instantly, she felt a warm glow throughout her body. She knew they were together and at peace. Charles had waited such a long, long time to be with his "sweet Louise." As those thoughts traveled through her mind, she knew that now she could begin to compose his eulogy.

Mike Christonelli slammed down the phone. "Goddamn son of a bitch," he murmured between gritted teeth.

Marnie's head shot up from the blocks that had held her attention for the past twenty minutes.

"Sorry, pumpkin." Mike smiled down at her and placed another block on top of her haphazard stack, then fingered through the Rolodex and picked up the phone. When the receptionist at Carlingdon's administrative offices answered, he gave his name and asked for Shirley Niquist. He was put straight through to the vice president of sales promotion.

"Shirley," he began. "I am so sorry, but I'll need to reschedule today's meeting. I just got word that my sister-in-law is tied up at the boutique, and I don't have a sitter for my niece, Marnie." He felt like a fool.

"Mike, I really need to see you today. Don't worry about the child. Bring her with you."

He hesitated. "Are you sure?"

"Yes. Judy thinks we need two pages added to the website, but Lloyd and I think we can accomplish it all on one, and we want to maintain the simplicity of your original design." Mike had met during the planning stages with Lloyd Wilcox, Carlingdon's director of advertising, and Judy Ware, the vice president of fashion merchandising. Both were tops in their respective fields, but they were not always on the same page. The supporter of cost-effective advertising often clashed with the detail-oriented fashion maven and her "vision."

"Okay, then," Mike said, pleased. "See you in a little while."

April and Madison stood at the cosmetics counter at Carlingdon's, inspecting the MAC face bronzer that the sales associate handed to Madison. "Are you sure this is the shade Miss Alison asked us to get for the dance competition?" Madison asked.

April nodded and handed the sales associate the card her mother had given her, indicating that she had an employee discount and the note giving her permission to use the account.

"Are you sure this will be okay with your parents?"

"Of course it is. It doesn't make any sense to get it at the MAC store, since I get the discount here. You paid for Caitlin's birthday present, so we'll just add the two together and I'll pay you the difference."

"Okay," Madison said. Then pointing toward the escalator, she cried out. "Hey, there's Callie! I thought you said her grandfather was sick, and she went with her parents to California yesterday?"

"She did."

"But there she is," Madison repeated.

April looked in the direction her friend was pointing and spotted Callie. She was heading toward the escalator, holding on to the hand of a dark-haired man April did not know. *But how did she get back to New York?*

"Callie!" April cried out. The little girl did not turn at the sound of her name. She and the man just kept walking toward the escalator. April raced to the escalator.

Callie and the man were already nearing the second floor. Flinging herself onto the moving staircase, April ran up the left-hand side and passed the two people ahead of her. At the top, she saw Callie and the man get on the next escalator, heading to the third floor. She was right behind them. "Callie!" she cried out once more.

Finally, the man turned toward April, a puzzled expression spreading across his face. "Were you talking to me?"

"No . . . I . . . ," April started and stopped. *What's wrong with her?* They had reached the third level and stepped off the escalator. She blinked and studied every feature of the child. It was Callie. But she was looking at April as if she had no idea who she was. "Callie?" April said in the very softest of tones.

The girl just stared at her, not uttering a single word.

"Is Callie the name of a child you're looking for?" the man asked April as he raised an inquisitive brow.

"Yes. Isn't . . . isn't this Callie?" But the child's eyes showed no sign of recognition. Her only reaction was a slight quiver in her lower lip.

"No," the man said. "Is your Callie lost?"

At that moment, Madison arrived. Short of breath, "Hi, Callie," she said. "I thought—"

Marnie began to cry and raised her arms to be picked up.

The man scooped her up and said, "This is my niece. She is not the child you are looking for. I suggest you call security to help you. Please don't upset her further, or I'll call them myself." He walked away without looking back.

April stood with her arms akimbo and her mouth open wide. "Did you hear what he said to me?"

"Guess he doesn't know who your dad is." Madison snickered as the little girl and the man disappeared around the corner.

April didn't move. It was as if she were rooted to that spot. *Something isn't right here.*

Suddenly, she knew. "Madison, Madison!" she cried out. "If that's not Callie, it's her twin. We've found Callie's twin!" She could hardly contain her excitement. Running to the nearest sales associate, she tugged on the woman's sleeve and said, "Call security . . . please! There's a kidnapper in the store."

"Excuse me?" the gray-haired associate said.

"A kidnapper. Don't let him get away!" April pleaded. "Please! Please hurry."

"Did you actually see someone kidnapping a child?" she asked, her brow creasing in a worried frown.

"Not today," April said. "It was four years ago, but the little girl he kidnapped has a twin, and we just saw the kidnapped twin."

"How can you be sure?" The woman looked skeptical.

"Please call security." If the lady kept asking questions like this, the man would get away. "Look, I know what I'm saying! I'm April Toddman. Mark Toddman is my dad, and he's the boss of your boss, Mr. Bradley. Mr. Bradley knows me. You can call and ask him, but please call security first. The man is getting away!"

The sales associate eyed them with curiosity, but picked up the phone. "This is Virginia Fletcher. Would you please page security to the St. John boutique?"

Almost immediately, they heard the sound of the pager. Two short bongs, a pause, and a single bong. The two-one signal continued for a few moments, then stopped. April's eyes darted all around. The man was gone. She wanted to run after him. How much longer could she just stand there and wait for security while the man who took baby Cassie was getting away? But finally, a plainclothes security agent walked into the department.

"Mr. Telford," Virginia said, "these girls want to report what they say is a kidnapping that happened a long time ago."

"A kidnapping. A long time ago." The man looked puzzled. "Young ladies, I am not a policeman. You need to report—"

Shaking her head, April said, "You don't understand. We just saw the kidnapper and the twin he stole four years ago. I know the twin who wasn't stolen, and I *know* the little girl we saw was her missing twin."

Virginia cut in. "Mr. Telford, this is Mr. Toddman's daughter. Perhaps you should call her father."

Marnie had fallen asleep in Mike's arms just before he'd boarded the crowded subway. The ride from Lexington to the stop closest to their walkup apartment was a relatively short one, but hanging on to the pole with the deadweight of the small child was a challenge. The heat of the tightly packed bodies was oppressive, and he nearly gagged from the strong body odor of the obese woman beside him, who held on to an overhead bar.

Glad to climb out from the underground station, Mike breathed in some fresh air. When the apartment building came into site, however, he began to dread the hike up three flights of stairs in the intense humidity. He cheered himself with the memory that the meeting at Carlingdon's had gone well. He was filled with new ideas he was eager to test out on his computer.

"Where have you been?" Erica asked when he stepped into the apartment. She kissed Marnie on top of her sweat-dampened hair and took her from Mike's arms. "I was worried. You didn't leave a note." Her tone was accusatory.

"No time for any note. I told you I had an important meeting at Carlingdon's today. Bill couldn't look after Marnie, so I had to take her with me."

Erica blinked. "Oh, Mike, I really am sorry."

His face softened. Erica was under enough pressure working for an egomaniac like Viviana De Mornay. "Not a problem. As it turned out, the VP of sales promotion has a secretary whose daughter is about the same age. The secretary fell in love with Marnie and entertained her while we had our meeting."

Marnie lay heavily against her mother's shoulder, still sound asleep. Erica took the few steps into the living room to lay her on the sofa. "The meeting went well." It wasn't a question.

He raised an eyebrow. "That fly on the wall. Was it you after all?"

Erica smiled. "You and Mario shared those expressive Italian genes. You're an open book. All I have to do is look at you to know how your day has gone."

"Well, you're right. The meeting was terrific. I can't wait to get started." He headed for the computer, but stopped midstride and turned back around. "Something very bizarre happened today in Carlingdon's. You know they say all of us have a clone somewhere? Well, Marnie was mistaken for hers today."

Erica took in a breath. The room swirled around her. She staggered to the sofa and dropped down. "What do you mean, Marnie's . . . clone?"

"Well, I didn't actually *see* the child," Mike answered. "But a young girl at the department store was convinced that Marnie was her. She said that the child looked identical to Marnie."

"I don't understand." Despite the heat, Erica felt icy cold.

Mike came over to the sofa but remained standing. "Don't look so panic-stricken. We all have a twin somewhere."

Erica felt sick. Her mind went back to the day she'd met the beautiful blonde in De Mornay's. She remembered her terror after Glenn had informed her that one of Mrs. Taylor's twins had been kidnapped from Long Beach Memorial Hospital. It was the same place and nearly the same time that Marnie had been given to Mario by the young mother, Rose, but Erica had shoved her misgivings to the back of her mind. How could that missing twin have anything to do with her own baby? She had buried it. *Mario could never have done such a thing.*

"I was running late as it was," Mike continued, "but was further delayed on our way up the escalator to my meeting. This pretty little preteen came rushing up to us like gang-busters. She was calling Marnie by another child's name, insisting that Marnie *was* that child. I told her she was mistaken and went on my way. She and her friend upset Marnie, but I don't think they meant to." He paused. "What's wrong? You look as if you've seen a ghost. It's just a case of mistaken identity."

"What was her name?" *Oh my God. This can't be happening. It has to be a mistake.*

"The girl who ran up to me?" He shrugged. "I have no idea."

"No. What was the name she called Marnie?"

He squinted his eyes as if it could help him squeeze out the memory. "Kelly. No, not that, but something with a K sound." Then, with a frown, he said, "What does it matter?" But just as quickly the frown lifted. As if the name suddenly materialized in his mind, he exclaimed, "Kallie! They called her Kallie."

Erica's mind reeled; that name sounded familiar. Was that the name of the Taylors' child? Erica strained to remember. She prayed that the Taylors' daughter had a different name altogether. She prayed that this preteen would realize she'd been mistaken.

"Hey," Mike said. "My story gets even crazier. When I went back to the office to pick up Marnie, I saw some photos on the bulletin board, from some big company picnic for the employees. And whose picture do you think I saw?"

"The girl who looks like Marnie?" Her voice was just a whisper.

"No. It was the girl who stopped me on the escalator. And guess who she is?"

Erica didn't want to guess. She felt as if she were bleeding inside.

"The daughter of the head of Consolidated. She's Mark Toddman's daughter."

Oh my God. Paige Toddman, Mark Toddman's wife, was the woman who had accompanied Ashleigh Taylor to De Mornay's. Her daughter had recognized Marnie as the missing twin.

Caroline felt like the proverbial third wheel. Ashleigh's and Conrad's efforts to make her feel important were transparent. They didn't need her input on her father's burial at Forest Lawn or the memorial service at the Long Beach Yacht Club.

As Conrad pulled into the driveway of her father's Naples home, a tidal wave of sadness washed over Caroline. She couldn't hold back the tears and didn't even try. She longed to get back to New Beginnings, where she could be her own person. No one walked on eggs around her there. They looked up to her, and she felt important.

Climbing out of the backseat, she noticed the next-door neighbor pull into her own driveway, not giving them a second glance. She felt even more invisible as Callie came running out to the car and straight into Conrad's arms. He swung her up, and Ashleigh gave her a quick kiss before Conrad set her on his shoulders. "I promised to read her a story when we came back," he said, and headed to the back door.

At least Ashleigh remembered that Caroline was with them, remaining in the driveway waiting for her.

Caroline turned her head away from the house and surreptitiously wiped her tears, straightened her posture to her full height, and reined in her emotions before turning to face Ashleigh. "After I finish packing, would you mind taking me home?" she said, her voice hard and bitter.

Ashleigh, a bit taken aback by Caroline's abrupt request and her tone, took a moment to respond. "Have I done something to offend you, Caroline?"

Caroline's face crumpled. With tears streaming down her face, she said, through choked sobs, "No. You have shown nothing but the utmost kindness toward me. I'm just a jealous bitch."

Ashleigh reached in her handbag and offered her a tissue. "Not at all, Caroline. Your father's passing has left a hole in all of our lives."

"I've done so many wicked and evil things in my life. I'm sure I'm going to hell."

"That is all in the past; you were sick. You aren't that same person you were then."

Shaking with silent sobs, Caroline's voice was unsteady. "I feel rotten. Damn it, I *am* rotten. You couldn't have been nicer to me."

Ashleigh led Caroline into the house and over to the kitchen table. Placing her hand over Caroline's, she waited for her to regain her composure.

"Now that Daddy's gone, I don't want to be here." Again her face crumpled, and she was wracked with heart-wrenching sobs.

Ashleigh shot to her feet, then knelt down beside Caroline, who was holding her head, sobbing into the palms of her hands. "We will take you back to New Beginnings, if that's what you want."

It took several moments for Caroline to emerge from her moans. After blowing her nose loudly, she looked up. "You are a good person. I know that, and yet I can't help but be envious of you and the relationship you had with my father. I know he loved me, but it was you he loved the most and was most proud of."

"Your father was enormously proud of you over these past few years. It made him very happy to see your successes."

"Forever the diplomat." Caroline's voice again had a hard edge to it.

Ashleigh did not know what to say, so she said nothing.

"Damn it. I'm sorry. You know, I've become my own best psychiatrist. I've read so much about my condition and talked to so many shrinks that I think I have a better handle on me than all those psychiatrists and psychologists put together. I'm even beginning to analyze and answer my own questions."

Ashleigh nodded, not sure what else to do.

"Let me try to explain. You and I can never really be friends. It's not your fault. It's mine. I can curb my jealousy, but it's always lurking about in the back of my head." She looked around as if to include the whole house in her explanation. "This house is a constant reminder that my daddy's gone. At New Beginnings, people look up to me. They are worse off than I am. I guess I am pretty normal now, but I fear getting angry and turning into a raving maniac again. At New Beginnings, I know I have something to contribute, and I like that. I like being somebody. If that's wrong, so be it."

"It's not wrong. It is the most normal desire in the world." Conrad had been so perceptive. New Beginnings was where Caroline felt safe, where she was looked up to. Ashleigh sighed and smiled at Charles's daughter, finally understanding. *It is where she belongs.*

The moment Terrence dropped the girls off at the Toddmans' Greenwich home, April, with Madison at her heels, flew in to find her mother. Paige listened intently while April expressed her frustration over being unable to reach either of her parents while at Carlingdon's. Then she and Madison excitedly told her about seeing Callie's twin and the man who was holding her hand.

Though April wanted to phone Ashleigh right away, Paige explained why this wasn't the right thing to do. In the midst of dealing with her grief over the death of Charles, Ashleigh certainly didn't need this thrown into the mix, the possibility that her lost twin had been spotted in Manhattan—and then lost to them again.

Madison joined them for dinner that night, and she and April repeated for Mark essentially the same story they'd told Paige the minute they'd raced through the door. When April described the man to her father, Paige noticed that she filled in details she hadn't mentioned earlier. Whether she had forgotten them before or was creating them the second time around, Paige was not certain. She trusted her daughter, but wondered if this wasn't simply a case of wishful thinking.

"Under no circumstances," Mark said after listening to their story, "are either of you to breathe a word about this to Ashleigh or Conrad." He looked them squarely in their eyes. "Or anyone else for that matter. Not before we have it investigated. Do you understand?"

The girls nodded, and he went on. "If that was Callie's twin you saw, we will find her. But it is too early to tell Callie's parents. It would be cruel to get their hopes up if it turns out that the little girl you saw is not their twin, or if she has already disappeared again."

After Madison left and April had gone to bed, Mark and Paige further discussed the possible sighting. It was a warm, pleasant evening, so the couple took their after-dinner drinks outside.

"Wouldn't it be a miracle if it turns out that the child the girls saw was the Taylor twin?" Paige began.

"Don't get your hopes up. Four-year-old girls can look pretty much alike." Mark dropped down on a bench and gestured for Paige to sit beside him.

Paige's heart sank. "But April and Madison are so certain. You're not dismissing it as a possibility, are you?"

Putting his arm across his wife's shoulder, Mark pulled her close. "Of course not. I've already called Landes. He's got two of his New York agents on it, and if they turn up anything, he's sending Pocino in. It would be tough to find anyone more motivated or savvy about this case. He wanted some more recent pictures of Callie, so they'd know what the missing twin looks like."

"I have several—"

"I know. Anna found some recent pictures of Callie and faxed them to Landes. And don't worry. I told him that under no circumstances was he to contact the Taylors. Not before they have a solid lead."

Paige pulled back an inch or two to meet his eyes. "Thank you." Then she said, "If it's not one thing, it's half a dozen more."

Mark reached out and took her hand, lifting it to his lips for a light kiss. "It was a damn shame I had to stay in town last night. I should have been here for you. Now, tell me more about meeting your mother."

"What I was about to tell you, before our umpteenth inter-ruption, was that my mother was diagnosed two years ago as having Alzheimer's."

Mark did not immediately respond. Slowly, he leaned forward and his eyes met hers. "Alzheimer's?" he repeated. "But isn't she only now in her early sixties?"

Paige nodded. Seeing the telltale twitch in his left eye, she hoped Mark wouldn't suggest that she stay clear of pursuing a relationship with the mother who had abandoned her. She knew it would add more complica-tions to their lives. With all Mark had on his plate, she couldn't really blame him if he wanted to avoid that possibility. But now that she'd found her mother, she found it impossible to turn away.

"I don't know a lot about Alzheimer's other than that it's a serious disease. It's not an easy thing for families to deal with." Mark hesitated again, then rose to his feet and pulled Paige to him. Wrapping his arms around her, he tilted her chin so that her eyes met his. "This relationship is important to you?"

"Very important," was all she could say.

"Then it's important to me. You're always on hand to support me; now it's my turn to be here for you. So, when do I meet your mother and her husband?"

"Well, since the memorial service for Charles Stuart is this Saturday, we'll need to schedule our visit to Queens for the following Sunday. Okay?"

"You've got it. We can have Terrence bring them here . . . ?"

"Hmm, no, our first meeting should be at their house," Paige said thoughtfully. "They live in a modest neighborhood, and I'm afraid that this estate might be intimidating. Especially for a first meeting. But once we get to know them—"

"Agreed. Most people are more comfortable on their own turf."

As the thought drifted through her head, she said, "On our turf or theirs, it doesn't matter to me. I'm just so relieved to have found my mother."

"Are you alright?" Mike held the cold cloth to Erica's forehead.

She hadn't actually passed out, but she'd come damned close. She was limp and so pale that Mike's bewilderment turned to concern. *What on earth is going through her head?* A case of mistaken identity was hardly reason for such alarm.

"Come on, Erica. Somewhere, we all have a double of some sort. It's no big deal."

She sat up straight. "Yes," she said stiffly. "It is a big deal."

"Erica, this isn't like you."

"I've never discussed this with you, Mike, but . . . What do you know about Marnie's birth?"

Mike stared at his sister-in-law. "What do you mean?"

"What, exactly, did Mario tell you?"

"You mean about the in vitro?"

She shook her head so violently that several strands of hair came loose from her fashionable twist. "I had a feeling you really knew nothing more than that. Well, I have a lot to tell you. Things you will find as hard to believe as I do. Things I've refused to believe until now. But I've got to take my head out of the sand and face the facts." She hesitated. "Mario lied to us."

"Erica." His voice was sharper than he'd intended, but she was talking in circles, making not one bit of sense.

"I have a lot to tell you," she repeated. "And I'll tell you everything. It'll actually be a huge relief. But before I get started, I think we'd both better get a glass of wine." She noticed Mike's incredulous expression. She hardly ever drank, except during business parties or social events. But she knew she needed something to soothe her nerves now.

"Sure. There's a bottle of Chardonnay in the fridge."

She followed him into the kitchen and pulled out one of the bar stools at the counter. He set two wine glasses on the counter and began to pour. Before he'd finished pouring the second glass, she had downed the first and was holding out the glass for a refill.

"What on God's green Earth has gotten into you?"

"Marnie is not my biological child," she blurted out.

With an expression of pure exasperation, Mike said, "Don't be daft. Of course Marnie is your child."

"I didn't say she wasn't my child. She is not my *biological* child." In answer to Mike's befuddled expression, she said, "I didn't give birth to Marnie."

Mike climbed on the bar stool beside her, picking up his glass of wine. "You'd better explain," he said.

Thirty minutes later, Mike sat in stunned silence. The kidnapping of the Taylor twin had been big news across the nation a few years ago. The snatching of any infant, from any hospital, would have hit the news wires, but the baby's relationship to Charles Stuart, along with the stellar reputation of the Long Beach hospital, guaranteed that the story made the headlines of all the newspapers, magazines, and periodicals in Southern California and beyond. Follow-up stories had continued to surface periodically over the years.

Finally, Mike's brain kicked in action and he shot to his feet, nearly tipping over the bar stool. "No way. I don't believe it. It just can't be. My brother—no way in hell. He was an honest and deeply religious man. He never lied. Even as a child, when telling the truth got him in a heap of trouble, his word was as good as money in the bank." He thought Erica had loved his brother. Why would she foul his memory in this way? "For you to even contemplate that Mario was capable of committing such a heinous act—well, it's beyond me."

"I understand how you feel." Erica slid down from the bar stool and reached out to lay her hand gently on Mike's arm. "Mario was everything you say he was. I couldn't believe it either. I refused to consider that my husband was capable of abducting an infant from a sleeping mother who had just given birth. Even when I was told the twin was stolen from Long Beach Memorial, I refused to look at the facts. But now, with this story of an identical child, the pieces of the puzzle have all come together. I can no longer ignore the truth."

"It's just a coincidence." Mike's voice cracked. He didn't much believe in coincidences, but the alternative was too terrifying to admit. He'd always looked up to his big brother. Mario had never done an evil thing in his life.

Erica continued, her face a picture of anguish. "I'm scared. I am so damn frightened. But look at the facts: We lost our baby. Mario told me about this young girl, Rose. I believed Mario when he said it was a win-win for all of us. At that point, we'd just lost our baby. I knew I could never have another baby, not even with in vitro. Meanwhile, Rose wasn't ready for a baby. She wanted a better life for her baby than the one she could provide. It all sounded reasonable—like a storybook case. Supposedly, Mario took Rose's baby out of the hospital before her parents could stop him, and he got away with it."

"You think he made up some tall tale? If he told you that this Rose gave birth to our Marnie, then that's what happened. Why are you borrowing trouble?" Even as he said this, however, doubt was creeping in.

"I don't want to believe that Marnie is the abducted twin. But do you really think that two newborns were taken from Long Beach Memorial Hospital at the same time, yet news of only one abduction ever hit the papers? What about this so-called Rose's mother and father? Did they just melt into the woodwork? The fact that the twin was kidnapped seems all the more reason—"

"So you're telling me that my brother—your husband—was nothing but a rotten liar and a kidnapper?" His voice rose so it was almost a shout.

Erica picked up the bottle of wine and her glass. "Please, Mike, let's go into the living room." She swayed a little as she padded across the hardwood floor and sank down on the couch. She set the wine on the end table. Then she seemed to fold in like an accordion onto the couch, weeping into her hands.

Mike dropped down on the couch beside her and cradled her head against his shoulder. "I'm sorry. I had no right to say—"

"No." Still shaking with silent sobs, she pushed out one broken word after another. "No, Mario was . . . he was a good and . . . and decent man. He was no liar, but he . . . he did lie about our baby. He lied to protect me. It's all my fault."

She sucked in a gulp of air and reached for a tissue from the box beside her. "When my appendix burst and I lost the baby, I fell apart. I wanted to die. Mario knew that. I told him I'd never feel whole without a baby of our own. I drove him to desperation. Whatever he did, he did for me. He was not the monster; it was me. Mario's love for me must have caused him to take leave of his senses, to disregard his ingrained sense of right and wrong."

Erica paused to blow her nose and met Mike's eyes. "Maybe there *was* a Rose. Mario wouldn't have made all that up. But something must have happened to mess it all up."

"So, in the end, he just took one of the Taylors' twins? Right from the bassinet beside the mother's bed?"

Covering her entire face with her hands, Erica sat silently for what seemed like a very long time. Neither spoke.

Mike wanted to shake her. *Stop talking nonsense!* he would say, and she would admit that this was all an exaggeration, caused by her insecurities as a mother, by her grief over Mario, by the stress of her job at De Mornay's, by the imagination of a mentally ill woman. But the cold, cruel sense of reality was closing in on him.

Yet Erica was Marnie's mother; Marnie belonged to Erica and Mike. They were the ones who'd raised her, who took care of her when she was sick, read stories to her at bedtime, held her when she was afraid . . . Mario had done a horrible thing, but four years later it was too late to turn back the clock. No one could love Marnie more than they did.

But now Mark Toddman's daughter had seen Marnie. It came to him like a flash: *We are no longer safe in New York.*

As if reading his thoughts, Erica leaned forward, placing her had on his arm. "We can't stay in New York. I want to talk about moving to Chicago."

"Chicago?"

"Bill's already there, without us. Be honest—you don't really want to do the long-distance relationship thing with him forever, do you? When he got that great job offer at John Stewart's, he wanted us all to come. Isn't that what you wanted, too?"

Is she really thinking about moving to Chicago? "The job as a divisional merchandise manager was a terrific opportunity for Bill. I know he didn't want to leave us, but he had to do what's right for him. But I just couldn't leave you and Marnie."

"But now we'll be coming with you. Mike, you can work from anywhere. It's not safe for us here."

Mike's head was spinning. He needed some time to pull his thoughts together. It was true, he'd considered moving with Bill to Chicago. What they had found together was the real thing—not at all like Mike's previous relationships in the Big Apple. Not like Jeff. Mike and Bill had fallen in love over the past two years and were committed to making a life together—a life that included his sister-in-law and Marnie. Bill was kind and sensitive. He treated Erica like a sister, and he adored her little girl. Other men in New York had actually become jealous of Mike's live-in "family," but Bill was different.

Finally he spoke. "Bill is aware that you and Marnie are my family, and it's a family he wants to be a part of. That's why he offered to share the new three-bedroom house with us and to explore opportunities for you to work in Chicago. But your life—our life—is here."

"I understand," Erica interjected. "But all that has changed." Then with a sudden expression of alarm she cried out, "Mike, don't you see? We have to leave New York! And the sooner, the better." She lowered her voice and tried to stay calm. "Do you think it's still possible? Will Bill still want us to move in with him?"

Shrugging his shoulders, Mike said, "Of course it is. Bill will be over the moon." It wasn't too late—but a move to Chicago couldn't happen overnight.

Yet he knew for sure that staying in New York was no longer an option. It was far too dangerous.

Viviana dropped down to the quilted satin chair in front of her dressing table to strap on her gold stilettos. She said a silent prayer, hoping that tonight's business dinner would go well and would not continue into the wee hours of the morning. She wanted Mitchell Wainwright energetic . . . and alone. Lately, he'd seemed remote and distracted; her libido hadn't been satisfied for nearly a week. *Well, that's about to change.*

Until recently, his sexual appetite had been as insatiable as her own. He'd brought her to heights she'd never reached before, and she'd done the same for him—or so he said. She believed him.

She leaned forward to check her makeup and hair. Satisfied, she picked up her Judith Leiber minaudière and bolero jacket and rechecked her appearance from head to toe in the full-length mirror. He wouldn't be able to resist her tonight—unless he'd already started in on the booze. She sighed. *If only he could get past the loss of his son.*

The doorbell rang, bringing her internal dialog to an abrupt end.

When she threw open the door, Wainwright's smashing good looks renewed her resolve to concentrate on the positives. She would not think about his bouts of drug use or alcohol abuse or about his frequent mood swings—his morose memories and the self-loathing as he recalled his son's death. Instead, Viviana would concentrate on his intelligence and know-how in the world of business—as well as in her bedroom.

He pulled her into his arms for a quick kiss and then stepped back for an appraisal. "My lady in red," he commented, the corners of his mouth turning up in a smile.

Viviana thought she detected a lack of approval. "What's wrong?" Did he think her strapless cocktail dress was out of place for his business dinner?

"Nothing that I can see," he said. "Gorgeous as always."

Viviana was relieved. *Why do I allow him to make me feel unsure of myself?*

"Are you packed?" Wainwright asked as he helped her into her jacket. They had plans to fly to Long Beach in the morning to attend the memorial service for Charles Stuart.

"All set," she replied. She'd packed photos of her high-class Fifth Avenue boutique to show those who had not yet visited Manhattan, and she'd also included pictures of her latest dress designs. Everyone who was anyone in the world of fashion and retail would be there. Viviana prayed that the presence of the Toddmans' young daughter wouldn't trigger painful memories. April Toddman was about the same age as Mitch would have been—the son whose loss still cloaked Mitchell in heartache.

"We leave at six A.M. on the dot," he reminded her. Stepping into the elevator, he pressed the button for the first level.

"I know," she said with mock irritation. "You've already reminded me a number of times."

"I assume Glenn will also be attending the Stuart memorial," he stated.

"Of course. But the shop will be in good hands; I can count on Erica Christonelli."

Wainwright had met the young associate on several occasions at De Mornay's. She seemed competent enough, though he knew Viviana had conflicting feelings toward her. "Isn't she the one who you said was getting too big for her britches?" he said teasingly.

"Not exactly. She has a way with the De Mornay's clients. And despite Glenn's accusations to the contrary," she added, "I'm delighted to give Erica name recognition on the De Mornay's label."

Wainwright cocked an eyebrow.

"You see? I am a generous spirit. Glenn was wrong when he accused me of being jealous. For me to be using her, she has to have something I need—which she doesn't. It was just that I didn't think she was ready until now." She hurried on to say, "You, of all people, know I have a reputation to uphold."

"You do indeed, and I understand. A perfectionist to the core! You can hardly risk anything but the very best bearing your label."

Not sure whether he was mocking her or he truly understood, she clarified. "Erica has been a fast and eager learner and has absorbed what I have taught her. She has rightfully earned name recognition."

"And with that bit of generosity, you've launched her career." He squeezed her hand. "If she's that good, though, you won't hold on to her for long, my dear."

"True. But if we can get our own exclusive boutique in Carlingdon's flagship store . . ."

The elevator halted, and the doors slid open to reveal the lobby. Viviana was silent as they traversed the polished marble floor. This was not the time to approach him about assisting her with her plans for expansion. Tonight the focus must be on him, not on his business. She would be his charming dinner companion while he eased the Chinese businessmen into his latest investment opportunity. Nothing must spoil this night . . . or their upcoming weekend together.

Ashleigh slipped the dress over Callie's head. It was a voile fabric with black polka dots on a white background. She had wanted Callie to have something special for Charles's service and had taken her to Luan's on Long Beach Boulevard, the same store where Charles and Gran had taken Ashleigh for special occasion dresses when she was Callie's age. The dress they'd selected was perfect; her daughter liked the fuzzy texture of the black polka dots.

After pulling on Callie's black patent leather Mary Janes, Ashleigh combed her hair into a high ponytail on top, clipped on the black bow, and kissed the top of her head. "Tell Elizabeth you're ready. Daddy and I will see you at Forest Lawn, at that pretty grassy area under the big tree that I showed you yesterday."

"Why can't we go with you and Daddy?"

Ashleigh gave her a squeeze. "Remember, I told you Elizabeth needs some company, so you will go with her to pick up Aunt Caroline, while Daddy and I take care of a few things at Forest Lawn."

Satisfied, Callie trotted out of the bedroom and called for Elizabeth.

Conrad and Ashleigh pulled past the kiosk at Forest Lawn at about nine thirty and parked in front of the main building. Once inside, they headed straight up the stairs to the viewing room to see Charles and say their farewells.

As they neared the blue satin–lined casket, Ashleigh breathed in the familiar scent of Charles's aftershave, which still lingered on his favorite suit. He looked young and at peace.

She leaned down and kissed his smooth cheek, unchecked tears rolling down her own.

Conrad, who stood close beside her, handed her his handkerchief. She used it to pat a fallen tear from Charles's damp cheek, then dabbed at her own eyes. "You'll always be with me. I'll hold our special memories in my heart forever," she said aloud.

She began to close the lid, then stopped and raised it again. "I almost forgot." She rummaged in her handbag until her fingers came across the folded paper. She opened it, and again read Callie's wobbly letters below the picture she had drawn. "Me and Grandpa going to the park," she had told her parents, pointing to the image. The letters spelled I LOVE YOU, and appeared under a tall stick figure beside a small one, the two of them holding hands.

Smoothing the drawing, Ashleigh placed it beside Charles and for a moment imagined that she saw a smile light up his face. Closing the lid, she said, "Give Gran my love. And tell her my glass is more than half full."

Elizabeth pulled Charles's vintage Rolls-Royce up to the curved curb nearest the area beside his plot and the graveside service, which had been set up by Forest Lawn.

As Caroline quickly climbed from the front seat of the Rolls, and Elizabeth made her way around the back of the car, Ashleigh and Conrad rushed across the damp lawn to assist. Conrad threw open the back door and leaned inside the car to free Callie from her car seat. He gave her a kiss and hug and gently set her down on the grass.

"Look what Auntie Caroline gave me." Callie held out a teddy bear—a collectable Steiff.

Ashleigh looked from the bear to Caroline. "Is that from your collection?"

"Yes." Caroline smiled. "I have well over a hundred of them. Daddy started my collection when I was about Callie's age, so if you don't mind, I'd like to help her begin her own collection."

"Of course I don't mind. That is very generous of you."

"Well, I'm a little old for bears, and I won't be having any children of my own." She gave a derisive laugh, then added, "That's for sure."

"Thank you. What a wonderful gift." After giving the bear a hug and handing it back to Callie, Ashleigh smoothed her daughter's dress and unclipped her bow, fanning out her hair before clipping the bow back in place. While Ashleigh fussed over her, Callie peeked over to the gravesite, a look of curiosity on her round face.

"What's all that dirt for?" Callie asked.

A sinking feeling lodged in Ashleigh's chest. She had not fully prepared Callie for this service. *How can I make her understand?* Maybe it was a mistake to have her here. And yet she knew that Callie should be here. It was important that she learn to say good-bye and that she focus on how happy she was to have been part of this wonderful man's life. She must know that he was now in peace and would never feel pain again.

"I'll show you." Ashleigh took Callie's hand and walked over to the casket beside the area of white plastic chairs, tiptoeing across the grass so that her heels did not dig in.

Conrad assisted Caroline, whose high heel had sunk deep into the damp grass, making it difficult to navigate to the area where the family service was to be held. Elizabeth, in her sensible shoes, trudged along beside them.

The casket, now closed, was covered with an enormous spray of red roses, sprinkled with baby's breath and white carnations. Callie tugged at Ashleigh's hand, her eyes large as coasters. "Is Grandpa in that box?" Her voice was filled with horror.

Ashleigh set her in one of the white plastic chairs and knelt down beside her.

"Open it," the little girl wailed. "Grandpa can't breathe in there."

Ashleigh hugged Callie to her, then pasted a smile on her face. "Grandpa is not in the box, sweetheart. Only his body is in the box. His spirit has gone to heaven. Remember what I told you? Grandpa is happy. He is with the people he loves who have already gone to heaven. Be happy for him, my love. Grandpa will never hurt or be tired again."

Callie didn't say anything for a moment or so, still appearing confused. "Mommy?" Ashleigh waited for her to go on. "If Grandpa doesn't take his body with him to heaven, how will everyone know him?"

As they made their way from Forest Lawn to the 605 Freeway, Conrad glanced over his shoulder into the back seat. "It appears that our little munchkin is sound asleep."

Ashleigh took a peak at their daughter, whose head was resting upon the teddy bear. "She's been a busy little girl, asking questions I can't begin to answer." Her eyes filled with love as she gestured to Callie. "I sure wish there was an instruction manual for this precocious package of ours." She repeated the child's question about heaven.

"That's a darn good question."

"I wasn't sure how to answer, so I talked to her about all the things she remembered about Charles. Not what he looked like but who he was—his kindness, his easy laughter, his love for her . . ."

Before turning off the Second Street Bridge onto Appian Way, Conrad's thoughts turned to his other daughter. *Who is teaching Cassie about life and death, and about the hereafter?*

". . . and Reverend West will do the invocation. I can handle the rest," Ashleigh was saying. Her focus brought him out of his introspection. She appeared calm and more relaxed than he'd seen her in days.

He turned into the members' parking lot at the Long Beach Yacht Club, where Charles had been a charter member. From the corner of his eye, he noticed that Ashleigh had only her small Chanel handbag with her. Concerned, he asked, "Did you forget your notes?" His wife, who usually managed to retain her calm, composed manner amidst the most dire circumstances, had spent the entire week stressed about the memorial. "I want to convey the essence of Charles and all he stood for, without sounding melodramatic," she'd told him as she started writing what he presumed would be a eulogy.

She'd written early in the morning and late at night. She'd filled legal pads with what she planned to say, then ripped up the pages and thrown them away. She'd written at the antique desk up in their room at the Stuart home; she'd written at the kitchen counter and at the dining room table. She'd filled one entire pad while Conrad drove her from place to place to do the myriad errands required to make this an event worthy of the wonderful man who raised her; they'd gone to Forest Lawn, to the florist, to the printer who was preparing the program, to the vocalist she had chosen to sing "It's a Wonderful World" at today's memorial celebration of his life. The song was Charles's favorite, and it conveyed his philosophy of life.

Starting over and over, she'd nearly driven herself crazy trying to figure out the right words. Now, she pulled a single index card from her handbag. "Thanks, love, but I have everything I need. I have no intention of giving a speech."

Thrown off balance, he said, "But I thought that was exactly what you'd been planning."

"That was the reason I was having so much trouble. I was attempting to do something totally out of character."

"I don't understand."

"I don't do speeches. I never have. Not even when I was in charge of the executive training program for Bentley's and in front of two or three hundred trainees."

"Sweetheart, you aren't making a bit of sense. Remember, I was a part of those programs too, and I recall that you did a magnificent job."

She shook her head.

"I know—this is not at all the same," he said.

"Yes, in a way, it is," she replied. "This is a lot more important and more personal. But all I want or need to do today is talk about the Charles everyone knew, loved, and respected. And everything I need to keep me on track is on this card." She held up the index card as Conrad pulled into the parking lot. Passing several spots reserved for flag officers or staff commodores, he finally found a place in front of the club.

Ashleigh looked over her shoulder as Callie's eyes popped open and the teddy bear fell onto the seat.

Elizabeth, close behind them, had reached out the window of the Rolls and inserted her key card to raise the security gate's wooden arm.

"Let us give you a hand," Elizabeth said as she hurried up to the car. But Caroline didn't stop; she continued straight through the yacht club doors.

When Elizabeth lifted Callie from the car seat, the child's eyes filled with tears. She leaned toward Ashleigh, her arms outstretched. Unable to resist, Ashleigh took her daughter into her arms and held her tight. It was at moments like this that she missed their Cassie the most. The girls would've gotten so much comfort from one another.

"Mommy has a lot to do right now," she said pointedly. "We want everyone to remember Grandpa. I am going to talk about my best memories of Grandpa, and so are a lot of other people, but first we have to put up all these pictures." She gestured to the photographs she'd gathered.

Callie's face brightened, and suddenly Ashleigh had a little helper.

Drifting through the crowd, Caroline Stuart felt uncomfortable and out of place. Round tables covered in alternating black and white table-cloths filled the main dining room, bridge deck, and quarterdeck. On each table were tasteful centerpieces: red roses and white carnations set upon round mirrors. And the tables were filling with people—people who were completely unlike her, people who didn't really know her and didn't want to know her.

Caroline's hand shook. On the memorial program she held, there was a photo of her father taken at his ninetieth birthday party. The image belied his age. He had thick white hair and a warm friendly smile on his handsome, relatively unlined face. On the back of the program was a picture of him with Ashleigh's grandmother, the Bentleys Royale tower in the back ground. The images were from Ashleigh's world. *Always Ashleigh.* Her confidence melted.

This is Ashleigh's show. She probably knows everyone by name. Caroline recognized quite a few of the men and women from the retail world who were present, but that unnerved her even more. They would associate her more with Morris Sandler than with her beloved father. As she took in the hordes gathered in various areas of the room—standing or sitting around the tables, in the bar area, out on the patio—she felt closed in. *How many of these people know about the pain I caused my farther? Most of them probably despise me.* She wasn't sure she would make it through the ceremony.

Clenching her fists, she began a silent mantra: *I can do this. Charles Stuart was my father. I am here to say good-bye. No one can make me feel inferior unless I allow them to.*

She tried to be fair. Ashleigh had made every effort to include her—she knew that. The collage included several photos of her with her father, most of them taken within the past four years. *Was that all she could find?* Ashleigh also had introduced her to most of the guests. Some of whom Caroline had known years before, but most acted as if they were just meeting for the first time. As she went through the motions of cordiality, an overwhelming sense of paranoia washed over her. It rattled her, but she did not flee. Instead she stayed, battling for control.

She could get through this. She must get through this for her father. Her father had believed in her, in her ability to get along in the outside world. If she left now, all his confidence in her would be meaningless.

As the yacht club began to fill with scores of people who had known and admired Charles, Ashleigh and Conrad made a point of talking with as many people as possible. Although the expressions of sympathy were plentiful, Ashleigh managed to lead most conversations toward recollections of fond memories. Everyone had a favorite story about Charles, many of which brought smiles to their faces. Most of the former and the dwindling number of current Bentleys Royale executives had turned up, as well as a large number of sales associates. Bentleys Royale had been their identity, and Charles Stuart had been their hero. Many others from the world of retail had flown in from the East Coast and from many points between the two coasts.

Ashleigh spotted Mark and Paige coming up the staircase and ran to meet them. Mark gave her a giant bear hug, followed by one of Paige's own. Looking around them to the bottom of the staircase, Ashleigh asked, "Where's April?"

"We were really torn," Paige said, her expression full of regret. "April wanted to be here, but she didn't want to miss Madison's twelfth birthday." Paige shrugged. "It's hard to say no, especially since Mark and I are planning to stay through Monday and didn't think—"

"Nonsense, Paige. Your daughter is growing up. Of course she should be at her friend's party. These things are important to our girls."

"Thanks for your understanding." Paige looked back over her shoulder at the long line that extended across the polished floor, down the staircase, and out the front entrance, and said, "What a wonderful turnout."

Ashleigh had to admit she was pleased. One thought ran through her head over and over: *This is for you, Charles.*

Glenn Nelson made his way across the room with Roger Stanton, a former buyer for Bentleys Royale. The memorial had been one to remember, and Glenn wanted to pay his respects to the Taylors—if he could make it through the crowd. He sighed and trudged on. *All these people . . .*

A little girl all dressed up in a white voile dress with black polka dots whipped across his path, stopping him in his tracks at the top of the stairs. Although he'd seen only the back of the child's head, he smiled when he saw she was making a beeline toward Ashleigh and Conrad Taylor, who stood midway between the staircase and a table of hors d'oeuvres. There was a string of people lined up, waiting to convey their condolences.

Glenn caught sight of Ashleigh leaning down to whisper something into the child's ear. The little girl, holding on to the hem of her skirt as if for balance, stretched up on her tiptoes. She turned then, her neck craning left and right, as if scanning the room in search of something or someone. That's when he saw the child's face, her sparkling brown eyes and the deep dimples accenting her happy smile.

It was Marnie, Erica's bright-eyed little girl. Puzzled, he stopped dead in the tracks for a second time. *Why is little Marnie here? And if she's here, where is Erica?*

In seconds, he had regrouped. It wasn't possible. He knew that. Viviana had trusted Erica to remain in New York and mind the store. Plus, she barely even knew Ashleigh Taylor, and she sure as heck had never met Charles Stuart. *She can't be here, and Marnie wouldn't be here without her.*

The child's face was turned toward him again. His heart came to a full stop. This child was the mirror image of Marnie. But she wasn't Marnie. A chill shot through him.

Leaning heavily on his cane, Wainwright studied the crowd—notable personalities from coast to coast who had traveled from far and wide to pay homage to Charles Stuart.

While Viviana reconnected with friends and acquaintances from her days at Bentleys Royale, he listened to snippets of conversations. Hearing one accolade after another for this legend of a man, his thoughts drifted to his own demise and how people might pay him tribute. Had he been the one to die—assuming anyone cared enough to plan a memorial service for him—he wondered who would go out of their way to attend. What would they say?

Watching Ashleigh chat with Duncan Bradley and his wife, Wainwright couldn't help but marvel at how beautiful and elegant she appeared in her simple black suit and pearl earrings. Her luminous brown eyes were clear and dry, and she wore a dazzling smile on her face. He turned away, suddenly sickened by the sight of her. *No matter what tragedy befalls her,* he thought, *that woman comes across unrattled and in control.* Now that she was no longer a part of his life, he found that trait even more irritating than her beauty. Today, as he'd mingled with all these legends and phonies, he'd overheard nearly as much praise for how well Ashleigh had handled this memorial as he had about the great man whom they had all come to honor. He shook his head, disgusted. *They're still talking about her goddamned poise throughout the ordeal of the twin daughter's abduction.*

But what did Ashleigh know of tragedy? She had always had at least a layer or two of protection. Raised by Charles Stuart, who had given her everything, she'd had more than money and prestige. She'd had unconditional love and acceptance, which was something he had never experienced in his entire life.

"Isn't she adorable?" Viviana said as she sauntered up beside him. Still thinking of Ashleigh, Wainwright turned at the sound of the tapping heels across the hardwood floor to find her walking up to greet them. A little girl scurried past and ran straight to her, lifting her tiny arms to be picked up. He nodded begrudgingly. *Even the goddamned child is picture perfect.*

"Thank you so much for coming," Ashleigh said graciously as she picked up her daughter. "This is Callie."

After the perfunctory greeting, while Ashleigh and Viviana chatted, Wainwright's mind traveled back to the time when Mitch was about the same age as Ashleigh's daughter. Wainwright would proudly introduce his young boy to his friends and acquaintances. That was before he'd been diagnosed with leukemia, before the roller coaster ride of fear— before Wainwright's own personal hell took over his life. As devastating as the kidnapping of that twin must have been, Wainwright knew it could not have had the impact on Ashleigh that losing a child like Mitch had had on him. She had lost an infant, not a child she had raised and nursed through a life-threatening disease. She had not been left childless. She had a perfectly healthy little girl.

It's not fair, he thought. So little ever was.

After the receiving line dwindled, and it seemed that everyone was upstairs, Ashleigh turned to see Dick Landes and Ross Pocino coming from the bar area. She threw her arms open in greeting. Seeing the hired professionals gave her a slight twinge, but today she wasn't going to think about anything other than celebrating Charles's marvelous life. Both of these men—despite being as different as apples and bananas—were not just hired professionals but good friends.

"Where's your Callie at?" Pocino asked.

"She's with Elizabeth and Caroline." Ashleigh gestured toward the table beside the raised platform. "Put your things down, and get some refreshments."

Once Dick and Ross were on their way, Ashleigh walked over to the microphone. Not wanting the formality of the podium, she'd asked that the mic be placed on a tall stand at far the side of the platform. Conrad and Elizabeth helped quiet the crowd and tried to get everyone seated. However, far more people had come to pay honor to Charles Stuart than the three rooms could hold. The club was packed—standing room only.

Ashleigh waited a few moments for the noise echoing through the dining area to die down. She felt fairly relaxed—until she noticed the absence of Caroline from their table. *Where is she?* Her eyes scanned the room once, and then again, before she saw her. Over by the sliding door leading to the patio, Caroline stood off by herself, a wine glass in her hand and a haunted expression in her eyes. Ashleigh, frozen in place, wasn't sure what to do.

Conrad strode to the edge of the platform and whispered, "Is every-thing alright?"

She leaned down close to his ear and said, "Would you mind going over to check on Caroline?" Her heart in her throat, she flicked her eyes toward Charles's daughter.

Conrad looked over at Caroline, nodded, and took off in Caroline's direction. Ashleigh took a deep breath and refocused. Nothing must spoil the celebration of Charles's extraordinary life.

When Conrad looked over at Caroline, he saw what had most likely alarmed Ashleigh. Caroline had a terrified expression on her face. *Oh my God, is that a glass of wine she's holding?* Caroline's face softened and her body seemed to relax as Conrad approached. Apparently noticing that Conrad's eyes had taken in her wine glass, she said, "Don't worry. It's Perrier."

"I wasn't worried," he lied. *Is she really as stable as Ashleigh claims? If not, she'd better not fall apart today.*

"Like hell, you weren't." The words were sharp, but there was no malice in Caroline's tone. "Ashleigh was worried about me, wasn't she?"

No longer seeing the tension he'd observed in her posture only moments before, Conrad saw no point in hiding the truth. "A little."

"Well, there's no need. I think the crisis has passed. At least I hope to hell it has."

Not sure how to respond, he made no comment. "Let's go back to the table," he said and held out his arm.

"Conrad, I didn't mean to be a cause of concern. I was feeling a bit overwhelmed, so I thought it best to get away from the crowd." She took a sip of her Perrier. "I feel better now. I would like to say a few words about my father."

Paige flopped down on a plump sofa in the Stuart home, immediately kicked off her shoes, and sank into the soft pillows.

Mark had gone with Conrad to take Caroline back to New Beginnings; Elizabeth was in the kitchen making some tea; and Ashleigh had taken Callie upstairs to get her into her nightie. Paige sighed. *What a week this has been.* The turnout to honor the memory of Charles Stuart had been overwhelming. At least twenty-five people had taken the mic to tell their favorite story about the retail icon or to express how he had touched their life. And Ashleigh had shared such wonderful memories about growing up with her grandmother and Charles. *Now that I've found my mother, we'll create loving family memories for April, too.*

Callie came running across the carpet, throwing herself into the sofa beside her and yanking her from her introspection. "My, haven't we got a lot of energy," Paige said, pulling the child up on her lap. Callie gave a big yawn and rubbed her eyes with her closed fists.

Ashleigh smiled as she entered the living room. "Give Auntie Paige a goodnight kiss."

Callie wrapped her arms around Paige's neck and gave her a sloppy kiss, then pulled back. A thoughtful expression came over her face. "A lot of people came to say bye to Grandpa," she said.

"Yes, they did," Ashleigh responded, her eyes fastened on her little girl.

"A really lot of people said they'd miss Grandpa."

Ashleigh nodded, a quizzical expression crossing her brow.

Paige watched the exchange with amusement, wondering what was on the child's mind.

"Does Grandpa have that many friends in heaven?"

Ashleigh broke into a broad grin. "Yes, I'm sure he does, darling. Now, it's time to say goodnight." She took Callie by the hand, and together they tramped upstairs.

By the time Ashleigh returned downstairs, Elizabeth had set out the tea on the coffee table and had gone up to bed. Ashleigh dropped into an armchair next to Paige and poured herself a cup.

The two friends talked about the celebration and smiled over some of the shared memories. Paige caught Ashleigh up on her future plans to introduce Mark to her mother and to welcome Helen and Rupert into their lives. Switching subjects then, she asked, "How is Caroline doing?"

"She seems to be doing extremely well, but she's still battling a few demons. She's frightened of a relapse, but she is quite open about it. Today she said she was afraid the paranoia might have returned." Ashleigh took another sip of tea. "But when we talked about it, I couldn't see anything abnormal about her feelings."

"Meaning . . . ?"

"She felt that people thought badly of her, especially those who knew about her part in Charles's loss of Bentley's and Bentleys Royale to Consolidated. That's hardly paranoia; it's simply facing the facts."

Paige nodded. "So, have you decided what you'll do with this lovely home since Caroline isn't going to live here?"

"Conrad and I talked it over and have decided not to sell it. It's been Elizabeth's home for the past nine years, and it will continue to be her home as long as she wants to live here. She will continue to take Caroline to her various art shows and galleries and to the classes being taught in the area."

"That's very generous of you."

"I'm no Mother Teresa. It was actually Conrad's suggestion—and a good one at that, don't you think?" It was indeed the ideal solution. Elizabeth had been a jewel with Charles, and she and Caroline had become very close and were about the same age. "Having her here is a godsend. I know that's what Charles would have liked . . ."

Ashleigh broke off, and with a mischievous glint in her eye, leaned over and poured more tea for both of them before announcing, "Change of subject."

Curious, Paige waited.

"Remember the question you posed last week?"

"About?" They had talked about so many things; flitting from one subject to the next, as they always did when there had been a long stretches between their visits.

Paige was puzzled.

Her friend continued, "Other than Conrad, you are the first to know."

"To know?"

"To know that there's another little Taylor in the oven." Ashleigh ran her palm across her belly.

Chills ran up Paige's arms as tears of happiness filled her eyes. "Oh, Ashleigh! That's the most wonderful news!" She sprang to her feet and ran over for a hug.

Later on, after the husbands had returned and they had all said their goodnights and gone to their rooms, Paige found that she could not sleep. She was delighted with Ashleigh's news. She knew how strongly her friend felt about not leaving Callie as an only child. But she couldn't help but think about April's claims to have seen Cassie at Carlingdon's just the other day. Landes's men in New York hadn't come up with any leads yet, but perhaps they would by the time the Toddmans returned to the East Coast . . . Perhaps there was another reason Callie would not be an only child for long.

Paige couldn't stop thinking about Cassie being returned to the Taylors, about how positive April and Madison had been about seeing her that day. How wonderful that would be if it turned out to be true.

Viviana tossed her jacket and beaded Judith Leiber evening bag onto the sofa in the hotel suite. "It totally threw me when you took the microphone today."

"Why's that? I meant every word I said. Charles Stuart had no equal," Mitchell Wainwright said in a matter-of-fact tone.

Tears stung her eyes as his uncharacteristic self-deprecation replayed in her had: *If I could possess even one-quarter of the qualities and accomplishments of Charles Stuart, I would consider my life to be one worth living.* "But how could you speak so flatteringly of a man who had disapproved of you?"

"How could I fault him for disapproving of my engagement to Ashleigh? The man was perceptive as hell. We would have been a match made in hell. But enough of the past."

The phone shrilled. Viviana did not move to answer it. "Who could be calling either one of us here?"

"Don't answer it," he said. "It can wait." He haphazardly propped his cane against the end table and pulled her into his arms.

Her breath caught in her throat as she leaned in for his kiss—gentle, yet erotic. Since leaving New York, he had been charming, attentive, and miraculously, even on the plane, sober—more like the Mitchell Wainwright she remembered prior to the death of his son. Reaching up, she loosened his Hermès tie and deftly slipped it from beneath his collar. He gazed into her eyes as if he wanted to devour her. She wanted him to—but not yet. *Make it last.* Her fingers fumbled with the cuff links in the tight button holes of his dark blue silk shirt. She felt Mitchell's fingertips at the back of her neck, hot and urgent.

"Turn around," he mumbled into her ear, still nuzzling her neck.

She turned, an intense heat searing through her center. *Hot, so incredibly hot.* She heard the rasp of her zipper, and then her body-hugging black dress fell to the floor. She turned slowly to face Mitchell and began undoing the buttons down the front of his shirt. *Why doesn't he say something?* Why didn't she?

Running his fingertips down the length of her body, he said at last, "I like your choice of underwear."

Arching a well-shaped eyebrow, she murmured, "But I'm not wearing any." She reached down to take the phone off the hook and stepped closer, leaving no space between them.

Wainwright awoke by five the next morning, unable to bear the intense, throbbing pain in his right leg. He glanced across to Viviana, her auburn hair splayed across the pillow. The tone of her breathing announced that she had not yet awakened.

What a woman. He couldn't help but be impressed. Neither coy nor cold, Viviana was brimming with passion and a sex drive that surpassed his own. To his chagrin, he had to admit that when he'd had a bit too much to drink or taken one painkiller too many, he was no match for her. As intelligent as she was glamorous, she put up with no crap and had walked out on him twice already. He couldn't blame her. But they were damn good together, and making up to her those times had been a mind-blowing experience. Unless she was one hell of an actress, she'd been as hungry for him as he was for her. And thank God, she was no more interested in marriage than he was.

As gently as possible, he slipped one leg out from under the covers. Instantly, Viviana's eyes blinked open.

"It's early," he said. "Go back to sleep. Just getting something for this goddamn pain." He slapped his bad leg and tried to smile.

When he climbed back into the bed, Viviana snuggled up to him. He held her close until the cadence of her breath signaled she'd fallen back asleep. Adjusting his position, he attempted to divert his mind from the unrelenting pain. Finally, the Percocet took effect and he too drifted back to sleep.

The respite was all too brief. An insistent blaring of the phone had him squinting at the clock. Only six ten. He reached across Viviana to pick up the receiver.

"Who is it?" she asked sleepily before registering that he was still grappling for the receiver.

He did not respond but finally managed to pull the receiver to his ear. "Hello," he said in a tone that was less than civil. Then he heard a familiar but unexpected voice. "Erica?"

Making her way across the upper parking structure, Paige took in the vivid mural of the porte cochère, then turned her eyes to the brass plaque. She smiled at the vague trace of the apostrophe that had been removed— establishing the unequivocal "luxury" identity of Bentleys Royale from its larger upscale, yet more moderate, parent.

Before climbing into the rented El Dorado, Paige gazed up at the magnificent tower, its top sheathed in copper, tarnished green. Her eyes misted as she was flooded with nostalgia. She knew her husband was right, but her emotions battled with her brain. Bentleys Royale was a California icon.

Mark held open the door and tossed their bags in the back seat. Paige slid into the car.

She had so wanted to talk with Ashleigh about what she knew of the future of Bentleys Royale, but the time wasn't right. Ashleigh had enough on her plate, on the heels of having lost Charles; she certainly didn't need to worry about the fate of his legacy as well. But just as quickly as that thought crossed Paige's mind, she realized that her friend was too bright and perceptive not to have read the handwriting on the wall.

Mark dashed around the car and eased into the seat beside her. "Paige," he said. "I know what you're thinking. It's like a death. This has been a gut-wrenching decision. If I had a snowball's chance in hell of saving this place—this majestic monument to quality and excellence in retail—I would. But to attempt it would be financial suicide for Jordon's."

Without thinking, spurred on by pure emotion, Paige said, "But bringing the Carlingdon's headquarters store up to par is going to cost a blooming fortune."

Mark did not respond. Instead, he gave her an indulgent look, reached across the console, and took hold of her hand. He gave it a gentle squeeze and brought it up to his lips. "I understand. It's like losing an old friend, and this is only the beginning. We're bound to experience a whole heap of backlash."

He turned the key in the ignition and headed for LAX. Paige was anxious to return home, though her husband would be staying another week to pop in on the remaining Bentley's stores in Southern California.

The car phone rang, and Mark pressed the TALK button. "Hi, Lynn." He turned his face toward Paige, and covering his mouth, he whispered, "It's Lynn Gee."

Instead of listening to his one-sided conversation with Consolidated's store property manager, Paige tuned out. Mark would fill her in later.

She regretted challenging his decision to close Bentleys Royale. She knew it was not one he'd come to rapidly or easily. He had lamented the fate of these stores that he had nurtured through good times and bad, but in his position, it had been the only rational choice.

Paige loved Bentleys Royale nearly as much as Ashleigh did. While Carlingdon's represented the same high standards and quality, it was not the same. It could never take the place in her heart that Bentleys Royale held. And yet, when she allowed the logical side of her brain to kick in, she understood why Bentleys Royale rather than Carlingdon's was the icon that must be sacrificed. Carlingdon's had about the same number of specialty department stores on the East Coast as Bentleys Royale did on the West Coast, but its name was known nationwide. Its headquarters store in Manhattan was known worldwide as well. "Carly's" was a well-known brand, located in the heart of the largest tourist destination in the United States. As much as she hated to admit it, it was the better investment.

Vaguely aware of Mark pulling onto the Santa Monica Freeway, Paige continued to tune out his phone conversation about the fate of Bentleys Royale, though she was ruminating over the very same subject. Unfortunately, the demographics had changed considerably in the Royale corridor. This had become a major concern while Mark was at the helm of Bentley's. The area became known for violence; drug dealing, shootouts, and the occasional rumor of a drowning became commonplace.

In the mid-1980s, the MacArthur Park was closed down for a period of time, driving the homeless further west along the corridor. Some of them had been discovered urinating on the sides of Bentleys Royale and taking shelter under the porte cochère and doorways of the building. The entire area had gone downhill.

And yet, for the many loyal patrons, Bentleys Royale was still the essence of luxury. All the ugliness disappeared once they had stepped inside the etched-glass doors. They drove from miles away to enjoy the ambiance of the tearoom, the elegance of the building with its wonderful murals, the Lalique chandeliers . . . and the extraordinary service and high-quality merchandise. After the Los Angeles riots, even Charles had to admit that Bentleys Royale's days were numbered. Yet he'd told Ashleigh of his hopes that it would be made into a museum rather than being allowed to slide into deterioration. Yesterday, just before the memorial service at the yacht club, Ashleigh had opened up to her about Charles Stuart's final moments. Mercifully, he had been allowed to die with dignity. On that count, he'd wanted no less for Bentleys Royale than for himself.

Mark disconnected from his conversation and picked up with his wife as if he'd never left off. "Although the Bentleys Royale stores will be operating under the leadership of the P. G. Marshal's banner until we find buyers for the various properties, the flagship store will not drop the Bentleys Royale name."

She nodded. "As a bona fide California monument, isn't it under the protection of the California Heritage Society?"

"It is. But even if that were not the case, I wouldn't attempt to change it. Too many people would be after my head." His smile broke into an all-out grin. "Including my own wife."

"Would you really want to if you could?"

Mark shook his head. "The only buyers under consideration for the headquarters store are those who are committed to maintaining its integrity. Lynn Gee told me he has a couple of buyers in mind. We need to sell the P. G. Marshal's properties as well as those of Bentleys Royale to meet the antitrust laws and reduce our debt. I'm not crazy about changing the branch store names either, but I have no choice. If I don't go forward with store branding in my old territory, I lose credibility."

"I get it, but if I were still living in the L.A. area, I'm afraid I wouldn't like it. Maybe it doesn't make a lot of financial sense when you are running a group of stores and have to satisfy your stock holders as well as your customers, but many of us are attached to our regional brands. I know Bentley's is not a nationally known brand like Jordon's. I am well schooled in the added cost of advertising. I'm aware of the diminished clout at the bargaining table when the buyers represent only twenty-six stores and are outnumbered by the Jordon's buyers. But—"

"But when that Bentley's name is removed and replaced by Jordon's," Mark interjected, "there's bound to be more than a few whispered objections,"

Paige thought about that and decided her husband wasn't quite right. *It's bound to trigger an ear-shattering roar of outrage.*

April could hardly keep her eyes open. The words in her book kept blurring, and she found herself reading and rereading the same sentences over and over again. She double-checked her wristwatch. It seemed to be standing still. She felt as if she were in a time warp. The sleepier she became, the more slowly the hands moved across the watch's face. The clock on the end table wasn't cooperating either.

In her drowsy mind, she replayed events from the weekend at Madison's. After all their friends had departed, Madison had nodded off to sleep the minute her head had hit the pillow. But April had been thirsty and wanted a glass of water, so she'd padded down the hallway toward the kitchen. Tiptoeing past the game room where Madison's father and three other men were engaged in a game of billiards, she'd heard her father's name mentioned.

Naturally, she had stopped short.

One of the men, the one with the enormous belly, was saying some crazy things about her father, unkind things: that he was greedy, a money-grabber. April couldn't wait for her mother to come home from California and was relieved she'd be back tonight instead of tomorrow, as originally planned. April wanted to tell her mom what she'd heard, wanted to hear that it was untrue. Her father was a kind and generous man—she knew that. But still . . .

Why does Mom's flight have to be late tonight? The sound of Wilma's sensible shoes scuffing down the tiled corridor that led to the library, though barely audible, jarred April from her thoughts. The sound died when Wilma stepped onto the area carpet. Sure that Wilma had come to tell her she must go to bed, April pleaded, "I know it's a school night, but I really need to talk with Mom tonight."

"I know. Terrence told me. I just wanted to see if I could make you some hot chocolate."

The tension drained from April's body and a smile spread across her face. "I'd love some. Thanks, Wilma. You're the best."

April unwound her long legs and followed Wilma into the kitchen, taking down her favorite mug. Instead of returning to the library, she downed her cocoa while Wilma finished cleaning up.

Finally, at the sound of her mother's key in the lock, April dashed to the entryway.

Before Paige had taken more than a couple of steps inside, April threw her arms around her and began tugging her toward the library.

"Well, apparently, you have something important to tell me," she said, her eyes inadvertently checking the hands of the grandfather clock in the entry.

"I know it's late," April said, speaking at an unusually rapid pace, "but I really need to talk to you. You just can't believe what—"

"Slow down," Paige said, still pulled along by April's hand. "Is Wilma still up?" Usually, Wilma's day ended right after dinnertime.

"I am indeed," Wilma called out from the doorway of the kitchen, "but I'm off to bed now."

Paige and April bade her a good night's sleep and continued into the library. Two of the walls were lined with floor-to-ceiling shelves of books: classics, books on fashion and retailing, general business books, biographies, and scores of the latest best sellers in fiction and nonfiction.

"I have something important I want to talk to you about," April repeated, lowering herself onto a chair next to the one her mother had chosen.

"If this is about Callie's twin—"

"No, Mom. What I want to talk to you about is Dad."

"Dad?" Perplexed, she asked, "What do you want to know?"

"Is he suing Consolidated?"

Taken aback, Paige studied her daughter. *She sounds so grown up.* "Well, yes, he is. Did you hear something about the lawsuit?"

April nodded, then told her about overhearing part of a conversation at Madison's house. "A big, fat man said Dad was greedy and that he was paid plenty of money."

Dismayed but not shocked, Paige asked, "Do you think your dad is a greedy man, April?"

"No way. He's awesome. I know he's always working for the community to fund better education and to help abused women. And he's donated a ton for medical research."

"I'm sorry that you had to hear such negative things being said about your dad. He does not deserve any of that. Of course, this man could not possibly know the circumstances. It's all pretty complicated."

April straightened her back and folded her arms in front of her. "Mom. Please, don't treat me like a baby. I'm twelve years old."

It was true. Paige was the first to admit that April was very bright and mature for her age. She'd skipped the fifth grade the previous year and, as a sixth-grader, had already joined the middle-school debate team. "You're right, darling." Paige wondered just how much to tell her daughter about what she wanted to know—and how to explain it. "I'm not quite sure where to begin."

"Well, you know what Dad always says."

Paige smiled. "Okay, so I'll start at the beginning. First of all, you know how much Consolidated has always meant to us."

April nodded.

"Your dad has spent the greater part of his life at Consolidated, beginning as a management trainee in their executive training program in New York. Since then he has held many positions at the company. You know how much your dad has done for the company and how well respected he is. Right?"

April nodded again and adjusted her position in her chair, saying, "We have an amazing home and lots of nice things, and we take great vacations, so I guess he must make a lot of money. So why is he suing them?"

"That's true. He does make a great deal of money. Waging a lawsuit against Consolidated was one of the hardest decisions he's ever had to make, but what I'd like you to understand is what a risk he took in returning to Consolidated."

"Risk? What do you mean?"

"Your dad was very sad when Consolidated fell victim to a hostile takeover. Your dad was CEO of Bentley's and Bentleys Royale in Southern California. He was one of two regional vice presidents and was in line to become CEO of the entire company, until—"

"Until that crazy Australian snatched it." April sighed. "I know all that, Mom, but why is Dad suing the company he works for? The fat man said he's biting the hand that's feeding him."

Paige laughed. "You are so like your father; all you want is the bottom line. Fair enough. I'm getting there as fast as I can.

"Your dad left Consolidated in 1988 because he did not want to work for Philip Sloane. The man knew little about running a retail company, and your dad didn't like what was happening to the other group of stores he'd taken over. He had a lot of job offers in and out of the retail industry. He decided to accept the offer to become CEO of Michael Nason's. Your dad always likes a challenge, and his challenge at that company was to regain its reputation for exemplary customer service. He made an immediate impact."

Noticing that her daughter kept fidgeting, Paige said, "Honey, I'm trying to explain, but it's not easy. If you don't know the background, you won't understand the risk."

"I kind of understand. But let me tell you what I already know. Consolidated came after Dad when he still had a contract with Michael Nason's because he was the only one who could save the company, and he saved it."

"Wow," Paige said, "I guess your dad has taught you to cut to the chase." She stretched her arms over her head, trying to get the kinks out of her shoulders and neck. "Okay. The bottom line is, your dad had a fabulous job with a very nice salary. He had turned Michael Nason's around, and we were very secure. When the Consolidated board came to him, Consolidated was deeply in debt and had filed for bankruptcy."

"And no other group of stores had ever made it out of bankruptcy," April filled in.

Paige stared at her daughter. "You've picked up a lot more than I realized."

"Well, duh. It's not like I've been under a rock."

Paige grinned. "I guess you haven't. Well, that's where the risk came from. Since no one had managed to bring a company that size out of bankruptcy, your father had very specific safeguards written into his employment contract. He was to be paid a specific amount of money based on how much he increased the value of the company. The problem is, there is a disagreement on how that value should be calculated."

April held up her hand. "Okay, Mom. I sort of get it. Dad saved Consolidated and has made it the greatest group of department stores ever, but now they don't want to pay what they promised."

Paige smiled at her daughter. She had summed up their dilemma.

"Holy shit!" Ross Pocino exploded. The phone nearly slipped from his beefy fingers. "Run that by me again." He listened carefully to his colleague, grunted a few responses, and signed off. A grin spread across his face.

No sooner had he hung up the phone then it blared again, and he immediately snatched up the receiver. "Pocino."

"And a very good morning to you." Dick Landes's voice rang with amusement.

With no apology for his lack of manners, Pocino said, "We've got our first legit lead. I'll check it out ASAP, and if I hit pay dirt, we can bring the Taylors into the loop."

"Hold on. You're talking about the lead that was called in last night?"

The previous day, the two New York agents—whom Landes had assigned to canvass the area adjacent to Carlingdon's—reported that neighbors at an apartment complex near Lexington knew of a child matching the description of the Taylor twin living in their building. There was no question about it. Landes kept his voice deadly calm. Before Pocino had a chance to respond, his boss continued, "I can't read between the lines, so you'd better fill me in."

Pocino sighed and heaved himself to his feet. With phone in hand, he paced in front of the floor-to-ceiling windows of the Landes Agency's New York office, thirty-two stories above Times Square. It was Monday, and he'd just arrived from Los Angeles, not expecting to have much to follow up on.

"You're not going to believe this twisted web of convoluted facts. Since no one answered when our two agents rapped on the door of that third-floor apartment last night, I'm taking over on the follow-up. It will be my pleasure to handle the questioning." He hurried on. "In running down the details, we discovered that the guy who rented it is dead. But apparently his wife and his brother are shacking up, and they have a four-year-old girl."

"So?" Landes said. "We agreed not to go off the deep end with this sighting."

"True," Pocino confirmed. "I still say that kids, with their baby features, tend to look pretty much alike."

"Since you haven't gone to investigate yet, what is it that's turned this into a legitimate lead?"

"The sighting isn't what has me hot to trot. I intended to fill you in after I had a visit with Mr. Michael Christonelli."

"The guy in the apartment?"

"You got it. Apparently, this guy just happened to design a website for Carlingdon's. And his sister-in-law, whose name is Erica Christonelli, just happens to work for Viviana De Mornay. How twisted is that?"

A beat of silence followed his remarks. Finally, Landes said, "That's a lot to take in. Convoluted is an apt description, but I don't see how it ties into a kidnapping. A kidnapper with even a quarter of a brain would stay clear of anyone who could tie him or her into that kind of crime. How dumb would you—"

"Hang on, boss. I've no fuckin' clue how this ties in, but I intend to find out. I'll fill you in after I pay a visit to Mr. Christonelli, but boss, this has to be more than a coincidence. You and I agree, coincidence has no place in our business." Pocino sighed into the phone. "And real life is a damn sight stranger than any goddamned fiction that anyone's ever penned."

Impatiently tapping the toe of her Prada boot, Viviana heaved a sigh of relief when the limousine pulled into the stream of cars lined up in the arrivals area at JFK. "It's about time," she muttered, moving rapidly toward the curb.

Mitchell cocked a thick brow and glanced down at his Rolex. "Actually, our driver is ahead of schedule," he said, taking hold of her elbow as she lowered herself into the vehicle. Their flight had touched down fifteen minutes early, and Viviana was more than eager to get to her boutique as soon as possible.

"After all I've done for Erica, I can't believe the ungrateful bi—woman would leave without notice! And I don't buy her lame story. She's never once mentioned a sick mother." *Where can she have gone? And even more critical, what has she taken with her?*

"Relax," Wainwright said, trying to calm Viviana. "When she called, Erica seemed genuinely overwrought with concern for her mother." And for both women's sakes, he hoped that her story was true.

But why would she resign with no forwarding address? Why wouldn't she ask for a leave of absence? he thought to himself. Aloud, he said, "She doesn't seem to be the type of young woman who would steal your designs or be stupid enough to try to peddle them as her own. You have pictures of all your fashions and the ones she designed while working for you. Besides, you said Glenn has duplicates of all the sketches."

Viviana rolled her eyes. "The duplicates are all in a file cabinet at the store, not at another location. As you say, it would be a stupid move for Erica to try to pass off my designs as her own. It couldn't be done. Not in this country, at least. But Erica is out to make a name for herself, so she could use those she'd designed with the De Mornay's label to get her foot in the door in the upscale market, if that's her game."

Wainwright listened to her carefully, but knew he had a more clear understanding of the situation. The upscale market wasn't her greatest worry—knockoffs in the mass market could be a far greater danger.

The instant they pulled up in front of De Mornay's, Viviana threw open the door and climbed out of the limo while rummaging in her handbag for the keys.

Noticing the shaking of her hand, Wainwright reached for the key.

"Thank you," Viviana said. "Sorry to be so uptight. But ever since Erica dropped her bombshell, I've had nightmares of walking into a Target or a Kmart and seeing knockoffs of the De Mornay's label hanging on the racks."

Once inside the upscale boutique, she headed straight to her office and pulled open the desk drawer. She pulled out a leather-bound folder. "They're here," she cried out, leafing through the pages. Then, dashing to the file cabinet in Glenn's office, she flung open the drawer where he stored the copies. Tugging on the folder labeled FASHION DESIGNS 1994, she announced, "I think they're all here. But she could have made copies."

While Viviana riffled through drawers and files, Wainwright picked up a photo that sat on Glenn's desk. Before setting it back on the desk, he took a second look; then he actually stared at the snapshot. *This can't be right.* Taken aback, he opened his mouth to ask Viviana about it when he heard heavy footfalls advancing toward the office.

Glenn Nelson dashed in. Clad in a pair of jeans and a rumpled shirt collar beneath his Armani sweater, he was uncharacteristically unshaven. His eye fell on the picture frame in Wainwright's hand. "Oh, shit," he said without even uttering a greeting.

Viviana whirled around to face Glenn, surprised by his uncharacteristic use of profanity. She first stared into Glenn's bloodshot eyes and then shifted her gaze to Wainwright. "What is going on?"

Wainwright held out the picture. He hadn't been wrong. Erica stood in between Glenn and another man. The little girl in Erica's arms was a carbon copy of Ashleigh's little girl.

Glenn swallowed hard, looking from Wainwright to Viviana and back again. He wasn't prepared for this—not now. Maybe not ever.

Flopping down into his leather chair, Glenn stared up at his business partner and Wainwright. He gestured to the two chairs in front of his desk. "Please, sit down."

Ignoring him, Viviana took the picture from Wainwright's outstretched hand. With a frown, she bit down on her bottom lip and said, "This is Ashleigh's little girl?"

For nearly a full minute, no one spoke.

"Oh . . . oh my . . . my God," Viviana stammered, stumbling backward slightly. "It's the missing twin."

Wainwright guided her into one of the cushioned chairs in front of Glenn's desk and lowered himself into the other. "How long have you known about this, Glenn?"

"I was hoping to have a bit of time to think this through."

Wainwright glared at him and repeated the words more forcefully. "How long have you known?"

Glenn raked his fingers through his hair. "Barely twenty-four hours. In working on our website with Mike Christonelli, Erica's brother-in-law, I've gotten to know Erica and her little girl pretty well. I saw Ashleigh's twin for the first time Saturday at Charles Stuart's memorial." He hesitated, not certain how much he should tell or whom he should protect. "Look," he finally said, "Erica and Ashleigh are both victims—there are no bad guys—at least, not among the living."

Wainwright sprang to his feet. "No bad guys? Are you out of your fucking mind?"

"Please, sit down," Glenn repeated. "I came here straight from Christonelli's apartment, and I'm still trying to wrap my mind around what he told me."

"Please, Mitchell." Viviana reached out and touched his arm.

Reluctantly, Wainwright slipped back into the chair.

"First of all, you need to know that Erica did not know that her baby was abducted."

Wainwright clucked his tongue in disgust. "That's absurd." But before he could utter another word, Glenn held up the palm of his hand, anticipating their reaction.

"I know it sounds impossible, but hear me out. The baby was taken by Erica's late husband four years ago . . ."

Wainwright looked across to Viviana, perched on the edge of the chair. Clenching his fists, he leaned back to give the impression that he was listening. And maybe he actually *would* listen. *How in the hell is Glenn going to rationalize the motives of a goddamned kidnapper?* His stomach clenched, and then, slowly, he began to relax. This was going to be good.

". . . and Christonelli was finishing packing up when I arrived," Glenn was saying. "He has a morning flight to Chicago tomorrow. He claims he doesn't know where Erica has gone."

"Doesn't know where she is," Wainwright scoffed. "Not likely. He's lying through his teeth."

"I tried my level best to find out. Said I was prepared to help if I could, but—"

"Prepared to help a kidnapper?" Viviana sprang from her seat. "I can't believe you haven't already turned her in!"

"Calm down," Glenn said. "I want to find Erica, talk to her. Then . . . I don't know what. I sure as hell don't want to keep Ashleigh's daughter from her. On the other hand, taking Marnie . . . that's the name they've given the girl." He cleared his throat and continued. "Being responsible for having Marnie taken from Erica is the most horrible thing I can imagine. It's unthinkable. It would be devastating for Marnie as well as Erica."

Viviana raged on. "But Ashleigh is the little girl's mother, not Erica! Ashleigh gave birth to the twins. And I don't buy the fact that Erica had no idea she was raising another woman's baby. She knows nothing about motherhood. She's never given birth. The police should be notified immediately, and the Landes Agency—before she gets away."

"Hold on," Wainwright cut in. "Let's not get into a knock-down-drag-out on nature versus nurture. Let's think this through. If what Glenn was told is the God's honest truth, Erica thought the baby was hers to raise—"

"You don't understand!" Viviana shouted. "Giving birth is . . ." Her voice trailed off. If she said any more, she would be in danger of revealing a secret she would do anything to hide.

"If giving birth is the only thing that makes a person a caring parent," he said with derision, "where does that leave the father?"

With an expression of abject horror, Viviana said, "Oh, Mitchell, I didn't mean—"

"Forget it. Let's not rush into any action until we have all the facts and can guess how those facts will play out." He turned to Glenn and asked, "Where did you say that Christonelli and his friend were moving to? Chicago?"

Wainwright wasn't sure what to do about the situation. It certainly was a sticky one. But when he thought about it, why shouldn't he be prepared to help the woman keep the child, if her story was true? Why should the fates always favor Ashleigh?

Mike Christonelli sealed the lid of the last carton and considered the boxes strewn across the kitchen and the countertop, wondering about his next move. Glenn Nelson's visit had left him rattled and filled with uncertainty.

Should he call Erica or wait until he was with her? Now that Glenn knew the truth and knew the destination of his move, Erica and Marnie would not be safe with him. He hadn't wanted to tell Glenn where they were moving, but it couldn't be helped. His business could not survive anonymity. And he'd seen no way of lying about the child and her origins—not when he was confronted by Glenn's account of his recent encounter with the Taylor girl.

Without Bill, Erica, and especially Marnie, the kitchen clock and the sound of the running refrigerator appeared unusually loud, and Mike was aware of the whistle of the wind and the tapping of tree branches beyond the kitchen window. The past two days, since the departure of his small family for Chicago, had seemed like an eternity. Fortunately, with the movers scheduled to arrive in the next hour, and a six thirty-five flight first thing the next morning, he'd soon be with them. But for how long?

Mike began shifting boxes from here to there in preparation, when he heard footfalls pounding their way down the third-floor hall. They stopped at the front door. *The movers?* He stood in place, expecting the sound of the door knocker. He didn't have to wait more than a moment before the knocker banged loudly against the metal plate.

He strode rapidly to the door and peered out through the peephole. A large ape of a man blocked his view. "Who is it?"

"Ross Pocino," the man said. "I'm a private investigator. I need to talk with you. It will only take a few minutes."

Private investigator. Private investigator. The words rang in his head. *Had Glenn already turned them in?* "What do you want?" He hoped his voice didn't sound as shaky to the man as it did to his own ears.

"I need to talk with you." The man's husky voice repeated, loud and insistent.

"Who is it you're looking for?" *Let it be the wrong apartment.* Mike's stomach knotted. Why hadn't he let the movers pack the household items, as Erica had suggested, and left with her and Marnie?

"Michael and Erica Christonelli."

Gathering what little courage he had left, Mike opened the door. "Erica is not here. How can I help you?"

The heavyset investigator, wearing an ill-fitting suit, stepped inside, introduced himself, and glanced around the apartment. "It appears that you are in the midst of moving."

Mike nodded, not wanting to say more than necessary.

"Where to?"

"Chicago." No point in lying now. Perhaps Glenn had already told the man. He couldn't remain incognito and run a successful business. That was for sure.

"Is Mrs. Christonelli also moving to Chicago?"

"No," he lied. Erica had given no notice to Viviana, telling her that there was an emergency and she had to go to take care of her mother—indefinitely. That's what he told the burly investigator.

"Where is that?"

"You mean where does Erica's mother live?"

The investigator gave an impatient nod, as if that were the most stupid question he'd ever heard.

"Uh . . . England," Mike stammered. It was the first thing that came into his head.

"England?" The investigator's brow furrowed. "Where in England?"

"Look, Mr. Pocino. I don't know."

"What do you mean? Was there a falling out between you?"

"No. I just don't know the exact place." It sounded lame, but he'd been totally unprepared for this line of questioning—he hadn't thought Glenn would betray them, and so soon! Starting to panic, he did the best he could to explain, just making things up as he went along. "I was out of town on a job when Erica received the call from England. She left a message on our phone, but she didn't mention the name of the town in England." A bead of sweat ran down his brow.

"Did she take the *little girl* with her?" the investigator asked pointedly.

"Little girl?" Any one of their neighbors could have told the investigator about Marnie. *But what does this guy actually know?* Mike's T-shirt stuck to his back, and he wiped his damp palms on his beige chinos. "Of course she took her daughter."

The man glared at him. "How about *this* child?" He pulled a photo from his inside pocket.

Mike stared at the picture. It looked just like Marnie. The crooked little smile, the big doe eyes, and dimples, but the child wore an outfit Mike had never seen. *It's the twin. He's trying to trick me.*

"Well?"

Caught like an animal in the bright lights of an oncoming car, Mike felt paralyzed, but he forced himself to speak. Somehow, he managed to keep his voice steady. "I'm sorry. I don't know that little girl."

The investigator continued to glare at him, thrusting the photograph even closer. "Doesn't she look a little . . . *familiar?*"

Mike gathered himself inwardly and replied, "Gee, that little girl does look a little like my niece. But not enough so as to ever mistake the two of them."

"You're sure about that?"

"Absolutely," Mike lied.

"Your neighbors seem to think this is the child who lives here."

"Well, they're mistaken. My sister-in-law and niece lived here. In fact, it was my brother who rented this apartment. The four of us were planning to live here together, but . . ." Mike hesitated a moment to regroup. "Sorry. You don't need to know all the background. The point is, the only similarities between this little girl," he said, pointing to the picture, "and

Marnie are that they both have blond hair and brown eyes. But then, there must be thousands of little kids this age who look like that."

He paused, realizing he should probably ask something about the other child. "Who is that girl in the picture?"

Pocino eyed him for several beats before answering. "This is the photo of a little girl whose *identical* twin was stolen within hours of her birth." He emphasized the word identical.

"How dreadful," Mike said, meaning it. "For the parents' sake, I sure hope you find her." Just as he was about to suggest that the investigator be on his way, the phone rang. Mike froze.

"Go ahead," Pocino said, gesturing to the phone with his head. "I have a couple more questions."

Mike wished he could either ignore the call or ask the man to leave, but he wanted to do nothing that would create further suspicion. Grabbing the receiver before the next ring, he held it so close that his ear felt numb. His blood turned to ice at the sound of Erica's voice, but before she had a chance to say more than a few words, he said, "Hi, Jean. I have some unexpected company. Let me call you back."

He quickly disengaged the phone and said to the detective, "If there's nothing more—"

Pocino, who had been scanning the room and trying to see beyond the boxes, asked, "Mind if I take a look around?"

"Yes, I do. I'm in the process of moving." With a last effort at controlling his strained nerves, he said firmly, "So if you don't have a warrant, I'd like you to be on your way."

The investigator slowly headed toward the door. Then he paused, turned on his heel to face Mike, and pulled a small notebook from the inside pocket of his jacket. "Do you have a phone number in Chicago?"

Mike's heart skipped a beat. But before he could utter any kind of response, the burly investigator said, "I'll also be needing your new address."

When Mike finally closed the door behind the man, his rubbery body trembled and, as if he were boneless, he sank to the floor.

Erica stood in stunned silence. Gripping the edge of the kitchen sink, she took in one deep breath followed by another.

Seated on a bar stool at the end of the high countertop, Bill set down his coffee and asked, "What is it?" Since moving to the cozy little starter home he had found for the four of them in Arlington Heights, it seemed like nothing had gone right.

Erica looked across the room, but her eyes did not meet his. "Something has gone wrong in Manhattan. I think the police were with Mike when I called."

Sliding down from the stool, Bill crossed the few steps between them and touched her elbow gently. With his index finger, he lifted her chin so she was unable to avoid his eyes. "Did he say the police were there?"

Erica shook her head. "But he called me Jean. That's his sister's name." Her voice shook. "If they've found out about Marnie, we won't be safe here. I can't stay with you and Mike." *What can I do? Where will we go?*

"Slow down. It's probably nothing. You know how Mike felt about the narrow window for this move. He was stressed over getting everything ready for the movers. Remember, he told us that everything was being picked up this afternoon."

"Yes. I remember. But why would he call me by his sister's name?"

"As I just said, stress. When Mike's concentrating on one thing, everything else is forgotten. If he didn't have that kind of skill, his website business wouldn't have taken off like it has."

Erica wished she could buy into Bill's explanation, but her stomach churned with apprehension.

Planning his next move, Pocino descended the stairs from the third-floor apartment at a fraction of his usual speed. Christonelli was lying through his teeth. Although the detective hadn't been allowed to peruse the rest of the apartment, the folded high chair beside the stack of packed boxes told him plenty. Unless Mike was planning to take all of his sister-in-law's and niece's worldly goods to Chicago for safe-keeping during their time in England, it looked like the threesome was relocating to Chicago as a comfy family.

Even before he reached his rain-spattered Mustang, Pocino spotted the ticket plastered to the windshield. "Son of a bitch," he muttered, not quite to himself. He knew better than to park in a thirty-minute zone. *But there was no other fuckin' parking spot!* He crumpled the ticket and shoved it into the pocket of his suit jacket. Since he'd been back and forth to New York for the Taylor investigation, he'd collected enough parking violations to wallpaper his entire studio apartment. Sure, the transportation system here was much better than in L.A., but he had to leave the car somewhere. And when he didn't have a clue where he was going, he didn't have the luxury of leaving his old chariot in public parking garages.

He turned up his collar to ward off the light drizzle and was just about to open his car door when he hesitated. *I already have one ticket; might as well leave the car here.* Getting to De Mornay's by subway was a no-brainer. He placed the ticket under the windshield wiper once more and headed for the nearby underground station.

CHAPTER

99

In the tenth-floor suite of his Long Beach offices on Ocean Boulevard, Dick Landes leaned back in his plush leather desk chair, the back of his head cradled in the palms of his hands and interlaced fingers. Pocino hadn't been off the mark when he'd labeled this case a twisted web.

The more pieces to the puzzle he assembled on this case, the more convoluted it became. After uncovering the fact that Mario Christonelli was a nurse practitioner at Long Beach Memorial Hospital at the time of the kidnapping, Landes now had enough facts to determine that on the evening of August eighteenth, 1990, Christonelli had had both the means and the opportunity to abduct Cassie Taylor. What he did not appear to have had was a motive: His wife, Erica, had just given birth.

Since the Carlingdon's sighting of a little girl who appeared to be identical to the missing twin, the trail had led straight to Mario Christonelli's wife and brother. These were more than just coincidences that didn't add up.

Riffling through the sheets of notes piled neatly on his desk, he found the number for Dr. Ian McDonald, and picked up the phone. No point in traveling down to Laguna Niguel before checking to make sure that the Christonelli woman's brother could be reached there.

"Oh God, Leslie," groaned Ian McDonald. "I don't know how to tell you this. Don't even know where to start." Following the call from the investigator, he had gone straight home from a midafternoon surgery without changing out of his scrubs, in the hope of intercepting his wife before she went to pick up their children from school.

"Why not take the advice you give so liberally?" Leslie paused, her expression wary. "Begin at the beginning, and take it one slow step at a time."

"It's often easier to give advice than it is to take it. What I have to tell you—it's going to be a shock. I can only pray that you will find it in your heart to forgive me."

Leslie sucked on her bottom lip. *Ian is having an affair.* No, that couldn't be. Or could it? Were there really that many late-night meetings at the hospital? And wasn't it always the wife who was the last one to suspect?

He continued, "I had no real justification for keeping something so vital from you, but I felt caught between that proverbial rock and a hunk of granite. I actually lied to you, and for that I am very much ashamed."

"For heaven's sake, Ian, stop talking in circles."

Ian took in a huge breath, stared at the ceiling for a second or two, and then said, "It's about Marnie. She's not the infant of the young mother I told you about. The one who wanted a better life for her daughter than the one she could give her . . ."

Leslie listened to Ian's story without comment. His words struck her as though she were hit head-on by an Amtrak train. One thought repeated itself in her head: *Why? Why did he lie?*

When he'd finished his explanation, he reached across the table, but Leslie pulled away. "How could you, Ian?" Rising to her feet, she stormed over to the sink and washed her hands. She washed them a second time and then a third before turning to face her husband. "And how could Erica . . . ?"

"Erica doesn't know," Ian said in as calm and even a tone as he could manage.

Leslie glared at him. He could see the simmering anger bubbling up in his wife; he was sure she was about to explode. But instead, an expression of pure bafflement settled on her face. "Erica doesn't know?" she repeated. "How can that be?"

As he related all that had happened between Mario and him four years before, he felt more foolish by the moment. "Mario didn't tell Erica that the young girl's infant, whom he'd arranged to pick up at the hospital, had been spirited away before he'd arrived. Nor did he tell her that he had taken the twin daughter of Conrad and Ashleigh Taylor."

"But Ian, it was all over the news."

"If you recall, Erica was totally withdrawn at that time. She was severely depressed. She hardly left her room. She didn't know what was happening in our house, much less what was going on in the news. And then once the baby arrived, she was completely absorbed with her."

Ian came to his feet and strode across the kitchen to Leslie, wrapping his arms around her shoulders. "Leslie, I am so sorry. I hate what I put you through then and what I'm dragging you into now. All I can say is that what I did was dead wrong. Especially failing to tell you the truth. I let my concerns for the mental stability of my sister throw me off kilter, and I can't tell you how much I've rued that decision ever since."

Leslie leaned into him, placing her head against his shoulder. "So, what do we do now?"

Ian glanced up at the kitchen clock. "I have an appointment with a private investigator in about forty-five minutes. You can sit in, but you don't have to. It's up to you."

She nodded but made no vocal response.

"I'm not sure what I should do. I didn't sign Marnie's birth certificate, but Mario forged my name, and I knew about it. However, I did write a false name on the death certificate of Erica's stillborn. So I guess that makes me an accessory. I suppose I could lose my license if they can prove I was involved and withheld information."

He sighed, but then a determined look came over his face. "But I'm not going to worry about that now. First I must call Erica. I can't allow her to be blindsided by this. She can't be caught unprepared."

But how in the name of God can I prepare her for this?

Viviana stayed near the front of the boutique, keeping her eye trained on the Fifth Avenue entrance.

"What's up?" Glenn asked, stepping back from the mannequin. "You've been hovering around here for the past half hour." He folded the red patent leather belt and clipped it discreetly in back, under the jacket. The lipstick-red Donna Karan ensemble now fit the mannequin to perfection.

"Ross Pocino is due any moment."

Arching a brow, Glenn stared at her. "You didn't tell him about Erica, did you?"

"Not yet, but that's who he wanted to talk to us about."

"What's his interest? What does he know?"

"He was vague. Just said he had a few questions about her—and her reasons for leaving."

Glenn's brows knit together. "Vague? Doesn't sound like the Pocino I know. Subtlety is not his game." He smoothed the Hermès scarves on the shelf beside him. "What do you intend to tell him?"

"Well, he's not likely to be interested in her leaving us without notice, so he must already have some sort of clue. Otherwise, he wouldn't be hotfooting it on over here."

"Please don't mention Chicago. Not yet."

She nodded. "I told Pocino that everything I know about Erica or her abrupt departure could be discussed by phone, but he insisted on stopping by. Said he had a picture he wanted us to look at."

"Oh, no. What kind of picture?"

"He didn't say, but I think we both know." Mitchell had asked her to promise that until she heard from him, she would reveal the truth to neither the police nor the Landes Agency. She hadn't quite decided how to handle it. She secretly prayed, however, that Pocino was already onto Erica. *Ungrateful little bitch deserves it.*

Glenn had already removed the incriminating framed photograph from his desktop, just in case the investigator decided to take a look around. "Afraid so. But I hope to hell it isn't true. Erica's entire life was wrapped around her little girl and becoming a top designer here in New York. I don't think she even dated, although her husband died two years ago. She's obviously giving up her own dreams now to keep Marnie from being taken from her."

"Well, that baby isn't hers. She's Ashleigh's. And another thing; you know Erica had access to all my fashion sketches. I'm worried she'll . . ."

Before Viviana could finish her sentence, however, Pocino ambled through the doorway and greeted them with his customary "Ciao." After returning his greeting, she moved to usher the untidy investigator out of the salon area and directly into her office.

"Hold on," Pocino said, stopping midstride. "Glenn, I'd like to talk with both of you. It will just take a few minutes."

Glenn caught the eye of the sales associate who was temporarily taking over Erica's sales duties. "We will be off the floor for a short time. Buzz me if you need me," he said, then he followed Viviana and Pocino to the back office.

"What is this all about?" Viviana asked immediately after she closed her office door. "I've already told you everything I know about Erica Christonelli. She had everything going for her, yet overnight she gave notice and was gone."

Glenn added. "We've wracked our brains trying to make sense of it. Seems like Erica could have asked for a leave of absence to take care of her mother rather than giving no notice and just disappearing."

"Did you ever see the little girl?" Pocino plopped down in the chair in front of Viviana's desk, while she rounded the desk and slipped into her desk chair.

Glenn nodded, taking the chair beside Pocino. "As smart as a whip."

Viviana shook her head. She wanted to add that she'd seen a picture of the child, and that Erica's daughter looked exactly like Ashleigh's, but she'd promised both Mitchell and Glenn that she'd hold her tongue until they located Erica.

Glenn continued as if there was no question on the table. "I talked with Mike, Erica's brother-in-law, yesterday. He confirmed that she'd gone to take care of her mother. She'd already packed up and left town. Mike's a real decent guy and crazy about his niece. He devoted as much if not more time to raising that kid than Erica did."

"Did he tell you where the mother lives?"

"No," Glenn said. "But they're such a tight-knit unit, I'm sure she'll be in touch."

Pocino leaned against Viviana's black lacquered table, pulled out a photo from his jacket pocket, and handed it to Glenn. "Does this look anything like the Christonelli woman's little girl?"

Glenn took the picture. "Sure, this girl looks something like Marnie. Where did you get this?"

Pocino's broad, round face broke into a grin and he snapped his fingers. "Bingo!"

Viviana rose, stepped around the desk, and took the picture from Glenn. Mitchell was so determined that information about the missing twin not be leaked. She decided to play along. "Ross, I think you'd better tell us what's going on."

"Are you saying you didn't see this child at the memorial in Long Beach on Saturday? This is Ashleigh and Conrad Taylor's daughter. You know, the twin?"

Nodding, Viviana stared from the picture to Pocino and back again. She allowed a gasp to escape from her lips, and slipped back into her chair, but it was all for effect. She knew exactly what this was all about.

"Mom," April said. "Can we have Terrence and Wilma help us with the decorations?"

This year the annual dance team party, a tradition that began when April and Madison made the mini-competition team when they were still in kindergarten would be at the Toddman's. Now that they were older, they were doing the planning. April had started making plans several weeks earlier, going over everything they wanted to repeat and improve upon from last year's affair at Madison's.

Before the car came to a full stop, the two girls bolted from the car, bags of decorations in hand. Shaking her head in amusement, Paige smiled as they disappeared into the house. She scooped up the remaining parcels and followed the girls up the front steps. As she approached the front door, she heard the distant ring of the telephone. At first she ignored it, expecting either Wilma or Anna to answer, but when the phone continued to shrill, she dropped the bags on the living room sofa and picked up the phone on the end table.

Following her greeting, she heard a familiar "Ciao." And before she could inquire about any new developments, Pocino gave her an earful. By the time he'd brought her up to date on all he'd discovered, her head was whirling. Weak-kneed, she lowered herself onto the sofa.

"Erica Christonelli?" The moment she heard the name, a vision of the young designer floated into view. She remembered the bright, vivacious woman Viviana had introduced to them when Paige had accompanied Ashleigh on her first visit to De Mornay's.

"You say she left De Mornay's without notice?"

"Right," Pocino said, without elaboration.

"Since her dress designs were first-class and causing quite a stir in the fashion market, she had to have a darn good reason for taking flight."

"There's little doubt in my mind that she has that kidnapped twin. Tell me what you know about the woman."

She filled him in on their first meeting. "But after that, something happened. When I ran into her at various fashion events over the next two years, she didn't seem at all the same person we'd met at De Mornay's. She displayed none of the friendly, easygoing manner we'd found so charming. She was polite but seemed somewhat removed, and she made no effort to join in the conversation. In fact, although I wasn't aware of it until now, she seemed to avoid me.

"Glenn had mentioned to me that Erica had a daughter about Callie's age. Now that I think about it, Erica did not bring her little girl to any of the Carlingdon's family parties. Not at Easter or Christmas. Most of our employees and vendors came with their entire families; she came alone. Now, I guess we know why." Hardly able to contain her enthusiasm, Paige said, "We've got to tell Ashleigh and Conrad!"

"I agree," Pocino said, "but not so fast. We're ninety-nine percent certain we're on the track of the Taylors' kid, but Landes is still following a lead. He's talking with Erica Christonelli's brother in Laguna Niguel, in California. It seems he's an M.D., and he claims his sister gave birth to a baby about the same time as the kidnapping."

"Do you think that could be true?"

"It's pretty convoluted. The Christonellis had tried to adopt two or three times. It seems the adoptions fell through. Then they tried in vitro."

"Was that successful?" Paige slumped back in the chair. Maybe this wasn't Ashleigh's baby after all. She reached up to her forehead to see if it was as hot as she imagined.

"Don't know. But I seriously doubt it." Pocino cleared his throat before rattling off his series of facts. "Her husband just happens to work at Memorial Hospital. His last day just happens to be the day the kid disappears. After years of failed attempts, his wife just happens to give birth to a baby girl, who's the spittin' image of Ashleigh's little girl, and that's on or about the same day Ashleigh's twins are born." As he ticked off the string of coincidences, Paige felt the tension in her head begin to ease.

"When can we tell Ashleigh and Conrad what's going on? With all you and Landes have uncovered, I no longer feel right about keeping any of this from them."

"All in good time. First, I need to talk with your daughter and her friend. The one who was with her when they saw the twin at Carlingdon's."

"Why? You have a recent picture of Callie."

"It's not the twin we need identified. It's the man."

In a darkened bedroom of the new home that wasn't to be hers after all, Erica sat on the bed beside her sleeping child. The frenzied action of the last few days—the packing, the traveling—had taken its toll on the little girl. The sun had begun to set, but Erica hadn't bothered to turn on a single light. Beside her on the bedside table sat an open bottle of Chardonnay and a nearly empty wine glass. She refilled her glass.

While Bill had full knowledge of her predicament, he simply couldn't fathom how dangerous her situation had become. She hadn't meant to, but she'd hurt him to the core. If only she could take back those angry words after Mike's phone call. "Don't be stupid!" she'd screamed at Bill when he'd tried to comfort her. "There's no way I can live here in Chicago now! I can't be anywhere near you and Mike. Do you want me to lose Marnie? Do you want to have her taken from me?"

Why hadn't she told him how much he and Mike meant to her? She loved them with all her heart, but she hadn't told him that. She had been too frightened and too angry. Mike and Bill were her family. They loved Marnie, and she loved them. But since the Toddmans' daughter had seen Marnie, and now with Glenn and an investigator linking Mike with the abducted twin, it wasn't safe to be anywhere near him.

Stroking Marnie's baby-fine hair, she saw her entire future begin to crumble. She'd resigned herself to forgoing her dream of becoming a dress designer and nearly talked herself into being happy over landing the possibility of a position as a personal shopper for John Stewart's, a fantastic Chicago icon housed in an awesome historical building—a pillar of the retail community. She had looked forward to settling in Arlington Heights with Mike and Bill. Their cozy new home was less than twelve miles from Chicago and only twenty minutes from John Stewart's, in a neighborhood with great schools for Marnie.

Tears washed down her face. She dried them with the back of her hand. All those plans must be abandoned. Her job at John Stewart's was over before it began. She dare not show up for a single day's work. She couldn't use her Social Security number. She'd seen enough movies and read enough crime novels to know that if they had linked Marnie to the missing twin, the police would soon be able to trace her through that number.

Now what am I to do? Where are Marnie and I to go?

The sound of Bill's movements in the adjoining room diverted her from further contemplation, but not for long. He came to the door and looked in at her with compassion. "Bill," she said quietly. "Do you know where I can get a false ID?"

Openmouthed, Bill stared at Erica. "A false ID?" he repeated. "Please tell me you aren't serious."

"Dead serious." He had no idea just how desperate she was.

Bill flicked on the bedside lamp. "Aren't you overreacting?" He looked down at the sleeping child. As he watched Erica pace back and forth near the bed, he continued, "Well, perhaps not. Look, I have no idea how to get false papers, but if you are really serious, I'll look into it." His eyes took in Erica's empty wine glass, but he made no comment. A stricken expression shadowed his face. "You don't really intend to leave Chicago, do you?"

"I don't have a choice. I didn't mean to bark at you earlier. I'm just so stressed; I don't know what I'm doing. But it's clear that I've got to distance myself from Mike and the detective that came to talk with him today. And I have to do it right away."

Bill stared at the floor, running a hand through his thinning hair. "The thought of losing you and Marnie makes me feel physically ill. If only I could assure you that you'd be safe here, I would. But I'm clearly out of my depth."

Pulling herself to her feet, she gave him a hug. "Me too."

"Where will you go?"

"I've been racking my brain. There's only one thing that I can do. I don't want Marnie to be isolated, without family . . ." Cutting off midsentence, she grasped Bill's arms. "God, this is so hard. It's best that you don't know where we are. That way, if Glenn Nelson, or that detective, or the police come to Chicago looking for me and Marnie, you won't have to lie to them. Even if Mike guesses where we've gone, tell him he can't call."

Her heart pounded so hard against her chest, she felt the thunder in her ears. "Promise to tell Mike that he mustn't contact any of my family or friends. In a month or so, I'll get in touch. We will work out something. Just as soon as I'm certain it's safe."

When there was nothing more to say, Bill hugged her tight and headed for his own room. Erica waited until she heard the click of his door, then picked up the phone.

Ian picked up before the second ring. "Erica," he said. "I've been trying to get hold of you. I talked with Mike, but he said he didn't know when you'd return."

What's going on? Why is my brother trying to get in touch right now? Other than on a holiday or a special occasion, he seldom called. Attempting to keep all signs of alarm out of her voice, she asked, "Are Leslie and the kids alright?"

Not responding, he asked, "Where are you?"

"Ian," Erica began, "I need your help. I can't give you all the details right now, but I need to get away from New York. I might come back to Southern California for a little while. Wherever I go, I need to do it right away. As early as tomorrow morning."

"No. You can't come here." His tone was harsh, his message emphatic.

Stunned, Erica walked to the window, looking at the billions of lights of the Windy City twinkling back at her, and feeling utterly lost and alone. Her stomach clenched, she asked, "Why not? I have a little savings. I have to get away from . . . from here right now, and I don't know where to go." She hurried on. "I plan to get my own apartment, though. I didn't say we planned to move in with your family. We won't be in the area for long. I didn't even say I planned to come to Laguna Niguel. I just . . . just wanted to let you know. I might need a little help."

She tucked a stray strand of hair behind her ear and waited. The silence lingered a beat too long. "Ian? Did you hear what I said?"

"Yes. I heard you. But there's a problem." A muffled sound drifted though the line. "Give me a number where I can reach you. I'll call you back."

"Ian? I don't understand. What is going on?"

"Please," he said. "I'll call you back within the hour."

She gave him the number. Just before the call disconnected, Erica thought she heard the sound of Ian's front doorbell.

There was no doubt about it. The impeccably groomed founder of the Landes Agency was not buying Ian's story. Landes sat in the chair across from him, his right ankle resting on the knee of the other leg. He had listened without comment, his eyes never drifting from Ian's. Eyes that did not reflect trust.

How can I protect Erica and the child without jeopardizing my own family and my position as a respected doctor? It was clear to Ian that there was no way. The best he could do was withhold the "whole truth" and make sure that Erica did not return to the area.

After answering Landes's preliminary questions, Leslie had excused herself to take Ilise to her piano lesson, leaving Landes and Ian alone in the spacious living room.

"Look, Mr. Landes. I haven't been completely up front with you."

Landes nodded, waiting for Ian to continue.

Wiping his hands on the front of his cotton trouser legs, Ian tried to think of the best way to begin. *There is no best way,* he realized. He badly needed some caffeine. Needed something to put in his clammy hands. "How about a cup of coffee? Or can I get you something else?"

Landes apparently saw this as a delay tactic, but he said, "Sure, coffee's fine, if it's already made."

Ian dashed into the kitchen, filled two large mugs nearly to the top, and returned to the living room.

"What I didn't tell you earlier, which I should have," he said with unconcealed chagrin, "is that Erica's appendix burst and she lost her baby."

Landes didn't move a muscle. "So the baby she's raising is not her own."

"Not exactly."

"Not exactly!" Landes repeated, setting his cup down hard on the end table. He rose to his feet and stood towering over Ian. "There's no 'not exactly' about it. Either she is or she isn't!" His no-nonsense tone rattled Ian into silence. "Your sister is raising a girl, right?"

"Yes, she is. It's true that Erica is not the birth mother, but—"

"The child is adopted?"

"I think so," Ian lied.

"*Legally* adopted?" Landes asked. His dominant, unwavering stare told Ian that the investigator had him pegged as a liar. "Dr. McDonald. My agency is following a lead on the sighting of the abducted twin of Conrad and Ashleigh Taylor." Landes's tone was serious and professional, not accusatory.

As his words hung in the air, Ian felt the silence close in around him. For several heartbeats, he was unable to conjure up a single word to fill the void. Finally he said, "What does that have to do with my sister?"

"It appears that the child is the spitting image of your niece."

From that point on, their conversation went further downhill. When confronted by the investigator about his name appearing on the birth certificate of a Marnie Christonelli, Ian said that he had signed no birth certificate in that name. That was the God's honest truth. What he failed to say was that he knew of such a birth certificate, knew his name had been forged on the document, and knew by whom it had been forged.

"So," Landes said. "I assume you filed a death certificate for your sister's stillborn?"

Swallowing past the hard dry knot in his throat, Ian said, "Of course I did." Again he gave a distorted piece of the truth. He had indeed filed a death certificate for the stillborn, but he did not mention that it did not bear the Christonelli name. He'd deal with that lie if the investigator dug into the death records.

While Ian lied as little as possible, he knew that his story was full of holes. Holes the investigator surely saw through. And it was obvious that Landes didn't put much stock in Ian's expressed concern over his sister's mental state following the loss of her last chance to have her own child.

So in the end, he repeated the scenario his brother-in-law had related to him. Mario's original plan—the one Erica believed to be true. And he admitted to Landes that he could not confirm that what he'd been told was true. But he did not admit to one thing: knowing the true identity of the infant. It was the one piece of information he knew could damn them all.

Erica pushed her feet into her furry slippers. She'd put on her night-gown and quilted robe hours ago, even before the sun went down, when Marnie went to bed. She peeked in on her daughter now. *She's bound to be up bright and early tomorrow.*

It was her last pleasant thought before heading for the kitchen. It had been almost two hours since Ian had ended their call, saying he'd call back within the hour.

With no energy to cook—not even one of the TV dinners she'd picked up that afternoon—Erica popped a slice of bread into the toaster and dropped the empty wine bottle into the trashcan. *It's past seven on the West Coast.* Had Ian not acted so strangely, she would have called him back by now. The toast shot up, and she rechecked the clock. Only twenty-two minutes after nine.

Opening the refrigerator, where she'd stored a jar of jam, Erica spot-ted another bottle of Chardonnay. She stared at it for a moment, then pulled it out and picked up the corkscrew sitting on the counter. The phone rang. In her haste to pick up the receiver, she nearly knocked over the wine bottle.

"Ian?" She prayed it was.

"Sorry it's taken so long . . ."

She couldn't make out his words. Static blared in her ear, then another sound. *Is that the sound of traffic?* "Where are you?" There was a soft bang, and then the background noise broke off.

"Is this better?" he asked. "I had to shut the door. I'm in a phone booth outside the 7-Eleven by the strip mall on Crown Valley Park-way." He sighed loudly. After a moment's silence, he began speaking rapidly. "I hoped never to have this conversation with you, but I'm afraid I can no longer remain silent. What are you doing at a Chicago phone number? Something's gone wrong, hasn't it?" He didn't wait for her to reply. "It's far too dangerous for you to be kept in the dark. There are things you must know." Another silence. Then Ian said, "It's about Marnie."

"What about Marnie?" *What does Ian know about my daughter?* Could he know that the baby Mario had brought into his home had not been given to him voluntarily? That in fact she was the missing twin of nationwide notoriety?

"We were all so worried about you after you lost your baby. No one was thinking straight. Mario would have done anything to make you whole, but what he did was unforgivable. And knowing what he did, it was even more unforgivable that I remained silent.

"The story Mario told you about the baby—about the young mother who wanted you to have her—it was true. It was no tall tale. That was his plan, but it all went wrong. When he came to get the baby, the girl's parents had already taken her away from the hospital with the infant. You need to know that it was never Mario's intention to abduct a baby. He knew it was wrong. But he was blinded by his love and concern for you. He said he simply could not return to you without a baby. He felt it was the only way to save you."

"So this whole abduction is . . . *my* fault?"

"Of course not. You didn't know, and I wasn't man enough to put a stop to it when it would have done the least damage."

"You knew?" Erica couldn't believe what she was hearing. "You knew he'd abducted an infant—an identical twin—and you said nothing? How could you?"

"It was wrong. I knew it then. And now, it's a thousand times worse."

The pounding in her head made it nearly impossible to concentrate. "I can't believe it. My own brother. You pretend to care so much about me, but you remained silent. And without any kind of warning, you allowed me to move into the very circle where Marnie was sure to be spotted. My God, Ian. She's an identical twin."

"What are you talking about?" He sounded bewildered.

"The world of fashion and retail is incestuous. Mark Toddman and his wife are best friends with the Taylors. I actually met Ashleigh Taylor in De Mornay's; she knows both Viviana De Mornay and her partner, Glenn. My God, Glenn was arranging a playdate for Marnie . . . with her own twin! The only reason it didn't happen was that the Taylors were returning to Dallas. What were you thinking?"

"I don't know anything about the fashion circles you moved in there in New York City, Erica. But had I told you, would you have returned Marnie to her parents?"

"You know I couldn't have done that. But had I known, I most certainly would not have gone to work as a fashion designer in New York."

"I'm so sorry. I tried to talk Mario into returning the baby. I was going to insist on it, but before I had a chance, he'd taken the baby in to you. That baby transformed you almost instantly. Your depression lifted. Before I saw that baby in your arms, I vowed that no matter what it took, I would get the infant back to her mother where she belonged. But looking into your glistening eyes, I was powerless. After Mario confided that you told him you felt like a useless vessel, that you feared you were turning into our mother, that you would end up just like her in a mental ward . . ." He halted. "Erica, the investigator who came to see me said you had gone to England to take care of our mother."

"What investigator?" *First an investigator in New York, and now in Laguna Niguel.* Nowhere was safe. *What am I to do? Where are we to go?* She listened as her brother told her about his meeting with Dick Landes.

"I told him that our mother died two years ago. Then he informed me that you had told your employer you'd gone to England a few days ago to take care of her."

"I did tell Viviana and Glenn that I had to leave to care for our mother. I couldn't think of any other excuse on such short notice. But I didn't tell them she lived in England. That must have been Mike's fiction." She told him about the incident in Carlingdon's last week and the detective who had visited Mike today in New York.

"My God, Erica. You can't come here, and you can't stay in Chicago. I came to this pay phone because I was afraid my phone might be monitored. I don't believe that there's been sufficient time for the police to bug my phones, but I'm sure they could subpoena phone records. I didn't tell Landes I had any knowledge of any kidnapping. I told him the story Mario told you, but I had to tell him you had lost your baby. That you did not give birth to Marnie."

"You goddamned S.O.B.!" Seething, Erica uncorked the wine and poured another glass. "You had no right. Do you know the danger you've placed us in?"

"I had no alternative. I'm a doctor. Bloody hell, I have a family, Erica! I'm a doctor. I must protect them. I can't jeopardize—"

"So you just throw Marnie and me to the wolves, and protect your own precious family," she shot back.

"Erica, be reasonable. If I could swear that you'd given birth to Marnie, I would. But there's no way to conceal the truth for long. It's bound to be uncovered. I can't allow my family to be ruined."

"Well, don't worry about us. You won't be bothered by me or your niece. Not now, not ever. Rot in hell, Ian." She slammed down the phone, tears coursing down her cheeks and splashing onto the collar of her robe.

Ian stood in stunned silence, watching the traffic whoosh by. Erica's slurred words only added to his concern. She could be a strong woman when necessary—she'd shown that since Mario's accident—but at present she was frightened nearly out of her mind. He redialed Mike Christonelli's New York number. Erica must not be left alone to take care of the little girl.

In a flash, however, he came to his senses and disconnected. He needed time to think. Neither he nor Mike was in any position to offer support. At present, contact with either of them would ultimately throw Erica and Marnie into grave danger. At least two investigators had discovered who they were and their connection not only to the abductor but also to the missing twin. His mind shot ahead to what that could mean. The police departments in at least two cities and maybe even the FBI could be notified. Soon they would have enough facts together to be fairly certain that Marnie was the kidnapped twin.

When that happens, Ian thought sadly, *it will be better for everyone involved if Erica and Marnie are nowhere to be found.*

Mitchell Wainwright heard the insistent ringing of his phone while he was still in the shower. Grabbing a towel, he wrapped it around his waist and made a dash for the bedroom.

"Mr. Wainwright?" a man inquired when he picked up the receiver.

"Yes," he answered, trying to place the deep voice.

"Richard Venterini. We've located the woman and child here in Chicago, like you said."

"Where?"

"Days Inn, a stone's throw from O'Hare. How do you want us to proceed?"

"Don't approach them, but don't let them out of your sight. I'll be out on the next flight."

He tapped the disconnect button, then dialed his secretary. "Stella, I won't be in today. Get me reservations from JFK to O'Hare. Doesn't matter which airline. Just book the earliest flight. I'm leaving for the airport now. I'll be there in less than an hour." Leaving her no opportunity to ask questions or protest, he said, "Call me back on my car phone when you have the itinerary."

MISSING TAYLOR TWIN FOUND AND REUNITED WITH FAMILY. He envisioned the headline on top of a quarter-page photo of Ashleigh, standing beside Conrad Taylor and her two happy, *healthy* twins. *No matter what, that dame always comes out on top.* The very thought of all those heart-wrenching stories about poor Ashleigh's personal tragedy—it made his stomach clench like a goddamned ulcer flaring up. Sympathy was one thing, but the media was bound to turn her into some kind of saint for soldiering on with only one *perfectly healthy* child. *What utter bullshit!*

Ashleigh McDowell Taylor was no goddamned heroine. She'd never had to nurse a child through a life-threatening disease. She'd never lost her only child, her only reason for getting up each morning.

Why should she be allowed to take Erica's only child from her? *Why shouldn't I help her? No one else is going to.* But Wainwright knew full well that Erica's plight was not his real motivation. Well, maybe Ashleigh's problems wouldn't magically disappear this time. *Not if I have anything to do with it.*

It had taken the Chicago-based private investigators he'd hired less than a full day to locate Erica Christonelli and the little girl, but he was taking no chances. The woman was desperate. She could take off for anywhere, at any time. She was bound to leave Chicago as soon as she could come up with a plan. Sitting in that hotel room, she was probably coming to terms with her fugitive status. And it was a good bet that she wouldn't use her credit card the next time around.

Just a few hours later, turning his rented Buick into the parking lot of the Days Inn O'Hare, Wainwright glanced around the area until he spotted the detective's black Taurus. He pulled up beside it, along the west side of the rambling building.

"Venterini?" he asked. "I'm Mitchell Wainwright."

Nodding as he rolled down his window, the slim agent with the deep baritone said, "Haven't left their room since they checked in." He handed Wainwright the paper where he'd jotted down the room number; then he gestured to the door five yards away, at the far end of the building.

"Good job. That'll be all for now. I'll be in touch," Wainwright said, and headed for room 901.

Outside the door, he stopped to gather his thoughts. It was unlikely that Erica would respond to a knock on the door. He took several steps back and began knocking loudly along the wall, right up to and including her door.

"We have a leak in our gas line. Vacate the premises immediately. We have a leak . . ." He continued to boom out those phrases repeatedly, waiting for people from the neighboring rooms to begin pouring out into the hallway and spot him. He was willing to take the chance. The door to room 901 finally swung open, and Erica, carrying the child, almost ran straight into him.

"Mr. Wainwright!" she gasped, clutching the child close to her. She'd told no one where she was, not even Mike or Bill. "How did you find us?" *Did Glenn tell Mitchell Wainwright about me and Marnie?* Her eyes darted down the corridor as Wainwright grabbed her elbow firmly and maneuvered her back into the room.

"Please, call me Mitchell. Sorry to frighten you, Erica, but I didn't think you were likely to open the door."

"Why are you here?" she asked in as brave a tone as she could muster. She watched his eyes travel over several empty bottles of wine in the plastic trash basket and settle on the packed suitcase that lay on the bed. To her horror the room literally reeked of "the morning after." Even though it was an odor she was sure that Wainwright was more than a little familiar with, she felt a burning sensation creep up the back of her neck.

"Looks like you're all packed and ready to go." He smiled. "So where is this ill mother of yours? You were so concerned about her."

Erica took an unsteady breath. So he knew that the story about her mother being ill was a lie. *But what else does he know?* "I'm sorry. I just had to get away. It's personal."

"I'd say that bringing up an abducted baby as your own could trigger all sorts of personal problems."

Her throat constricted, too dry to swallow, but she tried. Wainwright's smile was mocking and unsettling. She stepped to the window and pulled back the drape just enough to peek out. She was to relieved to see that the parking lot was free of police cars. What did this man want? *I've got to get away. Far, far away, where no one can find us.*

"Erica, I'm not the enemy. Please sit down. I'm here to help you." He gestured to the chair beside the small desk, but remained standing.

So did she. *Is this a trap? Why would he help me?*

"I know you did not give birth to that little girl, but giving birth is not what makes a person a parent," Wainwright began.

Erica recalled his tragic story: first the leukemia, then the accident. A father may not give birth, but surely this man's bond with his son was as strong as any mother's. *Could he be saying that he truly understands?* But Wainwright was the boy's biological father. Could he truly understand that the bond between Erica and Marnie was as strong, if not stronger, than any biological ties?

Marnie squirmed in her arms; she wanted to be put down. While Erica whispered in her daughter's ear, Wainwright strode to the window, pulling the drape closed again. He caught a glimpse of the parking area.

"Damn it!" His voice rang out with alarm. "Get the child. I'll grab your suitcase."

Confused, Erica spun around to face him.

His looked at her intently as he said, "There's a dark blue Ford Escort pulling up to the front entrance of building. Close behind it is a police car."

Erica froze with fear.

"Hurry! My car is right outside." Limping slightly, Wainwright rushed them out the west door and into the backset of his rented Buick, closing the door behind them. As Erica and her daughter crouched on the floor, their heads down, he sailed out of the parking lot and into the busy airport traffic.

Pocino flung open the door of the rented Escort and took off for the hotel entrance, charging into the lobby on the heels of Lieutenant Bob Hess of the Chicago Police Department. A second CPD officer cruised from one end of the building to the other in his white-and-blue police car.

Pocino hoped the goddamned Christonelli woman was still at the hotel. He stood back while Hess introduced himself and inquired about the room number of the woman and child, his gaze shooting around the lobby and small dining area. This was no time for protocol. He had a strange feeling. The ranch-style building had exit doors all over the damn place, and Hess was taking too much time on niceties. Pocino wanted to bolt down the corridor, but he didn't know which direction to choose. *Better hold tight.*

Stalking up and down the lobby beside the floor-to-ceiling windows, he saw a beige Buick speed through the parking area. It was coming from the west side of the building. The police car had headed east.

As the car streaked by, Pocino had time to take note of the driver's thick silver hair. "I'll be damned!"

Hess whirled around to face him. "What is it?"

"The man in that car. I know him." *What in the hell is Wainwright doing here?*

"Anyone with him?"

"Not that I could see. But that doesn't mean much; if Wainwright's helping the Christonelli woman, he'll make sure she isn't seen."

The wail of a siren pierced the air. Hess frowned at the sight of his Crown Vic tearing across the parking lot. "Brennan seems to be in pursuit of the Buick." Switching back to the task at hand, he said, "It's room number 901. Fill me in on the way."

As they headed toward the room, a crackle came from the police radio that was hooked through Hess's belt loop. "Hess," he barked into the radio.

"There was a Buick peeling out of the parking lot, so I gave chase. Unfortunately, I lost him, but the man appeared to be alone."

"Copy that."

Hess turned to face Pocino. "Do you think the man you saw in the Buick is involved?"

"He lives in New York, so I can't figure why in hell he'd be at a Days Inn on the outskirts of Chicago if there weren't some sort of connection." *I wouldn't put it past that bastard to keep Ashleigh Taylor's child from her.*

"Nine-oh-one," Hess announced. Then he banged on the door and called out in a loud voice, "Police, Mrs. Christonelli. Open up. This is the Chicago PD." After a few more attempts, he slipped the key card into the slot and opened the door. The room was empty.

Pocino pulled out his cell phone and scrolled down to Wainwright's office number.

"This is Ross Pocino." He used as gracious a tone as he could muster. "May I speak to Mr. Wainwright, please?"

As expected, Pocino learned that Wainwright wasn't in. The secretary offered no information as to where he had gone, but before he signed off, Pocino asked, "Do you have the phone number of the hotel in Chicago where he's staying?"

She said, "He's not staying over; he's expected back this evening."

Holding up one of the wine bottles, Hess said, "Other than this, the rumpled bedspread, and some cookie crumbs, there's little sign that this room was recently occupied. Tell me about this Wainwright character. How is he connected?"

Pocino parked himself on the side of the bed. Sucking air through his teeth, he said, "Let's see if I can make this simple." It was damned complicated, but Hess didn't need to know everything. "Erica Christonelli worked for Wainwright's girlfriend, and he has some history with Ashleigh Taylor, the kidnapped twin's mother."

"You didn't mention this guy earlier. How long have you suspected him?"

"Not until ten minutes ago. I never figured him as being involved. But now that I think about it, it computes. And his secretary didn't deny that he came to Chicago today. He's involved, alright!"

Behind the rented Buick, a siren wailed, though the sound faded as Wainwright made turn after turn.

"Mommy!" Marnie cried. "I don't like it here. I want up."

Erica's head pounded and her hands shook. "Just a few more minutes," she whispered in her daughter's ear.

Finally, Wainwright looked back over his shoulder and announced, "It's okay to sit up now. We're not being followed anymore. But we'll have to get rid of this car soon, in case they got the plate number."

Terrified, Erica pulled herself up onto the backseat and set Marnie beside her. "Mr. Wainwright, I left a rental car back at the hotel."

"Did you rent it in your own name?"

"I had to. They wouldn't rent me a car without my driver's license."

"Do you have the paperwork?"

"It's in the car."

Wainwright sighed and said, "I'll call Hertz as soon as I get you a new hotel. I'll have the car picked up." He paused. "On second thought, forget about the car. The police will be all over it by now."

"Mr. Wainwright, why you are doing this?"

"Mitchell. Please. Is it so hard to accept a helping hand?"

"Don't get me wrong. I appreciate all you've done. Had you not come today, Marnie might have . . ." Erica hesitated, not wanting to frighten her daughter any more than she already had. "I don't know what we'd have done if you hadn't been there. But why are you opening yourself up to this? You could be accused of being an accomplice."

"Don't worry. I know how to take care of myself."

"Where are we going?" She wasn't afraid of him, but could she trust him? *Can I trust anyone?*

"There's a Holiday Inn in Skokie, on the outskirts of Chicago." He explained that he would check them in. There would be no record of a mother and child. He would pay in cash, and from now on she mustn't use either her credit cards or her driver's license for any reason.

As she listened to Wainwright outline his plan, Erica felt as if she were in the middle of the ocean, with wave after wave washing over her and pulling her down. She didn't have much cash, and with no usable Social Security number or other identification, how could she hope to get a decent job?

After stopping at a small grocery store to buy food and drinks for the harried fugitives, Wainwright drove to the Holiday Inn, parking the car at the far end of the building. "Wait here until I check in." He flung open the door, fumbled for an instant with his cane, and then walked toward the entrance.

He soon came back with a key in hand. "We're about twelve miles from downtown Chicago. You two will be safe here, at least for tonight," he said as he handed her the key.

Without her credit cards, Erica knew, she didn't have enough money to pay for the hotel for even one night. *If he hadn't come along, my daughter and I would be separated by now.*

He went on, "You two go ahead through that door, and I'll join you in a few minutes. Just take Marnie. I'll take care of the luggage when I come back."

Erica set Marnie on the ground and took hold of her hand. Glad to be out of the car, Marnie skipped happily beside her. Erica could only feel relief that her daughter had no idea how close they'd come to disaster.

Wainwright returned in a new rental car later that evening, after Marnie had fallen asleep. He knocked on the door and announced in a loud voice, "It's Mitchell Wainwright."

After Erica cautiously opened the door, he cleared his throat. He wanted to—*had to*—gain her trust. If she were caught, he would likely be dragged down with her. When he had seen Pocino at the Days Inn earlier that day, Wainwright realized he'd taken an uncalculated risk in coming to Chicago. Had Pocino spotted him? If so, he couldn't think of a single plausible reason for his being there. But no point in worrying about something he had no control over.

He paused before speaking. "You asked me why I'm helping you."

Erica nodded.

"Well, there are a number of reasons," he began. "First of all, you have raised your daughter since she was an infant. I know you love her and she loves you. When I heard about your predicament . . . I don't know, it just hit a sore spot with me." *That was probably true enough.* "I didn't go through labor either, but I loved my little boy far more than his mother ever did." *That part was the God's honest truth.* "Ashleigh Taylor has a daughter, and she is young and healthy enough to have more children if she desires. Not like me. Not like you." Seeing the tears rolling down Erica's cheeks, he pulled out his handkerchief and handed it to her.

"Erica, I am willing to help you, but this has to be between you and me. No one else, not even your brother-in-law, can know of our arrangement. If you want to keep your little girl, you can let no one know where you are. I realize that you can't stay here in Chicago and I don't imagine you have money to travel or to support yourself and the child. Nor can you get a job without a new identity. I can help with all that."

"But where will I go? I can't stay here. I can't go to New York. I can't even go to my family in Southern California. Marnie and I are totally alone."

"Not so. I said I was willing to help you."

"But why? Does Viviana know you're here?"

He bit down on his tongue. "No. And she must never know. You are a talented designer, and it would be a shame to lose that kind of talent in the fashion world. However, you cannot continue to design for De Mornay's and maintain your anonymity. I can get you a new identity and even a job as a designer. The stores I have in mind don't have the upscale prestige of De Mornay's, but by the time your daughter is on her own, you will have a sizable portfolio."

"Do you really mean that?" Erica's eyes were filled with hope.

"I do." Wainwright said, warming to the idea. What had begun as a vengeful plan of action just might be turning into a viable plan and a good business decision.

"In the 1980s, when leveraged buyouts were making their way into the business community, I was one of the first to step into that arena. I happen to still own the Melody dress stores, a small retail chain in the Los Angeles area. Although I am not a hands-on manager, I have the ear of my management team. Currently the stores carry only ready-to-wear clothing, but developing some of our own brands would be a smart business move."

Her eyes lit up for an instant, but then Erica became wary.

Wainwright asked, "What's troubling you?"

Erica hesitated. "Are you sure you can get me a new identity?"

"Not a problem. I'll set you up in your own place, and I'll make sure you won't be living too close to the Melody stores in L.A., just in case." Wainwright removed a thick envelope from the inner pocket of his suit jacket and laid it on the table.

Erica stared at the envelope as Wainwright told her his plan.

"I'll have a new identity for you tomorrow afternoon at the latest. I'll take a taxi to the airport now and leave you my rental car. I want you to start for L.A. the first thing tomorrow morning. Drive as far as you can. Get a hotel room and then call me at this number." He handed her his business card with his unlisted number written on the back. "I'll have the new identification papers overnighted to your hotel. Then, purchase airline tickets to L.A. under your new name." He grinned. "I almost forgot to ask. What names would you like to go by in the future?"

"I don't have to change Marnie's name do I?"

"Yes. If you want to stay under the radar, both your name and hers will need to be changed."

This appeared to trouble her. "Four-year-olds can be pretty unpredictable."

"If you're worried about Marnie blurting out her old name, turn it into a game. She will love it."

Erica nodded. "You're right. My past life is over. I imagine this is just the first of a long string of things I'll just have to get used to."

Wainwright pointed to the thick envelope. "There's enough cash in there to tide you over for the next few weeks."

"I'll pay you back every penny," she said, her voice shaky and filled with emotion. "If not for Marnie, I would never consider . . ." Her voice trailed off.

"Sure," he said. "Consider this an advance." He stood and picked up his cane. "Call me tomorrow night," he repeated.

"I don't know how to thank you," she said, and impulsively gave him a hug.

Wainwright briefly returned her hug and then stepped back, steadying himself with his cane. "I know what it is like to lose a child. I don't want to see you lose yours." He winced at the thought of his own loss, but a small part of him felt noble for being the one to help this woman out, even though he knew that his intentions were not one hundred percent noble. *Is this why the fates brought us together?*

They had driven more than four hundred miles when Marnie's piercing wails from the backseat told Erica it was time to find a place to stay for the night.

"Help Mommy find someplace to eat," she told her fretful little girl.

Instantly, the crying came to a halt. "McDonald's. There's one right there." Marnie pointed to the famous yellow arches on the other side of the freeway.

"Let's look for something on this side." She pointed to the right.

Erica vaguely recalled driving through Iowa once before, with the newborn Marnie, but she hadn't a clue where they were now. There was a sign coming up, and she strained to read it. As they neared the sign, she saw that the town they were approaching was called Neola—and that there was a Motel 6 just off the interstate.

"Let's check into our motel, then I'll find you a McDonald's with a nice play area."

Later that evening, after getting Marnie into bed, Erica poured herself a glass of wine to calm her nerves. And then another and another. Then she finally picked up the phone and called Mitchell Wainwright.

"There's a problem," Wainwright said immediately after answering the phone. "But we'll work it out."

Erica's breath caught in her throat. "What kind of problem?"

"It turns out I was seen at the Days Inn by one of the investigators. I told him that we'd never connected, but this bulldog of an agent is nipping at my heels. He works for the Landes Agency . . ."

As Wainwright filled her in on the details, Erica felt her blood turn to ice. Another dream job had come to an end—one that had had no beginning. And now she must sever all connection to Mitchell Wainwright. The disappointment was crippling.

With an edge to his voice, Wainwright told Erica, "I'm afraid you won't be able to work in one of my enterprises. At least not at first. But I will make sure you and Marnie are safe. Where are you now?"

There was a silence before Erica spoke. "I appreciate all you've done for us, Mitchell, but I can't let you or anyone else know where we are. You can probably trace this number, but please don't." Her words came out slowly, and she tripped over them. "Besides, it won't do any good, because we are leaving. I don't know how, but I will pay back every dime you've loaned us."

To Wainwright, she sounded as though she'd been drinking. "Erica," he implored, "please don't do anything hasty. I said I'd help you, and I will."

"I'm sorry. I know you mean well, but I can't take the chance. No matter what I have to do to protect us, no one is going to take my daughter from me."

"I understand," Wainwright conceded, "but you need to slow down. Listen, I can get around Landes and his agents." He paused. "Erica, I know you're scared, but I can help. Get settled and call me Saturday morning about ten. I don't want you to lose your daughter. I know what I'm doing, and I'm not about to do anything that might put you in jeopardy."

In a voice that he had to strain to hear, Erica said, "Let me think about it."

She'll call. She has nowhere else to turn. "I'll be expecting your call." He thought of the empty wine bottles in her trash at the hotel, and though he hesitated for a heartbeat, he said, "I understand your struggle. I know how tempting it is to turn booze for escape . . ."

He heard a sharp intake of breath on the other end of the line.

"Erica. Don't take this the wrong way. I've been down that road, so I'm the last person to criticize. All I'm saying is, watch it." Then, abruptly, he dropped his friendly-but-firm advice. "By the time you call on Saturday, I'll have the paperwork you need and a fail-safe plan."

"Okay," said Erica.

But Wainwright detected a note of uncertainty.

Edith hurried down the corridor toward the small conference room. Members of the store-branding task force streamed out, followed by Conrad Taylor.

"Mr. Toddman is on line one," she announced.

"Thanks, Edith. I'll take it in my office." A moment later, Conrad tapped the door shut with the heel of his shoe and grabbed the phone on his desk. "You're not calling to say you're snowed in, are you?" he joked. The plans for the current holiday season had been put to bed by the end of July and implemented in October. Assured that all was on track, Toddman and his family had been on a ski vacation in Hemsedal, Norway, for the past two weeks.

"Not a chance," Mark said. Instantly switching to business mode, he asked, "How did the meeting go with Ralph Lauren?"

"Better than expected. I met with Roger Sharp and Tim Chopin over breakfast. They attempted some fancy footwork with some pretty attractive incentives, but I held our purchases to the lowball figure. They definitely got the message. I'd be surprised if we ran into any more employee defections instigated by Lauren or any other vendor."

Conrad had heard Mark say on more than one occasion that he would greatly curtail purchases from any vendor who attempted to entice any of his people to abandon Consolidated. He meant it. The crew at Ralph Lauren had crossed the line and were learning their lesson the hard way. The usual holiday purchases from Consolidated had been cut in half. Toddman had not ordered that they be cut off entirely; that would've been a poor business decision. Instead, Consolidated had reduced the purchases from Lauren and found another superb vendor to fill in the gap.

"Conrad, that's great news. Anything else I should know before we board the plane tomorrow morning?"

"Nothing that can't wait."

Before Conrad had a chance to ask about the skiing, Mark proceeded with his own agenda. "How did your meetings with Landes go?"

Conrad had demanded that Landes set up the opportunity for him to speak directly to both Mike Christonelli and Dr. Ian McDonald. Neither had heard from the missing woman in the past three months—at least, that's what they claimed—but Conrad was determined to follow every possible lead right to the end.

"About like Landes predicted, but it wasn't a complete wash," he replied. "Neither Christonelli nor McDonald were the sleazeballs I'd conjured up. Landes and Pocino don't believe they had anything to do with the abduction, and neither do I. They seemed as appalled as we are that Mario Christonelli could have done such a thing. Both his brother and his brother-in-law described Mario as a good man. Hard to believe, but he has no criminal record. He was a nurse, for God's sake! Strange as it seems, I have to believe now that the woman—Erica Christonelli—was also in the dark until way after the fact."

"Hold on," Mark broke in. "If the Christonelli woman didn't give birth to her baby, where did she think the kid came from? Some pumpkin patch?" His tone signaled not humor, but derision and disgust.

Conrad told him the story as it had been told to him.

"So where do you go from here?"

"Not sure. The only thing I know is that this Erica has very little savings. She hasn't as yet tapped into her account at Citibank here in New York, and she may be too smart to do so. Which means she's going to have to get a job somewhere, and soon. In order to get a job, she'll need to use her Social Security number, and that's been faxed to Social Security offices and employment centers nationwide." Conrad sighed. "We have no idea where the woman is now. If she's working off the books, there's a good chance that she and our baby could fall straight though the goddamned cracks."

"Hey, this is a substantial lead. I know it hasn't panned out the way you'd hoped these past few months, but it's not like you to look—"

"So, how's the snow?" Conrad interrupted.

Mark paused, then went on as if nothing had changed. "Phenomenal. Great powder, but at minus six degrees, it's a bit chilly for the women in my life."

"Has April improved as much as she hoped to?"

"She's turning into a terrific little skier, but she shies away from the icy early-morning starts."

"Can't say as I blame her. Besides, with this year's Tremaine Winter Dance Convention quickly approaching, I bet the dance director has promised that the wrath of God almighty will be upon her if she sustains any type of injury." He laughed. "Callie told Ashleigh that Miss Debbie warned all her classes to stay off their skates until after the Christmas recital." Conrad shifted his view to the clock on his desk. "Got another meeting in five, Mark. Give Paige and April my love."

"Right," Mark replied. "See you Saturday, then, about six thirty."

Conrad dropped the receiver back into the cradle. After their precious daughter had been sighted in New York and the FBI had stepped in, assigning actual agents to the case as well as their considerable resources, Conrad's hopes had skyrocketed. But that was nearly four months ago. They hadn't shared a single lead with them, so he had to assume they, too, had come up empty. Erica Christonelli had fallen off the face of the Earth, it seemed.

From coast to coast, Pocino, Landes, his other agents, and law enforcement are searching for my daughter, but the bottom line is Cassie is growing up as Erica Christonelli's daughter.

Amused at the sight of her six-foot-three husband sitting cross-legged on the floor, stringing popcorn, Ashleigh smiled.

"When will April be here?" Callie asked for the umpteenth time. In her red velvet dress and red ballet flats, she was wearing a path between the Christmas tree and the bay windows in the entryway. On her tiptoes she would peer out the window to the snow-covered ground, discover that the Toddmans had not yet arrived, and then tear back to the living room. The fully lighted but otherwise bare Christmas tree stood eight feet tall. Boxes of their familiar decorations, along with a number of new additions, were stacked beside it, ready for the evening's festivities.

Despite all the ups and downs of the past few months, the Taylors' move to the East Coast had gone fairly smoothly. Conrad had assumed his new position with Consolidated, and things were going well. Ashleigh was delighted with their wonderful property in Greenwich, just a couple miles from the Toddmans' estate. It was a comfort, knowing her best friend was once again so near, and she looked forward to tonight's tree-decorating party, which Paige had suggested as a new annual tradition.

Their musical door chimes rang out with "Frosty the Snowman," which sent Callie scurrying to the door a step or two behind Elizabeth, who was spending the holidays with them and had appointed herself the official greeter. Caroline would be joining them on Christmas Eve, accompanied by Don Munz, the curator of a Long Beach art museum, whom she had befriended over the last few months.

Despite the fact that Erica Christonelli seemed to have fallen from the face of the planet with their little girl, Ashleigh focused on all the positives in her life. The half-empty portion of her life could drive her to despair, but only if she allowed herself to dwell on it. For the most part, she managed to detach from the areas of her life over which she had no control. Gazing at her precious daughter, she rubbed the slight protrusion in her belly and felt a glow of satisfaction, which flatly refused to leave room in her heart for depression.

Conrad looked up from his strand of popcorn and grinned at his wife. "Why am I the one sitting with this needle and bowl of inedible popcorn when it appears that Callie could care less?"

"Well, it's nice to know that our tradition is being carried on." Bradford Taylor strode into the room, his Boston accent announcing his arrival.

Callie held on tightly to Mary Taylor's index finger, pulling her toward the boxes beside the tree. "Gran, this one is the one you and Grandpa gave me," she said, taking out the gold bear, dated 1993, from the top box.

"So it is." Conrad's mother gave her granddaughter a hug, then greeted Ashleigh and her son.

"Jingle Bells" rang out, and Callie took off for the entryway again. One of her ballet flats slipped from her tiny foot, but she didn't bother to stop to pick it up, and made it to the front door a few steps ahead of Elizabeth. Knowing better than to open the door herself, she peered through the glass panel while Elizabeth pulled open the broad double doors.

111

The entire Toddman entourage stood on the other side, their arms full of wrapped packages. "Merry Christmas," they said in unison.

Callie peered around Mark, looking for April. Mark chuckled and handed his package to Paige, then scooped up the giggling Callie and thrust her upon his shoulders. "Guess you were hoping to see a playmate instead of just us old folks," he said with a note of amusement. "April will be right back; she left a package in the car." Then, with a twinkle in his eye, he said, "It's something for a little girl. I think her name is something like . . . Allie?"

"No, silly. It's for me. My name is Callie, spelled with a C."

Mark set her on the ground, and Paige gave her a big hug.

Taking in the rest of the party, Callie turned to Paige's mother, who stood shivering in a heavy faux fur coat, and said, "Merry Christmas, Nana." Turning to Rupert, who was stamping the snow from his boots, she said, "Merry Christmas, Grandpa." It seemed to please Paige's mother and stepfather that they had been made honorary grandparents for the little girl.

Callie, still wearing only one shoe, called out to April, who came running up the steps, slipping and sliding on the icy surface.

"Slow down!" Mark bellowed. "We don't want any trips to the emergency room tonight."

In front of a roaring fire, Paige and Ashleigh collapsed on the sofa, each with a glass of Amaretto in her hand. Mark had followed Conrad and the others down to the basement to see the Lionel trains he'd set up in the playroom.

Paige kicked off her shoes and folded her legs beneath her.

Ashleigh began the conversation. "This was a super suggestion for a party, Paige. It's a wonderful start to the Christmas season."

"Well, don't get too relaxed. We start all over again next Saturday to decorate *our* tree."

"We'll be ready."

Ashleigh stared into the fireplace for a few moments, then reached out for Paige's hand. "I miss Charles, of course. But tonight it seemed as if he were very close. I couldn't be in a better place this holiday season. You've become the sister I never had, and it's great to be part of a big family."

Paige's smile transformed her pretty face. "Same for me. I've never felt this kind of closeness before. Our friendship is fantastic for us, but even better for our girls." But her smile soon faded, and her expression darkened.

"What is it?" Ashleigh asked.

"I was just thinking about Helen's lack of diplomacy. I know you understand, but I really am sorry."

Ashleigh stretched out her long legs. "You know, Paige, like a child, your mom asks what everyone else is afraid to ask. More than anything, I hate people thinking they have to walk on eggs around Conrad and me." She took another sip of her Amaretto. "I know Mark talked with Conrad a couple of days ago, and he must have brought you up to date."

"He did," Paige confirmed.

"We still haven't heard anything, and we may never know what's happened to Erica Christonelli or Cassie." Leaning toward Paige, she said softly, "It's actually much easier dealing with your mother's candid questions than with the lack of them from Mary and Bradford Taylor."

"I understand; I really do. I just wish there were something I could do."

"There is," Ashleigh said. "Just listen to me. You're the best sounding board I've ever had."

Paige nodded, a curious expression on her face.

"Paige, what kind of person do you think Erica Christonelli is?"

For a long moment, Paige did not respond. "I really don't have enough information to make—"

"First impression."

Paige glanced up at the ceiling and then at Ashleigh. "You mean, what I thought before finding out that she had Callie's twin?"

Ashleigh nodded.

"She seemed nice enough. And judging by the garments Viviana showed us, I'd say she was extremely talented." Paige halted. "What is it you're after?"

"I've gone through hundreds of different scenarios in my head. The bottom line is, Cassie is my daughter, and if we can find her, I want her back."

"Of course, you do."

"But what if Cassie doesn't want to leave the woman who raised her?"

Paige stared at her. "My God, Ashleigh, Cassie is only four years old."

"So is Callie. But how happy do you suppose she'd be—and how messed up could she become—if she were told that Conrad and I were not her parents and that she had to go and live with strangers?"

Paige frowned. "Ashleigh, are you saying you would just allow the woman to keep your child?"

"No! Well, I don't know what I'd do. But we'd have to think about what would be in Cassie's best interest." She paused, thinking of an analogy that might strike a chord with her friend. "What if you found out that what you were told about April's mother having been killed—it wasn't true? That she had in fact not died from the gunshot wound; that she was still alive and wanted April back."

It took a long moment before Paige exhaled. "Wow. You sure know how to bring home a point."

Visions of finding Cassie, only to have her cling to Erica Christonelli, had become a constant, unrelenting nightmare for Ashleigh. A nightmare from which she could not detach herself, no matter how hard she tried.

Viviana felt trapped, but she responded on the offensive. "I've never asked *you* to account for *your* time, Mitchell, and—"

"Come off it, Viviana. I'm not asking you to clock in. We have a good thing going. A relationship that allows both of us companionship, sex, and a world of freedom. Plus some damn good business perks. So it's important that you attend the dinner meeting I've set up with the Evanovich brothers. Keep your damn secret rendezvous to yourself, but make it *after* tonight."

Viviana had heard plenty about the brothers—they were giants in the industry. "Didn't the Evanoviches support Toddman's White Knight campaign?"

"Yes, as I recall, they did. And they are our best bet as investors in your boutiques." Wainwright paced the room. "Would you *please* switch your tickets to tomorrow morning? I'll pick up the tab for the change."

"Not this time, Mitchell. I have to leave tonight. It's important."

"What's so goddamned important that you'd risk offending potential investors? I thought getting your boutiques in Carlingdon's stores nationwide was a priority?"

"It is. Believe me, it is."

"So you'll make the switch?"

"I can't. I want to, but I just can't." She was mortified to find unchecked tears flowing down her cheeks. *I can't tell you about it, but it's much more important than my boutiques, than my label, than anything.*

Mitchell didn't know of her son. No one knew about Mason, who had been born severely autistic and had been in a Southern California facility since birth. No one knew but her former lover, David Jerome—the first and last man to whom she'd given her heart and with whom she'd shared her secret. Only David knew she had a son. Only he knew that Viviana had given birth to Mason, but he believed it was after she had been gang-raped at the age of thirteen. Even though she had not shared the whole truth, when their affair came to an abrupt end, she had regretted her candor. She did not want to make that mistake again.

Since moving to Manhattan, dealing with her failed marriage, and juggling her many business and social engagements, Viviana had not been able to see her Mason more than once every month or two, generally flying out on a red-eye one night and returning the next day. Only an hour before Wainwright stopped by to remind her of the evening's engagement, however, she had received word that Mason was critically ill with pneumonia. The doctors weren't able to give her much hope. She couldn't let him die alone.

Anger flashed in Mitchell's hazel eyes. Dramatically throwing his arms in the air, he said, "Don't ever ask me to get involved with your god-damned business again. You can't expect me to work my ass off while you take off on secret missions to God knows where. I'm through." He picked up his cane and headed for the door.

"Wait. Please, Mitchell," she cried out. "My son . . . he has pneumonia. He may not make it through the night." The words tumbled out before she could hold them back. Her secret was out. A sense of relief settled over her. She hadn't realized how much energy it had taken to keep everything hidden inside.

He stopped. Open-mouthed, he stared at her. "Your son? What in the hell are you talking about?" He slumped down to the arm of the couch and listened as Viviana told him the story. The same version of the story she had told to David.

But it was a lie. She had not been gang-raped. She did not—no, she *could not* tell him the truth. She was too ashamed to admit that since the age of eleven, she had been intimate with her older brother, whose name was also Mason. That he, not a faceless stranger, was the father of her child.

Nor did she want to think about how horribly Mason had died at the hands of those teenagers—gang members—while rescuing her. Getting pregnant had been her punishment; monthly visits for the rest of her life her penance.

Viviana told her story while standing rigidly beside him, her suitcase at her feet. When she'd finished, he reached out to her. "I won't ask why you didn't tell me before."

He stood and picked up her suitcase. Leading her by the elbow, he said, "Come with me. I'll get my attaché case and a change of clothes from my condo. I'll be ready in five minutes. I'll get whatever else I might need at JFK. We'll leave tonight. I'll call the Evanovich brothers on the way to the airport and reschedule our meeting for next week."

Viviana didn't say a word. She simply followed him, wondering if she should have told him long ago.

PART FOUR: 1998

In the cold November night air, Pocino stood in front of the Tuscany Arms, outside the street lamp's circle of illumination, planning his strategy. He had a full view of the security desk through the floor-to-ceiling glass doors, but he wanted to avoid having his visit announced. Come hell or high water, Wainwright was not going to sidestep his questions. Tonight, he was going to tell him the God's honest truth.

Four goddamned years, and he was no closer to bringing Cassie Taylor home to her family than he'd been on the day that he'd uncovered the identity of the kidnapper. How the Christonelli woman had managed to slip under his dogged radar and stay there was beyond him. Neither the FBI nor law enforcement in cities from here to the West Coast had done any better. But that failed to bring him one iota of comfort. He'd promised Ashleigh that he'd get her baby back damned near eight fucking years ago. That baby was now a little girl living God knew where and calling Erica Christonelli "Mom."

If the woman had held a single legitimate job, her Social Security number would have flashed across the screen of a social service or employment center, setting off an alarm. And a dame whose only known skills appeared to be in the fashion business sure as hell couldn't make it on her own. She had to have some sort of financial help. With the close tabs they'd kept on her brother and brother-in-law, the assistance didn't appear to be coming from them. That left only some new liaison—or perhaps Mitchell Wainwright. The sleazy negotiator had lied through his expensively capped teeth in the past, and it wasn't likely he'd turn over any information that might lead them to Erica Christonelli.

A woman clad in a sable coat, holding a medium-sized grocery bag in one arm and the leash of a well-groomed white poodle looped over the other, stopped a few feet from him at the door to the Tuscany Arms. She was awkwardly fishing for something in her purse.

Seeing that the security guard had gone on his rounds, Pocino dashed to her side. Thrusting his shoulders back, he sucked in his stomach and straightened to his full six feet. "Looks like you've got your hands full," he said. "Could I help you?"

She took a step back, and eyed him with suspicion.

"I'm on my way to see Mr. Wainwright in seventeen-oh-three," he quickly explained, then introduced himself.

On the seventeenth floor, Pocino heaved a sigh of relief as he rang the bell. Wainwright was a long shot, and it had been a long time since they'd spoken, but long shots often paid off big time.

"Who is it?" a woman called out from the other side of the oak door.

Before he could respond, the door was flung open, and a stocking-footed Viviana De Mornay confronted him, a look of astonishment on her face. She must have seen him through the peephole in the door.

"Is Mitchell here?" *Are they now living together?*

"Ross. I don't know what this is all about, and I don't know why security did not announce your arrival, but Mitchell is in the shower, and—"

"I'll wait," Pocino said, edging between Viviana and the open door.

"Who is it?" Wainwright's voice boomed from somewhere beyond the living room of the spacious condo. In a moment, he appeared barefooted, clad in a pair of gray wool trousers and a blue, unbuttoned dress shirt.

"What brings you here?" he asked while buttoning his shirt. There was not a hint of friendliness in his tone.

"I have a few questions."

"About?"

"Your current relationship with Erica Christonelli."

Wainwright shot a look in Viviana's direction and then glared back at Pocino. "I'm getting damn sick of you showing up unannounced and asking the same blasted questions. From day one—"

"Erica worked for me," Viviana interjected. "Mitchell has no *re-la-tion-ship* with her. He hardly knew her."

Noting the rigid set of Wainwright's shoulders, Pocino quickly weighed the pros and cons of Viviana's presence. *She knows Wainwright hotfooted it to Chicago to find Erica Christonelli. What else might she know? And what has been hidden from her?*

"Give it a rest, Pocino. I've told you everything I know. Didn't you cause enough upheaval a few years back with your groundless suspicions?" Anger hung in the air as a bitter frown registered above Wainwright's thick brows. "The Chicago PD, the NYPD, the blasted FBI," he rattled off without taking a breath. "I've got nothing more to say."

"Well, the Christonelli dame hasn't managed to remain undetected for the last four fuck . . ." His gaze shot to Viviana, who now stood beside Wainwright. He apologized and began again. "No one just evaporates. She'd need a bit of cash to stay undercover. And since—"

"For Christ's sake, I don't have time for all this bullshit." He turned to Viviana. "Sorry." Then he asked, "What time are our dinner reservations?"

After she told him, he said, "I'll handle this. Give me about ten minutes, then I'll come straight down to your place." He gestured for Pocino to take a seat on the couch and then eased himself into the armchair beside it.

Reluctantly, it seemed, Viviana slipped into her shoes and picked up her mink stole. She turned to Pocino. "This is an utter waste of your time. Not just for you but for Mitchell as well. We wish that Erica had been found, and we would help if we could. That child should be with her mother, but Mitchell had nothing to do with her disappearance. He followed her to Chicago to—"

"Viviana. Please. I'll take care of this."

Wainwright's expression appeared stained. There was something he was hiding from Viviana. Something he didn't want her to know.

The instant the door clicked behind Viviana, Wainwright said, "I don't know a damn thing about Erica's whereabouts. I wish I could get that through your thick skull." The moment the words slipped out, he regretted them. *No point in getting into a pissing contest with this bulldog.*

"Like I should just take your word, since you were so up front with me in the past?"

"Can we just put that behind us?" Wainwright pulled out his gold cigarette case, flipped it open, then extended it toward Pocino.

Pocino scowled and shook his head. "I'm putting nothing behind us until you are totally up front."

Withdrawing a cigarette, then tapping it on the initialed case, Wainwright observed the hard set of the pudgy investigator's jaw as he sank into the leather sofa.

"Let's cut to the chase," Pocino said. "You lied to me about the woman and the money back in ninety-four. You never would've come clean if the NYPD hadn't come up with the proof of that ten thousand dollars cash you withdrew the same day you hightailed it to Chicago."

That had been a big mistake—one he'd lived to regret. And apparently Erica hadn't needed his protection anyway. "I gave you chapter and verse on my rationale at that time." Wainwright lit his cigarette with the Ronson table lighter, inhaled, then continued. "In case it's slipped your mind, I believed that Erica needed time to wrap her mind around the fact that her daughter belonged to someone else. She had no idea she was harboring the Taylors' abducted twin. She'd devoted her life to that child."

Pocino let out an audible *harrumph.* "And for those few weeks, while she came to terms with the fact she must return the child to the Taylors, you figured she needed ten grand?"

"I've no intention of spelling that out for you again."

Pocino sprang to his feet with surprising agility for a man his size. "You sick fuck. You expect me to believe that you gave her that money so she could move back to New York, return the child to her parents, and resume—"

"Sit down, Pocino. For the last time, I was giving her the benefit of the doubt and buying her a little time. The Taylors weren't the only victims in this particular case, and I don't happen to be a believer that what is lawful is necessarily what is fair."

Pocino crossed his beefy arms in front of him, his narrow set eyes intent. "Come on, Wainwright. What were your real motives?" he asked. "And what part did the fact that the missing child belonged to Ashleigh play?"

Wainwright glanced down at his wristwatch, reached for his cane, and rose to his feet. "This meeting is over. My past relationship with Ashleigh is irrelevant. The fact is, I haven't heard a peep from Erica Christonelli since one day after she took flight from Chicago."

"And if you had?"

"Enough," he said, leading Pocino to the door.

Pocino grinned and, in the style of the infamous Terminator, said, "I'll be back."

Following Pocino's departure, Mitchell slipped on his jacket and headed for the elevator, the investigator's persistent inquiries replaying in his head. *I would have helped Erica in the past. But not now.*

The truth was that he'd come to terms with the loss of his son and, with that, the need to lash out at others. He didn't exactly see motherhood in the same light as Viviana did, but observing the peace that settled over her following the monthly visits to her son—healthy again in Southern California—he could not deny the power of that connection.

He didn't understand all the subtle nuance of Viviana's behavior, but it piqued his interest. The Viviana he knew was beautiful, a creative and intelligent businesswoman, not to mention great in bed. *Tonight we'll talk about that after-Christmas cruise she suggested.* He wanted to get to know her in a deeper sense.

CHAPTER

114

It was a beautiful November day—sunny but quite cool. The air was filled with the delicious scent of the surrounding pine trees.

Marnie stopped at the mobile home park's bank of mailboxes and dug in her jeans pocket for the key. On tiptoes, she opened the box labeled BAKER. It was jammed full of advertisements, an electric bill, and the envelope she'd been waiting for. The one with her scholarship certificate. Heaving her beat-up backpack over one shoulder, she swept her hair off her face and headed for their low-rent mobile home. Never quite sure what she might find when she arrived home, she mounted the two wobbly steps to the front door and called out, "Mom. I'm home."

Pushing open the unlocked door, she was assaulted by the stale odor of booze. Dishes she'd washed that morning still lay in the dish rack where she'd left them to dry when she'd hurried off to school. She fanned the door back and forth to clear the air, and then left it standing open. "Mom," she called out again, not able to keep the note of irritation from her tone. She opened the window above the kitchen sink, then noticed the unemptied trash can. It was filled with empty bottles. Again.

"Gross," she muttered under her breath. Then she dropped her backpack to the floor and went in search of her mother. This she accomplished in a flash; the one-bedroom mobile home was not much bigger than a studio. In fact, she heard her mother before she actually saw her: Erica was lying on the sofa bed, snoring lightly and reeking of alcohol.

Marnie felt like crying. "Mom!"

Erica's eyes blinked open. She took in the vague outline of her daughter, already home from school, and wanted to die. "You're home early, sweetheart," she said, trying to make her tone light and coherent.

"No, Mom," Marnie said. "I'm not home early." Her eyes swept the small room. "Looks like you forgot to go over to Mrs. Wells's house to clean today. *Again.*" Sotto voce, she murmured, "You're drunk. *Again.*" She sighed. "You never keep your promises." Dropping the large unopened envelope on the sofa bed, Marnie turned on her heels and ran into the bedroom, slamming the door behind her.

Erica sat up. Still in her bulky fleece robe, she heaved herself to her feet, then made her way to the bathroom. Her wood-soled Ugg slippers clunked across the hardwood floor, the sound echoing off the walls. With more than a degree of self-loathing, she pulled the door shut and squinted into the mirror.

What have I become? The words reverberated in her head. She couldn't go on like this. She hadn't gone to a single AA meeting, though she'd kept promising herself that she would. And yet she'd found one excuse after another. *If I don't pull myself together, I'll totally lose my daughter's respect.* Maybe she already had.

Not being able to follow her own dreams of becoming a fashion designer was no excuse for what she had become. *No damn excuse!* Tears streamed down her cheeks. Her eyes, red and bloodshot, felt as if they were filled with sand. Her mouth tasted like the inside of a birdcage. Staring into the mirror, she spoke to the image looking back at her. "You worthless piece of shit. You've really hit bottom."

From the corner of her eye, she saw a cockroach crawl up from the drain of the bathtub and cringed. Squeezing her eyes shut, she threw back her head, trying to expel the dark thoughts. *I'm not a fit mother. It's not fair to condemn Marnie to this kind of life. She deserves more than I can give her.*

The following morning, Erica woke with the sun streaming down upon her. Her head ached, and her mouth felt as if it were filled with cotton. She tried to remember the night before. She'd only had two glasses of wine—three at the most. Pushing back the covers from her sofa bed in the living room of their small mobile home, her gaze took in the two empty wine bottles on the countertop. She cringed. Now she was even lying to herself.

"Marnie," she called out as she squinted at the clock on the living room wall. "Oh my God. It's after ten," she said to no one. Looking around the cramped space, she was filled once again with self-loathing. *What has become of me? Again, my little girl has gotten herself off to school, and I don't even know if she's eaten breakfast.*

She picked up the phone and quickly punched in the numbers. She needed this job, and she hoped she hadn't blown it. The phone was picked up on the second ring.

"Mrs. Long? Julie Baker. I was delayed this morning, but I can be at your house by ten thirty," Erica said as she pulled on a pair of jeans and a cable-knit sweater and slipped into her boots. The air crackled with electricity as she tugged a brush through her curly hair.

She'd felt ambivalent about their move here four years earlier. Not knowing which way to turn, she had brought Marnie back to California, to the mountain community of Big Bear, which seemed like a good place to raise a child. With the ten thousand in cash that Mitchell Wainwright had loaned her, she and Marnie had flown to San Bernardino and taken the bus to Big Bear. To conserve as much of the cash as possible, they had moved into Lakeview Pines, a mobile home park right on Big Bear

Boulevard, calling themselves Julie and Marnie Baker. Erica had had grand plans for their modest mobile home—had even dreamed of moving up to a two-bedroom in time—but her job possibilities had been limited. *If I had it all to do over, I would have . . . Stop that.* No point in ruminating on what she should have done.

Erica dashed out to her four-wheel-drive Jeep Cherokee, which she'd purchased secondhand from a neighbor shortly after they'd arrived. The snow had melted by now, but she had to be careful not to fall in the ice-slicked parking lot. She climbed in the Jeep and nosed her way up Big Bear Boulevard, turning on Fox Farm Road toward the rambling Long home, which looked nothing like a mountain cabin. In front of the ranch-style home, there was a plastic deer beside a tall pine tree decorated with Christmas lights year-round. Mrs. Long, an elderly widow, was a full-time resident, and she loved to talk. Erica cleaned her house every Tuesday.

"Come in, my dear," Mrs. Long said when Erica climbed out of the Jeep. "I've made you a nice cup of tea."

Erica needed this job, and she did not want to offend Mrs. Long, but she had no time for tea. She wanted to be home when the bus dropped Marnie off from school.

"Thank you," she said. "If you don't mind, I'll take it over to the sink while—"

"No, dear. I think we should talk." Mrs. Long pulled out a chair from the breakfast room table, nodded toward it, and lowered herself gingerly into the one next to it.

I really don't have time for this. Erica sat down and raised the cup of tea to her lips.

"My dear, you do a wonderful job cleaning my house, but I believe you have a serious problem."

The hot tea burned Erica's lip. Startled, she set it back in the saucer. "Excuse me?" she said.

"You were late again today, and you look a bit . . . disheveled. I'm sure I don't need to tell you that you have a drinking problem."

Erica was stunned. *How would this woman know what I do in the privacy of my own home?* "I sometimes have a glass of wine at home, but—"

"Please don't be defensive, dear. I'm not trying to be critical. I believe you need help." She hesitated, then said, "My daughter is Barbara Bower. You know, the principal at Big Bear Elementary? She told me she was concerned."

"Concerned about what?" Finding herself on the defensive, Erica said. "Marnie has never been neglected. She dresses well and is always well groomed. And I make sure she is well nourished, which is not at all easy, in this fast-food generation and with our limited budget."

"Julie, I know you love your daughter, and she loves you. I wouldn't have brought this up, but it seems that your little girl—Marnie?"

Erica nodded.

"Barbara knows you clean my house each week, so she asked me if I knew of anything that might have happened to make Marnie so . . . sad. She told me that your daughter had been such a happy, vivacious little girl, but in the past few months she seems to have withdrawn."

"Nothing that I know of," Erica replied. "But I will certainly look into it." Before she could get to her feet to begin cleaning, Mrs. Long reached out a bony hand and touched her arm.

"Please, Julie, sit down," she said. "I did not mention this to Barbara, but I think I know the problem." Not leaving a space for comment, she went on. "I've seen you with your daughter, since she was just a wee one and you brought her with you to clean. That little girl adores you. And now if you will allow me to be blunt, I must tell you what I think. I have a very sensitive nose, and I know you've had more than a glass of wine many nights before you come to clean my house."

Erica sat in stunned silence.

Mrs. Long continued, "I know, my dear, because I am an alcoholic. I haven't had a drink for more than twenty years, but I know the signs. I don't know what has made you so unhappy, but I can tell you that the answer in not in the bottle. When your daughter sees you sad, it makes her sad." She rose and opened one of the kitchen drawers, pulled out a business card, and handed it to Erica.

Erica immediately saw that the card had two large capital As at the top. It gave multiple addresses for meeting of Alcoholics Anonymous.

Her first reaction was to deny it, but when the tears began running unbidden down her cheeks, she knew there was no point in denial. "Thank you, Mrs. Long. I appreciate your blunt talk. I've been struggling with this—knowing that I have a problem. I've told myself I should start attending meetings. I guess I needed someone to say it out loud, and now that you have, I plan to follow through."

Mrs. Long said, "It's not an easy road, but I am here for you. And you will find others. When you feel like pouring just one little tiny drink, call me. There is a meeting just up the street tonight. If you'd like, I will go with you."

"Thank you. I'd like that." Then, realizing it was Tuesday, she said, "Wait, I can't tonight. Marnie has a dance lesson down the hill." But she quickly asked, "Are there meetings on nights other than Tuesday or Thursday?" Before Mrs. Long had a chance to respond, Erica asked more specifically, "Is there one tomorrow night?"

The older woman nodded.

"I'll go." She paused, then said, "And thank you for offering to go with me." Then, as Mrs. Long stepped out to do her weekly shopping, Erica slipped on some rubber gloves and got on with the cleaning. *Could I actually be reeking of liquor and not know it? How disgusting! And how embarrassing.*

As she cleaned Mrs. Long's house from top to bottom, one question after another crossed her mind. She had tried to give up her nightly intake of wine. It had begun right after she'd discovered that her daughter was the abducted Taylor twin. *And now I'm going to put an end to it.*

As she dusted the mantelpiece, she thought of the prim and proper Mrs. Long and could not picture her as an alcoholic. Then again, she couldn't picture herself as one—nor did she want to.

Paige toed off her Ferragamo flats and flopped down on the oversize sofa. Leaning back against the arm rest, she swung her legs up on the cushions. *Thank God, I have nothing scheduled for the entire day.*

Clad in a bulky, white cashmere sweater and wool slacks, she breathed in the heady scent of pine from the roaring fire in their massive fireplace. Feeling a chill in the early November air, she pulled up the afghan over her legs. April had spent the past weekend at the Grand Hyatt in Manhattan with Madison and her mom at the Tremaine Winter Dance Convention. She wasn't due home for a couple of hours, but Paige planned to take full advantage of her rare day of freedom and simply relax by the fire.

Her eye fell upon the English Teddy, with its tall, furry busby, sitting in the armchair beside the fireplace. She remembered her mother's first visit to their home, when April had shown her grandmother her collection of bears. When Helen had picked up this English bear, it had sparked some long-forgotten images. Bears from Paige's early childhood danced through her head. It was not a false memory, but one that her mother confirmed. "Oh, yes, you had a lovely collection of bears. I spent way too much money on those bears! We would often have to live on canned soup until my next paycheck. But it was well worth it to see your precious eyes light up and the smile on your adorable little face. You loved those bears. You took them to bed with you every night." So much had happened over the past few years since she'd found her mother. So much had changed since she'd discovered she had not been a horrible, unwanted child.

When she and Mark had asked her mother and Rupert to consider making the Greenwich guesthouse their new home, she had feared her stepfather's pride would cause him to refuse. But to her delight, his resistance melted away at the sight of Helen's response to her grandchild. The man cared deeply for her mother, and Paige supposed he realized that she would have better care with them in Greenwich than he could provide for her with his Social Security and small pension. Rupert had swallowed his pride, and they had moved into the guesthouse in early 1995.

In these past few years, Helen had blossomed. While she had not necessarily gotten better, as far as Paige could determine, she had shown no signs of deterioration. In the beginning, the adjustment had been tough on Rupert, but not for long. Terrence and Wilma, the loyal members of the Toddmans' staff, had become friends and companions to Helen and Rupert Sheldon, and although they were about the same age, Wilma fussed over Helen as if she were her mother. She looked after her and took care of most of her personal needs. It had been a godsend for Paige.

The melodic door chimes jolted Paige from the past. Whisking the afghan from across her legs, she straightened up and dropped her feet to the floor.

"Mom?" April called out as she charged into the living room.

Paige rose to her feet. Although April had been away at the conference for only a few days, she appeared so grown-up all of a sudden. Her dark hair and big brown eyes reminded Paige of one of those Keane paintings. Swelling with pride, she crossed the room to throw her arms around her daughter. "You're home early. How lovely."

April took a step back and raised one dark brow. "I see you've been busy redecorating. This room is truly 'lover-ly,' " she said, parroting a favorite adjective of her grandmother's.

Paige's mouth turned up in a grin. "Well, I guess it's contagious." She chuckled. "I've missed you a lot. It's seemed really strange to be rattling around here without you bopping in and out."

"Missed you too." April laughed. "How's Nana and Grandpa?" That was always April's first question, even if she'd been away only for one night.

After filling her in, Paige asked, "Any exciting news in your life?"

"Sure is." April gestured toward the sofa. "Let's sit down."

April loved the world of dance and had excelled on the dance floor since she was only four. She had even thought about entering college as a dance major. But since becoming part of the high-school debate team, her long-term goals had changed. She still loved dance and had no intention of giving it up, but her goal was to be a TV anchor. She had her route all mapped out and was prepared to begin as a radio newscaster or host. April was looking forward to her future.

Paige's pulse tapped out a wild tattoo. *Sit down? Why does April think we need to sit down?*

"Mom. Please." With deep frown lines creasing her dewy, young skin, she said, "What was it you used to tell me?" She paused, then filled in, " 'Don't go borrowing trouble.' " She dropped down on the sofa beside her. "I have some really good news—with just a little hiccup."

Paige dropped back onto the sofa beside her daughter. *Get a grip.* "So, spit it out. And get to that little hiccup fast."

"The good news is, I won another scholarship for the Tremaine Dance Convention this year."

Paige leaned over and gave April a quick hug. "Way to go." Not for the first time, she marveled at the way her daughter's expressions mirrored her own. More and more over the years, she found herself discounting the importance of biological birth. "And now . . . the hiccup?"

"I realize you were planning on me being home, but I have a chance to assist for Miss Alison's jazz classes at the convention in Washington, D.C., and I'd really like to do it. Please say you don't mind."

Letting out the breath she hadn't realized she was holding, Paige asked, "When is it?"

"Next Saturday and Sunday. But I need to be there Friday night." Her big brown eyes sought understanding. "It's just three days. We can use frequent flyer miles, can't we? I can go with Miss Alison. She said I can share her room. I will come right back here and spend loads of time with you and Dad and everyone."

"Your dad will be home before six thirty. We'll ask him then. But April, neither of us has stood in your way of doing anything that's important to you, so I don't suppose we're about to start now."

"Thanks, Mom." April threw her arms around her, a bit awkwardly due to their positions on the sofa, and gave her a kiss on her cheek. "And guess what?" she added. "Callie called me yesterday. She said she's going to the convention, too. Even though she's just eight, she's been moved up to intermediate, so she'll be in my class."

"That's wonderful. She really is a talented little trouper."

April nodded. "She went to the New York convention last summer, and Aunt Ashleigh is taking her to this one." She paused for just an instant. "Hey, maybe you'd like to come too? It would be such fun. We could all share a suite, and while we dance, you and Aunt Ashleigh can spend some time together. I'm sure you will find lots to do and plenty to talk about."

"I'll think about it," Paige said, adding with a mischievous grin, "it would be lover-ly."

After dropping Marnie off at the dance studio for her five o'clock Tuesday class in San Bernardino, Erica found a pay phone at the local Target. Since moving to Big Bear, Erica had not let Ian know where she was, but she had kept in touch as much as possible with Mike and Bill. It was with their financial help that Marnie had been able to participate in various school activities and continue her dance lessons. Yet Erica always was careful to use a pay phone so the call couldn't be traced.

"Erica." Mike's voice had a tone of exasperation. "We've gone over this a thousand times. I don't know what to tell you. You are a fantastic dress designer, but you can't afford any kind of publicity. At first I thought you were being paranoid, but after seeing the Taylor twin the last time I was in New York, I'm every bit as paranoid as you are."

What was he saying? Mike went on quickly, "Glenn tells me the Taylors' private investigator is still on the case. Seems he's not about to give up."

"Wait—you actually saw Marnie's twin?"

"I did. But I wish I'd kept my goddamned mouth shut."

"Where did you see her? Did she look a lot like Marnie? Why didn't you tell me?"

She took a breath. She knew exactly why he hadn't told her.

"Whoa. One question at a time. The last time I went to the city, I accompanied Glenn to see his niece perform at the High School of Performing Arts. The twin was in some group dances and had a solo. And yes, the girl looks exactly like Marnie."

"I know you were trying to protect me. But you can't do that by keeping me in the dark. Promise me, if it has anything to do with Marnie or might affect her, that you will let me know about it."

"Okay," Mike said. "But the fashion industry, as well as that of the performing arts, falls into tight, practically incestuous webs. Everyone knows everyone else. You must steer clear of both of these tangled worlds, where the risk of being caught . . . it's almost unavoidable."

"Damn it, Mike. I've never once said I was considering pursuing a career in fashion. It's just that I've got to find something, anything. I feel so isolated, and it has nothing to do with the mountains." The real danger lurked from within. "The temptation of just one glass of wine to help me unwind—it always leads to another and then another and another."

Erica paused as the walls of the phone booth began to tremble. It was not another earthquake. A few yards from the flimsy structure, she saw that a Shell Oil truck had pulled up to the stoplight and was gearing down.

"And . . . and I haven't done a good job of hiding it from Marnie," she continued. "Seeing that look of disapproval in her eyes breaks my heart, and I vow I'll never do it again, but then I do. I love Marnie with all my heart, but every day she slips further away from me." Her voice caught once again. "I . . . I don't want her to think of her mom as a . . . a drunk. I've got to find something meaningful before I turn into my own mother. I feel utterly worthless."

Mike swallowed past a large lump in his throat and wished with all his heart he could comfort his sister-in-law. He and Bill missed her and little Marnie in their lives; their rare visits to Big Bear were not nearly often enough. He wanted to tell Erica that Marnie was growing up, and it was only natural for her to begin pulling away and gravitating toward friends her own age. But the truth was, the child was only eight, and it was a bit early for that kind of independence—no matter how mature Marnie had become. Erica's drinking was a problem that should not be ignored.

He'd seen this coming years ago, but he felt powerless. He and Bill were simply too far away to have the impact they'd once had on Erica's and Marnie's lives.

"I've been trying to go to AA meetings," Erica was saying, "and it's helped a little. I stay away from the booze for a while, and then I fall off that proverbial wagon and I'm too embarrassed to tell my sponsor."

"We'll figure it out, Erica" was all Mike could muster by way of response.

He prayed for guidance, as he prayed to God each night that Marnie would not discover she had an identical twin. At least, not until Erica was able to share that devastating news with her. He had relentless, recurring nightmares, invading even his daylight hours, of Marnie coming face-to-face with her twin. But Mike agreed with Erica that they must wait until she graduated from high school before shattering her world with the truth of her birth.

Even so, there was a very real danger of the girls meeting before Erica would have the chance to explain. As identical twins, they had already made some of the same life choices. When Glenn had called earlier that year to check on Mike in Chicago, he'd mentioned attending a dance performance and raved about the Taylor twin.

"Boy, Mike, that little kid can really dance. For her age, she's phenomenal; she never missed a beat."

That comment had turned Mike's legs soft and spongy and set off bells in his head. Marnie too was a superb dancer for her age. She had been dancing half her life, since she'd moved to Big Bear and Mike had started sending money for classes. For months after seeing the movie *Fame,* she'd set her heart on attending the performing arts high school in New York where the movie had been filmed. Mike could only hope that dream would fade before Marnie reached that age. But with her talent, according to her teachers, her dream of becoming a dancer when she grew up was not unrealistic.

Six months ago, in May, he'd sent money for Erica and Marnie to travel to Chicago so Marnie could attend a top-notch dance convention. Marnie had loved every minute of it. Since then, she'd won a dance scholarship that would allow her to attend an upcoming convention in Washington, D.C.—at no cost. They were all happy for Marnie, yet apprehensive. Within the world of dance was a web every bit as tangled and tightly knit as the world of retail, with the same dancers and families coming into contact and overlapping between one competition and the next. Participating in a convention on the East Coast was far too great a risk.

Was there no way to protect his niece? The thought made his heart ache and turned his blood to ice.

With a sigh, Wainwright nosed the rented Lexus into a parking space in front of the main entrance of the Hillside Long-Term Facility. Climbing out, he pulled his cane from the backseat and rounded the car to open Viviana's door.

"Give me about an hour," she said, gathering her Fendi handbag and the stack of comic books.

Watching Viviana disappear into the building through the sliding door, Wainwright wondered if he should have forced himself to accompany her—but only briefly. *Never again*, he'd sworn to himself after his second visit to the facility. Mason had not appeared to be such an abomination on the first visit; after all, he was very ill. Following his recovery from pneumonia, however, the second visit had been another thing altogether.

What had rattled Wainwright at that point was Mason's response, or rather his lack of response, to his mother as she turned the pages of the books she had brought with her and chatted about what was taking place on each page. Although Viviana's son might be thought of as handsome, with his well-sculptured face, smooth skin, and thick brown hair, the dead expression in this man-child's eyes made Wainwright's skin crawl. *Can't Viviana see that she might as well be talking to a wall?* What made her feel obligated? She was a victim and only a child herself when she'd given birth to this creature. Why Viviana religiously put herself through this was more than Wainwright could understand.

Steadied by his ubiquitous cane, he made his way to the top of the grassy knoll beside the entrance and lowered himself to the ground. Viviana usually made this pilgrimage to see her son in Southern California midweek and always on her own. Since the gala opening of her boutique in the Carlingdon's Newport Beach store would be this evening, however, they had flown together, and it seemed sensible to combine the two events.

Thinking about what Viviana had gone through and her hang-up on motherhood brought Ashleigh and her twins to the forefront of Wainwright's mind, as it so often did, which inadvertently led him to thoughts of Erica Christonelli. Pocino's recent visit had rattled him. *Where is she?* The money he'd given her couldn't have taken her far. He'd expected a call as soon as the money ran out, but that call never came. Erica Christonelli and Ashleigh's twin daughter both seemed to have vanished into the wind. He never would have suspected the young designer had what it took to evade the law, not to mention the Landes Agency. And then there was Pocino; like a dog with a juicy steak bone, he was not about to let it go. *What has it been now, four or maybe five years? For the past couple of years he'd lived to regret the roll he'd played. Well, she can't hide forever.*

"I hate you!" Marnie cried out. "You always say no. At least Uncle Mike was happy when I won the scholarship."

"Marnie . . . ," Erica started, looking sadly at her daughter.

"You always break your promises. Why can't I use my scholarship? Marissa doesn't even have a one, but she's going! Her mom is paying for her to go to the convention, and she said that I can stay with them in the hotel."

"Marnie . . . ," Erica started again. Her stomach was doing cartwheels. Marnie had said she hated her, something she had never said before. Her head throbbed, and she couldn't string a coherent thought together.

"You're a terrible mother." Marnie glared at Erica's empty glass. "I wish I could live with Uncle Mike and Uncle Bill. They care about me, and they'd let me go." She whirled around and stormed into the bedroom, slamming the door behind her.

Erica sat in stunned silence, the floor of the mobile home rocking beneath her feet.

Moments later, Marnie emerged from her room, carrying her duffel bag.

"Where do you think you're going?" Erica asked with a note of alarm.

Marnie stared back at her. Her hand on her hip, she gave an annoyed sigh and said, "Mom."

Then Erica remembered. "Oh, I'm sorry, darling. I forgot about Marissa's slumber party. Do you need any money?"

Marnie shook her head and headed out the door. Erica knew she shouldn't allow her daughter to leave in such a manner. *No hug. No parting words.* But she didn't stop her.

After Marnie had left, Erica sat quietly in the dark for some time. When she finally got up, she emptied the cupboards of the wine bottles and thoroughly cleaned their small home. She was so frightened that her entire body shook, yet she knew she was doing the right thing.

She hesitated near the phone. *Tomorrow. I'll do it tomorrow.* She would call Mike the first thing in the morning. If he and Bill couldn't help her, she could always turn to Ian if it came down to that.

Next, she took out a scratch pad and ballpoint pen from the kitchen drawer. Lifting herself onto the bar stool at the counter, she began scribbling a few notes. She certainly didn't intend to give Marnie a piece of paper explaining things, but she needed to write it all down. She'd have to rehearse what she would say.

Erica wrote:

> *From the moment I held you in my arms and looked down at your precious face, I loved you and you were irreversibly mine . . .*

No, I can't start there. Erica crumpled the paper and set down the pen. She must start by letting Marnie know she had something important to tell her. Then she'd tell her daughter how much she was wanted and how much she was loved. She hoped Marnie wouldn't hate her, wouldn't blame her for the terrible life they had lived these past few years. *But she already said she hates me.* Of course she did. Without knowing the truth, how could Marnie understand why Erica had tried to prevent her from attending the dance convention? It made no sense to her. She had won a scholarship doing what she loved most, and she deserved to go.

It was natural for Marnie to think that her mother was cruel, that she didn't understand what was important to her. Her love of dance was every bit as strong as Erica's devotion to fashion design. *How can I let her know that I do understand?* Leaning against the cushioned backrest of the bar stool, she gazed up at the ceiling, praying for inspiration. She scolded herself. *Waiting could take all night.* If authors waited for inspiration, there would be little to read.

Picking up the pen, she leaned over the small pad of paper and began to write once more.

Blurry-eyed, Erica raised her head from atop her arms on the kitchen counter. This time as she woke, she knew for certain that she hadn't had a drop to drink the night before. Yet the stiffness in her body announced that she'd managed to fall asleep at the kitchen counter.

She attempted to remove the kinks, rolling her shoulders and rotating her head. Looking across at the kitchen clock, she saw that it was just after six. *After eight in Chicago.* She riffled through the Rolodex, picked up the phone, and dialed Mike's number.

"Christonelli Web Productions," a smiling voice said.

"Mike, it's me."

"Erica?"

"Yes. I didn't wake you, did I?"

"No, of course not." He hesitated. "It's early. Is everything alright? Where are you calling from?"

"Home, but—"

"Erica—"

Cutting him off before he could caution her, she said, "Mike, it's over. I am no longer in hiding. It's not fair to Marnie. It isn't even fair to me. I'm through with this . . ."

As she told him about what had happened the day before and about the resolutions she reached, Mike listened and made very few comments.

"The life we've been living these past four years must come to an end. I know what I need to do, and I intend to follow through, but . . ." She hesitated, then blurted out, "I can't do it alone."

"You want to come here?" he said, his voice tinged with apprehension.

"No. That doesn't make any more sense than it did four years ago. Besides, I need more help than you or any single person could give. More help than AA meetings can provide. There's only one way to guarantee that I'll be able to remain sober for the rest of my life."

"Which is . . . ?"

"I need to go through an in-patient rehab program. But to do that, I may need a loan. I am going to turn my life around, and if you can help me, I will pay you back—every penny. I promise. I've looked into it—it's just thirty days. I know I can lick my problem if I attend this program."

"I understand," Mike said. "I'm proud of you. That sounds like the responsible decision. But what about Marnie?"

"I have that figured out, but first let's talk about the rehab. I found one in New York that's—"

"New York? Have you lost your mind, Erica? New York is the last place you should be."

"That's the other thing I have to discuss with you." She remained silent for several seconds, listening to the rhythm of her own rapid heartbeat drumming in her ears. "Later today, when Marnie returns from her slumber party, I'm going to tell her the whole truth about her birth."

Not looking forward to returning home, Marnie walked slowly through the mobile home park, wondering in what condition she might find her mother. Her anger had not lessened overnight; it was a hundred times greater. Her friend Marissa, who had never won any dance awards at all, had a really neat mom who was taking her to the dance convention next week in Washington, D.C. But now Marnie wouldn't be sharing their room at the Renaissance Hotel. *I wish my mom was more like Marissa's.* Marissa's mother understood how important this was. She had even paid for her daughter to go—more than three hundred dollars! *But Mom won't even let me use my scholarship. Why does she have to be so mean? If we were still living with Uncle Mike, he would let me go. He would probably go with me himself.*

Approaching the two wobbly steps in front of her home, Marnie began to feel sort of sorry about all the ugly things she'd said to her mom. Maybe she really was sick. In school Marnie had learned about alcohol. Her teacher had talked about being dependent on it and said it was a sickness, but Marnie didn't really understand. *Mom's an adult. She can do whatever she wants. She doesn't need to get permission. So why does she keep drinking when she says she wants to quit? If she didn't go to the liquor store . . .*

As Marnie swung open the door, her internal monologue came to an abrupt end.

"Hi, honey," her mother called out, turning from the kitchen stove directly in front of the doorway. "I hope you're hungry. I fixed all your favorites."

"Am I in the right house?" Marnie said, then instantly wished she hadn't.

Ignoring her remark, Erica began rattling off the menu. "Creamed corn, chicken, and Caesar salad."

The distasteful odor that usually assaulted Marnie when she entered their mobile home was gone. Instead, she was greeted by the aromas of a hot meal. The table was set, and her mom was dressed in a pretty emerald-green cable-knit sweater and white wool pants. Her hair was pulled up into a ponytail, and she was smiling.

Looking from one end of the cabin to the other, Marnie noticed a warm glow from the lamps throughout the living room, a crackling fire in the fireplace, and a total absence of the usual clutter. Even her mother's bed was tucked away in the sofa. "What's going on?" she asked. "Is Uncle Mike here?"

"Honey, your mother isn't totally inept. Cleaning houses is my job! I know I haven't done my job in our house, but that's going to change. You are never again going to see me the way you did a couple of days ago. I promise. And you will never see your home in such disarray. I want you to be happy and to feel comfortable about bringing your friends home with you."

Marnie shrugged and gave her mother a skeptical "Okay." She'd heard it all before. Then again, she hadn't seen their house this neat and tidy for a very long time.

Erica came over and wrapped her arms around her daughter. Marnie thought she smelled Dentyne chewing gum. "I really mean it, Marnie. I know that I've broken promises in the past, but never again. Our lives are going to change."

Marnie nodded and pulled away, still suspicious. *You always mean it.*

Stepping in even closer, until she was only inches from her daughter's face, Erica said, "I've registered you for the dance convention in Washington, D.C."

Marnie stared at her. "Do you mean it? Do you really mean it?"

"I do. And I also booked a room at the Renaissance Hotel. And Uncle Mike and Uncle Bill are going to meet us there."

Marnie felt a tingle all the way to her toes and threw her arms around her mom. "I'm so sorry about last night. You're a good mom. I know you do the best you can, and I love you."

"I love you too, darling," Erica replied, hugging her daughter tightly. "And I'll never let you down again."

Throughout dinner, Marnie talked animatedly about the winter convention. "I can hardly wait to take classes from the awesome teachers there. Did you know that Garret Minniti is teaching? And Alison Dambach, and . . ." As she rattled off names of former teachers she'd met or heard about, she left no space for comment, so Erica just sat back in her chair and listened.

"Mom," she cried out, "I almost forgot. The strap on my costume for 'Diamonds Are a Girl's Best Friend' needs fixing." Only five girls from Marnie's studio would be at the convention, so they would be competing with only one number. But their choreographing was terrific, and the team had won two local competitions.

Marnie seemed so excited and happy that Erica regretted having taken so long to figure out what was right for daughter—and what was in her best interest. After dinner she suggested they make hot chocolate. She poured milk into a saucepan and set it on the stove while Marnie began to clear the dishes.

Erica helped her daughter clear the table so they could do the dishes together like they used to do. She felt herself drawing out the process. *Am I just procrastinating?*

"How about taking our hot chocolate into the living room?" Erica said finally.

"Sure."

She cleared a space on the coffee table. And before Marnie could flop into her usual armchair, Erica patted the seat beside her on the sofa.

Marnie raised an eyebrow, making her soft brown eyes appear enormous. She dropped down beside her mother, her legs stretched out and resting on the edge of the coffee table.

Erica had thought she knew just where to begin. Now that the time had come, though, she found she couldn't remember even one of her well-rehearsed sentences. "Darling, I love you with all my heart."

Marnie's face flushed. "I know, Mom."

"I'm glad you know. What I want to tell you—I mean, what I must tell you—it has me frightened almost out of my mind."

Marnie frowned.

Erica raised both hands, her palms out. "I'm sorry, I'm doing this all wrong."

Bewildered, Marnie said, "Just tell me, Mom." She leaned back on the sofa and set her mug of cocoa on the flat of her stomach.

Erica took a deep breath. "Before you were born, your father and I had wanted a baby for a very long time." This was probably the last time she would refer to Mario as Marnie's father, but the concept was still ingrained in her mind. "I miscarried three times, and we tried to adopt . . ."

"What does 'miscarried' mean?"

"I lost the baby." She did the best she could to explain to her daughter how much she had wanted a child and how sad she had been when she couldn't have one.

Marnie nodded and put her mug back down on the coffee table. Her face sad, she pulled her legs up on the sofa and wrapped her arms around them. But still, she was growing impatient. Of course, she had no idea why she had to know all this. It wasn't the kind of stuff that grown-ups usually talked about with kids.

Erica tried to talk a little faster. Finally, she got to the point where her appendix had burst. "And then the doctors told me I would never have a child," she said slowly, trying to prepare her daughter.

Marnie's brow furrowed and her eyes grew damp and wide. The truth had sunk in. "You're . . . you're not my real mother?"

Erica grabbed her daughter's hand and continued, "Your father thought I was going to—well, lose my mind, or maybe even die from sadness. He was very scared, and when people are scared, they do things they wouldn't normally do. He talked to a young woman named Rose, who was too young to keep her own baby. But when your father went back to the maternity floor to pick up Rose's baby—"

"My real mother is someone named Rose?" Marnie said as tears began to spill from her eyes.

"No, Rose is not your mother." *Oh my God. How could I have messed this up so horribly?*

"What do you mean? You just told me my father . . ." Through her tears, Marnie's eyes had turned hard. "I mean the man you were married to."

Erica reached out for her daughter's other hand, but Marnie pulled away.

"If Rose isn't my real mother, who is? Where is she? Can I meet her?"

"Oh, darling. I'm doing this all wrong. I knew this was going to be hard, but—"

"Tell me the truth! You aren't my mother! First you said Rose was my mother, and she gave you a baby. But I'm not the baby . . ." Marnie was reaching the point of hysteria.

Erica tried to take her in her arms, but her daughter's body had turned to rigid steel. "Darling, I love you! I'd rather cut off my own arm than hurt you. I didn't know—"

"You didn't know what?"

"I didn't know—" she started again.

"You didn't know I wasn't your baby?" she shouted, backing away. "You don't know who my mother is? Where did I come from? How did you get me?"

Erica pulled herself to her feet and silently looked down at her daughter's tear-ravaged face, having no idea what to say or what to do next. "I know this is confusing, darling. It's hard for me, too."

Marnie turned and shot down the hall toward her room.

"Please, don't!" Erica called after her. "I can tell you everything, it's just going to take a little time."

Marnie whirled around to face her. She stood for a very long moment, then at last she returned to the sofa and folded herself into a neat ball, clutching the outside of her legs.

Erica sat down on the sofa and placed a hand on her daughter's arm reassuringly. By the time her story neared the end, Marnie had calmed down and was as curious as any eight-year-old would be. "I have a twin sister?"

"Yes, darling. You do. But I never knew you were that kidnapped twin until you were four years old. I believed you were Rose's baby, and she'd arranged for your father to take you so that you'd have a better life. And I wish with all my heart that you *were* Rose's baby, that you were not that twin missing from that other family."

"But my fath . . . Mario . . . he stole me from them? How could he do that?"

Erica tried to explain, but she found it nearly impossible to explain what she herself could not begin to understand.

"Mom?"

"Yes?"

"I can still call you 'Mom,' can't I?" Tears streamed anew down Marnie's cheeks, falling on the legs of her jeans in big, wet circles.

This time when Erica folded her into her arms, she met no resistance. "I will always be your mom." Tears welled in her eyes, but she blinked them back.

CHAPTER
122

On Friday afternoon Ashleigh hurried from the train to her Lincoln Town Car, which she had parked at the Greenwich station for the day. She noticed it was badly in need of washing, but that could wait. She didn't want to be even a moment late for tonight's play, and she hoped that Conrad was also winging his way home. Although they often took the Greenwich train to and from Manhattan together, today had been one of Conrad's days for visiting a couple of the suburban stores. She just hoped he remembered tonight's important event.

Their youngest daughter, Juliana, was performing as one of the pilgrims tonight in the Thanksgiving play at her preschool. It was hard to believe that Juliana would soon be in kindergarten and Callie in the fourth grade. Time flew by at such a rapid pace, Ashleigh could barely keep up. But she seemed to have the best of two worlds—both personal and professional—something that was hard to come by, she knew.

Following Caroline's marriage to Don Munz, Elizabeth had come to live with the Taylors in Connecticut. Elizabeth loved Callie and Juliana, and they adored her as though she were their grandmother. And now that both girls were in school, Ashleigh had been able to go back to the type of meaningful work she loved; her position as head of human resources with John Stewart's could not have been more ideal. John Stewart's was synonymous with the high-quality merchandise and service for which Bentleys Royale had also been known. William Uniack himself, the CEO of John Stewart's, had actually gone out of his way to recruit her. And even though their headquarters were in the heart of Chicago, he'd allowed Ashleigh and one other key executive to work from their Manhattan location.

When she came within a few steps of the Lincoln, she spotted a paper under the windshield wiper. Whisking it from the glass, she smiled when she recognized that it was a note in Conrad's illegible, hurried scrawl: SEE, I WAS LISTENING. IN FACT IT APPEARS THAT I'LL ARRIVE HOME BEFORE YOU. Checking her watch, she noted that she still had plenty of time.

She arrived home soon after and dashed up the front steps to announce her arrival. Stopping at the entryway table, she picked up the small stack of mail and riffled through it. Advertisements, bills, and a hand-addressed envelope bearing the postmark of Big Bear Lake, California. Ashleigh stopped to consider. She could not recall that they knew anyone who lived in Big Bear.

Juliana came tearing into the entryway. "Mommy, look at my costume." She wore a long beige skirt and blouse, her pilgrim collar askew.

Ashleigh set the mail back down on the table and gave her youngest a hug. "Here, let me help you," she said.

Juliana smiled up at her. "Do you like my costume?"

"I especially like the pilgrim inside the costume."

Conrad descended the stairs. He'd already changed out of his suit and was wearing her favorite blue shirt, some casual trousers, and Italian loafers. "Better get a move on. We don't want to be late for the play."

Forgetting about the mail, Ashleigh headed upstairs to change.

That night, after the play, Conrad went down to his study with a pile of paperwork to go over. Ashleigh gave Juliana a kiss good-night and tucked her into bed, then strode purposefully down the hallway to Callie's room to check on her progress. "How's it going?" she asked. "Do you need any help?"

Callie sat on the floor in the middle of her room, a bottle of fabric glue and a lot of Austrian crystals spread in front of her. Tweezers in hand, she placed a crystal on the bodice of her jazz costume. "Almost have this one finished," she said without looking up. "And April said she'd help me with my costume for the lyrical routine."

With the last crystal in place, she lifted her eyes and grinned. "I don't know how you glued all those crystals on the jumpsuit I had when I was Juliana's age, Mom. There must have been a thousand."

Ashleigh laughed. "At least. That was a job and a half." She remembered sitting up most of the night, gluing crystals till she was seeing double. She leaned down and kissed Callie on the forehead. "Don't stay up too late," she said, and was about to start down the hall toward her own room when she remembered the mail.

At the bottom of the stairs, the stack of mail sat piled on the entryway table where she'd left it. She left the bills on the table and headed back upstairs with the rest. In her bedroom, she tossed the junk mail in the trash, picked up the letter opener, and flipped on the floor lamp beside the lounge. She quickly slit open the envelope with its neat and precisely penned lettering. Inside, there was a letter written on plain white paper—a single sheet, both sides filled. Curious, she turned the page over to see who had signed it.

Ashleigh stared at the signature.

Outside, the wind howled loudly, sending the branch of a nearby tree tapping into the window over and over again. She was chilled to the bone, and her hand shook uncontrollably. *Can this letter actually be from Erica Christonelli?* How could it be? Lowering herself onto the lounge chair, she pushed firmly against its sloping back.

This is silly, she chided herself, her no-nonsense outlook still intact. *I'm behaving like a Victorian lady in need of smelling salts.* She took a deep breath. The envelope was addressed to her; the letter was without the typical greeting.

There is no right way to begin to describe a crime that has had such a devastating effect on you and your family. By now, you must know that the little girl I have raised as my own is the twin who was taken from you in August of 1990. All I can say for myself is that until my daughter was four years old, I had no idea that she had been abducted. What I had been led to believe is a long story—one I'm sure you have no interest in. Nor would it justify your loss.

You may not remember me, but I remember you. We met in De Mornay's about six years ago. It was after that meeting that I learned your baby had been kidnapped from Long Beach Memorial Hospital. I told myself it was only a coincidence that your baby was abducted from the same hospital where a young mother had turned over the care of Marnie (that's what we named her) to Mario, my husband, who was a nurse practitioner. That young mother, I was told, was unprepared to have a child and wanted a better life for her baby than the one she could provide. All I knew was that I loved that child with every beat of my heart from the very first moment I held her in my arms.

I will never know exactly what happened or why

Mario took your baby, because I never got a chance to ask him.

Never got a chance to ask him? Ashleigh's eyes traveled back up the page, wondering if she'd missed something. Seeing that she had not, she read on.

We were already preparing to move to New York for Mario's new job at St. Vincent's Catholic Medical Center. He had gone ahead of us to begin work. Since Marnie was too young to fly, Mario's brother, Mike, drove us to New York. Before we arrived, however, Mario was in a near-fatal car accident. That happened barely two weeks after he put Marnie in my arms. Mario was in a coma for many months, but he never woke up. He was a good and honorable man. My depression over losing my last chance to have a baby must have driven him over the edge.

Marnie did not know she was not my natural child until today. I've told her everything now. She's taken it very hard, but she's also curious about her "missing family," especially her twin.

What my husband did was wrong. And hiding Marnie from you after I learned the truth was wrong, but for Marnie's sake, I pray that you will find it in your heart to do what is best for her. I honestly don't know what that is, but right now she is a very frightened girl. She has asked me if she would have to live with her twin's family. I know that legally she is yours, and in the past four years since I went into hiding, I have experienced some severe personal problems and have been far from a perfect mother. But I have arranged to get help, and I plan to get my life in order starting now.

Why am I telling you this? I'm sure this is a question you must be asking yourself. Number one, I love Marnie with all my heart, and I want what's best for her. Number two, I know that you and your husband want what's best for her. Number three, quite honestly, I know that if I didn't tell you now, you would find out someday. My sincere hope is that you can put yourself in my place: Imagine if, four years ago, you found out that your daughter belonged to someone else. Would you have been able to hand her over to the rightful mother? I don't think you would have been able to do so any more than I could. So please find a way to forgive me for the past, and let's see what we can work out for the future.

Marnie and I will be checking into the Renaissance Hotel in Washington, D.C., on Thursday the nineteenth, a couple of days before the dance convention. Marnie will be attending on a scholarship. From what I understand, your daughter is likely to be attending also. I have no right to dictate how we can arrange our meeting and will do whatever you suggest. However, if possible, I would like to meet with you and your husband on that day—the nineteenth. If not at the hotel, you can suggest another place by leaving word for me at the front desk. After we have spoken, I think the girls should meet.

It is not surprising that the girls have chosen a similar path in dance. Until now, I have avoided allowing Marnie to go anywhere I believed you or your daughter might be, but that was wrong. The first meeting will be a difficult one for both girls, but if all I've read about twins is true, it might not be as devastating as I've imagined. And what better way for them to meet than at a dance convention, doing what they love best? I look forward to hearing from you.

Laying her head back, Ashleigh closed her eyes. Rather than a sense of elation, a hollow unreality spiked though her. The Renaissance Hotel. Cassie was no longer missing; she was within her reach. In less than a week, Ashleigh would be reunited with her baby for the first time in more than eight years.

A cold knot of fear settled in her stomach. *Cassie is no longer a baby. There is no Cassie. Cassie is gone; there is only Marnie. Who is Marnie? What is she like? How will Callie relate to her? And where will Juliana fit in?* Dragging herself to her feet, Ashleigh tried to sort out her feelings. It was all so strange and surreal.

Clutching the note, she drifted slowly down the stairs toward Conrad's study.

The fierce November wind had raged throughout the night. The following morning, small tree branches littered the ground and piles of fallen leaves danced about on the lawn.

"Drive carefully, love," Ashleigh whispered in her husband's ear, before she pulled away.

Standing on the front porch, Conrad gave her another tight hug. "We will work it out. I'll think about what you've said. I want us both to end up on the same page."

"Of course. Take your time. I know how hard this is." She stepped back, pulling the sash on her robe tighter.

Her husband pulled up the collar of his heavy cashmere coat. "Be back before noon," he shouted, just before he dashed into the open garage.

Ashleigh hadn't slept a wink the night before, but she didn't feel at all tired. Luckily, Callie wouldn't be sleeping in this Saturday morning. Ashleigh had set her daughter's alarm so she would be up and about in plenty of time for her ten o'clock rehearsal. She turned back into the house, closed the door firmly behind her, and headed for the kitchen. It was only seven thirty. She put on a pot of coffee and returned to her bedroom to get dressed, leaving her door open wide so that she could hear any signs of activity from Callie's room.

Donning a white cashmere sweater and wool pants, Ashleigh ran a brush through her hair and then heard water running in Callie's shower. That meant she'd have plenty of time to get a cup of coffee.

Coming into the kitchen, she saw Elizabeth pouring the coffee into white mugs.

"Thank you so much," Ashleigh said, ready to head back upstairs.

"Is everything alright?" Elizabeth asked.

She must have overheard them last night. "Yes . . . at least . . . We will work things out." Conrad's response had been explosive. He had been vocal about his views; he wanted their long-lost daughter turned over to their care immediately. Over the last few years, Ashleigh knew how hard he'd struggled to conceal his anger. And for the most part, he had managed to hide it from them all. But at what cost? Last night the dam broke—none of his pent up anguish had remained unspoken.

Seeing Elizabeth's distress and genuine concern, Ashleigh quickly brought her up to date.

"It is wonderful that Cassie has been found." Elizabeth's eyes were moist as a warm smile lit up her face. Then, in her typical manner, she added, "I do understand your dilemma. I'm sure you and Mr. Conrad will do what is best."

"Thank you, Elizabeth. I sure hope so. It's the talk with Callie I'm concerned about right now." Callie wasn't aware of all the drama surrounding the abduction. But as she had grown older, she had been told that she had a twin sister. The Taylors had neither encouraged nor discouraged Callie from asking questions about her twin. She had asked few questions, basically just accepting in her child's way the fact that her twin was missing. Now, Ashleigh wasn't sure what to expect.

Upstairs, she gently knocked on the door of her daughter's bedroom. Hearing the roar of a hair dryer, she knocked louder. Still no response. Stepping inside, she called out her daughter's name.

"In here, Mom." Callie's voice wafted out through the open bathroom door. "What's up?" She was still drying her hair.

As Ashleigh waited for her to finish, her mind raced, filling with all the possibilities. The negatives began to fade. If she handled this right, this need not be traumatic. Callie would get to know her twin. Amazingly, they were both very good dancers. What else might they have in common?

Callie strode out of the bathroom in her black leotard, skin-toned tights, and slippers, placing the final hairpin into her bun.

Ashleigh sat on the edge of the bed and gestured for Callie to sit down beside her.

"What's up?" Callie repeated. "Am I in trouble?" Her smile belied her concern.

"Not at all," Ashleigh said. "I have some exciting news." Without embellishment or delay, she took hold of Callie's hand and said, "Your twin has been found." She paused, waiting for this to sink in. "We will be meeting her next weekend. There is a long story about what happened to her, and I will share that with you. But I wanted you to know right away . . ." She looked intently at her daughter.

Callie drew back a little and her large eyes met Ashleigh's. For a moment, she said nothing. Then a smile lit up her face. "Wow. That's great, Mom! Do we really look alike?"

"I'm sure you do," Ashleigh said, a little stunned. "You are identical twins, but you're both individuals with your own personalities. She might dress differently or have a different hairstyle. But you have at least one thing in common: Your twin is also a dancer." Her daughter's questions seemed natural, though she was taken aback by Callie's immediate acceptance of this new reality.

"So when can I meet Cassie? Will she come to live with us?"

"Her name is Marnie now. I'm not sure. We'll have to see—"

"But she's my twin. Doesn't the person who took her have to give her back?"

Ashleigh had to smile. *If only it were that simple.* "It's more complicated than that. The woman who has raised her didn't know she was kidnapped. And—"

"How could she not know?"

Ashleigh looked down at her watch. "If only you could miss this morning's rehearsal . . ."

"Mom! The competition is next weekend."

Smiling, Ashleigh said, "I understand. Grab your dance bag. We'll talk in the car."

Mike Christonelli and his partner flew into Dulles early on the morning of November nineteenth. When Bill had taken Marnie to the Smithsonian's National Air and Space Museum that afternoon, Erica had commented, "I am so happy that Bill was able to get away from John Stewart's." She was glad to have him there—to bring a bit of culture into Marnie's life for an afternoon, but also to give herself and Mike a chance to smooth the way for her first encounter with her biological parents.

Erica would have liked to feel she was strong enough to handle her meeting with Conrad and Ashleigh Taylor on her own. She had set it up that way in her letter. But she realized she was only fooling herself—and doing so poorly. She was grateful when Mike insisted on being at the initial meeting with the Taylors. The very thought of coming face-to-face with them on her own turned her body to mush.

"Bill loves this city, and he loves Marnie, too. We miss her a lot," he said, quickly adding, "and you too."

Ignoring his little faux pas, she replied, "Mike, I hope you know how much Marnie and I appreciate all you've done for us."

"Wish I could do more."

"No one could have done more. You know, I got to the point for a while when I hated your brother for the position he'd put me in. I was angry and looking for someone to blame for me turning into—into the Big Bear bag lady."

"Erica, for the love of God!"

"Well, not a bag lady, exactly, but pretty damn close." Seeing that he was about to cut in, she said, "Wait. Please, I want to explain. Maybe that was the alcohol talking back then. I didn't want to take responsibility for what was happening. I was looking to lay blame. But that was wrong of me. It was all wrong. I don't know why Mario turned to kidnapping, but I do know it was my fault."

Mike made a motion to interrupt her, but she raised her hand, palm out. "Let me finish. I've come full circle. Mario gave me the most wonderful gift of my entire life. I'm sorry Conrad and Ashleigh Taylor's baby was abducted. It is a crime to take someone's child. But I'm not one bit sorry that Mario gave Marnie to me to raise. I wouldn't give up the last eight years of my life for anything in the world."

Mike stared at her and didn't say a word for several long seconds. Then the corners of his mouth turned up in a tentative smile. "Me neither."

While Conrad checked the car with the valet and saw to their luggage, Ashleigh secured the room keys from the front desk. Conrad would be staying with Ashleigh and Callie in the suite of rooms tonight, but would be flying back to New York the following day. Then they would be sharing the suite with Paige and April, who were due the next day. Ashleigh also had arranged for Elizabeth to have the adjoining room.

On the way to the hotel, they had dropped Callie and Elizabeth off at the Smithsonian's Air and Space Museum. It had been Elizabeth's suggestion, and Callie was delighted; her role model, April, had told her how cool it was.

Unable to keep her hands from shaking, Ashleigh held one with the other.

"Are you ready, sweetheart?" Conrad asked as he met her in the lobby.

Ashleigh smiled. "Just a touch of the jitters."

Conrad looked at her for a long moment. And then with a deadly serious expression, he said, "I can't imagine why."

She playfully punched him in the arm. At times like this, she realized how grateful she was to have him at her side.

At exactly four o'clock, Mike knocked on the door of room 1711. Erica stood at his elbow, praying for strength.

Conrad Taylor opened the door. He wore a blue silk dress shirt and no tie. His unblinking eyes did not waver from Erica's even as he greeted Mike. He introduced himself and said, "I believe you and my wife have met."

Unable to respond, Erica merely nodded.

Coming to her rescue, Ashleigh said, "Yes, we met at De Mornay's. Please, come in." She gestured for them to sit at the round table in front of the large window, where she had pulled out a couple of chairs.

When everyone except Conrad had been seated, he mercifully broke the silence. "There is no point in skirting the issues." He looked directly at Erica. His gaze was so direct that she felt as if he could see straight through to her soul—that he could see all her deficiencies.

"Mrs. Christonelli, I—"

"Please, call me Erica." Her voice came out in a squeak, and she cleared her throat. Mike moved his chair closer to hers.

"Erica. I understand in certain respects that you have also been a victim of your husband's crime. That is unfortunate for you and unfortunate for our abducted daughter, but we must now rectify the situation. Our daughter, who has been missing from our lives since almost the moment of her birth, deserves to have a better life than then one you have provided for her."

"Hold on." Mike shot to his feet.

Ashleigh, unable to hold her silence, took hold of her husband's arm. *This is starting out all wrong. What is Conrad thinking? Why is he putting the woman on the defensive? I thought he understood.* Her voice just above a whisper, she spoke directly to Conrad. "Please, darling. May I say something?"

"Go ahead," he said, lowering himself into the empty chair.

Mike sat back down and focused his attention on Ashleigh.

"My husband is correct when he says that, in a way, we are all victims. However, what we must all keep in mind is that this meeting isn't about us. It is about what is in the best interest of our daughter." Ashleigh met Erica's eye. Though the room was cool, beads of perspiration stood on the poor woman's forehead. "You say your husband was a good man. And from all that our investigators have learned of him, he was a respected member of the hospital staff. How he could have stolen our newborn is beyond my understanding."

Seeing Mike lean forward, Ashleigh held out her hand. "Please. I'm not trying to lay blame. No one in this room is to blame. I wish there were some sort of divine intervention to guide us, but I'm afraid we will just have to sort it out as best we can." Her eyes sought Erica's. "I know this has to be a nightmare for you. And as you suggested, I thought about the situation being reversed. The ramifications for Callie and for me—it would be devastating." Feeling Conrad's unease and noting the muscles clinching in his jaw, she reached over to lay her hand on his arm. He was used to being in control, but they were both out of their depth in this situation.

"Thank you, Ashleigh," Erica began. "I am so confused. I don't know what is best for Marnie. What I do know is that I love her more than anything in the world." Tears streamed down her cheeks. "I know she's yours, but she's mine, too. You could give her a much better life than I can, than most anyone could, but I don't want to lose her, and she's afraid. She doesn't want to live with . . . strangers."

"My God! We aren't strangers. We are her parents," Conrad protested.

Ashleigh remained silent. Her husband had a right to vent.

"I'm sorry," Erica continued. "I know you are her parents, and I know she has sisters, something I can't give her."

Mike began pacing the floor.

Ashleigh rose from her chair and knelt down beside the sobbing woman. "Erica," she said with a sad smile. "You will always be a part of . . . of Marnie's life. We will work things out. I don't know how, but we will. Marnie will have to set the tone. We will not force her to be with us full-time, but she must be a part of our lives. She must get to know her sisters. But you will not be left out. I promise."

As the words spilled out, Ashleigh realized that their family would now include Erica, the wife of the man who kidnapped her child.

"Would you excuse us for a few minutes?" Conrad said, rising to his feet.

When Ashleigh looked up at him, her smile faded. Instantly a cloud of unease enveloped her. Her husband's hands were balled into two tight fists. His jaw was clenched, and it appeared that he was ready to explode. She reached out, slipping her hand into his, and said a silent prayer as she stood to meet him. When she glanced back, she caught an unsettled look of anxiety pass between Erica and Mike. "We will be right back."

With her hand still in Conrad's, she rose, and without a word they headed to the bedroom to their right.

Conrad waited until he heard the door click securely behind them. *How could Ashleigh be so damn forgiving?*

Ashleigh had dropped down on the edge of the bed and was patting the space beside her. She looked up at him expectantly. He remained standing, however, doing his best to rein in his temper. He took a deep breath. He must not spoil the return of their daughter for his wife, but he had to make her understand. To consider the kind of people they were dealing with.

He chose his words carefully. "Sweetheart, while I agreed not to press charges against Erica Christonelli and her brother-in-law for harboring our kidnapped daughter . . ." He lowered himself to sit beside her and attempted to clarify. "I understand that neither of the people in the next room is literally guilty of abducting Cassie from the hospital." Just voicing the name he and his wife had given their kidnapped infant—a name she'd never known—left a bitter taste in his mouth. "But I'll be damned if I'm prepared for them to become members of our family."

Tears welled in Ashleigh's eyes, and he saw that she was trembling. But when she spoke, her voice was steady. "Darling, I understand how hard this is for you. It's not easy for me, either, but I've been thinking about this day and preparing for the complications and—"

"For God's sake, Ashleigh," he spat. "Erica and Mike Christonelli are guilty of a heinous crime. They knew the identity of our daughter four years ago. When she was four years old, not eight!" Raking his fingers though his hair, he said, "But instead of doing the right thing, the woman went into hiding to keep her from us."

"*The woman* was desperate. She loves—"

Leaping to his feet, he turned and glared down at his wife. "Don't defend that woman! Don't you dare defend her. Erica Christonelli had our daughter living in a goddamned trailer park."

Ashleigh stared down at the carpet as tears fell down her cheeks. For a while, she did not respond.

Conrad sat down again beside her. *So much for well-chosen, unemotional words.* "I'm sorry, sweetheart." Wrapping his arm around her, he said, "I didn't mean to raise my voice. We all have a very challenging period ahead of us. You, me, and all three of our daughters. We don't need to take on more. If our information is correct, and I have no reason to believe otherwise, Erica has had a severe drinking problem."

Ashleigh blinked back tears while gulping in an unsteady breath. When she raised her eyes to meet his, her voice was barely above a whisper, "I know, love. Ross's report was unsettling, but—"

"But nothing!" Conrad's voice exploded. "You know that this has to have had a devastating effect on our daughter. The woman denied Cassie the type of childhood we could have provided. The child has missed growing up with her sisters, Ashleigh, and . . . so much more.

"And I still think it was wrong to keep Pocino on such a short leash this past week when he was in Big Bear. I'd feel a lot better if you'd let him question—" He broke off. It felt as if he were on an emotional teeter-totter. He wanted to know everything there was to know about the woman who had kept their daughter from them, and yet he wanted to support his wife, to avoid doing anything to make this untenable situation more difficult for her.

Ashleigh straightened and gently pulled away so that her eyes again met Conrad's. She seemed in control of her emotions when she repeated, "Darling, I know how difficult this is. Everything you're saying is true. I can't fight that, and I can't turn back the clock. What I suggested, though, is not for the benefit of the Christonellis. We must all work together to do what is best for our daughter. Please, give me a few moments to explain. I've been thinking about this for a long time, and I've come up with a rather complicated analogy that might help to explain my feelings.

"Suppose that four years ago we discovered Callie was not our daughter." Before Conrad could interject, Ashleigh continued, "Forget about

Callie being a twin, and just suppose there had been a mix-up at the hospital, and we didn't discover that we weren't Callie's biological parents until she was four years old."

Conrad swallowed his retort, knowing that his wife was generally level-headed and not prone to wild supposition. He asked, "And how did we discover this?"

"Suppose," she repeated, "she needed some sort of transplant, and her DNA did not match ours." Taking his chin in her hand so that their eyes met, she said, "Would you love Callie any less?"

He sighed. "Of course not. But what you are laying out is not at all similar. We did not abduct Callie from her birth parents."

"I know. I'm not finished. Let's say there was a reason for the mix-up— say there was a disaster, an earthquake or a fire at the hospital, and everyone had to vacate. Say we took the wrong infant from the nursery."

"Sweetheart, we have some important decisions to make. It's certainly not the time for creating impossible scenarios. This is not at all like you . . ."

"Conrad, do you trust me?"

"Of course I do." *But what is going on in her head?*

"Then please let me finish. I realize it's an *unlikely* set of circumstances, but not an *impossible* one. But that's not the point. What I'm trying to do is get to the type of feelings Erica Christonelli must've had when she found out that her child, the one she's raised and thought of as her own, was the missing twin she had heard and read about."

Conrad pulled out the desk chair and sat down, leaning back into it.

"Say that, following the disaster at Memorial Hospital, we read about a couple who had lost their child that night. We had empathy for the parents but didn't know it had anything to do with us, until four years later when we discovered that the child we had raised was not our own."

"Wow. That's quite a leap. Perhaps you should write fiction."

Ashleigh bolted to her feet. "Conrad, I'm serious. If you had that kind of knowledge, would you try to return Callie to her biological parents?"

Of course not. The very thought of someone taking his Callie from him gave him no less a jolt than the Northridge earthquake of 1994.

Suddenly Ashleigh's analogy made a strange kind of sense. He could see her perspective—making the leap to grasp the Christonelli woman's actions would take more than a little time. The situation they were facing was not at all the same, and yet in a way it was. He sighed and reached for his wife. "Life truly is stranger than fiction, by a long shot," he said.

After making polite apologies for their brief absence, Ashleigh sensed that a great deal of the tension had dissipated from the room.

Conrad met Erica's eyes. "Let's put the past behind us and all focus on what's best for our daughter."

An expression of relief swept across Erica's brow. Then, glancing down at her watch, she said, "Marnie is due back in the next hour. Do you still want to meet her before she sees her twin, or do you think we should just all meet together?" When no immediate response came, she went on. "I've prepared her for the possibility of meeting with just the two of you, but she might be more comfortable if Callie were with you. With their love of dance, they have a common interest. That is bound to make things easier."

"I think you're right," Ashleigh said, looking to Conrad, who nodded his agreement. "Callie is at the National Air and Space Museum, but she should be—"

"The Air and Space Museum?" Erica and Mike cried out in unison.

Shivering, Callie turned up the collar of her faux fur coat and pulled her gloves out of her pocket.

A light drizzle bounced off the taxi window, and her breath made tiny circles on the glass. Their visit to the museum had been fun, with so many interesting exhibits to see, but she was really curious about meeting her twin. Hundreds of questions ran through her head. *Will we like each other? Will I have to share my bedroom?* She'd thought of little else throughout the day.

The taxi pulled into the semicircular drive in front of the entrance to the Renaissance. Her souvenir book slid to the floor. She picked it up and shoved her gloves back in her pocket while Elizabeth dug in her handbag for her wallet to pay the driver.

They stepped out under the porte cochère, the wind snapping Callie's hair into her face as she ran for cover just inside the electronic doors. Elizabeth hustled in behind her and they headed for the bank of elevators. When Callie noticed the events directory just ahead of them, she stopped. It read TREMAINE DANCE CONVENTION: GRAND BALLROOM. Looking up at Elizabeth, she asked, "Please, can we go and take a peek in the Grand Ballroom?"

Elizabeth checked her watch. "Sure. We have plenty of time. It says it's on the lower level." She pointed toward the escalators.

They descended one floor and stepped off onto the paisley carpet, immediately spotting the GRAND BALLROOM sign above the open door. The room was empty. Chairs were set up in lines along the walls, facing the dance floor. In the center, the entire floor was available for dance. Callie took a few steps inside the room.

"Cool," she said to Elizabeth, who stood behind her, just inside the door. Callie took in the full length and width of the room, and then she turned, nearly running into a tall man with thinning brown hair.

"Sorry," Callie said to the man entering the room. She was about to return to Elizabeth when she found herself staring into the big brown eyes of a girl about her own age. No, this girl was *exactly* her age. Exactly her height. Exactly her . . . everything.

Both girls stood stone-still, staring at each other.

Elizabeth and the man also stared. No one spoke.

"Wow," Callie finally said, "it's like looking into the mirror."

The other girl didn't say a word.

She tried again. "I'm Callie, so you must be Marnie. This is crazy!" She burst out laughing, and after a few seconds, the other girl did as well.

"You really do look exactly like me," Marnie said, looking her twin up and down, her eyes wide and her mouth open in a bemused smile.

"No," Callie said with a serious face, "*you* look like *me*." At her twin's bewildered expression, she giggled and said, "Mom says I'm seven minutes older."

The adults hadn't moved and appeared to be stunned speechless. Callie turned to Elizabeth and said, "This is my twin."

Elizabeth stood motionless in her sensible shoes, her wool coat buttoned to the neck, her face flushed. "Oh my!" she said. "I don't believe this is how your parents intended for you two to meet."

The man walked toward them, his face as red as Elizabeth's. "I guarantee they did not. Marnie and I have spent the day at the Air and Space Museum to avoid any such accidental meeting."

"Oh my!" Elizabeth repeated. "We've just come from there too."

Callie had never seen her so flustered. She and Marnie looked at each other and broke out in giggles all over again.

"Small world," he said, extending his hand to Elizabeth. "I'm Bill Reynolds."

Elizabeth took his hand and introduced herself. "Well, I suppose God does indeed work in very mysterious ways. At least the girls are getting together in a place where they have much in common. Perhaps it was meant to be."

Callie and Marnie were already talking about their upcoming dance routines and their competition schedule. Callie slipped off her coat and set it on the chair beside her. "What kind of dance do you like best?"

Marnie shrugged out of her fitted wool coat and tossed it on the chair beside Callie's. "I do all kinds. Jazz, lyrical, ballet, tap," she rattled off. "But my favorite is lyrical, and then jazz."

"Me too," Callie said. "I have a jazz and a lyrical solo for competition."

"They don't do solos here, do they?" Marnie asked.

"No. It's for another competition. They just do groups here. I'm in three groups. How about you?"

"Just one. There are only four other girls from our studio here. California is too far away for some of the girls."

"Bummer," Callie said. "Do you do solos?"

Marnie shook her head, her gaze dropping to the floor. "Mom says it costs about a thousand dollars to work with a dance teacher to learn a solo, and then there are extra costumes to pay for and competition fees . . ."

"Oh," Callie said. She had no idea of the cost. "Well, my cousin, April . . ." Callie hesitated, a frown creasing her forehead. "Uh, she's not really my cousin, but her mom is Auntie Paige, my mom's best friend. So we've always been sort of cousins." She paused, biting down on the bottom corner of her lip. *My mom is Marnie's real mom. That feels really weird.* She decided to think about that later. "Anyway, April is one of the assistant teachers here at the convention. She's doing the jazz and lyrical sessions. She taught me my first solo."

Marnie nodded. "Great, she sounds like fun."

"You'll really like her. She's coming with Auntie Paige tomorrow. They're sharing our rooms, so you'll meet them both." Callie suddenly grew silent, remembering that it was April and her friend Madison who had seen Marnie at Carlingdon's when she was just four. She wondered what might have happened if April and Madison hadn't seen her that day. *We might never be meeting today!* She reminded herself to thank April later for being such a good "cousin."

A curious expression settled on Marnie's face. "What's wrong?"

Callie's stomach was sort of jittery. She didn't want to talk about serious stuff now. There would be plenty of time for that. "I guess there's a lot we have to learn about each other." She paused, then the grin returned to her face. "Can you do an elliptical?" she asked.

Marnie scrunched her nose and peered up at the ceiling, then asked, "What's that?"

"You know," Callie said, "sort of a cartwheel without hands. In gymnastics they call it an aerial." The puzzled look remained on Marnie's face, so Callie said, "Let me show you," and led her to the big hardwood circle in the center of the room.

Callie's flawless elliptical elicited an audible gasp from Elizabeth, who came rushing over to them. "I'll never get use to seeing you perform that trick. I'm so afraid you could fall and break your neck."

Callie looked up at her and said, "Don't worry. I've had lots of practice."

"Awesome!" Marnie was still jumping up and down, clapping her hands. "Will you teach me how to do that?"

Turning to Marnie, Callie smiled. *It's going to be great fun to have a sister my own age!* "Sure. It's easy once you get the hang of it. April taught me. We can teach you this weekend."

"Girls," Elizabeth said, looking worried. "I'm afraid it's time for us to join your parents."

"Okay." Callie grinned. "Let's go up to see everyone together," she suggested. "Our parents will really be surprised." It was turning out to be a great day. She could hardly wait to see her Mom's and Dad's faces when she walked through the door holding Marnie's hand.

EPILOGUE

Erica spotted Ian's tall, lean frame beside the baggage carousel and nervously wound her way through the meager group of passengers. It was the day after Christmas, and JFK, while not deserted, was no longer teaming with hordes of holiday travelers.

Throwing her arms around her brother, Erica said, "I've missed you so much." Ian's hair was a bit thinner, but he hadn't seemed to have aged a day in the past six years.

He squeezed her tightly and stepped back, giving her a warm, appraising look. "God, it's good to see you. You look terrific."

"I feel terrific." It was a bit of an exaggeration, but not exactly a lie. Things were working out far better than she'd dared to dream. While the path they'd all chosen was not problem free, she was learning to cope with her occasional bouts of jealousy and focus on her positive emotions—in particular, her gratitude for all that Ashleigh and Conrad Taylor could provide for Marnie. "I would have loved to see Laura and Ilise. Maybe next time."

"Just wait until Marnie becomes a teen—"

"I understand," she said, then changed the subject, not wanting to think about Marnie growing up and going her own way. "I've made it through rehab, and you won't ever have to worry about me again. Even if you put a gun to my head, I'll never touch another drop of liquor. Ever."

"No guns." He gave a chuckle. Then his expression turned serious. "I'm proud of you, Erica." Raising his hand to his forehead to shade his eyes from the fluorescent lights overhead, he peered out into the sparse crowd. "Did you see Leslie?"

"Oh, there you are," Leslie called out as she threaded her way toward them. "I must have just missed you." She wrapped Erica in a warm embrace. "Please forgive me."

"Forgive you?"

"Yes. When you most needed a friend, I was an absolute bitch."

Erica didn't know what to say. She had been hurt deeply by Leslie's coldness, which she hadn't understood at the time.

Ian grabbed their second bag from the carousel. "Hope you don't mind, but I asked Leslie to read the letter you sent from rehab."

Before Erica could respond, Leslie broke in. "It was incredible. And I feel so ashamed. With all you've been through, my holier-than-thou attitude was not only wrong, it was unkind."

Meeting Leslie's troubled eyes, a wave of understanding flooded Erica. "I'd probably have felt the same way if the situation had been reversed."

"Well, that's all in the past now. Right now, I'm glad we'll have some time to talk before meeting your . . . *extended family*," she said. Her eyes darted around the baggage area. "Where's Marnie?"

Erica gulped. She had tried to explain their situation in the letter, but there was so much more to tell. "She's still at the Taylors'. April, the Toddmans' daughter, is choreographing a duet for the girls while they're on school vacation."

Noticing Leslie's expression, she said, "I'll fill you in on the cast of characters on our way to Greenwich."

Turning to Ian, who had loaded the luggage onto one of the carts, she said, "The limo driver is just outside the door."

"Limo driver?" Leslie's voice telegraphed her surprise.

As Erica led them through the electronic doors and to the open trunk of the limo, she reminded them, "Marnie and I spent Christmas at the Taylors', and Ashleigh insisted on taking the limo to pick you up."

The temperature had dropped below thirty degrees, and Ian shivered as they climbed into the limo. "I'm looking forward to hearing all about these new family members of yours," he said, amused—and perhaps a little incredulous. Then he paused midstride and turned to Erica. "The Taylors don't know that I knew Marnie was their abducted twin, do they?"

More relaxed now, Ian gazed out at the thick, feathery snow, which fell rhythmically against the windows of the limo as they drove, rendering the road nearly invisible. In the background, he heard the hum of Erica's voice. She was filling Leslie in on all her new relationships—names, how they fit in, and who was related to whom. Observing the two women in his life in animated conversation, a wave of relief washed over him, and he relaxed into the comfortable, warm leather seat.

His mind drifted back to the long letter he'd received from Erica during her last week of rehab. Her opening sentences—"I am no longer in hiding, and you will no longer have to fear a detective or police officer knocking at your door to talk about a missing twin. Nor will you ever have to worry about an alcoholic sister. That is all in the past"—had set his nerves on full alert. He had barely dared to hope it was all true.

In the letter, Erica had been candid about her slide into alcoholism, and she had given him a fairly detailed account of the events in her life and Marnie's over the past four years. To have overcome all that, he knew, she could no longer be the depressed teenager she once was—or the weak, vulnerable woman he'd seen at the start of all this mess. But was that really possible? She'd written that the Taylors were fantastic, especially Ashleigh, and that Marnie had the best of all worlds now. But how did she actually feel about sharing custody with Marnie's biological mother? And he had to wonder, what did Marnie call Ashleigh and Conrad Taylor?

"We're here," Erica sang out.

"Oh my God." The words were out of Ian's mouth before he realized it. Even compared to their own large, prestigious home in Laguna Niguel, the home and grounds of the Taylors' estate were phenomenal— straight from a Hollywood movie set.

Erica let out a nervous laugh. "Don't worry, you will be meeting a group of warm, friendly people. They're not in the least bit pretentious. You'll love Ashleigh and her best friend, Paige. And Paige's mom, Helen, is a real kick. She has early-onset Alzheimer's, but most of the time, you'd never know it."

Ian smiled. His sister was talking so fast, he wondered who it was she was trying to convince. "I trust you."

Ashleigh ran to the door before the bell filled the entry with a frenzy of holiday tunes. She had done her best to make this a wonderful holiday for Erica as well as for Marnie. Their situation was unusual to say the least, but she wanted so much for her long-lost daughter and the girl's "second mom" to feel comfortable. Swinging open the door, she saw a tall man and a red-haired woman standing beside Erica, stamping the snow off their shoes. She saw immediately that Erica and her brother bore a strong resemblance, although Erica's curly blond hair softened the angular shape of her face.

Following the introductions, Ashleigh took their coats.

"Here," Elizabeth said, stepping up quietly behind her. "Let me take these while you bring your guests to meet the others."

Ashleigh smiled and introduced the McDonalds to Elizabeth.

Before the coats were hung, Erica was swept off her feet by her brother-in-law. Bill was right behind him. "Mike! Bill!" she cried. "How. . . ?"

As she struggled to assemble a coherent sentence, Mike said, "Ashleigh invited us."

Tears streamed down Erica's cheeks as she turned toward Ashleigh.

"I thought it would be nice for you and Marnie to have all your family here," Ashleigh said. "It was Mike's idea to make it a surprise."

A round of giggles sounded from above, getting louder and louder. When Marnie and Callie finally dashed down the winding staircase, Ashleigh noticed the way Ian stared at the girls. Both were wearing black leotards, and each girl had her hair pulled back in a ponytail. Ian blinked.

Even knowing that Marnie and Callie were identical twins hadn't quite prepared him for just how identical they would look.

Halfway down the stairs, one of the girls called out, "Aunt Erica, we want to show you our duet before dinner."

"I'd love to see it." Turning from Callie to Marnie, she said, "But first I'd like you to meet your aunt and uncle. This is your Uncle Ian and Aunt Leslie. You haven't seen them since you were just a toddler."

Ashleigh registered Ian's unasked question. "It isn't always easy to tell them apart, although they don't usually dress alike in their everyday clothes. But somehow, Erica and I have no trouble telling them apart, at least not when they're together." Callie's face was just a bit fuller than Marnie's.

Marnie said shyly, "It's nice to meet you." Then turning to Callie, she said, "Uncle Ian and Aunt Leslie, this is my sister."

Callie smiled. "I'm Callie. What should I call you?"

Ian's mouth turned up in a broad grin; he could see which was the more outgoing of the twins. "Well, if you don't mind, we'd like to be called Uncle Ian and Aunt Leslie."

"Got it," Callie said. "Hi, Uncle Ian. Hi, Aunt Leslie."

Conrad greeted Ian as he stepped down into the spacious living room, and in turn Ian introduced Conrad to Leslie.

Ashleigh began to relax as her husband took over the introductions. Soon after, everyone fell into companionable conversation. Glancing down, she took in the progress Juliana had made on her puzzle; its pieces were spread out on a low table in front of their fragrant, ten-foot-tall Christmas tree. Then she returned to her position on the floor beside Paige and Helen.

Erica and Leslie sat together, catching up on events they'd missed in each other's lives over the past few years. Their eyes occasionally swept over to the Winter Wonderland puzzle, and one woman or the other would point out a piece that had been overlooked. Helen, too, attempted to squeeze in a puzzle piece now and again, and Ashleigh was proud of how kind and diplomatic Juliana was when it turned out to be the wrong spot.

"Thanks, Grandma Helen," she said. "That's the right piece, but it goes here." And she would turn the piece in the right direction and lay it gently in the spot where it belonged, asking Helen to help her pat it into place.

Helen's emerald green eyes glowed with delight. She looked as excited as a child at Christmastime, dressed in the new red dress Paige had chosen for her. She and Rupert, in his usual wool trousers and dress shirt, were a joy to be around, and it seemed as if they had always been a part of the Toddman family.

Paige looked up from the puzzle and gave Ashleigh a wink, then handed her mother another puzzle piece. Pointing to an open spot, she said, "I think it might fit here."

At the sound of the door chimes, Juliana jumped up and skip-hopped to the door. Cracking it open, she squealed.

It was Uncle Sonny and his friend Brad. Their arms were loaded with packages.

"Aye, colleen. You goin' to let your pal Brad and your ol' Uncle Sonny in the door?"

Juliana flung the door open wide, jumping up and down, her eyes on the wrapped packages.

Sonny wore a red cap, which he whipped off his head the moment he stepped inside. Setting it down along with the packages on the entryway table, he made a face at Juliana, who saw that his red hair stood up in spikes. She giggled when he leaned down to give her a hug.

"You better comb your . . ." She cut off, distracted by the big box wrapped in pink paper that he was extending toward her. Her eyes widened. "Is that for me?"

Brad jumped in. "We just got back from Bermuda a few days ago. But while we were away, we thought about our favorite little lassie and your sisters." Before Juliana could thank them, the door sounded again.

Seeing that Juliana's hands were full, Sonny grabbed the knob and flung open the door.

Mary and Bradford Taylor stood on the porch, wiping the snow from their shoes.

Conrad strode in and gave them all a hearty greeting. Then he ushered them into the living room after Juliana, who ran ahead to inform everyone of their presents—and to get permission to open hers.

April and the twins, who had gone upstairs to practice their duet, reappeared. "Is it okay if we set up the dance floor?" Callie asked.

"Sure," her father answered, and then he turned to Ian. "Can you give me a hand?"

Ian followed Conrad back into the game room, and they wheeled the circular hardwood dance floor into the living room. It was hinged in the middle, and they unfolded it before arranging it at the far end of the living room.

"Showtime!" Ashleigh announced as she helped Juliana carry the puzzle table over to the wall beneath the bay windows.

Mark stood behind Paige, massaging her shoulders as the girls huddled together.

Ashleigh watched as her loved ones gathered close to enjoy one another's company. She'd decided that Erica's family were people she would like to get to know better. Suddenly she felt very lucky. She smiled as she felt Conrad's arms wrap around her waist and a kiss being planted on the top of her head.

April stood to the side of the circular dance floor and announced, "Tonight we are honored to have Callie and Marnie Taylor performing 'Best Friend.' " She pressed the button on the boom box, and music filled the room.

Call me when you need a friend,
'Cause I'm your sister,
And always know that I'll be there for you . . .

A lump formed in Ashleigh throat, and chills ran up her arms. Had April chosen this song? It was the perfect number for her identical twins. Surreptitiously, she glanced over to see Erica wipe tears from her eyes with the back of her hand. The girls were terrific. They looked as though they'd been dancing together for years.

After dinner, while her guests were gathered in several noisy conversations, Ashleigh made a point of singling out Ian. She was aware that he had more or less raised Erica, and she saw that he had a lot of unanswered questions on his mind. "Ian," she said. "Let me show you the girls' room."

As they climbed the stairs, Ashleigh turned to Ian and asked, "So, what would you like to know?"

Ian grinned. "Well, you sure don't beat around the bush."

"I don't see much point. We have all found ourselves in a very unusual set of circumstances, but I want you to know that I do not hold your sister responsible. She was as much a victim as we were." She purposely made no mention of Mario Christonelli as she led Ian into the girls' bedroom. Sitting down on one of the double beds, she gestured to the other.

Wordlessly, Ian lowered himself onto the edge of the second bed. "I haven't had much time to talk with Erica," he began, "but she wrote us a very long letter, explaining everything as best she could. She has told us that you and your husband have been unbelievably kind and understanding."

"We'd like to make Erica feel more comfortable around us. The simple fact is that Erica loves and cares about Marnie no less than Conrad and I do. To remove her from Marnie's life would be devastating for our daughter as well as unfair and unkind to Erica. At first, Erica was intimidated by us and very much afraid of losing Marnie." When Ian did not respond, Ashleigh went on. "I'd like to assure you, there is no danger of that. Marnie loves Erica, the only mother she'd ever known until recently. So while I am Marnie's mother in many important ways, so is Erica. I think we're all coming to terms with that."

"May I ask you a rather straightforward question?" asked Ian.

"By all means."

"I understand that Marnie is now going by the last name of Taylor. But she still calls Erica 'Mom.' What does she call you and your husband?"

It was a reasonable question, but not one with a straightforward answer. "She began calling Conrad 'Dad' shortly after we were reunited. There was no conflict there. But for the first couple of weeks, she didn't call me anything. That was awkward for us both, so we talked it over. She suggested calling me 'Mother Ashleigh,' but that made us both laugh. It made me sound like a nun. So for now she calls me 'Mom Ashleigh' most of the time we are all together. But occasionally, when she's excited or in a hurry, I often hear her say 'Mom.'

"The point is, Ian, whatever she's comfortable with is alright with me. I'm just so glad to have her here with us."

Ian's forehead furrowed. "So she lives here full-time?"

Ashleigh shook her head. "No. Taking her away from the mother she's known all her life would not be in her best interest. Fortunately, the girls have bonded." She grinned. "I mean *really* bonded. Conrad and I often feel like outsiders. At first, when Erica started rehab, we set up a separate bedroom for Marnie. We didn't want to force the situation and throw them together. Besides, Callie has always had her own room, and we weren't sure how she'd feel about sharing, even though she said it would be okay. But in less than two weeks, the girls asked to share both rooms. This is their bedroom," she indicated with the sweep of her hand. "It was originally Callie's bedroom. The one we decorated for Marnie is now their computer and study room."

She paused, hoping that Ian understood their dilemma. "We know how much Erica and Marnie love each other, and we're working things out. And it seems to be a lot less difficult than any of us anticipated. Since the girls like the dance studios in Manhattan better than here, since Erica returned from rehab, they've stayed with her almost as often as they are here."

Ashleigh paused again, seeking Ian's serious blue eyes. "Erica and I agree that the twins belong together, and we are making it happen."

"That's what Erica told us in her letter. I must admit that I'm a bit of a skeptic. I've found that things that seem too good to be true usually are. However, perhaps this is the exception."

"I understand. We are pretty much taking things one day at a time."

"I guess there's a great deal of uncertainty for all of you," Ian said. "But you seem to be working it out together. Erica mentioned that you were helping her find a job."

Ashleigh nodded. "I work with John Stewart's. She has an appointment with the personnel director for our Manhattan store on Monday. She is an excellent candidate for the personal shopper position that will be open after the first of the year."

Ian smiled. "That's terrific. I assume you know her background."

"Erica has been very honest and straightforward with us." She smiled back at him. "We actually met in De Mornay's several years ago, and I saw some of the fashions she designed. She's very talented." Ashleigh was pleased that she had something to tell him that Erica could not have included in her letter. "Tonight, I was able to give her some more encouraging news. When I ran into Viviana De Mornay a couple of days ago, I filled her in on the situation, and she said she'd be willing to look at some of Erica's new dress designs when she returns from her two-week cruise in the Greek Isles."

"Oh, there you are," Conrad said as he strode into the room. He pulled Ashleigh to her feet and wrapped his arm around her shoulders.

"I was just bringing Ian up to date," she replied.

He turned to Ian with a twinkle in his dazzling blue eyes. "That must have been an interesting conversation."

A chuckle sounded from each of them.

"Although we've traveled an unimaginable road," said Ashleigh, "I was just about to tell Ian that perhaps we've been blessed."

Ian and Conrad looked at her, each with a questioning expression on his face.

"I've been thinking of that old African proverb 'It takes a village to raise a child.' There is so much truth in it that it inspired the penning of at least two books using that exact title." The thought had just come to her, but in her heart, she knew she was on the right track. "No matter how twisted the route, we have established a tremendously powerful village."

AUTHOR'S NOTE

What has happened to my favorite department store? and *Shopping used to be a lot more fun* are laments that can be heard from coast to coast.

According to a survey of American buyers, published in *The Wall Street Journal* more than a decade ago, shopping has become such an unpleasant experience that people hate browsing in stores more than doing household chores.

The ordeal of making a purchase, along with the disappearance of many (or in some cases, most) of their favorite shopping destinations, has consumers too stressed to enjoy shopping. In the past, department stores provided an escape from the everyday pressures of life. When customers must endure clogged elevators and escalators, low-quality merchandise, sky-high prices, and uninformed and unmotivated sales help, however, the magic vanishes.

The days of "shop till you drop" are over. With the advent of the special midnight openings, early-bird discounts, and all other sorts of sales, the magic of the "after-Christmas sale" has evaporated. The shopping environment and mentality has significantly altered. Today, you are far more likely to hear people from all economic levels talking about how much they saved rather than how much they spent.

Beginning in the fourth quarter of 2007, as the longest recession in the history of the United States unfolded, we saw not only mom-and-pop retailers but large national chains go down or shutter thousands of locations around the country. Big chains such as Circuit City, Linens 'n Things, and Mervyn's declared bankruptcy. Then, unable to come up with money to restructure, liquidation was their only alternative. But it was more than the recent economic climate that caused many of these closures. That train started moving toward disaster more than two decades ago.

The environment of perpetual sales, which began in the mid-1970s as department store merchants fought to gain or retain their share of the market, brought about a new shopping climate. While consumers were finding lower prices, retailers were losing profit and therefore became ripe for hostile takeovers by predatory corporate raiders. In the wake of these leveraged buyouts, many retail organizations were left heavily in debt. Those that were unable to come up with fresh capital were forced to liquidate or to close a number of locations.

However, I see light at the end of this long, dark tunnel. At the end of 2009, Federal Reserve chairman Ben Bernanke announced that the recession was already over and that recovery was just around the corner. What does this mean? Things are less bad than they were. However, some very specific things have to take place in order for retailers to put their recession woes behind them. This is not going to happen overnight. It will be a long, slow recovery. Things may not completely fall in place for some time to come.

To recover from the bloodbath of the past few years, the first thing we needed to do was to begin posting gains again—not huge gains, but gains of some kind. We couldn't move forward until we were able to stop the bleeding. We accomplished that in the fourth quarter of 2009. Christmas of that year was better than expected. Many sectors beat Wall Street's predications, which helped the nation's retailers turn the corner. It was the biggest December gain since 2006, and the best monthly showing since April 2008.

All this bodes well for our economic recovery, which depends heavily on a revival in consumer spending—seventy percent of our economy is based on retail sales. Although the gains were not as high as most retailers desired, currently we are off the critical list—for the most part.

For true recovery to be imminent, consumer confidence must be restored, and the "value" shopper must reemerge from the discount stores and head back to the department stores.

In the world of retail, there are essentially three kinds of consumers:

1. There are *price shoppers,* whose primary concern is the cost of goods. They are typically middle-to-lower-middle-class, blue-collar consumers who have tight budgets, so they tend to shop at big-box discount stores like Walmart, Costco, and Target.

2. At the other extreme are *luxury shoppers,* who have money regardless of the economic conditions. They summer in the Hamptons, buy a new automobile each year, and are willing to pay for luxury in both goods and services. However, in our present economy, even these consumers are buying differently, since it is now somewhat gauche to be a conspicuous spender.

3. In the middle is the *value shopper,* who is typically middle to upper-middle class. This consumer doesn't mind paying a few extra dollars for extra service and better quality. But during the Great Recession that began in the fourth quarter of 2007, value shoppers became price shoppers. They fled the mall department stores so they could push a cart at Walmart or Target instead.

What is on the horizon for our traditional upscale department stores? Has the influx of big-box discount stores, the rise of the Internet, and the increase in mail-order catalogs turned them into so-called dinosaurs? Are they now irrelevant in the current environment and thus candidates for extinction?

My answer to that question is a resounding NO. Not by a long shot. New store openings, which were put on hold during the recession, are now underway or on the drawing board for the not-too-distant future. Among those opening new stores are Nordstrom, Bloomingdale's, Belk, and Saks Fifth Avenue. At a more moderate level is Forever 21, which has done well by offering low-priced, trendy merchandise and has moved into some of the big box locations vacated by other retailers. Kohl's also has several new stores scheduled to open in the near future. Since it is less expensive to remodel than to build from the ground up, Kohl's is taking advantage of some of the turnkey locations left by big-box closures.

We have all played a part in the demise of our favorite department stores, and we will continue to play a part in their future. Faced with the post-recession, pre-recovery shopping landscape, retailers have been forced to cut costs everywhere they can. Most of the stores that survived the mass closings of 2009 have fewer staff and less of a selection. Managers have cut down on excess inventory in order to lower operating costs, and they have raised the bar on their everyday pricing. Savvy retailers are in tune with the fact that all the high-low pricing has driven consumer confidence to an all-time low—and they are armed to meet that challenge.

At this point, knowing the obstacles the retail community must overcome, I can only wish I had a crystal ball. Since department stores cater more to consumer desires than to tangible needs, management must retain the loyalty of these patrons or motivate them to return. To accomplish this they must provide quality, service, and value. The conundrum remains no different than in the 1980s when I was on the management team of the Bullocks Wilshire Specialty Department Stores in Southern California—actually, no different than it has been since the evolution of department stores in the mid-1850s. To put it simply, department stores must provide excellent service. To provide service, they must have a sufficient staff of knowledgeable, well-motivated sales associates. To provide an adequate sales staff, they must generate enough store traffic to pay for that staff and, if they are to survive, to provide profit to their shareholders.

I have worked with the CEO of the largest conglomerate of department stores in the United States. I know for a fact that his number one priority is customer service. You can often find this man popping into one or more of his locations unannounced to observe everyday customer service—the look of the department, the level of service, cleanliness, etc. He retains the unique management style we enjoyed at Bullock's/Bullocks Wilshire, which includes selecting the very best executives, empowering them to do their job in their own way, and giving them one hundred percent accountability. You may be surprised to learn that this man is the CEO of Macy's, Inc. (previously Federated Department Stores).

Macy's, I have found, is a store that people either love or hate, depending on their orientation. If you've lived in Manhattan, or you think of the Thanksgiving Day Parade or *Miracle on 34th Street,* you are most likely a fan. If, on the other hand, you lost your favorite store, the one you grew up with and have a strong relationship with, you are not likely to be fond of Macy's, which in recent decades has replaced many of these local stores. When I mention customer service as the number-one priority, your personal experience—wandering around in one of that store's locations, unable to find someone to ring up your sale—may tell you that it just isn't so. Remember that with more than eight hundred locations, accomplishing excellent service and also bringing profit to the bottom line is a whale of a task. Although I do not happen to be a regular Macy's customer, and I know the organization has fallen short of its goal, from what I've seen and what I've heard among the various groups that I've spoken with recently, it is making significant inroads.

Store management at Nordstrom report that this organization, too, has reduced expenses to the bone, but it also has kept customer service as the number-one priority—a goal shared by all our surviving traditional department stores—a goal that is not optional.

I am often asked, "What can shoppers do to prevent their favorite stores from closing? Is it as simple as buying more stuff, or can they appeal to senior management?" Although my view into the future is not crystal clear, my advice for those of you who enjoy the ambience of quality department stores is to refuse to abandon your favorite store. If the merchandise selection or service is not what you expect, don't just walk away. Get in touch with store management. Even if this store is now a part of a large conglomerate, they desire and depend upon your feedback to maintain or improve their customer service. They certainly do not want a negative incident with an uninformed or unmotivated sales associate to color your perception of the entire store.

As I mentioned, from coast to coast I've heard a cry for the return of our favorite department stores, which translates to the return of excellent service, quality merchandise, selection, and exciting merchandise displays. In 2006, when the Macy's name was placed on Chicago icon Marshall Field's, the patrons of that store did more than complain about it. They gathered 9,800 names on petitions, demanding that their name be restored. They continue to wear buttons, hand out flyers, go to stockholders' meetings, run a website, and hold midnight vigils. While Macy's is known nationwide (and I certainly understand the importance of branding), in my opinion, changing the name of this significant landmark was a big mistake—one that has cost Macy's an approximate thirty percent of its profit in the Chicago area. The protesters are still going strong and gaining momentum. They do not appear to be giving up. They want Marshall Field's to come back, and they believe that it can. Whether they will be successful or not, only time will tell.

On a brighter note, department store retailers are resilient. They weathered the Great Depression and a number of recessions prior to the one from which, as this book goes to print, we are now emerging. They were actually more prepared for our recent recession than they were in 1991. They responded more quickly in cutting expenses and reducing inventories. It appears that the majority of our top retailers have regrouped and are meeting the challenges ahead. If you feel that the day of department stores are a thing of the past, check out some of the malls and see how difficult it is to find a parking space, or if you're an upscale customer, just walk into Bloomingdale's on one of that store's Insider Days. You'll see a full parking lot and patrons walking out with their arms loaded and smiles on their faces.

The need and desire for quality department stores has not been replaced. The rapidly growing Internet (which surprisingly accounts for less than eight percent of total retail spending in this country), mail-order catalogs, and the big-box discount stores are now a part of our retail world. However, they fall short of filling the needs of a large portion of our population.

The department store is here to stay. It will be what we make of it.